Dark Child: Omnibus Edition

Adina West

momentum

First published by Momentum in 2013
This edition published in 2013 by Momentum
Pan Macmillan Australia Pty Ltd
1 Market Street, Sydney 2000

A CIP record for this book is available at the National Library of Australia

Dark Child: Omnibus Edition

EPUB format: 9781743341834
Mobi format: 9781743341841
Print on Demand format: 9781743342701

Cover design by Jon MacDonald
Copyedited by Ali Lavau
Proofread by Glenda Downing

Macmillan Digital Australia: www.macmillandigital.com.au

To report a typographical error, please visit momentumbooks.com.au/contact/

Visit www.momentumbooks.com.au to read more about all our books and to buy books online. You will also find features, author interviews and news of any author events.

Adina West grew up on a remote property on Australia's east coast, in country New South Wales. She spent most of her childhood curled up with a book, and her first teenage job was shelving books at the local library, where she was cautioned more than once for reading them instead of putting them away.

Her first stories were laboriously typed up with two fingers on her parents' old typewriter. Her dream of one day being a published writer progressed much faster after she learned to touch type and switched to a computer.

Adina lives in Sydney's leafy north-west with her IT guru husband, two children, and a couple of unwelcome possums who really don't know how to take a hint. *Dark Child* is her first novel.

Adina loves to hear from readers. You can contact her through her website, www.adinawest.com.

For Susan Gai, best and only aunt. You will always be remembered.

Prologue

Amarok left his tower room the moment dusk fell, and descended the winding stairs to the entrance hall.

Anton stepped out from the shadow of the doorway. "Leaving so soon, brother?" His voice held the faintest hint of reproach.

Without speaking, Amarok kept moving toward the door. He'd hoped his departure would be unobserved.

"You know we are all concerned for you." Anton reached out to lay a hand on Amarok's shoulder and he tensed, his skin unused to touch.

Of course Amarok knew that. He had been away so long, living dangerously wild, watching over this human girl.

"We all understand what you are doing, Rok," Anton continued softly. "Keeping faith with Amber's last words to you. But you have shut us out, and that is so dangerous. The more time you spend as the wolf …"

… *the harder it is to return*. Oh yes, Amarok lived with the terrible strain of balancing man and beast every day.

At last he spoke.

"Brother, what Amber foretold … it is beginning. And who can protect this girl but me?"

Chapter 1

That day, for the first time in her life, Kat fainted. She woke to find herself staring up at the fluorescent lights of the meeting room ceiling. She was stretched out on the floor, with something soft beneath her head – a cushion maybe? The carpet beneath her smelled faintly of cleaning chemicals. She'd never noticed that before. She usually didn't get this close.

Her boss, Paul Gibson, hovered above her. Stephanie too, with her fine brown hair hanging around her face and her glasses almost falling off her nose as she bent over.

"Hey. Welcome back." Paul's voice was gentle.

"Gee, I'm sorry – how long was I out?" Kat slowly sat up, feeling a little queasy.

Paul leaned over her and searched her eyes. He was in physician mode, hand beneath her chin to hold her steady while he checked for signs of concussion.

"Several minutes. Have you eaten anything today?"

Kat heard the worry in his voice, and thought back to the single spoonful of oatmeal she'd had that morning before scraping the rest of the bowl into the bin. She'd had another of those seriously vivid dreams last night. As soon as she'd woken, she'd rushed outside into the snow-dusted front garden in her slippers. She'd been crazy to think her wolf, that she'd only ever seen back home in the mountains, would be curled there in a hollow beneath a thicket of dogwood branches. And of course, he wasn't. After that dawn escapade she really hadn't been hungry. "No," she admitted.

Paul made a sound of disapproval. "Breakfast is the most important meal of the day. Might just be low blood sugar then. You gave us quite a shock."

Stephanie kneeled and put a supportive arm around Kat's shoulders. "Here, have this. I keep them in my desk drawer for emergencies." She handed Kat a granola bar, and a glass of juice to go with it.

Kat obligingly finished both, and let Stephanie help her to her feet. Her head seemed okay, but her stomach was still churning.

Paul ushered them both out of the meeting room and switched off the light. "Go and sit down for half an hour or so and take it easy, okay? And if you're not feeling better soon, you really should go home."

Kat gave him a grateful smile, and she and Stephanie headed off along the corridor back to the pathology lab.

"You are gonna go home, right?" Stephanie made it sound like there was no other reasonable option.

"I think I just need to eat, Steph. I'll have lunch early, and see how I feel after that." She was going with the low blood sugar theory, because she was normally *never* sick. Her mom always said Kat had a super-charged immune system.

"You should go to the doctor, get a general check-up," Stephanie said. "Make sure you're not anemic or something."

"I guess so," Kat said. She didn't plan on taking the advice though. She wasn't the type to visit the doctor when she was perfectly healthy.

"Oh, hang on," she said as they approached their lab, and detoured via the vending machine. She bought a couple of cinnamon granola bars, and tossed one to Stephanie with a wink. "Never let it be said I don't pay my debts." The machine ran out of the best flavours every other week, so around here, the things were like gold.

As Kat went about her routine tasks that morning, her mind kept wandering back to the same topic. *Why* had she fainted? Low blood sugar might have been a reasonable explanation, but she'd been feeling queasy since first waking up that morning, and she'd eaten a perfectly good dinner last night.

Even now, after Steph's granola bar and juice, she still wasn't feeling fantastic. Definitely a bit wooly-headed and tired, and she'd found it really hard to concentrate during the staff meeting that morning, before she'd fainted.

She slid a tray of samples into the hematology analyzer and started the cycle, then leaned against the bench top, frowning at the frosted-glass wall in front of her. Working in pathology, one easy way of checking if there was anything seriously wrong *without* going to the doctor did kind of leap to mind. She could take a look at a sample of her own blood. Easy to see straight away if she was anemic, or fighting off some sort of infection. A viral thing, maybe.

Later that morning, Stephanie headed off to a half-day training course at the University of Charleston medical center down the road, and Kat found herself alone in the lab, feeling restless and a bit bored – not for the first time.

You can do this work standing on your head, Kat.

She sighed. It was true enough. She didn't mind the job most of the time, but it wasn't even vaguely challenging. And there wasn't much scope for advancement to a more interesting role – not here in quiet little Charleston, West Virginia, anyway. She knew, because she and Paul had had that discussion at her last annual review meeting. That was months ago, though. She really needed to raise it with him again.

She glanced at the wall clock. Work was quiet, and she was ahead of schedule. Plenty of time to pay a quick visit to the pathology collection clinic next door. She reached for her bag, and headed out.

The receptionist at the clinic recognized her straight away. "I wasn't expecting a pickup this early. Did someone else here call for one?"

"I'm not here to pick up samples." Kat made a face. "Actually, I'm here as a customer. I wanted to get a blood sample taken, if you can squeeze me in."

"Sure." The woman eyed her curiously, but professional courtesy evidently forbade her asking any questions. "You'll need a request form from your physician."

"Of course," Kat said. Internally, she cursed herself for having forgotten something so basic. "I'm seeing my doctor tomorrow." The lie slipped out surprisingly easily.

The receptionist tapped a few keys to bring up her appointments screen. "Okay, so you want to come in tomorrow at what time?"

"Actually," Kat said, with what she hoped was a winning expression, "I wondered if I could get the blood taken today? I've already been fasting, and I can drop around the paperwork tomorrow." She did feel a twinge of guilt at how smoothly she was compounding one lie with another.

"Oh." The woman looked doubtful. "That wouldn't usually …"

"Just this once?"

The woman wavered. "You're going to take the samples back with you today?"

Kat nodded.

"I'll still need your insurance details," the receptionist said.

"Sure."

The woman's eyes went back to her screen. "I can squeeze you in right after this next lady."

"Thanks. I really appreciate it."

Minutes later, Kat had a pressure tie around her upper arm and a pathology nurse bent over her, prodding the flesh inside her elbow. The nurse looked up, giving Kat a wry smile.

"Josie said you work next door. Not every day we have pathologists in here ordering their own blood tests and getting a physician to rubber stamp it afterwards."

Kat decided to make light of the comment. "Call it a job perk."

"You had much to drink today?"

"Only a little."

The woman sighed. "You have to be hydrated for a blood test, otherwise I have trouble finding a good vein." She went back to work.

"Okay," she said a moment later. "Just a little sting now."

Kat turned her eyes to the wall and concentrated on a decorative poster of Blackwater Falls someone had thoughtfully put up. Despite working with blood every day, she still didn't want to watch herself getting jabbed.

It didn't hurt so much when the needle first went in, but the nurse started fiddling with it, moving it around. After a moment, she shook her head. "Sorry, honey, I'm not having any luck with this vein. I'm gonna have to try the other arm." She pressed a cotton ball firmly over the puncture site and withdrew the needle. "Press down on this for me, for about a minute." She stuck a strip of surgical tape over the cotton ball, and then turned away to get another needle ready.

This time they had better luck, and the nurse filled three sample tubes before pressing a cotton ball over the site and slapping on some tape.

"There. All done. Press on that for me." The nurse picked up the first sample tube and the sheet of labels printed with Kat's personal details. After a moment, she made a frustrated sound. "These darned things are so hard to peel off sometimes."

"Just leave them. I can do that for you later," Kat said quickly.

The woman shrugged, and slid the sample tubes and labels together into a zip-lock bag. "You taking these back with you now?" She held out the bag.

Kat nodded, and slipped it into her handbag. "Yes. Thanks."

"Next time, remember to hydrate," the woman chided.

Kat rolled down her sleeves and slid from the chair. If she had her way, there wouldn't be a next time. She gave a guilty smile and headed for the door.

Back at the lab, Kat pulled the samples out of her handbag. After a moment's thought, she threw the labels with her name on them in the wastebasket, then put the unlabeled tubes in the sample fridge. Better to keep the fact that she was doing her own blood analysis off the record, she decided.

She pushed up her sleeves and peeled the tape and cotton balls from her arms. Glancing down at her left arm, she traced her fingers lightly across her skin, searching for the spot where the needle had entered. Feeling nothing, she frowned and held her arm up for a closer look. Then she looked at the other arm too, with growing consternation. On the delicate, almost transparent skin of her inner elbow, where there should have been an angry red spot, there was no hint of a needle mark.

*

Stephanie was still at her course when Kat got back from lunch, so she processed the next batch of samples, and then retrieved her own blood vials from where she'd tucked them away at the bottom of the sample refrigerator. Her actions were automatic, her mind still pre-occupied with what she'd seen – or hadn't seen – on her arms. No bruising, no redness, no puncture marks. It didn't make sense, and she'd checked both arms twice.

She prepared a slide and slid it under the microscope to begin a full blood count. No way she wasn't doing this one manually. A quiver ran through her; anxiety and anticipation combined.

Her eyes narrowed as she looked down at the slide, professional training coming to the fore as she began recording her counts methodically on a piece of paper. But even without doing the calculations, she knew straight away that there was something very, very odd about her blood.

Paul entered the lab a few minutes later, but Kat was so intent on the microscope she didn't notice him until he'd walked right up beside her, with a sheaf of papers in his hand.

"Your notes from the staff meeting, Kat. Lab protocols for our new client. After all the drama this morning, you left them in the meeting room."

"Oh! I didn't hear you come in." Kat hoped she sounded normal, because she felt completely flustered. "Thanks." She took the offered papers.

"How are you feeling now?" Paul asked. "You have a bit more color."

Probably because her face was flaming – pretty much the way you'd expect someone to look when they were caught doing something extremely unorthodox at work.

"I'm feeling much better," Kat said, with perfect honesty.

"Good to hear." Paul glanced at the sheet of paper she'd been recording her counts on. "Doing a manual FBC?"

"Ummm … yeah." *Move along now. Nothing to see here, folks.*

Paul's forehead creased as he scanned the figures. "What's this sample you're working on? These numbers aren't typical."

"Just something I came across," Kat said.

"Mind if I take a look?"

Kat's heart missed a beat. Great. On the one occasion she really *didn't* want anyone looking over her shoulder, her boss had to happen along and take a friendly interest in what she was doing.

"Go ahead." She stepped away from the microscope.

Paul leaned over the eyepiece, and after a moment gave a low whistle. He looked back down at the list of figures she'd been recording. "This has to be an oncology patient or something similar. Right?"

Kat's head was whirling. Working in pathology she knew enough to realize how strange her results were … which explained Paul's reaction. What could she safely say that wouldn't make this any worse than it already was? "Uh, I'm not sure."

"This blood composition indicates someone with an advanced illness or infection," Paul said firmly. He gazed again at the page in front of him, then shook his head, as if discounting what he read there. "Do you mind if I double-check this?" He pointed to her red blood cell count figure.

Kat shook her head, and passed him the desktop calculator.

Paul looked through the eyepiece again, and then did his own calculation. Finally, he looked up at her and nodded. "Your figure is pretty much spot on. With a red blood cell count this low, you're looking at a patient who is seriously anemic at the very least or, at worst, comatose. As you know, the body can't function without enough red blood cells. It needs them to transport oxygen …"

He broke off, picking up the page to stare down at it again. "Platelet count is off the scale too. Over two million per microliter. I've never seen figures that high. And as you've noted down here, they're oddly shaped, elongated, though they seem fully functional. Hemophilia I've seen plenty of times before, but this is the clinical opposite of a clotting issue like that. Very unusual."

"I wasn't sure what to make of the platelets either," Kat said.

Paul frowned. "White cell counts are abnormally high as well – which, as I said, usually points to some sort of severe and advanced infection." He reached for the sample tube. "Where's this from?"

"I'm not sure," Kat said again. *And there we go with lie number three, out into the big wide world.*

"It's not labeled." Paul looked up at her questioningly.

"It came in like that," Kat said. At least *that* wasn't a lie. Strictly speaking.

"Odd." Paul's expression turned thoughtful. "I remember reading something about a study on platelets like these in a bulletin from the corporate head office. I'll see if I can dig it out later this afternoon, because I'm sure they'd be interested in recruiting another subject."

He passed her back the tube. "Great initiative, by the way. If you hadn't thought to do a manual analysis on this, the abnormality in the platelets probably wouldn't have been noticed."

"Thanks." She got the word out, even though she wanted to choke on it. The irony in the fact that she was standing here accepting her boss's congratulations for showing such wonderful initiative didn't escape her. If she hadn't decided to get all creative and test her own blood, none of this would be out in the open right now.

"Oh, and you'll need to do a full audit of your current batches of samples to find out where this is from. It's got to be missing from somewhere."

"Absolutely," Kat said. "I'll get right on it."

Paul dallied a minute or so longer before going back to his office, and by the time he left, Kat was sure her smile was about ready to crack off her face.

As soon as she was alone again, she got the two other sample tubes containing her blood out of the refrigerator, and threw them in the hazardous waste disposal unit where they couldn't cause her any further trouble. Then she slumped into a chair. She could easily enough tell Paul she couldn't identify where the sample had come from. But still the troubling question remained. A few odd dreams, momentary nausea and fainting *once* hardly constituted a reliable symptom list for a life-threatening illness. So *why* did both her red and white blood cell counts indicate she should be seriously ill – when she clearly wasn't?

Chapter 2

Traffic was light as Kat headed home from work that evening. The private pathology lab she'd worked at for the last couple of years was near the university on the south bank of the Kanawha River, and she followed the river back toward the city center, then veered off toward where she lived in South Charleston.

The two-bedroom house she shared with Tiffany was on one of many streets that backed on to the wooded hills. The hill behind their house was green through summer, and awash with the yellows and reds of beech, oak and poplar in fall. She loved that about Charleston. The city was a ribbon of densely settled river plain that followed the Elk and Kanawha rivers to their juncture downtown, and then spread outward, with tendrils winding their way through every accessible valley into the surrounding hills. Wherever you went you were never far from the river or the trees.

She pulled into her driveway less than ten minutes after leaving work, and turned the engine off. A sudden wave of nausea rolled through her, so acute that she doubled over at the wheel. After a moment, she cautiously straightened up. The sensation seemed to have passed for now, but this, coupled with her strange and inexplicable blood results today, definitely had her feeling uneasy. She was pensive as she walked slowly to the door and let herself inside, and she went straight to the kitchen and took a couple of iron tablets with a glass of orange juice. They certainly couldn't hurt.

When she went through to her bedroom, there was an envelope taped to the door. It was printed with the logo and address of the beauty salon where Tiffany worked. Kat pulled it off, and went to sit on the bed.

Inside was a page torn from a women's magazine – the horoscope section, folded around a business card. It was a full-page spread for Kat's star sign – Cancer – and Tiffany had circled a paragraph in what looked like pink lipstick.

Kat read it quickly.

You are approaching a time of change, and dream states will prepare your subconscious and inform your waking hours. Your instinct for self-protection may not be your best ally though, as it encourages you to look inward, while your answers lie with others. This is a good time to seek outside counsel from an expert or a friend to clarify your future direction.

Kat gave an exasperated sigh, instantly regretting talking to Tiffany about her strange dreams. She'd been having them for years now, though lately they'd become more frequent. More real. But her housemate's views on things spiritual were on a different planet from hers.

A bright pink sticky note was attached to the bottom of the page, covered in Tiffany's sloping writing.

I know you're free tomorrow night. Taking you to visit a psychic so she can sort this dream thing for you. No ifs or buts. My treat, to thank you for all your good advice about Jason.

She'd signed it "Tiff", with a love heart.

Jason was Tiffany's charming ex-boyfriend, and he'd kept on going with the late-night booty calls long after telling her he needed some time to "figure things out". Kat had been there right through their recent messy breakup. She sighed. This wasn't the first time Tiffany had raised the idea of her seeing a psychic. If she didn't go along with it now she was going to look like a total wet blanket, and ungrateful too.

She didn't believe in this stuff. Not really. At a logical level, she knew psychic predictions were just clever generalisations and wish fulfillment – which seemed to suit Tiffany just fine.

Kat wished her housemate could have gone with the same gift as last time she'd been feeling generous: a voucher for a deluxe manicure at the salon. There was something to be said for a gift that was safe, non-threatening, and easily removable with acetone.

She looked at the business card. Pretty standard; the kind you could get done cheaply at any printing place. The psychic's name was printed in a flowing script.

Kat frowned. Candice Brown. Ordinary enough … not Madame Giselda or something equally loopy. This Candice Brown would probably spin her some line about her dreams being the window to her soul, and purple being her favourite color, and whatever else they usually came up with. Tiffany would be happy. And Kat could continue in her comfortable skepticism. It would all be fine.

*

Kat was preparing a dilution when Paul stuck his head into the lab late the next morning. When he saw her, he made his way straight over, with the briefest of absent-minded smiles for Stephanie.

"Kat, I found the reference to that platelet study I mentioned yesterday. Any luck tracking down where that sample came from?"

Kat shook her head. "No, I audited all the paperwork and sample batches from yesterday and couldn't find anything missing." Maybe it was a little childish, but she had her fingers crossed behind her back as she said this – so did it still count as lie number four?

"Hmmm." Paul glanced at the pipette she was holding with a preoccupied frown. "Hopefully something will turn up later. Anyway, could you come to my office? I wanted to run through the parameters for this study, and see if you agree the sample we have fits."

"Sure. I'll need to be back here in ten minutes though to do the count on this once the stain takes."

Paul shook his head abruptly. "No. It might take longer than that. Can you get someone else to finish it off?"

"Um, yeah, I guess so." Kat looked around. Stephanie was standing by the centrifuge. "Steph, can you babysit this one for me? If I'm not back in ten minutes it needs an eosinophil count done."

Paul was still hovering by the door. Stephanie caught her eye, and motioned her head at him, raising her hands in a questioning gesture. Kat shrugged, and shook her head. Seemed she wasn't the only one who'd noticed their usually easygoing boss was a little distracted.

Paul seemed to be fighting the urge to hurry as she followed him to his office, but he still moved fast for a short, plump little man.

When they reached his office, he shut the door behind them and ushered her into the spare seat, then sat behind his desk. He gave her a conspiratorial smile.

"I didn't really need to discuss the study's parameters with you, Kat. Sorry for the subterfuge. It's just that I have an exciting opportunity I wanted to discuss with you privately."

He reached across the desk to pass her a printout. "Here's the relevant section from the research bulletin, by the way. I've made a copy for you. The study examines the relationship between certain platelet types and accelerated healing. The description of elongated platelets in very high concentrations clearly matches the sample you identified."

Accelerated healing? Kat filed that thought away for later reflection as she took the sheet. *Get to the point, Paul.* Being so intimately involved in the outcome of any investigation into this particular sample was making her feel jumpy.

"So," Paul said, settling back into his chair. "I called through to our research lab in New York yesterday afternoon about our sample."

My *sample*, Kat thought glumly.

"I got a call back last night," Paul continued, "from the hematology research director. He's taking a personal interest in this study. Incidences of this blood condition are extremely rare, apparently, so he had all sorts of questions for me, most of which I couldn't answer. He'll be visiting in person to take custody of the sample and any information we can dig up on it.

"But the reason I particularly wanted to talk to you, Kat ..." He broke off to give her a sympathetic smile. "Well, I haven't forgotten the discussion we had at your last evaluation, and I've been giving some thought to your future – not just here, but within the organisation as a whole. I think we both know that you've outgrown your current position, but there aren't many opportunities for you to move into a research role, or take on more responsibility here in Charleston – particularly since Stephanie has been here longer, and it would cause bad feeling if you were promoted above her." He cleared his throat. "But I do see you as the more, ah ... *capable* employee. You see where the need for delicate handling comes in, I hope."

Kat murmured something she hoped was appropriate, but mostly she was glad the discussion was heading in a safer direction, meaning anything that wasn't about her weird blood.

"Anyway," Paul went on, "it's not every day we see a senior director of the company making the trip down here to little ol' Charleston, so I casually dropped a few comments about you into the conversation, and he'd like to meet you when he visits." He beamed at her, obviously pleased with himself.

Kat's eyes widened slightly. "Wow! I wasn't expecting this."

"Don't get your hopes up," Paul warned. "But there's a chance we might be able to open some doors for you in another part of the organisation. Some sort of internal transfer – if you're willing to relocate."

Kat made a face. "At the risk of sounding unprepared, I have to admit I hadn't thought that far ahead."

Paul gave her a jovial smile. "I'm glad you haven't been sitting around fine-tuning your résumé and planning how to leave us. You're a valued member of our team, Kat, and there's always a place for you here. But now I've given you the heads-up, you *can* give some thought to this. Decide if it's something you're interested in."

"Thanks, Paul. I really appreciate it." This definitely earned him a place in the Great Boss Hall of Fame as far as Kat was concerned.

"Now – logistics. The director will be here tomorrow, and he's only available in the evening. Can you stay back late tomorrow?"

"Sure." Tiffany was dragging her out to visit the psychic tonight after work, but tomorrow night her schedule was clear. The only thing she wasn't looking forward to was the fact that this visiting director would undoubtedly ask her again about where she'd found the blood sample that was attracting all this attention. She'd have to stick to the story she'd already told Paul – that a single tube had just turned up in the sample refrigerator, unlabeled, and with no paper-work. What other option did she have?

Chapter 3

The psychic operated out of a modest little shop facing the river on Kanawha Boulevard, in downtown Charleston.

Kat eyed the shop dubiously. "How did you hear about her?" She'd driven past here many times but never noticed this place before.

"She dropped some cards off at work," Tiffany said. "She's new in town. One of the girls has been to see her already. Apparently she's the real deal."

"Okay." Kat still didn't make a move to go in.

"I'll wait out here." Tiffany shooed her toward the door. "I'll just walk along the river or something. Go on."

The bell on the door made a discordant jangle when Kat entered. There was nobody else inside, just a small bookshelf, a sofa that had seen better days, and an indoor plant. A curtain partitioned the room floor to ceiling, and a woman came out from behind this to greet her.

"I'm Candice," she said. "You must be Kat?" She ushered Kat through the curtain, and motioned to a seat on one side of a small table next to another laden bookshelf.

She took the chair opposite, and gave Kat an encouraging smile. "Give me your hand."

Feeling totally ridiculous, Kat held out her right hand, trying to do it with good grace. She still didn't feel comfortable going along with this whole fortune-telling charade.

The bells in the psychic's earrings gave a silvery chime as she leaned over Kat's hand. Her name might have been ordinary enough, but everything else about her was pretty much in accordance with the Gypsy Fortune Teller manual, if there was such a thing. Wavy dark brown hair contained by a colorful scarf, dark eye makeup, red lipstick – and she was wearing tight-fitting black gloves, with rings and dozens of bracelets worn over the top. She straightened up and frowned without raising her eyes, clearly focused on her task and unaware of Kat's scrutiny of her.

"May I see your other hand?" she asked.

Kat wondered if the woman could sense how tense she was. She really didn't want to be here, but Tiffany had been so excited when Kat had picked her up after work that she'd done her best to be at least, well, *pleasant* about the whole thing. Kat began to mentally prepare herself for the raft of questions Tiffany would be sure to ask afterward.

The psychic subjected Kat's left hand to the same minute examination she had given the right, and then reached to the shelf behind for a book.

The Art and Science of Chiromancy and Palmistry Kat read on the book's spine as the woman leafed through to the page she wanted. *Great, so she's consulting a book in the middle of a reading. Very professional.*

The woman looked up, and Kat blushed, almost as if she'd been caught saying the thought out loud.

"You have strong hands." It was spoken almost as a challenge, and Kat didn't reply. What could you really say to that? "Ummm, thanks. I work out a lot." Maybe not.

The woman continued speaking, looking at Kat's hands, and it sounded like a discussion of Ancient Greek and Roman gods, with Apollo this, and Mercury that, and something about the girdle of Venus.

She examined Kat's long fingers, her fingertips, and thumbs, and pronounced her thoughtful, intuitive, and idealistic. Kat relaxed. Well, that wasn't so bad.

"I know you don't want to be here," the woman said abruptly, looking up. "It's quite clear your friend outside is the one with all the enthusiasm for this. There's something different about you, isn't there? Something you hide from others?"

Kat stiffened. Well, how about that? The woman *was* psychic after all.

"Shall I just look at what your future holds, and we can go from there?"

"Fine," Kat muttered, and the woman nodded.

She released Kat's hands and sat back, her face wreathed in shadows. Kat couldn't see her clearly in the dim light, but she sensed the woman was deliberating.

"Perhaps ... the cards will shed more light." The psychic was speaking as much to herself as to Kat, and she reached for a pack of cards she'd had ready at the side of the table.

Even wrong way up, the words on the box jumped out at Kat.
Rider Waite Tarot Deck.

The woman hesitated though, after weighing the deck in her hand for a moment, and put it back on the desk. She reached instead for a well-worn wooden box on the bookshelf, and lifted out the cards inside.

The psychic selected a card, and laid it in the center of the table, smoothing the black lace tablecloth beneath it as she did so. She shuffled and held the rest of the deck out to Kat in a fan.

Kat felt an odd reluctance steal over her. A sense of crawling misgiving. She didn't want to select any cards. Didn't want to hear whatever it was the psychic was going to say about her future. She didn't even want to *be* here. But it was too late to back out now, and her hands moved automatically, reaching out to pull the requested number of cards at random from the deck.

The woman placed each card face down on the table as Kat passed them to her, forming a cross, then a line to the right of that. She carefully straightened them, lining them up neatly with black-gloved hands, and then she began her reading, her voice low and melodious.

At first Kat let the words wash over her without really taking them in. She heard some mention of heritage, and the woman paused over the Wheel of Fortune card, telling her that destiny was about to take a hand in her future. But then there was a silence. Kat blinked, and looked up to find the psychic eyeing her pensively.

The woman's eyes narrowed, as if she was thinking, and she seemed to reach a decision, though she didn't look completely happy about it. She leaned forward, clearing her throat.

"Normally, I soften the way I present things in a reading, but with you I need to be completely honest. To warn you about what is to come. Because I've never seen such a clear agreement between what is shown in your hands, and the cards you've drawn. You must prepare yourself for a time of transformation."

The psychic touched the Wheel of Fortune card with one finger. "You've been marked by destiny."

She paused, as if expecting a response, and Kat nodded. Whatever her feelings about the authenticity of this sort of reading, she was caught by the deadly serious expression on the woman's face.

The psychic leaned forward and reached for Kat's hands, once more turning them palm upward.

"You see here? And here? This curved line is the life line, and this vertical one represents fate. On both your left and right hands, these lines are broken, and there is a clear gap before they continue."

"What does that mean?" Kat was fascinated despite herself.

The psychic closed her eyes for a moment, and pressed her own palms against them, then opened them again and looked straight at Kat.

"A significant gap in your path like this shows that in your future … well, the best way to describe it is that your life energy will come to a halt. Not an end to life; that's an old superstition based on a lack of knowledge. But you should prepare for a radical change in your life's direction."

She released Kat's hands, and reached for the deck again. "I'd like you to draw three more cards, to clarify exactly what you can expect in your near future." The woman fanned the cards out before holding them toward Kat.

The first card Kat drew was labelled "The Moon". She then drew "The Lovers" and, finally, "The Tower".

The psychic drew breath at that one. She laid it on the table between them. "This is considered an unlucky card. It confirms again that you face a time of chaos and turmoil, of revelation and transformation, whether you want it or not."

She pointed to the card showing a couple holding hands. "Then the Lovers. This means you'll have difficult choices to make. Your path to love will be filled with obstacles, and tangled with desire."

Kat shifted in her seat. *Just great. How come I get the doom and gloom prophecies?* It really wasn't fair. Last time Tiffany had been to see a psychic, she'd got the classic feel-good stuff about meeting a tall, dark, and handsome man.

"And the Moon." The woman touched the final card. "You should expect vivid dreams, even nightmares, as your imagination struggles to give form to animal impulses deep within you. You may already be having such dreams."

Kat felt a ripple of unease. Surely it was just coincidence that the reading had strayed onto the subject of dreams when she'd been plagued by vivid and unnerving ones for the past few weeks. Anyone could have drawn that card. Still, she found herself listening more intently.

The woman ran her gloved finger down the side of the tarot card. "But the moon can also bring you calm, if you can trap its power."

She looked up at Kat. "You were born under a full moon, so you're strongly affected by lunar energy. More than most. And highly intuitive, with psychic tendencies."

Kat relaxed a little at that, because they were safely back into territory she could easily discredit. Intuitive? A little, maybe. But she was about as psychic as the average brick. Which put Candice Brown squarely on the loopy side of normal.

The psychic gathered up the cards and placed them carefully back in their box, then began to remove the many rings from her fingers and unclasp her bracelets. She placed them one by one on the side of the table, then slowly removed both her gloves.

"I don't usually do this." Her voice was pitched low. "Direct touch can be too overwhelming for me. But before we finish, I think I need to …" She reached out to touch Kat's hands.

A shudder passed through the psychic's body, so sudden Kat was sure that it had to be put on, and she pressed down on Kat's hands.

"You are a Dark Child." She went very still, her eyes wide, like she was staring at some faraway place – then she spoke again in a low voice, almost muttering, with her words tripping over each other. "You will not walk alone. A seer will guide you, and one more yet to come. But the path ahead is tangled and your guide can guide no one. She is trapped, and you must find her. Find the one who is lost."

She drew breath in a sharp gasp, and pulled her hands away from Kat's, and her eyes … her eyes looked really strange. Glassy, as if she wasn't really there anymore. "Silver chains on her feet," she said. And then she let out a groan, and closed her eyes. "They burn – oh, how they burn!"

Kat watched her nervously. Was this all a normal part of a reading? It wasn't like she had much experience. But yeah, she was officially a bit freaked out now. This lady's brand of crazy made Tiffany look conservative.

The psychic's eyes opened and she blinked a few times, then she gave Kat a strange look.

"This session is over," she said abruptly. She stood, reached for her gloves, and escorted Kat to the door.

*

The next day at work passed quickly and uneventfully. By half past six, the labs and offices were all but deserted. Kat was completely up to date with work, which left her with far too much time for worrying about the meeting tonight. Or was it an interview? Paul hadn't really made that clear.

Paul had said this study they'd be discussing was analyzing the relationship between accelerated healing and a certain type of malformed platelets. Elongated platelets like hers. And she'd just experienced accelerated healing herself only two days ago. That was definitely no coincidence. But of course she had no idea what it actually meant, and she was hoping she could find out more in this meeting – while still not revealing the fact that the blood sample they'd come to collect was actually hers. She really wished she hadn't gotten herself into such a damned tangle.

She was feeling a bit sick again. She checked her watch. Twenty to seven. She really should eat something – although eating didn't seem to help with this strange nausea. She took a couple of iron tablets from the bottle she'd taken to carrying in her handbag, and gulped them down with water. There was a light on in Paul's office down the corridor, and Kat headed in that direction.

She knocked on the open door, and then stuck her head in. "Paul?"

He looked up. "Yes?"

"I'm all ready for the meeting, but I just wondered if I still have time to go out and grab a bite to eat first?"

Paul glanced at his watch. "That should be fine. He's not due until around eight."

"Okay. I'll be back before then. Did you want anything?"

Paul shook his head, and gave a rueful smile. "My wife has packed me some leftovers and I'll get in trouble if I don't eat them."

Kat grinned at that. "See you soon, then."

She had a vegetarian calzone at an Italian place a few minutes' drive away, and was on her way back to the office shortly before eight. When she turned into the lab's parking lot, she noticed a dark and very expensive-looking limousine parked next to Paul's car. As she drove past it she saw the passenger door on one side was ajar and the internal light was on. A pair of long male legs, clad in dark suit pants, extended out onto the bitumen.

Kat parked her car, and got out. The evening air was cool against her skin, a slight breeze catching her hair as she slammed the car door. The rest of the lot was empty, and thick with gathering shadows as dusk fell. She felt a sudden crawling unease that made her hurry to the safety of the lighted foyer.

When she reached Paul's office, she paused at the open door. Paul was facing her, while his visitor had his back to her, his hand resting on the sealed shipper that probably contained her blood sample.

Paul made eye contact, and motioned for her to enter.

"We've already discussed the blood sample, Kat," Paul said. "We don't need to go over that again. But did you have any luck finding any identifying paperwork?"

"No," Kat said as she walked into the room, sending a mental thank you to the fates. It seemed she was going to escape the twenty questions she'd been dreading.

The other man turned to face her with a smile. "This isn't the first time we've had identifying data go 'missing'. Even entire sample tubes have been known to disappear before we can get there to pick them up." He shrugged. "Paperwork's not critical. This blood profile is rare enough that we take any and all samples, regardless."

"Director, let me introduce Katerina Chanter," Paul said. "Kat, this is Director Norris."

"Pleased to meet you, Ms Chanter." Director Norris reached out to briefly shake her hand. "You know, plenty of people wouldn't have taken the time to identify that platelet abnormality," he said. "It's a credit to your attention to detail."

"Thank you." Kat felt her face heat as two sets of male eyes studied her.

"Mr Gibson here speaks very highly of you, Ms Chanter." The director nodded toward Paul. "He feels you have a great deal of untapped potential, and thinks your initiative, thoroughness, and exemplary laboratory skills would well equip you for a research role with us."

Kat cleared her throat. "Research work is ... it's certainly something I've thought about."

"Given your role in identifying this unusual blood sample, Kat, the director and I were discussing the possibility of a secondment for you to his hematology research lab in Manhattan," Paul said.

Norris nodded. "You'd be working on this platelet study of ours, and you could start ..." Norris looked at Paul for confirmation, "... well, pretty much as soon as you want to, as it's an internal transfer. We do urgently need hematology researchers with the right experience."

Paul smiled. "It wouldn't necessarily be permanent, unless you decide you want it to be, but I could spare you for six months initially, and get a contractor in to cover your position here in the interim."

Kat's eyes widened, and she took a deep breath. "Wow – I, ah, I might need some time to think about this." This was happening a whole lot faster than she'd expected.

Director Norris opened his mouth, as if he was intending to add something, but then his eyes moved away, startled, as his attention was caught by a movement at the door.

Kat turned her head to see what he was looking at, and saw another man – a very tall, very well-dressed man – filling the doorway.

And he was looking right at her.

Director Norris took a step in his direction, and faltered. "Sir, is … is something the matter? I understood you'd be waiting in the car."

The man didn't immediately acknowledge him.

Norris held out the sample shipper. "I have the sample right here."

Finally, the man broke his unblinking focus on Kat, and glanced at Norris. "I'll take over now." He made a dismissive gesture with his hand, as if shooing away an annoying fly. "Take that to the car."

"Yes, sir." Director Norris scurried away down the corridor carrying the shipper.

Kat looked back up at the man in the doorway. "Country club material," her grandmother would have said. A perfect match for the limousine outside. Even without his height, he was the sort of man who commanded instant attention, with all the confidence of bearing, the charisma, of one used to leading others. But who *was* he? And why had just seeing him been enough to make Director Norris jump to do his bidding – behaving more like a junior associate than the director of an entire research division?

"I am Ionescu," the man said, somehow knowing to answer the question she hadn't asked. His dark eyes glittered. "Director Norris reports to me." He took a step toward them.

"Your name isn't familiar, Mr Ionescu," Paul said, looking baffled. "Do you work in our corporate head office?"

Ionescu turned to face him with an expression of mild surprise, as if he'd only just noticed him standing there. "Indeed," he murmured. "Would you excuse us?"

Kat saw the strangest expression cross Paul's face. Shock, then an odd blankness, then bewilderment. "Of course," he said, and walked out of his own office without another word.

Kat swallowed, and felt a flutter of nerves as Ionescu again turned toward her with those darkly fascinating eyes.

"Ms Chanter," Ionescu said, with a caressing smile. His voice was cultured, the vocal rhythm strangely soothing. If she'd thought otherwise when Paul had first mentioned it to her, the attention Ionescu was paying her showed that this part of the meeting was most definitely not an afterthought.

Then a sudden chill ran up her spine. Ionescu hadn't been in the room when Paul had done the introductions.

So how do you know my name?

"I saw your photograph in the foyer," Ionescu continued smoothly. "Last year's employee of the year. Quite remarkable."

Again, it was as if he'd anticipated her question and answered it before she could ask it.

"Oh," she said, her anxiety dispelled. "Thank you."

Ionescu crossed the room to stand in front of her, and she automatically held out her hand, expecting to shake with him.

"Meeting you is a most … unexpected pleasure," Ionescu murmured. She caught a flash of dark eyes as he bent over her hand with a brief inclination of the head – a remnant of what perhaps would have been a gentlemanly bow in years gone past. It seemed perfectly in keeping with the rest of him, somehow.

"P-pleased to meet you," Kat said in return, finding herself surprisingly tongue-tied.

Was that because of his old-fashioned courtliness? Or because he was still holding her hand? She had no idea of the etiquette on this. Most people she knew just shook hands and then let go. Should she … pull away?

Finally, he smiled and released her hand. Again, he made that half-bowing motion in her direction. "As I am sure Norris has communicated, we would be privileged to have an employee of your caliber join us."

Kat smoothed her palms down the sides of her thighs. "The platelet study does sound very interesting, though I only know the little I've read about it in the research bulletin."

"It certainly is … interesting." Was there a glimmer of humor in his eyes? "And our research is cutting edge. Research subjects with blood matching this platelet profile are quite unique, with a fascinating list of correlating attributes."

"What attributes do the subjects share?" Kat said. She couldn't resist asking the question. *Tread carefully, Kat,* an inner voice warned.

"Certain dietary sensitivities and accelerated healing, among other things." Ionescu's mouth curled slowly into a smile. "I'm afraid I can't disclose any more details in general discussion. The subjects in this study value their privacy, and we request all employees to sign a non-disclosure agreement when they join us." He paused, and his eyes, thoughtful and assessing, briefly met hers. "Perhaps I should also mention that this position would attract a significant salary increase."

"Oh!" Extra money would be nice, particularly if she had to pay for accommodation in a big city.

"I hope I can count on you accepting our offer?" Ionescu's voice was smooth as silk.

Kat blinked. It was a little too early to be asking for a commitment, surely? She wasn't sure why he was being so pushy. "As I was saying to Director Norris when you arrived, I'll need a few days to think it over. But I'm very grateful to be offered the opportunity."

For the merest instant, Kat thought she saw discomfiture on Ionescu's face, as if he'd actually expected her to agree immediately, to give her acceptance on the spot. But then that momentary lapse was cleanly erased, and his expression became benign once more, so she almost thought she'd imagined it.

"Of course." Another charming smile. "Anything involving relocation requires some thought. But I hope you will not take too long to make your decision."

He held out a business card, and Kat took it and slid it into her pocket.

Moments later, she was out in the hallway, heading past the

dark, quiet, offices and deserted labs toward the building's exit. She passed Paul, hovering in the alcove next to the vending machine, and gave him a wave.

"'Night, Paul. I'm heading home now. Thanks for letting us use your office. I really appreciate it."

Paul gave a befuddled smile. "Happy to help. Goodnight, Kat."

Outside, the chill of night was setting in, and she hurried to her car across the dark lot. Before she slid into the car seat, she reached into her pocket for the business card she'd put there, and read it as she swung the door shut. Her eyes widened. Despite Paul's talk of head office she realized she knew almost nothing about the parent company that owned the pathology lab here in Charleston and a string of others like it. Given the speed with which companies changed hands in the corporate world, that probably wasn't surprising.

Seeing what was written there in black and white, though, gave her a jolt. Not so much the main part of the card, which identified Leander Ionescu as the Chairman of the Research Division, Manhattan. No, it was the corporate insignia in the top left corner, the well-known inverted ankh symbol, that surprised her.

Hema Castus Institute. Yeah, she'd heard of the institute, with its reputation for corporate secrecy and its state-of-the-art premises in the mountains south of Pittsburgh. It was an industry byword for quality. The word "prestigious" wouldn't do justice to the carpet in their reception area, and though it was probably much smaller, she guessed their hematology research division in Manhattan would be no different.

She stared out at the dark parking lot, eyes narrowed. If this Ionescu was the chairman, he had to be really, really high up, especially judging by the way Norris had reacted.

The confused expression she'd seen on Paul's face just before she'd left was starting to make a whole lot of sense. Maybe he was wondering, like she was, why this project they were recruiting for was so important to them that senior executives were picking up blood samples and sourcing staff in person?

Which brought her to a more pertinent question: why choose her?

She tapped the end of the card against her lip, thinking, but no easy answer came to mind. With a sigh, she reached for her bag, and carefully slid the card into her wallet.

She fastened her seatbelt, then started the car and reversed out of her space. It was all a little weird, but she couldn't argue that the end result wasn't good for her. She was being offered a fantastic position with a well-respected employer. And as a bonus, Paul would hold her job here for her, in case she didn't like it. Definitely win–win.

As she pulled out onto the road, the psychic's words from yesterday came back to her. *Destiny is about to take a hand in your future.* And here she was, the very next day, being headhunted and offered a sizeable pay increase by the chairman of one of the nation's finest research laboratories.

She shivered. The timing was just … coincidence, right?

In the car on the way home, Kat's phone beeped as a text message came in. She waited until she'd pulled into the driveway before checking it. It was from Tiff.

Out with friends. Candice Brown the PSYCHIC called me, has something U 4got RU home?

Kat texted back *Yes*, and then grabbed her bag and headed for the door. As she stood there fumbling for her door key, the phone beeped again, and Kat glanced down at the new message from Tiffany.

She will B there soon.

Kat frowned. She didn't remember leaving anything behind after her consultation, let alone something important enough for the psychic to track her down and deliver it to her at home, at night.

She got the door open just as a car pulled up in the driveway behind her own, its headlights briefly illuminating the hallway. As she switched on the porch light, she heard a car door slam, then the faint rustle of someone approaching across the grass.

Kat recognised the woman's face as she drew closer. Tonight, though, Candice Brown the psychic looked very different. She had her hair pulled back in a simple ponytail, no makeup or jewellery, and she was wearing faded jeans and a dark shirt.

"Hi," Kat said, as Candice stopped near the front door. "My housemate texted to say you'd be coming."

"I have something for you," Candice said abruptly. She looked down at the brown paper parcel she was holding, and then up at Kat. Her face was pale, eyes tired – like she'd seen too much lately.

"Our Arcana. It's been passed through my family for generations," Candice said. "Kept hidden. My grandma had the gift too, and when she gave me the book she told me I'd know when it was time to pass it on." She held the parcel out to Kat. Not like she was handing over a present – more like she was passing on a wearisome burden.

Kat reached out to take it from her, but her face must have betrayed her bewilderment.

"You're a dark child," Candice said. "I know it's meant for you." And then she turned on her heel and walked back to her car.

Kat waited until the twin red spots of the car's rear lights had disappeared down the street before going inside and closing the door behind her. This was her second piece of weird for the night. She carried the parcel to the kitchen, her curiosity well and truly piqued. She had no idea what she was expecting to see as she unwrapped the brown paper, but she breathed out in a soft exhalation of wonder when she saw what she was holding. This book was old – probably hundreds of years old – and was beautiful in every way. The cover was hand-tooled vellum, the spine embossed with faded gold. Metal latches, black with age, held the book closed.

Kat turned the book gently in her hands, and read the single word on the spine.

Arcana.

She carried it into her bedroom and flipped on the light, then took the dictionary from her desk. Arcana apparently meant mysterious or specialized knowledge – in plural.

She put the dictionary aside and rested the book on her knee to undo the latches, then opened the cover and began to read. It was mostly snippets, journal fragments, recorded miscellany collected over many, many years, probably by successive generations of Candice's family. One of the early segments caught her eye, dated *Yule, 1603.*

We have moved to a new village, and I heard the children singing and skipping in the square yester morn.

Dark Child walks the night/Pray you for the morning light/Lest when the moon's hid by a cloud/You should feel the darkling's bite.

Foolish are they that make light of things they know not.

Kat shivered. *Dark Child.* That was what Candice had called her.

The next entry, in the same handwriting, was dated *Midsommer Eve, 1604.*

Superstition is gone mad in the village, for two women are called witch, and ask'd to account for sundry evils attributed them. If they burn them both in the bonfires tonight, we can do nothing, for we fear to draw attention to ourselves. We make our plans to move once more, to another house, another unknown village.

She continued flicking through the pages, but the other entries weren't exactly enlightening. Much of what was written seemed to assume inside knowledge, or to reference a world view and a culture she had no understanding of.

One later entry from the 1850s did jump out at her though, a passage apparently quoted from another text, titled *Arcane Mysteries.*

Medieval scholars referred to them as Dark Children, though others, notably those within the Church, called them Devil's Spawn. Some believed such children to be tainted by malevolence, and others thought they were simply gifted. Only a handful of Dark

Children have been born, and all are plagued by dreams of worlds outside human experience, and lives of violence ... in some cases, even an unexplained lust for blood.

Kat shut the book after reading that. Her eyes went to the window, and suddenly the darkness outside seemed oppressive. Yeah, okay, so she was feeling a bit ... spooked.

If in doubt, throw science at it prompted a dry inner voice. Scientific rigor. Evidence. *They* were things she understood. This psychic may have believed her to be a dark child – whatever that was – and linked in some way to the world in this book, but that was just *her* belief. People came up with crazy theories for things every day of the week, and it didn't make them true.

So, Kat decided, she'd consider the matter empirically. A family record like this had to be of some historic importance, given its age, but it was full of old-fashioned superstition, and really, did it actually tell her anything useful? Anything she could independently verify? Nope.

So she'd take the book and give it back to Candice tomorrow after work. No need to be rude about it; she'd just say that she felt it wouldn't be right to keep something of such significance to someone else and their family. End of story.

Having made the decision instantly cheered her up, and she re-wrapped the book, then went to make herself a bedtime mug of hot chocolate.

*

The next morning, Kat slid the parcel into her handbag. She was glad Tiffany hadn't arrived home before she went to bed the night before and wasn't up when she left for work. Tiff would want to know why the psychic had needed to see her so urgently, but for some reason Kat didn't want to have to show the book to Tiff and have her flick through the pages, theorising about why Candice had given it to her.

That afternoon, after work, Kat drove across the bridge spanning the wide brown river and continued on to the parking lot near the little shop where she'd seen the psychic. She slung her bag over her shoulder, with the book inside, and walked the half-block to the shop.

The door was locked, though, with no lights on to indicate anyone was there. Kat stepped back, and then saw the realtor's sign fixed to the top corner of the window. It proclaimed the shop's new status in large letters.

VACANT. FOR LEASE.

Kat looked around to make sure that she was standing in front of the right shop. She was sure this was it.

She peered through the window. The interior was deserted, almost empty, but discarded papers and packing boxes on the floor and an empty bookshelf against the wall told her that Candice – or someone – had packed and left in haste. Kat had been here only two nights ago, and there hadn't even been a suggestion that the place was closing down then.

Kat swung around and began walking back to her car, mulling over the psychic's hasty departure. What would cause someone to shut up shop so suddenly, with no warning?

She felt her bag bump against her side, heavier than usual because of the wrapped book still tucked inside it. She'd been looking forward to giving it back, to getting rid of it and all the unanswerable questions it raised. But seeing as the previous owner was giving every indication that she'd skipped town, it looked like Kat would be keeping it after all.

Chapter 4

It was Friday afternoon, the end of the working week, and Kat hummed to herself as she uncapped the last sample in the batch and prepped a slide. The scent of blood hit her nostrils. Like always, her mind automatically sorted and categorized, gave the unknown patient an ethnicity, an age. Her own little guessing game to pass the time.

She realized she'd been too distracted to pay much attention to the smell of her own blood when analyzing it at the beginning of the week. But she recalled it hadn't been like the run-of-the-mill stuff she came across every day. Hers was a contradictory medley, a mixture of different notes forming an intoxicating whole like a fine perfume; moonlit midnight and sun-baked drowsy summer, dew-speckled unfurling petals and mossy stones and night-scented jasmine. There wasn't one thing which had risen above and defined the whole.

She smiled to herself, amused by her mental foray into poetry. Her sample might have smelled a little unusual, but it was still just blood.

The one in front of her now – this one smelled like a blend. *German*, she decided. *And Irish. Early twenties. Blood group …* It smelled like one of the less common ones. She sniffed. *Definitely B positive.*

She capped the tube, then turned it around to check her answer.

Bridget Ferber, born 1989. Blood type B positive.

A secret smile of victory touched her lips. Perfect score on the whole batch, and some hard ones too. Not that this was a skill she could go public with.

She reviewed the slide and updated the computer record, then began tidying up.

Stephanie wandered over and leaned against the wall near her.

"Join us for a drink, Kat?"

Kat lifted the rack of samples, and shelved them. "Thanks, Steph, but I'm heading to Mom's for the weekend. Next Friday maybe?" *If she was still here.* She wasn't any closer to making a decision about this research position in Manhattan. The opportunity to gain valuable research experience was a definite positive, but the thought of working directly with a group of research subjects with the same rare blood type as her was as intimidating as it was tantalising.

"Okay, enjoy your weekend."

Kat reached under her desk for her handbag. "You too. And have a good night, okay?"

"Thanks." Stephanie grinned. "See you Monday."

Kat was out of the building minutes later, heading straight home to pack a bag for the weekend. She threw in the bottle of iron tablets, as it seemed to be taking the edge off the nausea she was still experiencing. She jotted a quick note and stuck it on Tiffany's door. On her way out, she went to the fridge and grabbed the bag of cubed venison she'd bought as a treat for her mom and Walt at the market yesterday. Venison stew was a family favourite, but they couldn't always get the meat back home in Richwood.

She was on the road in her little car by five thirty, heading southeast out of Charleston on Highway 60. She'd made the trip dozens of times, knew every bend in the road as it followed the serpentine twists of the river, below wooded hills.

The sun was setting as she reached Gauley Bridge, and she drove higher as night fell. She turned northeast off the highway, and her mood slowly lifted as she followed the winding road into the Appalachians, leaving the city far behind.

Growing up, she hadn't been able to appreciate how beautiful it was up here. Mountain life was all she knew. It wasn't until she'd left to go to university in Charlottesville, Virginia, and begun coming back to Richwood as a visitor, that she'd seen it through fresh eyes. She'd noticed how strongly the seasons were felt in the mountains, especially in Richwood where the north and south forks of the Cherry River converged, and spring thaw could turn a burbling stream into a swollen and angry river in days. How the shadows lengthened so much earlier in the afternoon when you were tucked into a mountain valley the way Richwood was.

Moonlight glinted off the water as she crossed high above the river near Summerville Lake. Soon after she turned east on the road to Richwood with a final bridge crossing signaling the home stretch. She was deep in the mountains now, the surrounding countryside mostly heavily forested; oak, ash and maple with the occasional cleared stretch, and lights from farmhouses twinkling through the trees.

It was just before seven thirty when she rounded the final corner, and her headlights lit the front of her mom and Walt's place, a two-story white-painted timber house with black shutters and shingle roof. The house was dark, though.

She reached for her handbag, and the bag of meat beside it on the passenger seat, and then stopped, confused. She'd bought more than a pound of venison, and the bag had been heavy and full when she'd put it on the seat with her handbag back in Charleston. Now, the top of the bag gaped open, and a couple of lonely cubes of raw meat were all that remained.

It didn't take long to make the mental leap, even though her mind rebelled against the appalling thought. She swallowed, her throat suddenly dry. Really, there was no other logical explanation, was there? The bag was empty, and there was nobody in the car but her.

She'd driven home, watching the scenery whip by. And all the while, she'd been absent-mindedly devouring an entire bag of raw venison. She knew she should feel sick to the stomach at the thought of what she'd just done, but that was the scary part: she didn't. The fact was, for the first time all week she felt wonderful. Supercharged and warm and bursting with energy.

But it made no sense. She wasn't much of a meat eater at the best of times, and to do something like this, eating meat *raw*, was so totally out of character …

With a sigh, she reached into the back seat for her overnight bag, got out of the car, and walked over to the house.

She let herself in and dropped her keys on the hall table, and took her bag upstairs to her room. Then she went down to the kitchen, and found a note in the middle of the table.

Kat,

Gone out for ramps. See you there when you get in. Prepare for a surprise.

Kat smiled to herself as she read this. Her mother's handwriting, but undoubtedly Walt's idea.

Spring in the mountains meant the bulbous little native leek plant known to locals as the ramp would be pushing its green shoots up all over the Appalachians. Her stepfather wasn't one to miss out once his favourite restaurant started offering its springtime ramps menu. Ramps were a Richwood tradition, and locals swore the first shoots to show themselves at the end of winter were a cure for almost any-thing.

Walt lived and breathed the stuff for three months of the year, and the rest of the family had learned years ago it was easier to join him than endure the pungent odor exuding from his pores afterwards. With ramps, as with its relative garlic, it was definitely a case of one in, all in.

She headed back out to the hallway, scooped up her keys again and went out to the car.

As she drove the short distance into the center of town, her head-lights illuminated the road ahead and the familiar timber houses to either side of her, at least a few of them faded, a little worn around the edges. Needing a good coat of paint.

Things rarely changed in the center of Richwood, which in a mountain town like this wasn't necessarily a good sign; more an indication that money was tight, and the population was aging.

Richwood was well past its glory days, in decades past, when the lumber mill and the paper pulp mill, the tannery and America's biggest factory for wooden clothes pegs had together employed more than two thousand local men and women. As Walt reminded them proudly, his own great-grandmother had taken a job at the peg factory during the First World War to help make ends meet. But one by one these businesses had closed. Now, only the lumber mill was still operating. And with the number of local jobs falling every year, the exodus of young people continued.

As Kat drove into East Main Street, residential gave way to commercial, mostly nondescript two-story brick buildings dating from the early 1920s. Most of the Main Street commercial district had been rebuilt in a hurry when the bulk of the town's earlier wooden structures were destroyed by fire in 1921, and now, ninety years on, even their brick replacements were looking a little shabby.

Kat parked, and walked toward the welcoming light of the diner. She pushed open the door and looked around. She heard her family before she saw them. Her brothers weren't the quietest of eaters.

"Hey, Kat! We ordered you a ramp burger, but Jez ate it." Ryan gave her a cheeky grin as she reached the table.

As usual, her little brother had finished his meal – and apparently hers too – before anyone else was halfway through theirs. Of course, "little" was a reference to age, not size. Neither of her half brothers could be described as small. Jez was nineteen, five years younger than her – but at six foot one, he towered above her five feet six inches. Judging by his appetite he wasn't finished growing yet. Ryan, at twenty-one, was six two, like Walt and broad-shouldered like his dad too.

Jez managed to look almost apologetic. "I was hungry … and we didn't know when you were getting here. I'll order you a hot one." He jumped up and went to the counter.

Walt nodded in her direction, then returned to his plate, piled high with potatoes, bacon, brown beans, and cornbread – all with plenty of ramps, of course.

"Where's Mom?"

"Gone to the bathroom," Ryan said with his mouth half full.

"Enjoying yourself?" Kat asked her stepfather as he dug into his food.

"You betcha." He grinned and took another mouthful. "Cornbread's good," he mumbled against his fork.

Tessa came up behind her. "Hey, darlin'. You got my note. It's good to see you."

"Hey, Mom." She turned and slid her arms around her mom's narrow shoulders.

"Jez ate your burger," her mom said, returning Kat's embrace.

"I know. He's gone to order me another one."

Kat sat in the spare seat next to her mother just as Jez returned. He reached across and snatched off Ryan's baseball cap.

"Kat, check out Ryan's hair. Got in a fight with a lawnmower." Jez ran his hand over his older brother's stubbly head, then twisted and ducked to avoid a punch in the shoulder.

Kat gave a low whistle. "Wow. It sure is short. What, clippers on number three?"

"Yeah. Getting ready for my survival course. It's more practical." Ryan looked a little defensive, and ran his hand self-consciously over his close-cropped hair.

"Now I'm the only pretty one." Jez grinned, and made a show of preening his thick, golden brown hair. He tossed the baseball cap back across the table, and Ryan caught it with one hand.

"Aw, shuddup. Age before beauty, bro." Ryan slid the cap back on.

"You used to have both. Now you won't stand a chance."

"Chicks dig a man who knows how to look after himself," Ryan said with supreme confidence. "After I've finished this course, *you're* the one who won't stand a chance."

"Yeah? After you've gone a coupla weeks without washing they'll be running *away* from you, bro." Jez grinned, and ducked again to avoid a headlock.

"Like I'll care, when a few months from now I could be halfway up a mountain, or on a river ... and getting *paid* for it. And I guess you'll still be working at the mill."

"Nothing wrong with being a timber man." Walt pushed back his chair and wiped his mouth on his napkin. He stood up, threw his napkin down next to his plate. "It's a good, honest job, whatever you boys might think." He stomped off in the direction of the restrooms.

There was an awkward silence for a few moments, until Tessa reached over and patted Ryan's hand. "You'll make a great wilderness tour guide, honey. Dad'll come round when he sees how happy it makes you."

Kat had been watching Jez speculatively. "Jeremy James, why I *do* believe you're going to miss him!" She grinned. "I know you weren't this upset when *I* left home."

Jez rolled his eyes. "I was in what, like, junior high."

"Of course he's gonna miss me," Ryan said, finally landing a good punch on his little brother's solid shoulder. "But we can still go fishing and camping on weekends."

"Yeah, I'm not sure how much fishing the two of you get done. Or how good you are at it," Kat said dryly. "Seems every time you stay out in the woods overnight, you come home dirty and hungry and eat everything in the fridge."

"It's the exercise," Jez said, rotating his shoulder and rubbing it. "Works up an appetite."

Kat's burger arrived courtesy of a smiling waitress she didn't recognize, who gave Jez an admiring glance as she left the table. Like everything else on the spring menu, the burger was topped with a large serving of the local wild-harvested ramps. They were the first of the season for her, and they smelled a little odd – stronger, even more pungent than usual.

She looked at her huge burger with misgiving. It really didn't smell very appetising, and she knew there was no way she could finish it. But if she didn't eat something her mom would ask questions. What was she going to say? I'm not that hungry because I ate a pound of raw meat in the car on the way here?

Jez and Ryan continued their horsing around while Kat took a few valiant bites, and when she stopped eating suddenly and put her hand to her lips, nobody noticed.

"Excuse me," she muttered. Pushing back her chair, she fled for the restroom. Moments later her roiling nausea reached its inevitable conclusion in the privacy of a toilet cubicle. She went back out to the sink, washed her hands and rinsed out her mouth.

For a long moment she gazed at herself in the mirror. She was a bit pale maybe, but the churning in her stomach had gone now, and she was feeling good again, buzzing with energy and warmth, like she had been ever since eating that meat in the car. She'd barely had a few bites of the ramps burger before feeling sick. What had suddenly made her throw up like that? An answer wasn't forthcoming, so she pressed a damp piece of paper towel to her cheeks and forehead, and then headed back to the table.

When she slid back into her seat, her brothers were still horsing around noisily and nobody commented on her absence.

The smell of the ramps was giving her a headache, so she pushed the remains of her food away and sat back, letting her mind wander while her brothers continued to create mayhem. Too many odd things were coming to light, converging on her from all directions. The weird dreams. The weird psychic with her sudden disappearing act. The aberrant blood test results, and hyper-speed healing. Devouring raw meat and, what's more, *enjoying* it. Was it just a random collection of symptoms, or were they all linked to each other in some way? It was as if the connection that would make sense of it all danced just out of her reach, taunting her subconscious.

*

Later that night, in her bedroom, Kat hung up her wet towel and put on her pajamas. The muted sound of a late news broadcast filtered up the stairs from the television, but she didn't go down again. She'd said goodnight to her mom and Walt before her shower.

Okay, yeah, so maybe she was avoiding one-on-one time with her mom. The moment she sensed there was something worrying Kat, Mom would worm it out of her. She'd always been too damned perceptive. Kat's brothers were going fishing tomorrow with Walt. It would just be her and her mom in the house. Maybe she'd suggest they go to Summerville to do some shopping and have lunch ... and while they were there she'd tell her mom about the job offer, and find the chance to ask some questions about her father.

She was hoping her mother would remember something that would shed light on Kat's weird blood profile. She'd prefer to be as prepared as possible before considering fronting up to this new job. But her dad was always a tricky subject, one much better raised when Walt wasn't around. She'd learned that at a young age, after her mother had once been unwise enough to make a fuss over her early artistic efforts, telling her what a gifted artist her father had been.

Walt had exploded. "She ain't special. Having an artist father who ain't around don't make you special."

Kat remembered the wetness of her mother's tears against her own cheek as Tessa held her close in bed that night, whispering stories to her and smoothing her hair with a gentle hand until Kat fell asleep.

That wasn't the last time Walt and her mother had argued about her father, either.

The facts, as far as Kat could ascertain, were that her father had left San Francisco, where he and Tessa had been living, to visit friends, and never returned. Her mother, desperate to share the news that they were expecting a baby, had tried to follow him, but she'd never been able to find him. Her mother had always suspected foul play. Walt, on the other hand, contended that her father must have got wind of the baby on the way, and hadn't *wanted* to be found.

Kat had no way of knowing whose version was right. And given Walt had met her mother when she was pregnant to another man, friendless and far from home, and had taken Tessa into his life, it wasn't likely that this was a subject they'd ever see eye to eye on.

Kat wriggled into bed with a sigh. She should have put socks on. The temperature was always a couple of degrees colder up here than in Charleston, not that either place was particularly warm at this time of year.

She closed her eyes, but sleep wouldn't come. This new job – well, *potential* new job – wouldn't stop buzzing through her head. She'd been to New York City once, as a child. She had vague memories of Central Park, the Empire State Building, and the subway, but that was about it. The thought of actually living there, working there, was both exciting and a little intimidating.

She rolled onto her side, and bunched the pillow up under her neck, trying to get comfortable. The bed was still cold, and until her feet warmed up she knew she'd find it impossible to sleep.

She rolled over again, and stared up at the dark ceiling. This wasn't actually the big deal she was making it out to be, anyway. She'd lived away from home for years now. So maybe she hadn't lived as far away as New York before, but after her senior year she *had* left Richwood to go away to college. And now she was working in Charleston.

Yeah, and both were close enough that you could come home all the time, an inner voice pointed out.

Oh, who was she kidding? Of course this was a big deal. For a start, Charleston was tiny compared to New York. Heck, the population of the whole state of West Virginia was probably only a tenth of the population of New York. If that. Given she felt most at home in the middle of a mountain wilderness, the thought of being surrounded by so many people was pretty damned scary. But with time, she'd get used to taking jogs through Central Park instead of her long runs through the streets of Charleston or the mountain wilderness. City lights instead of stars. And it wasn't ... forever.

She drifted off to sleep while imagining herself running through Central Park, and fell immediately into a vivid dream.

She saw a woman, black hair spilling untidily around a pale face. The woman was crouching near bars, inside some sort of cage. And then it was as if she gazed straight at Kat, with an odd kind of knowing in her golden eyes, and somehow ... pulled her inside. So quite suddenly, Kat felt as if *she* was there, inside the bars. She *was* the woman, sharing her thoughts, crouched down and looking at her own dirty bare feet.

Her gaze flicked upward as a man entered the room with a springing step.

Kulbart Roth. The name floated to the front of her mind. He always tried to please her, but oh, how she hated him.

"Ah, you're awake," he said, his face brightening still further. She ignored him completely, kept her eyes fixed vacantly on the far wall, where floor-to-ceiling shelves were laden with books and scrolls.

"Come, see what I've brought for you," he coaxed, moving toward the bars. "Fresh fish, caught this morning. And some braised fennel." The smell teased at her nostrils. She was so very hungry. But she made no move, gave no indication she was aware of his presence.

Disappointed, he pushed the steaming plate through the bars and turned away. He moved to sit at his desk against the far wall with his back toward her, and after a few moments she crouched and devoured everything with her fingers. She shoved the empty plate back through the bars, harder than she needed to, and it hit the floor with a clunk.

Roth turned. "There you are. I knew you'd like that." He smiled delightedly, and hurried over, bringing a black leather-bound notebook with him and pulling a chair close to the bars. Always with the book. The book and the damned questions, when she was so tired, and her mind filled with chaos. After so long in here, nothing was clear, nothing was certain to her, yet still he picked away at her mind, preying on her when she was weakest, writing everything down.

Tell him nothing. It was like a mantra in her mind. The one thing she could rely on. *Protect the girl.*

"Now, are you feeling better? Did you want anything else?"

She made no reply. She rarely did, but he sat anyway, and continued, in his delusional way, as if he was having a normal two-way conversation with her.

"Well then – as I told you, I've transcribed everything you said in your last trance." He tapped the notebook, leaned forward eagerly. "Now you're feeling better, I was hoping perhaps we could discuss again what it all means."

She remained crouching, staring away, making no response.

Roth stood, and moved right up next to the cage, cajoling her. "Come, surely you must agree this is exciting. After all these years, I really believe we are close to a breakthrough at last." He tapped the silver bars to get her attention.

Without warning she spun and sprang toward the bars, growling in fury. She sank sharp teeth into the back of his hand, and he broke free with a cry, and staggered over to get a cloth to staunch the blood.

Returning, face pale, he looked at her sorrowfully. "We've talked about this before. I feed you, I care for you. I am your friend. You must not hurt me."

Not my friend. She closed her eyes, concentrating on her pulse until it calmed to normal. *Tell him nothing. Tell him nothing. Protect the girl.*

He sat again, slightly further from the cage, and raised his notebook, flicking through it until he got to the page he wanted. Blood darkened the cloth bandaging his hand, but he seemed to pay no attention to it.

"Now, as I was saying, we must clarify the *meaning* of your words. You repeated many times, 'She is coming.' Is this 'she' you refer to the Mahra? And when and where will she appear?"

There were no windows in the room, but some instinct deep inside called to her, telling her that outside in the open air, it was night, and the moon was full and high in the sky. It was a perfect night for hunting, for those who could roam free. She made a sound between a sob and a wild howl, and beat against the bars.

Roth sat back with a frown. "This really isn't helping. You must stop this behavior … or I will have to bring the chains back. And you know you don't like the chains."

Then she screamed. And it was a terrible, gut-curling sound, filled with anguish and heartbreak.

With a wrench, Kat's connection to the woman was severed. Kat's sleeping consciousness drifted up and away, through a roof rendered flimsy as silk floss, and into the clear night sky under a full moon.

She woke with a start, surprised to find herself in her old bed at home in Richwood. The house was dark, and the distant ticking of the downstairs clock sounded through the slumberous quiet.

So real. So *immediate.* She'd never dreamed of this woman before, and now she felt as if she knew her. A woman imprisoned for so long that her clothes had worn to tatters, and her mind had become clouded. Touched by madness.

At that moment, the psychic's words danced into her head. She'd talked of a seer who was trapped. Lost. And silver chains. Chains that burned. But this was just another horrible dream, right? Surely … surely the images she'd seen, the scene she'd experienced couldn't be real? It was too awful to imagine.

Kat raised unsteady fingers to her eyes, and found them wet with tears.

Chapter 5

Jez and Ryan were up and finishing breakfast by the time Kat returned from her run the next morning. Nothing like a fishing trip to get them moving early.

"Mom up?" she asked as she pulled her dark hair out of its tight ponytail and began to plait it loosely over one shoulder.

Jez shook his head. "Nope. We even made her breakfast, but she wanted to sleep in."

"Yeah, I cooked her eggs, and you ate them," Ryan corrected dryly.

Jez shrugged. "Can't let good food go to waste, bro."

"How come you didn't cook any eggs for me?" Kat asked with mock indignation, flipping her hair aside and going to get herself a plate from the cupboard.

"Could have something to do with him not scratching the rear fender on *your* car last week, maybe," Jez said with a wink, and then dodged the arm Ryan swiped at his head.

"So ..." Kat said with a smile, "you been eating out a lot lately, Jez?" She raised her eyebrows suggestively.

"If you're talking about that waitress, Kat, apparently it's a taboo subject around here," Ryan told her.

"Her name's Jenna," Jez said, and then he clammed up.

"What's the problem?" Kat reached for the packet of bread and took out a couple of slices. "She obviously likes you."

"Yeah, well, I asked her out ages ago, and she said no, okay? Next thing I know she's going out with some guy from Fayetteville or something."

Kat slid her bread into the toaster. "Fayetteville? Long way to drive for a date." She passed the Fayetteville road on her way home from Charleston, but in mountain terms it was still considered a fair way away.

"He was working here at the timber mill," Ryan said, his tone offhand. "Until about a month ago," he added. This was clearly a subject he and Jez had discussed before, maybe several times.

"So is she serious about this other guy? 'Cos she was giving you the eye." Kat could almost feel the Big Sister sign taped to her forehead.

"I heard they, like, broke up or something. A few weeks ago." Jez's face was beet red.

"Okay, so ..." Kat let the sentence trail off.

Jez shoved the rest of his toast in his mouth, and looked up at her mulishly as he replied. "Dunno why you and Ryan are so interested. I don't see *you* going out with any of the guys who like *you*!"

Kat laughed. "Yeah, they're queuing round the block."

"What happened to that guy you used to go jogging with?" Ryan asked.

"My neighbor? From Charleston?"

"Yeah, the one who called here a couple times when you were back for the weekend."

"I don't know. It just didn't work out. And he moved, I think." Plus it'd been painful having to slow her running pace so he could keep up – though she'd liked him best when he was too puffed to talk. Conversation hadn't been his forte.

Jez gave her a look. "*Lots* of guys like you Kat. People ask us about you all the time."

"Really? Who?" Kat was honestly surprised.

Jez shot a look at Ryan, and Kat caught Ryan's slight frown and subtle shake of the head.

"Well, Mike does," Jez offered a little lamely. "I know Mike would love to go out with you."

Mike had been her brother's best friend since grade school, and had seemingly always worshipped her. When he'd visited as a kid he'd followed her around the house, asking questions. Kind of sweet, if a little annoying. More recently, though, he'd morphed into a tall, broad-shouldered young guy like her brother ... and he'd become increasingly tongue-tied whenever he was around her. Made sense to think he might have a bit of a crush on her. But he was only a kid.

"*Mike?* Is that the best you can do?" Kat grinned. "Maybe one day I'll ask *him* out. Poor boy would probably die of shock!"

"Well Mike isn't the only one who likes you," Jez said defensively. "Lots of other guys do too."

"Yeah, I'm sure there are broken hearts stretching from here to Charleston on my account," Kat said with a disbelieving smile. "I'm not exactly inundated with good offers." *But you're not exactly looking, either,* a little voice added. *One guess why.* A sudden mental image of dark-haired male perfection and eyes like a stormy ocean supplied her answer.

She had a favorite dream, one she'd had recurrently since her late teens. The dream scenarios had varied over the years: anything from dancing in a forest glade by moonlight, to a death struggle against some imagined enemy. But the guy by her side had always been the same. Blue-green, dark-lashed eyes, with a brooding intensity in their depths. A tousled mass of thick dark hair that fell to his forehead in tangled waves, just begging to be tamed.

Kat pushed the unhelpful memories away. Comparing every guy she met to a perfect dream man who didn't exist wasn't exactly a recipe for romantic success.

"Seriously, Kat," Jez insisted. "If you're not getting asked out all the time, it must be because you just … act equally friendly to everyone. You're not, you know, girly or flirty or whatever, so I guess guys don't think they have a chance."

"Maybe you need to remember to take your lab coat off when you leave work," Ryan suggested with a wink.

"Oh, very funny." Kat looked down at her chest, drolly self-deprecating. "It's not like I'm all that heavily endowed in the under-the-lab-coat department, boys."

Ryan grinned. "Trust me, not every guy wants to go out with Kim Kardashian."

"Just most of them," Jez added.

"You're not bad-looking, Kat, even if you are my sister," Ryan said. "And you've got the legs. Mike totally fantasizes about your legs."

"Okay, enough!" Kat raised her hands in the air. "For the record, my legs look just fine in a lab coat. Or so I've been told. But—"

"Who, Kat? Who's got the hots for you at work?" Jez begged.

She shook her head emphatically. "I am *not* gonna talk about this with my little brothers."

"But you never—" Jez protested.

"Nice distraction job, by the way." Kat interrupted. She laughed, and reached over to ruffle Jez's hair. "I can take a hint. The subject of you and Jenna the waitress is closed. And as for all the guys in love with me … well I'll let you and Ryan screen them for me and pass on any likely applicants."

Kat grinned, but Jez didn't smile back. He just rolled his eyes. "Whatever."

Kat's toast popped up, and she buttered it and sat at the bench with a stack of her unopened mail while her brothers dumped their plates and cutlery in the sink.

"We gotta go. Dad's waiting outside," Jez said.

"Okay. Have fun!"

"Hey, Kat?" Ryan paused on the other side of the bench as he was leaving the kitchen.

"Hmmm?" Kat was scanning through a credit card offer, and barely paying attention.

Two objects came whistling through the air at her head at full speed, and acting purely on reflex, she reached out and caught one in each hand.

"Would you not do that?" she said in annoyance. She'd thought by now her brothers would have tired of the old game.

"Still a *freak* of nature." Ryan's voice drifted back along the hallway, followed by a laugh, then the front door slammed shut behind him.

She raised both hands in front of her and opened them, frowning at the fragile pale shell of the unbroken egg she held in each hand. They were just eggs. And her brothers had been playing this game for years. Eggs, sticks, balls ... even a knife once, though Walt had given Ryan a hiding for that little stunt.

Normally, the comment really wouldn't have worried her. But with everything that had happened this week, the words seemed to take on a new weight. She *wasn't* a freak of nature, she was just ... different.

Yeah, really, really different, a little voice taunted, seeming to delight in pointing that out as much as her brothers did.

The more she thought about it, the more likely it seemed that her physical "differences" were related to her unique blood. They had to be. But that didn't bring her any closer to knowing *why* her blood was the way it was.

That was part of a larger puzzle. Some sort of cosmic-sized jigsaw – only she was missing most of the pieces.

*

"This is nice, having lunch together, just the two of us." Kat's mom settled into the chair opposite her at their table next to the window of the small Italian restaurant, and gave her a warm smile. "So, you mentioned you had a meeting with someone from your corporate head office about a research job? It's exciting you're looking at moving on to something new, honey. I always hoped you'd get the opportunity to travel, to work in different places before settling down."

"Really?"

"Of course. I was so young when I met your father, and then I came out here and met Walt. But I still got to do my little bit of travel. I hitchhiked all the way here from San Francisco, you know."

"I know, Mom, you've told me this story a million times. And you were pregnant with me too."

"Yes." Her mother's eyes were misty as she remembered that far-off time.

"You were crazy, you know."

"I was in love. I would have followed your dad anywhere."

Her mom had the look on her face that Kat couldn't bear to see, the look she always got when she talked about Kat's dad. Kind of wistful ... and sad. Yep, this was why conversations about her father never lasted very long.

Kat cleared her throat, and quickly changed the subject. "Anyway, the meeting went well. There were two of them in the end."

"Oh?" Tessa tucked a loose strand of her bobbed dark brown hair neatly behind her ear and took a sip of her peppermint tea, looking at Kat over the rim of the cup.

"They seemed to like me." Kat made a self-deprecatory face.

"Of course they liked you." Her mother gave a complacent smile. "So do you have any idea how many people you're up against, or how soon they're going to make a decision?"

"Umm ..." Kat looked down at the tablecloth, and started tracing one of the checks with her fingertip. "Actually, I was offered a secondment to a research lab in Manhattan, starting straight away. Well, as soon as I can organise to go, anyway."

Her mom's face lit up. "Seriously? Sweetie, that's fantastic. You should have told me right away!" Then she took in Kat's expression. "You're not happy about this?" Her sharp gray eyes searched Kat's face for enlightenment.

Kat sighed, and looked up. "It's just that the job ended up being a little bit different than I expected. It's kind of complicated."

The waitress arrived with their meals, placing the salad in front of her mom, and the plate of beef carpaccio in front of Kat.

"Oh, so that's what you ordered?" Her mom maneuvered some of her salad onto the tines of the fork.

Kat had decided to order the carpaccio at the last minute, purely because she'd seen a plate of it going to another table right when the waiter was standing there looking at her expectantly, and it had smelled so good.

Her mom eyed Kat's plate with interest. "I've never known you to eat raw beef, sweetie. I can't keep up with all these modern foods. Everything used to be cooked when I was a girl, and now all these actresses in California are eating raw fish sushi, and goodness knows what else." She stopped to take a bite of her salad.

"Probably raw fish sushi ... and not much else," Kat said with a wry grin. She'd never been much of a dieter. Her mom was even finer boned than she was, and a little shorter, but they shared the blessing of a fast metabolism.

Kat took her first bite, and the thin slivers of delicately marinated meat tasted every bit as good as they'd smelled, the sharp bite of parmesan shards and tang of fresh lemon juice marrying perfectly with the beef. Why had she never tried this before?

She swallowed her mouthful. "Mom, I have kind of a weird question. Do you remember what the moon was like when I was born?"

"What the moon was like?" Her mom wrinkled her nose and smiled. "You mean what point in the lunar cycle?"

"Yeah." Kat picked up her fork again, and toyed with another piece of meat. She had no idea why she was even asking this. What would it prove, anyway, if the psychic turned out to be right, by fluke, and she *had* been born under a full moon?

"There was a full moon the night you were born," Tessa said emphatically. She smiled, eyes seeking out a distant memory. "It was spectacular, truly spectacular. There was a blackout at the hospital that night, and the moonlight was all I had to see you by."

"Oh." Kat speared her piece of meat and raised it to her mouth, feeling a bit disgruntled. Pure fluke. It had to be.

"Why are you asking about that?" Her mother looked merely curious.

"Just, um, something that came up, because of Tiffany."

"Hmmm." Tessa frowned, but let it go. "So, enough changing the subject." She pinned Kat in position with her sharp eyes. "This job you've been offered. It's complicated … how?"

Stupid to imagine her mother would forgo getting the whole story out of her. "Apparently it's a specialized project, researching subjects with a particular rare blood profile."

Her mom nodded, and took another mouthful of her salad. While she chewed, she eyed Kat speculatively.

Kat shifted uncomfortably. "It wasn't coincidence that they were interested in me for this role. It all came about because I identified a sample with the same rare profile they're studying, and my boss, Paul, passed that information on to the team in New York." She looked down again. "And it's complicated because the blood sample in question was actually mine. It wasn't labelled, though, so they don't know that."

Her mother frowned. "What made you go and get the sample taken in the first place? You've always hated fuss like that."

"Well … I fainted at work. There's nothing wrong with me now, I feel fine," Kat hastened to reassure her mother. "But that day I felt nauseous, tired … all pretty unusual for me. And something else strange. Within an hour after the blood test my skin had healed completely so you couldn't see the puncture marks from the needles at all."

Her mom nodded. "You've always healed fast, even as a child, remember?"

"Yeah, but not that fast, Mom. You're talking about times when I healed in a couple of days. This time, the puncture mark was completely gone in only an hour, maybe even quicker – I didn't have any reason to check. The guy from the research lab in New York – well, he mentioned that people with the same rare blood profile I have often heal fast. It's got something to do with how our platelets function."

Tessa was silent for a moment, looking at her hands. When she looked up again, her expression was thoughtful.

"You know, your father was the same. I remember he got badly sunburned once – he told me he'd fallen asleep in a chair near the window. He was completely healed by the next morning."

Kat seized the chance offered, glad her mother had raised the subject of her dad again. "Did you ever ask him about it?"

Tessa gave a low chuckle. "That was just one of many unusual things about your father, but no, I never asked him about it. When we were together questions like that were the last thing on my mind."

"So you think maybe whatever this is – the weird blood, the healing – I inherited that from him?"

Her mom shrugged. "Could be. Your father was a mystery in so many ways. Now I guess he'll always be one." She took a sip of her tea, and made a face at the coldness. Putting the cup on the table, she reached out to take Kat's hand in both of hers. "Sweetie, I know you probably sometimes wonder why I fell for someone like your dad. I think I liked the fact there was something ... different about him. Your grandmother had so many expectations, so many rules. Your father was my escape from all that. And he had his own family issues, from what I gather. It was something we shared. Parents who disapproved of our choices."

"Grandmother didn't ever meet my dad, though, did she?"

Her mom gave a short laugh. "No. By that point I was living in a flat of my own. My 'little rebellion', she called it. But you should have seen her face when I told her he was an artist. And then later, when I told her he'd left … and I was pregnant." She looked down at the table for a long moment, the shadow of old memories passing across her face, and then she sighed.

"Walt's a good man, and a good father to your two brothers, but the truth is, if I had the chance, if I was twenty-one again, knowing what I know, knowing I'd lose him, I'd still choose to be with your father, for however long we had. Wouldn't think twice."

Her mom was looking melancholy now, and Kat knew her mind had flown two thousand miles west, back to that golden San Francisco summer. And her eyes were suspiciously shiny.

Tension clutched Kat's midriff, a heavy force robbing her of breath. She shifted in her seat. Why did this subject always make her feel guilty, as if *she* was the one who'd personally caused her mother pain? It was completely illogical. She willed herself to fill her lungs, and exhale slowly. The tension didn't disappear, but it subsided a little.

This guilt of hers was totally nuts. Not being born at the time should pretty much exonerate her of any blame in the whole thing. Then again, whether something was logical or not didn't really rate when emotions were involved – and like it or not, she was her mom's living reminder of the guy who got away. She gave a deep sigh of her own … which her mother obviously misread.

"Don't let this get to you, honey. And don't let it affect your decision on whether to take the job." Her mom's gaze was warm on her. "Your father was … special, I guess, and so are you. There's nothing wrong with being a little different. But if you feel more comfortable maintaining your privacy, you don't have to tell anyone the blood sample was yours."

"You're right. Thanks, Mom." She tried for a smile, and Tessa must have bought it, because she turned back to her salad.

Way to make me feel better, Mom.

It was such a long time since her mother had used those words.

Special. Different.

She remembered coming home from grade school once in tears, after a running race. Her teacher had accused her of cheating when she'd finished the hilly course before all the other kids without even breathing heavily.

Her mom went to the school to talk to the teacher, and came out of the meeting red-faced and upset. *Special. Different.* Yeah, her mom had used those words that time too. Trying to make her feel better. But all Kat took from their talk was the memory of the unshed tears in her mother's eyes. She knew with a child's certainty her mother was upset because of her, and she resolved at that moment *not* to be special or different – not to stand out in any way.

That was the end of her school sports career. By the time she reached junior high, she was known as the one who always had her nose buried in a book.

Academic. Quiet. Unremarkable. She'd have been happy to keep it that way, but this blood sample of hers would blow her cover completely if anyone ever found out about it.

Her mom looked up at her again, and Kat managed another smile, even while her hand was clenching around her napkin under the table. *Thanks so much for the genes, Dad.*

A moment later, her short-lived burst of anger burned itself out, and she gave another sigh – a rueful, internal one this time. Not much point blaming her father for anything. Mr Unexplained Mystery probably couldn't help having oddly-shaped platelets any more than she could.

"So … I should take the job, right?" Despite some lingering misgivings, she knew she couldn't pass up an opportunity like this. Researching the blood of others who were like her was her best chance of finding some answers.

"It sounds like a great opportunity – if you want it. I've always known you wouldn't be able to settle here. Not while you're so young. People come here to retire, not to start their lives."

"Except you," Kat noted with a smile, pushing her empty plate away and wiping her lips with a napkin. "You didn't quite get that right."

Tessa gave a wry smile, and settled back in her seat. "Well, maybe the land was calling me home."

"Maybe," Kat said. She didn't really believe it was anything more than coincidence that her mother, being one-eighth Iroquois, had come to live here on the fringes of the territory where they'd once lived.

"If you do go, I'll miss you, sweetie. But I want you to have all the opportunities you deserve." Her mom leaned forward, her expression serious, and a little sad. "Travel. See the world. Don't do what I did."

*

On Sunday evening, Kat silently watched the antics of a male cardinal from her familiar nook beneath a chestnut oak, high in the hills a few miles from Richwood. The bird's bright crimson was the only spot of color among the mist-shrouded branches as he flew from one treetop to another, crest raised, loudly whistling his claim to this little piece of Appalachian hillside. She doubted he even noticed her down here, tucked into the natural seat formed where the roots of the great oak grew over a rock.

The bird disappeared into the mist as suddenly as he'd come – probably flying away down the mountain to a warmer perch. Without him, the forest was still, silent, the mist a solid mass, bringing cold dampness to whatever it touched. Kat clasped her arms more tightly around her knees, glad she'd thought to put on a thick sweater and socks before coming out.

As the last of the light faded from the bare aspen branches, and mist deepened to shadows, Kat rested her cheek on her knees, gazing dreamily at the edge of the clearing. She always loved it here. If she sat still for long enough she felt merged with the mountain; the cool stone beneath her thighs, the moist rotted leaves beneath her feet – just like the tree roots curved around her. At peace.

A light wind touched her cheek and she blinked, the chill in the air bringing her back to the present. She lifted her eyes to the clear night sky, where the stars shone cold and brilliant.

When her gaze returned to the edge of the dark clearing, the wolf was there, a sudden dark shape lit faintly by starlight. Huge, between the slender trees. Larger still as he came loping straight toward her hiding place with unerring accuracy, until he loomed over her, tongue lolling out, long white teeth bared in a grin.

"Hey," Kat said, a soft welcome.

He turned, and lowered himself to his haunches on the ground in front of her rock. She slid down to stand beside him and slung an arm over his broad back, resting her cheek against his neck.

Richwood was surrounded by forest, but even so, it would have been strange to see a wolf so close to human settlement, let alone one so huge. The rational part of her had long ago decided that despite the lack of any collar, he was probably someone's pet. Someone's very overgrown pet. A husky, or a malamute – one of those wolfish breeds. But the whimsical part of her preferred to imagine he was a wild creature who for some inexplicable reason had chosen to trust her.

"I've got a new job. In New York." Kat spoke quietly into the darkness, but she knew he was listening.

She buried her face in the thick warm fur of his neck and wrapped her arms around him. His scent of pine resin and musk came to tickle her nose. After all these years, the smell was inextricably interwoven with him and with this patch of hillside. The smell of home.

"I'll miss you," she barely whispered.

He laid his big head on her shoulder, and nudged her as if to say he understood.

Chapter 6

Having her place in Charleston and the room at her mom's place too had always seemed convenient, but Kat was now frustratingly aware of the fact that it also meant twice as much stuff to pack up when she eventually left.

Still, she was pretty much done. She sat on the corner of the bed, mentally thinking through what she'd packed to make sure she hadn't forgotten anything important.

"Packed already, sis?"

Kat looked up to see Jez's face peering around the edge of her bedroom doorway. Her eyes went to the neat cluster of bags against the wall.

"Uh, yeah, guess I am."

"You're a whole day early." He sauntered into the room, and took a good look around. It was pretty bare. Just her pajamas for tonight on the bed, clothes for tomorrow neatly folded on top of the dresser. "Doing things at the last minute is healthy." He gave her a slap on the shoulder, and a cheeky grin. "You should try it."

"I *hate* leaving stuff till the last minute." She watched as he wandered over to the closet and opened it to reveal empty space. "What have you got there?"

Jez lifted the long, capped plastic cylinder up to eye level. "Fishing-rod holder. See, I can be organized too. It's for Ryan's birthday. Got it on sale. Can I hide it here?" He gestured to the empty closet. "You won't be needing the space anymore."

"Sure."

"Thanks." He deposited it with a thud, then closed the closet door. "See ya." He scooted out the door.

Kat, alone in her empty room, couldn't help feeling the tiniest bit aggrieved. What he had said was perfectly true – she wouldn't be needing her closet space anytime soon. But she hadn't even left yet and already he was moving gear in.

"Yeah, what will you want next?" she muttered under her breath. "Shirt off my back? My last breakfast?"

"Kat?"

She looked up quickly. Jez was hovering in her doorway holding a small flat package.

"Mmm? Something else you want to hide from Ryan?"

He shook his head, and came toward her. "Do you, ah, want to take this with you? When you move?" He thrust it at her.

She took it from him, and frowned. "Isn't this that picture ..."

Jez nodded.

"Of course I can't take it, then. It's not mine; it's Mom's."

"I ... I think you should take it." Jez's voice sounded urgent.

"Why?"

"Just ... Mom and Dad were arguing – about Ryan quitting his job or something. And later, I saw Mom looking at this picture. For a long time." He looked down at his feet. "She was, y'know ..."

"She was what?" Kat asked, confused.

"Crying," Jez said.

"Jez, you don't think ..."

"Just take it with you, alright?" He looked up again, his expression suddenly almost hostile. "It's better if it's far away from here. Otherwise it's just trouble."

"Okay. I'll take it. But if Mom goes looking for it and asks you where it is *you* can tell her I have it."

"Deal." Jez stuck his hand out, and she shook it briefly. "Thanks, Kat."

When he was gone, she unwrapped the worn paper to reveal the flat piece of artist's parchment inside, and studied the small charcoal drawing. Her mother's young face was instantly recognizable. The artist had captured her with her face tilted toward him. Laughing, flushed with joy. Illuminated by light, surrounded by shadows.

It was a while since Kat had seen it. Usually, the picture was kept safely tucked away in the front of her mom's old family photo album.

She held it a little closer. There was writing in one corner, in a curling old script. Odd. She knew her father had drawn it, because her mom had told her. But she'd never noticed the artist had signed it.

She squinted at the ornate letters, trying to make them out. *Tironik Vasilei.* Vasilei was her father's name, the only one she or her mom knew — or at least, the only one her mom had ever mentioned. She'd never heard the other before. So was Vasilei actually her father's surname?

Just add it to the list of mysteries, Kat, a wry little voice said. Because she sure as heck couldn't mention this to her mom after what Jez had just told her. It sounded like things were worse than normal with Walt, though judging by some of the discussions she'd had with her mom it'd been no bed of roses for quite a while now.

Kat frowned, and chewed on the edge of her lip, wondering whether she should tell them she'd changed her mind about this job. Stay in Charleston, closer to home, in case her mom needed her. After a moment's worried consideration, she dismissed the idea. If her mom ever found out she'd put a brilliant job prospect on hold for a reason like that, she'd never forgive herself. For now, the phone would have to do – and she could always come back home if things changed.

Tironik Vasilei. The name came back, tickled at the edges of her mind. A thrill passed through her as she realized what this meant. Tironik Vasilei. Or maybe Vasilei Tironik. Her father. She knew her father's *full* name, which meant she might actually have a shot at finding him. For a long moment, she crossed her forearms over her chest, hugging the secret knowledge to herself.

She'd never seriously considered trying to find him before. Not without a surname for him. Not when the very mention of him caused such trouble between Walt and her mom. But things had changed. She was moving away, and any efforts she made to locate her father wouldn't impact on her mother or Walt. And then there was all the weird medical stuff she'd been finding out about lately, which her father might be able to explain. Now seemed like the right time.

She carefully rewrapped the portrait, then sat on the edge of her bed, holding it. Conspiring with Jez like this made her feel guilty. Disloyal to her mom. Then again, her mom sitting crying over this particular picture was kind of like crying over a bunch of love letters from a high school sweetheart, or a wedding photo of an ex-husband. Seeing as her current husband happened to be Jez's dad, Kat supposed she could understand where he was coming from. She sighed. Did Walt have any idea how her mom still felt about Kat's dad after all these years?

Jez was right. Trouble. Definitely trouble. There was no need to involve her mom if she succeeded in contacting her dad. Not at first, anyway. Not until she was ... sure. She went and unzipped one of her bags, and after a brief hesitation slipped the thin package inside the cover of her still-to-be-attempted copy of *Anna Karenina*.

Downstairs, her mom was in the corner chair reading a book while Ryan watched television. She looked up when Kat walked past and smiled absent-mindedly. "Going for a walk, honey?"

Kat nodded. Her mother turned back to her book as Kat walked quickly out into the night. She knew exactly where she was going.

This time tomorrow night she'd be on the road to catch her bus to New York. Tonight was her last chance to see him. To say goodbye.

The wolf was there when she arrived, silhouetted by the full moon rising through the trees behind him, and rendered huge and grotesque by the long-legged black shadow he cast. As he stood staring off into the darkness with his head held high, he seemed less like an animal than he ever had. She began walking toward him, and he turned to face her.

What she saw in his golden eyes made her stop in her tracks; they were lit from within, glowing with a wild fierceness, a hunger she'd never seen in them before. Through all the nights she'd spent by his side over the years, she'd never worried about what might be lurking in the darkness. With him next to her she felt safe. But in that instant, as she stared into his eyes, for a split second she saw him as a predator. Her reflection was there too, in those eyes. Frozen. Silent. Aware she was prey.

Some part of her reacted to the new danger instinctively, screaming at her to run, but her feet were rooted to the ground, her eyes fixed helplessly on his, unable to resist the mesmerizing golden glow, the pull in their depths. He moved toward her, and though her hands were trembling, and her breathing was shallow, the rest of her was very still.

Even if her feet had been working and her mind had been functioning properly, she realized the moment for flight had passed. He was close to her now, and her eyes remained locked on his. For an endless moment, they gazed at each other. Then he sprang at her, a silver-gray blur in the moonlight.

She hit the ground hard, his great paws on her shoulders, his weight utterly immobilizing.

I'm going to die. The thought was only mildly surprising. That it should happen here. Like this.

His huge mouth was so close. Long sharp teeth. She closed her eyes.

A searing pain on her neck … then something warm, wet. Rough against her skin. Was he *licking* her?

Suddenly, the weight was gone from her chest, and the night air was cold against her neck. Stinging.

Her eyes flew open.

The wolf was gone.

Chapter 7

Amarok was grateful for the dark of a moonless sky as he loped up the hill, his paws unerringly finding purchase among the rocks and coarse grass. He didn't particularly want an audience for his arrival home. His destination was already visible; a large stone house, castle-like with its towers, built into the side of the mountain, with bright light spilling out of the many doors and windows. It was early, and he knew his family would have just risen for the night, and the house would be full. They would be coming together in the kitchen perhaps, at this very moment.

He paused, sitting back on his haunches. He couldn't bring himself to go any closer than this. It was too much for his night-accustomed wolf eyes, too soon for the bright light. Instead, he turned and followed a stone path to the side of the building, along a rocky promontory. There was a single small building where the promontory terminated, with sheer cliff face dropping away around it on three sides. In the darkness, the curl of wood smoke issuing from the chimney to the side wasn't visible, but he could smell it, and as he drew closer, the air around the stone structure was subtly warmer. Below the foundations, heated channels crisscrossed below the floors and up through all the walls. The radiating warmth was welcoming on this cold night.

He closed his eyes, overtaken by the exhaustion he had only just been keeping at bay for days. Summoning the last of his remaining energy, he let the change rip through him until he stood on two legs on the stone path, a gaunt, naked man.

With faltering steps, he entered the bathhouse, and slid into the hot, scented water. He stretched, his aching muscles luxuriating in the warmth. The stone step was warm against his back. He had the bathhouse to himself. Perhaps after a little while … perhaps he would be ready to follow the stone pathway to the house and face the others. He couldn't put it off much longer. He was already running dangerously behind. He closed his eyes for a moment, blocking out the candlelight. Even the soft, golden glow was far too bright against his eyes, acclimatized as they were to the darkness of a night forest.

"You should stop this, you know." His brother's voice came quietly from across the room. He opened his eyes to see Anton's figure in the flickering shadows near the arched entryway. He knew Anton wasn't referring to his visit here tonight, or to his avoidance of contact with the others, but to his obsession with the task that had kept him away from home for so many years.

A long, silent moment stretched between them.

"I can't," he ground out, his voice scratchy from disuse.

The specter of Amber rose between them unspoken. On this subject, Amarok was immovable.

Anton sighed. "You could come home more often at least."

He moved forward, shedding his robe, and stepped into the bath on the far side.

As his brother sank deep into the water, ripples moved across to lap at Amarok's chest and he shuddered, acutely and uncomfortably aware of his nakedness, of each and every sensation touching his bare skin. It was always like that after the change. It always took a while to get used to being without fur.

Anton caught his eye, his expression faintly reproachful. "We miss you, my brother. Especially Corrin, every Nochistide. Your absence throws his numbers out. And Della worries about you. We all do."

Amarok was glad his features were hard to see in the candlelight. It was impossible to explain to Anton how painful he found it to be around them all. How he had fled the pain, and only returned because he felt he owed it to them.

He let his eyes drift to the domed glass ceiling and, above it, the newly risen moon and the starry night sky. He found the rounded lines of this building soothing, and its isolation from the main building less threatening. Coming to the bathhouse first was his way of easing into civilization slowly. And after living wild for so long, he really needed the bath.

The man in him could still appreciate such balm for the body and soul as could be found in a dry dwelling and a hot bath. Even the thickest of fur couldn't keep out the chill of the winters he had endured as a wolf. In fact, at this instant, while stretched out in warm water, it was hard to remember he had been in enough pain to render the deprivation necessary. Perhaps time really did soothe such hurts.

The water lapped at his torso, washing away tension, and he spoke at last. "She is a young woman now, the girl I have been watching over. Her name is Katerina. Kat. I never told you, though, the whole of the vision Amber shared with me the night before she disappeared." Amarok glanced up to find Anton's eyes intent on him.

"Amber believed this girl would bring new vitality to our people, that she would unite us. She said we must protect her at all costs, as she is our only hope for lasting peace and justice."

Anton's eyes betrayed his shock. "Surely she didn't mean …"

Amarok spoke softly, finishing the half-uttered thought. "The rebirth of the Mahra. I have often speculated, but of course, I can't be sure."

Anton shook his head slowly, in disbelief and wonder. "I always thought that was just a *ganamar* myth, a way for the true-born to keep hope alive in the face of their slow extinction. We all know that if things continue as they are, it is only a matter of time before there are none of them left. The rebirth of the Mahra would mean the return of fertility to our people, the re-emergence of the true-born as a political force. It would change everything." His gaze sharpened suddenly. "But of course, Amber did not say that was what she meant – not in so many words?"

"No." Amarok frowned. "But there is something very special about Kat. I can feel it." He paused, and closed his eyes again, slowly sinking deeper into the water. "Anyway, you can stop your worrying. The wolf … it's over for now."

"I am overjoyed to hear that." Anton's voice was sincere, but clearly he was waiting for more.

Amarok sighed. "Someone else has found her. After all these years. It happened at work, perhaps. There's not enough cover for me to watch over her there. She told me she was taking a job in New York, and I – stupidly – didn't realize …" Amarok knew his voice reflected his exhaustion. He had run night and day to get here, without pause for food or rest.

"I didn't immediately see the need for urgency, or suspect any danger. Then a letter arrived for her. I smelled it the moment the postman removed it from his bag, and took it before she ever saw it. The whole thing was rich with the stench of a blood-made male. Everything had been organised for her. Airplane tickets to New York, accommodation …"

He opened his eyes to find Anton still watching him.

I have to ask him, Amarok thought. He had been wild too long, and the thought of being near a great city left him cold. He had to entrust this task to someone else. "Brother, when did you last take wing?"

Anton frowned at Amarok's question, the eagle-sharp intensity of his gaze resembling the bird whose form he favored. He shrugged.

"Not long ago. Why?"

"Whoever is behind this job offer will only have been delayed a few days, at most, by my taking the letter. Clearly they know where she will be working, and that she begins there next week. I need you to follow Kat to New York ... and find her before they do."

Chapter 8

Kat shifted her weight on the hard chair. Everything seemed to be about appearances here in New York. Even this space off the foyer of the real estate office was very ... well, fashionable. Dark, short pile carpet, modern art prints on the walls, and everything else stark white. The chair she sat on was definitely built for style rather than comfort. Or maybe the uncomfortable furniture they had here was to discourage people from lingering. She certainly hoped the real estate agent found something for her before the damned chair succeeded in completely cutting off the circulation in her leg.

The woman sitting opposite ran her finger down the list again, lips pursed. "This one might be suitable too," she said after a pause. "Also in East 72nd Street. One bedroom, washer and dryer, partly furnished ... but I know it's been popular. We've had more than twenty applications – I've shown it eight times this week already. You could try your luck, but I can tell you honestly that the landlord is close to making a decision in favor of one of the applications they've already received."

"I had no idea it would be this competitive," Kat said in dismay.

She'd only allocated herself a week to find an apartment and get settled. That'd seemed reasonable when she'd made the plan back in Charleston. Now, she was starting to recognise it for the mammoth task it was. This job had come up at short notice, so she hadn't exactly had much choice in the matter, but if circumstances had been different she'd have liked to start looking for somewhere to live a whole lot earlier.

"Are there any more you can recommend if I broaden my criteria a little?"

The agent shook her head. "You did say you wanted the Upper East Side? The smaller, less expensive ones here do tend to go the fastest. I'd advise you to keep checking the website for new listings though."

Yep, doing that already.

She'd searched online listings at the internet cafe until her fingers were sore, and she'd lost count of how many agents she'd visited over the last couple of days. They'd all said the same thing: there was almost nothing available for rent in her price range within walking distance of where she'd be working on East 67th Street. Unless she was willing to commute, paying more might end up being her only option, but it'd mean she'd be living on beans and rice. And saying goodbye to a social life.

No big loss. It's not like I know anyone here.

She sighed. "Thanks for your help. I'll keep looking."

The agent gave a polite but dismissive smile, and rose to her feet. "Let me know if we can help you with anything further," she said as she ushered Kat to the door.

So. Another strike-out.

Kat's steps were slow as she exited the real estate office. Outside, she stopped to look again at the glossy pictures and enticing descriptions of the multimillion-dollar Manhattan properties listed for sale in the window. Glorious brownstone townhouses. Spacious restored lofts. She shook her head in disbelief. Be nice to have that kind of money.

It wasn't like she was aiming high. All she wanted was a studio apartment, preferably furnished. Didn't matter whether it was in a walk-up or elevator building or a soulless modern high-rise – though if she had a choice, she'd prefer somewhere with a tiny bit of character. She wasn't holding out for a big place, either – not after spending the last few days in a shoebox of a room in a budget hotel on Bowery in downtown Manhattan. Just having her own bathroom again would be a luxury, especially if it was clean.

The last couple of mornings, she'd been woken early by the jack-hammer knocking of pipes coming straight through the walls of her room as someone took a shower in the shared bathroom next door. And then there was the dead rodent she'd almost stepped on in said bathroom. The place was cheap, but definitely not salubrious; the one-star rating was overly generous, she thought.

She was about to turn away and head to the next agent on her list when a gilt-edged noticeboard caught her eye. It was propped against the inside of the window, looking a little out of place in the modern setting. She bent to take a closer look. The font was hard to read, kind of old and ornate-looking, but when she looked closely it resolved itself into letters and words.

Listings. They were listings of properties for lease – ones she was quite sure the agent hadn't mentioned to her when she was in-side. A thrill of excitement passed through her, and a spark of new hope.

Two of the listings she scanned quickly and discounted as they were way outside her budget. But the third was exactly what she was looking for: one bedroom, fully furnished, alcove kitchen, bal-cony, elevator ... and it was available immediately. Even better, it was on East 66th Street, only blocks away from her workplace, and priced just a bit above what she'd originally wanted to pay. She felt buoyant with relief, as she quickly crossed the fingers on both her hands. She could do with a bit of luck this time.

At the bottom of the noticeboard just a few words were written. *Evening inspections. Ask for Cesca.*

She felt a bit conspicuous as she stepped back into the real estate office foyer again. The agent she'd just spoken to was leaning against the front desk talking to the receptionist. She looked up as Kat approached, and stepped forward to meet her, polite surprise on her face.

"Can I help you with something else?"

"I hope so. There's a property I'm interested in inspecting. It was on the noticeboard in the front window."

A strange look crossed the woman's face. "Which noticeboard?"

"The one with the gilt frame." Kat thought it was an odd question. She'd only seen one noticeboard in the window.

"Come back in the evening if you're interested in something listed there." The agent's tone was frosty, almost hostile.

"Oh. I'll need to see Cesca, right?"

The woman looked like she'd just sucked on a lemon. "Yes." She turned and stalked away.

Kat stood there looking after her for a moment, stunned by the woman's rudeness. What on earth had she said to provoke such a strong reaction?

She turned to leave, and as she passed the front reception desk, an odd tingle went through her. On impulse, she paused and smiled at the girl behind the desk, who gave a sympathetic roll of her eyes, and grimaced at the departing agent's back. Kat raised her brows, and mimed a helpless shrug. Moments later, she was outside in the lobby.

"Hey!"

Kat felt a tap on her shoulder and turned around. The girl from the reception desk had followed her out.

After looking around theatrically, the girl spoke in a low voice. "Come back in ten minutes, okay? Angela is going to lunch." She skipped backward, a conspiratorial grin on her face, and quickly disappeared through the office door.

*

The receptionist greeted Kat like an old friend when she returned.

"Hi. That noticeboard is only used for Francesca's clients. Special clients. She handles sales, rental listings, property management and leasing … all of it." The look she directed at Kat was frankly appraising and curious.

"Usually," she added, "Francesca's clients don't come here during the day."

"So she only works nights?"

The girl nodded. "She only works about ten hours a week, but she earns the highest commission in the agency. Our boss gives her whatever she wants. Angela – the agent you were talking to before – she always comes in at number two, so she absolutely *hates* Francesca."

"Oh. Okay."

"You know, I filled in for her once." There was pride in the girl's voice, as if she was reporting on a special honor she'd been granted. "For Francesca. She was expecting some big client to come in but she couldn't be in the office that night, so I covered for her. Nine till eleven. All I had to do was give some guy a key, only he never showed. She still paid me though. A hundred bucks for two hours.

"Francesca says her clients value their privacy, so they prefer to do stuff outside business hours." The girl paused to eye Kat again in fascination.

"So does that mean I'll have to come back tonight if I want to see this apartment?" Kat asked.

The girl snorted. "Forget what Angela said. Total bullshit. I mean, there are always exceptions – like when she gets me to give keys to one of the executive apartments to her married *boyfriend* and then takes a long lunch. She was just trying to get rid of you because you're one of Francesca's clients."

She leaned forward. "Angela is a total bitch. You noticed she recommended a whole lot of apartments on East 72nd, right? And not a mention of why they're cheap."

Kat gave her a questioning look, and the girl just looked back at her expectantly for a long moment, as if waiting for the penny to drop.

"East 72nd," she said again.

Kat was still mystified. Clearly there was something she didn't know that everyone else did.

The girl looked at Kat more closely. "You're not from around here, huh?"

"West Virginia," Kat said, feeling suddenly self-conscious.

"Oh, right!" The girl nodded as if that explained Kat's cluelessness. "East 72nd is one big construction zone for the next few years. It's where they're doing the Second Avenue subway. Underground blasting, like, every day ... and a thing happened a while back where they miscalculated the charge and a whole lot of windows got broken up on 72nd." She shrugged.

"Oh." Kat felt her face heat. The other agent, Angela, must have taken one look at her in her serviceable jeans and well-worn walking shoes and immediately known her for a total country mouse. How embarrassing.

"Like I said – she's a total bitch," the girl said. "She told our boss I was ringing my boyfriend on his cell from work, and got me in big trouble. Anyway ..." She grinned triumphantly as she pulled out a tray full of keys. "*I* have access to all the keys, and Francesca said if a client ever needs something when she's not here, I should look after them. I guess that applies even during the day. So, which apartment was it?"

Kat repeated the address, and the girl rummaged for the key. She looked up after a moment. "You know the Upper East is super quiet, right? Well, apart from 72nd Street!" She grinned at her own joke. "Mostly, young people prefer somewhere like the Lower East Side. Clubs, bars, cool restaurants ..."

Kat shook her head. "I'll be working on East 67th. I was hoping to walk to work."

The girl shrugged, and went back to key hunting.

"Do you live on the Lower East Side?" Kat asked.

The girl looked up, brows raised. "Me? I wish! No, I still live with my parents in Brooklyn. Ah! Found it." She grabbed a big key, and handed it to Kat. It was heavy, the metal blackened and pitted with age.

"Oh, and take this too …" The girl turned to flick through an index box and extracted a card. "You'll need the landlord's details so you can send your application directly. That's how Francesca normally does it." She glanced at the card with a wry grimace. "I guess you can read whatever's on there." She passed it to Kat. "You can keep it. We have more."

Kat took the card. It was printed with a jumble of characters. She blinked and held it closer. There it was: a postal address, again in that same ornate script. It kind of made her eyes tired when she looked at it for too long.

"What language is that anyway?" the girl asked. "It's nothing like Arabic. And I know it's not Russian, 'cos I asked a Russian friend if he could read it and he couldn't."

Kat frowned in confusion. "What language is what?"

The girl smiled knowingly. "I get it. You can't talk about it, right? Privacy and all that. Well, I can be discreet. You could put in a good word for me with Francesca if you get the chance. And I hope you like the apartment."

"Thanks." Most of what the girl had said really didn't make much sense, but clearly she thought Kat was some kind of special client. No need to mess things up by asking too many of her country-mouse questions. She could almost feel the silly smile bubbling to her lips as she pocketed the card and key. "I really appreciate this."

The girl put on a solemn expression. Gave a slow wink. "Hey, if you and Angela ever cross paths again, this never happened, right?"

Chapter 9

"Mr. Raddberg?"

At the soft voice of his assistant, Zeth Raddberg looked up. Portia was timid and respectful in his presence, but ruthlessly efficient and thorough in her own domain. In short, exactly what he liked in an assistant.

"There's a Mr. Roth to see you. He doesn't have an appointment. Should I tell him you're unavailable?"

He frowned. "Tall man? Excitable?"

Portia nodded, and he mentally assigned the right face and history to the name she had mentioned. It was a source of pride to him that he never forgot a name ... or a face.

Portia opened her mouth as if to say something else, then evidently thought better of it.

"Was there something else, Portia?"

"He seems ... agitated, Mr. Raddberg."

This was not news that caused any particular alarm for her employer.

"Very well. Send him in."

She bobbed her head and backed out of the room, a performance he watched with approval. He didn't consider himself vain, or particularly in need of meaningless shows of respect, but at a purely ideological level he enjoyed the old-fashioned observance of hierarchy.

Roth was shown into the room, and it was clear Portia had erred on the side of understatement in describing him as agitated. Distraught would have been a more accurate word – though he was clearly trying to hide the fact.

Raddberg rose to greet him. "Roth-arelli. It's good to see you." The honorific slipped effortlessly off his tongue in recognition of his visitor's status as the elder of the two, but neither was under any illusion as to who really wielded the power in the room.

"Raddberg! I had no idea you had become director. I remember when you started here at Hema Castus as a junior researcher. Brilliant. They all said you were brilliant."

Raddberg gave a polite smile. "Please, take a seat. It has been quite some time since we saw you here at the institute. Seventy, maybe eighty years?"

"Yes, yes. I was not sure whether there was anyone left who would remember me from the old days. I live quietly now."

At this moment, to Raddberg's observant eyes, the man seemed anything but quiet. He sat on the edge of the seat, his hands twisted together in his lap in a clear sign of tension.

Roth cleared his throat. "I have not stopped my work, but I carry it on privately, you know. Well, actually, that is what has brought me here. You see, some of your people from the institute came and took away my research subject. I am sure it was just a mistake of some sort ..." He trailed off, evidently discouraged by the complete lack of emotion in the colorless eyes of the younger man he faced.

"I'm sorry, but my people don't make mistakes." Raddberg's tone was crisp and, despite his words, not at all apologetic. "We have been consolidating records left by my predecessor for the last ten years. He left things a little ... untidy. It's likely your 'research subject' was mentioned in one of his files, and was needed to complete our own analysis."

"But you will return her to me after you have finished your inquiries?"

Raddberg took a dim view of the use of the gender-specific pronoun – and the desperation in the older man's voice. It showed, to his mind, a clear lack of scientific detachment.

"Unlikely. Times have changed, Arelli, and I'll tell you honestly I'm not in favor of unsanctioned private research, even when it's conducted by a respected former employee such as yourself. My predecessor's files – haphazard though they were – apprized us of private research projects spread across the continent. We've already brought a number of externally managed projects like this back in-house. At the request of the Directorate, I might add. The current administration prefers to keep things centralized."

Roth's face paled. "But I was the one who found her and captured her. She has been a great aid to my research for the past thirteen years. Invaluable. And I was close to a breakthrough. Nobody knows her like I do; how to look after her, how to handle her."

Raddberg eyed him disapprovingly. "We are not discussing a pet. Your 'research subject' must have been relocated for a reason. All our subjects are dangerous, with criminal inclinations, and need to be kept under close surveillance by trained professionals in an appropriate facility. I'm sure the subject you mention is no exception."

"But ..."

"If, as you say, this particular subject has been such a great aid to your research, perhaps you would be willing to share your findings with us? Your research to date? We are all working for the same cause, after all. For the greater good of scientific inquiry."

Roth blinked, trapped in a web of his own making. "I ... Of course. My notes are preliminary, but I ..."

"Your cooperation with the institute would be noted on your record," Raddberg added smoothly, "and I'm sure we can improve on your findings, if we find the right way to communicate with this particular subject. After all, we have all the best resources available to us, and many minds are better than one, are they not?"

Roth fell silent, and Raddberg, watching him carefully, could tell the exact moment he realized his cause was hopeless. Best not to give him any time to stew about it.

"Thank you for your visit, Roth-arelli. I'll send you home with an escort, and they can take custody of any relevant papers that might pertain to our joint research. I wouldn't want to trouble you with a return trip." He was smooth, polite, but very final.

After Roth had been escorted out, Raddberg sat in silent thought for a few moments. He unlocked his desk drawer, and pulled out the document he had received earlier in the night, with its distinctive black and red Directorate seal. He scanned it again, even though he had read it thoroughly when it first arrived. There seemed nothing unusual about this particular research order, and he had planned to pass it on to his head of Predictive Science. Still … some instinct told him perhaps he should oversee this one personally.

Leaning back in his chair, Raddberg considered his options. He himself wasn't particularly interested in Roth's area of specialty. Oracles, predictions … here at the institute they called it Predictive Science. To his mind, though, it was very imprecise. He preferred cold hard facts, and genetics was more to his taste.

Roth was quite clearly past his prime, and his methods were old-fashioned. It was questionable whether anything useful would be gleaned from the seized research notes. But to the best of Raddberg's considerable recollection, Roth had been a man with an unusually accurate instinct for research. If that meant this research subject of his was indeed a valuable asset, then perhaps the application of more modern interrogation techniques might yield results.

He tapped the edge of the request document against the desk, once, twice, three times, and then reached a decision. If both Roth and the Directorate were interested in Predictive Science, then he would take a closer look himself. Perhaps this so-called "science" would surprise him with an insight into the future.

Chapter 10

Kat sat in the back of the cab, watching through the window as the Manhattan streets passed her by. They were following 3rd Avenue northeast toward the Upper East Side, leaving her dingy hotel room far behind. She'd been counting off the streets since 10th, getting steadily more excited. The butterflies in her stomach told her that this *was* a big deal – her first New York apartment.

She caught a glimpse of a green street sign: East 47th Street – so still a fair way to go. Ahead of her, a stretch of high-rise commercial buildings continued up 3rd Avenue and into the distance.

Her cab driver honked at the delivery van in front and suddenly swerved across into the middle lane, and the car behind blasted his horn at them for cutting him off. Five lanes of traffic surrounded them, all going in the same direction; at least half of the cars were yellow cabs. Kat settled back in her seat and grinned. Definitely New York City.

She couldn't believe her luck in getting this place. She'd heard the good news quickly too – the day after sending in her application. "Not luck – angler's magic," Ryan would have said, because of the odd impulse that had made her smile at the receptionist at the real estate office, and how all her good fortune had flowed from that. A smile touched her lips now, thinking about her crazy brothers. They both swore they always knew in advance when they were about to catch a big fish. "I feel a tingle in my fingers," Ryan would say, "and I just know I need to let the line out a bit, or wind it back in real slow ... and then bam!"

Kat had no idea whether the odd feeling she'd had at the real estate office was like Ryan's "angler's magic". Maybe the receptionist would have bent over backward to help one of Francesca's "special clients" regardless. Whatever it was – luck, or fishy magic, or a well-timed footsore prayer to the god of small things and Manhattan apartments – the timing couldn't have been better. She'd done pretty well for herself, though it was scary how much even a tiny studio apartment cost to rent here.

The traffic thinned out in front of them, and the cab sped up. She glanced idly out the window, looking for a landmark. After all the walking around she'd done in the last few days, everything in this part of town was surprisingly familiar. Gleaming glass and stainless steel met her eye as they passed the Bank of America on East 59th, and then the shiny black facade of Bloomingdale's whizzed past.

Not far now. She wriggled in her seat, her excitement starting to escalate. They passed East 61st Street, and now there were street trees on both sides of 3rd Avenue. The buildings were more residential, some brown and cream brick, and some more modern high-rises stretching high into the sky out of her line of sight.

At East 64th Street, the cab stopped briefly at a red light, and then they were on their way again, flashing past East 65th. Moments later, they passed a little row of four-story brownstone buildings with shops at street level, and the cab pulled into the left lane, indicated, and turned left into the one-way street. Kat made a mental note of the Starbucks on the corner with a yoga place above it, because she'd be walking back past here to go to work every day.

It was much quieter on East 66th Street. Slender trees, green with fresh spring growth, lined both sides of the street, almost touching in the middle. All the buildings were residential, with not a shop in sight. They passed a big cream limestone church that stretched ahead of them to the next corner, and on the other side of the street there were a couple of big, older apartment buildings in cream stone and brick with awnings stretching from the entry to the curb – no doubt with uniformed doormen waiting to usher residents inside. It was that kind of neighborhood. Those sorts of buildings were totally, *totally* outside her price range.

The stretch she'd be living in wasn't that classy, though her building was more beautiful than most, if a little rundown. Her part of East 66th was similarly tree-lined, but her ten-story building was surrounded by other pre-war brick and brownstone apartment buildings, each with their own quirky vintage character. Only a few blocks to work, and a couple of blocks from Central Park, where she could go running. She'd really got lucky.

As they crossed the intersection and entered her block, Kat leaned forward in anticipation, waiting for the cab to pull over, but they continued on past her building, even though there was a space right in front.

"It's back there," Kat called to the driver. "You've passed it."

The driver pulled over a little further along, and shook his head as he shut off the meter. "I know this city like the back of my hand, lady. You have your street numbers confused. This has to be the one you want." He held out his hand for the fare, and she paid it, annoyed at his insistence when he was plainly *wrong*.

Moments later, she was standing by the curb, her suitcase and two small bags beside her. She looked up at the brownstone building in front of her, with its flight of stairs leading to the front door. The number 54 was emblazoned above the door in gold. She sighed as she looped the straps of one bag over her shoulder, and balanced the other on top of the suitcase, then trundled her way back toward her building. Unbelievable that the cab driver had missed it by half a block even though she'd told him the number so clearly.

She soon reached her building, and a flash of annoyance passed through her. Of course, *she* had been right, not the I-know-this-city-like-the-back-of-my-hand cab driver. She'd told the driver hers was number 64, and the number was right there on the front wall in plain sight. The place kind of stood out from the ones around it too. Handsome red brick and cream stone with gothic embellishments, shuttered windows, and ornate wrought-iron balconies on the sides of the building. Not exactly hard to spot.

She'd seen her fair share of buildings during her long treks over the last week, and this one looked old even by Manhattan standards. But old in an interesting, historic kind of way. A narrow strip of garden ran along both sides of the building, thick with mature trees, their branches almost brushing the balcony railings. That was one of the things she really loved about this place. Having something to look out on other than the featureless wall of the building next door was usually an expensive privilege in Manhattan.

She angled her way through the front lobby door back first, dragging her suitcase in after her, and crossed to the elevator. She pushed the button, and then waited for long seconds as gears slowly shifted into action, and the wire cage descended to her level with a rusty creak. She pulled it open with an effort, and got in, bags in tow. Okay, so a wire-cage elevator was slow, and it was noisy, and it belonged somewhere around the beginning of the last century ... but she kind of liked the romance.

The door to her apartment was a challenge. She spent a while trying to force the key to turn, then tried wiggling it a little. Finally, it turned in the lock, and the door swung open. She hauled all her bags inside, shut the door, and collapsed on the sofa – *her* sofa in her new apartment – with a sigh of relief.

After a few minutes, Kat got up and moved her suitcase and bags into the bedroom next to the generous built-in closet. Her next move was to open the wooden shutters that covered the large windows and the French doors leading onto the big balcony, letting the dappled sunlight that filtered through the tree branches come flooding into the bedroom and living room.

Unpacking her clothes was a quick task. It might have been the state capital of West Virginia, but Charleston was really just a big country town in many ways, and life there hadn't exactly given her scope for a high-fashion wardrobe. She ironed the creases out of her work shirts, skirts, and trousers, and hung them in the closet, then transferred her neatly folded piles of sweaters and jeans onto the shelves, and threw her pajamas onto the double bed.

There was plenty of space left in the closet for her to slide her empty suitcase in at the end. It was nice to get it out of sight. Having the closet full – well, half full – of her clothes meant she'd really arrived. It wasn't quite home yet, but she didn't feel like a tourist anymore either.

One of her smaller bags held her toiletries, the few books she'd brought with her, and assorted bedroom items. She put away the bathroom stuff, and as she was stacking books on the low shelf next to the bed, a flat packet fell to the floor. It was the picture of her mother, drawn by her mysterious father, Tironik Vasilei. She quickly slid it out of sight without unwrapping it.

No new insights on that one. He might be her father, but how on earth was she planning to find him knowing nothing but his name? She'd already tried Google and online telephone listings, but had turned up nothing. She didn't even know if he was still in the country.

Kat wandered through the living room and into the tiny alcove kitchen. There was a refrigerator and a funny ancient-looking microwave, but after opening a few cupboard doors, she realized there was very little in the way of kitchenware.

She pocketed her keys and made a quick trip to the nearest market, back on 3rd Avenue, for some food and cookware basics. She returned laden with bags, and stocked the fridge and the little pantry cupboard.

She surveyed her food supplies with a thoughtful frown. Cheap and nutritious had been her main criteria, so living on beans and rice was about right – at least until she got her first pay check. She pulled a tin of beans and some pasta spirals from the pantry, deciding minestrone was her best option.

She chopped some fresh vegetables with one of the two small knives she'd just bought, then took a glass of juice out onto the balcony and leaned against the iron railing while she waited for the stock to boil. It would be a little weird, eating by herself. At home, she was used to big family meals and plenty of noise, and even at the apartment in Charleston she and Tiff had usually pooled their resources and eaten together.

She closed her eyes for a moment, enjoying the glow of the late afternoon sunlight through her eyelids. Her balcony faced the building's side garden, and she loved being surrounded by green leaves. It was peaceful … and so quiet, too. She heard the distant hum of traffic going by on Park Avenue, and cars moving past on the street below, but there was no noise coming from any of the apartments nearby. Judging by the shortage of apartments in the area she had to assume they were occupied, but with the lack of noise it was hard to be sure.

There was no furniture on her balcony, something she hoped to remedy eventually. It'd be nice to be able to have breakfast and dinner out here when the weather was warmer. She cast an idle glance across at the other balconies, and then, with a sense of disquiet, she peered over to look through the leaves at the ones below.

There was nothing wrong with privacy, but *this* … Suddenly she felt uneasy and out of place, standing here all alone. Like an intruder.

Because every balcony was empty, identical.

No ashtrays. No forgotten coffee mugs or magazines. No pot plants, dead or alive. And across every window and every door, the thick wooden shutters were firmly closed.

Chapter 11

Amarok stood at the edge of the balcony, resting against the stone balustrade, and facing away from the brightly lit room behind him. This was the closest he had come to entering the building since being home. It would be dawn in a few hours, but he wasn't quite ready to go inside yet; to the wolf in him, it was too much like being trapped – though his logic questioned why he would prefer the thought of a damp cave to a warm dry bed. Even without looking, he knew the room behind him so well he could name every piece of furniture in it. What dominated was the long wooden table, heavily carved and inlaid along its length. Tonight, almost every seat at it was filled.

Three seats he knew would be vacant. One was his. As for the other two … Memories of those who had once sat there were undimmed despite the intervening years. Thirteen years. He forced himself to face the unpleasant thought that those seats might never be filled again.

At the head of the table was Aron's empty chair. Aron, who was the closest thing to a father most of them had ever known. His trips to Italy had given him so much pleasure in those last few years, so it had come as no surprise to them when a planned absence of a couple of months had become three months, then four. But after a year had passed without word, then two, they had had to face the fact that their maker wasn't coming back. Aron was dead.

And Amber? Amarok clung to the hope she still lived. She was his twin, each one half of the whole. He didn't believe she could have died without his knowing it. But clearly she was not free to return to them, perhaps never would be. If she was alive, she was imprisoned. That much he was sure of.

His fingers curled into claws as the anger rose in him, the impotent frustration of knowing she was out there somewhere, and he was unable to find her, powerless to save her. He wrenched his mind away from these thoughts. He had been glad to bury them by going wolf to protect Kat for all those years. But he had done enough running. It was time to find a new way to deal with the ache when it returned.

He forced himself to concentrate on the murmur of conversation filtering out through the paned glass door.

"How is he?" Della's soft voice, her concern for him clear in her tone.

Anton's baritone came in reply. "He is here. Our brother has returned. That is what matters."

"For how long? Is he staying?"

"Yes. I think so." Anton again.

"Has he any word on Amber? Did he find a clue to suggest what … what might have happened to her?" The desperation in the male voice was palpable. He had almost forgotten that Miklós, too, was suffering from his sister's disappearance – perhaps as much as he was.

Had it been cruel to leave them all behind to go and grieve in his own way? For him, this meant letting the part of him who had been a brother, the part who had lost a beloved twin sister, shrink until it was no more than a small speck buried deep within him. He had allowed the wolf to subsume his entire existence while he watched over this human girl.

Oddly, in many ways he felt more human as a wolf. More grounded, less … unhinged. Because Amber's disappearance had almost cost him his sanity.

At the time there hadn't seemed any other choice but to leave, to take on the task Amber had left him. Perhaps the compulsion was stronger because they had been the last words she had spoken to him, the last vision she had shared, the night before she disappeared.

"You must search for her. You will know her when you find her. And then you must protect her. We all must."

It had been easy to focus on that one task to the exclusion of all else – particularly as it meant going far, far away from where he could be reminded of Amber. Far from where her twisted and broken rune necklace, darkened by traces of her blood, lay curled together with his in a hidden drawer in the tower room he used on the rare occasions he was actually here.

For all he knew Miklós felt the same. Perhaps he didn't want constant reminders of the past either. Of the woman he had lost. Seeing Amarok night after night through these long, empty years might have brought more pain than healing. After all, Amarok shared Amber's golden eyes, her dark hair.

Anton's voice cut through his recollections, his tone scathing. "Do you really think I would ask him about Amber under the circumstances? Or that he would fail to tell us if there was anything to tell?"

Miklós was silent. Perhaps he also felt powerless and frustrated – the way Amarok did whenever he allowed thoughts of Amber to intrude.

"Why is he standing out there on the balcony? Won't he come inside? We are his family." Della again, sounding a little hurt.

"He will come in when he is ready, Dell. He should not be rushed." Corrin's tone was soothing, and Amarok could almost imagine him smoothing his big hand over Della's long brown hair to calm her. Those two were the strongest in the room in many ways, because they were the only couple. No matter what the passage of the years brought, they always had each other. In her way, his sister had been that for him too, once. A grounding influence. Resolutely, he pushed the thought to the back of his mind.

"So, Anton. Care to tell us why we're here tonight? We haven't met in full council for years." Alek's voice was impatient, aggressive. Amarok wondered whether the attitude was in honor of his arrival.

"Rok has asked for my help – our help. For my own part, I have agreed to give it. I leave for New York immediately after this meeting."

"So he *does* have information about Amber?" Miklós's voice was eager.

"When are you going to get it into your head? That's not what he's been doing all this time. He's been off chasing after some human girl. He couldn't care less that Amber's probably ..."

Amarok was through the door and had Alek's throat in his hand before the sentence was finished.

"You will take that back," he hissed.

Alek's hostile expression showed he hadn't won any new friends with his long absence. Perhaps they all felt the same way as Alek. Perhaps they all thought he shouldn't be here if Amber wasn't. But suddenly, he didn't care. He had good reasons for what he'd done. And no regrets.

"Apologize, Alek." Anton made no move to stop Amarok.

Alek muttered something that sounded like an apology, and Amarok dropped him back in his chair, only just realizing he had been holding him suspended in mid-air. The lights in the room, the enclosing ceiling, and the familiar faces staring at him from around the table all began to register now. His entry had been adrenalin-fueled; that was enough to get him through the confrontation with Alek, but now he was swaying on his feet, overcome by weariness and hunger. His fear of the lights and enclosure was gone though, blasted away in that moment of anger. The door he had entered through was still open, but the darkness outside didn't beckon as strongly.

He walked over to his chair, sheer pride keeping him upright. There was a collective hush as he sat down, taking one of the three seats that had been vacant for so long. He could sense the eyes fixed on him, but it was Corrin's gentle green gaze he met first.

"Am I too late for food tonight, brother?"

As Corrin left the room with Della in his wake, Amarok let his head fall forward onto his folded arms on the table and closed his eyes. He was home now. He would eat, then he would sleep. And Anton would find Kat and keep her safe. Everything else could wait.

Chapter 12

The Hema Castus Research Division was housed in a modern building near the corner of 67th and 2nd Avenue, midway between Hunter College and the University Hospital campuses on the banks of the East River. As Kat walked through the door on her first day, she paused for a moment, taking in her surroundings. The lobby was tiled in dark chocolate-colored marble, and lit with recessed downlights. A cluster of low bench seats upholstered in cream leather filled an alcove to one side, and there were large-leafed pot plants in oversized cream pots placed against the walls.

Director Norris must have been awaiting her arrival, for he hurried over to welcome her.

"Good morning! Everything all right with your travel here, your accommodation?"

"Yes, thanks." It was nice of him to ask, but she didn't think he really needed the whole involved story of her upgrade from grotty little hotel room to studio apartment.

He led her to a bank of elevators, and leaned across her to press the call button. Once inside, he held a security tag on a lanyard up to a panel before pressing the button for the eighth floor. "We're a secure facility. We'll pick up your tag at the front desk. You'll need to keep it with you at all times."

Kat nodded, and followed him out of the elevator as the doors opened. *Hema Castus Research Division* was embossed into the frosted-glass wall in front of her in elegant gold.

"Here we are." Norris held his security tag up to a wall panel, and pushed the heavy glass door open with a click. "Home, sweet home. My wife complains I spend most of my time here." He gave a jovial smile, and Kat politely smiled back.

The reception desk just inside the door was staffed by an attractive redhead.

"Jemma, meet Katerina Chanter. She's starting today."

Jemma smiled at Kat. "Nice to meet you. I have your security pass ready, and your orientation pack has arrived too." She passed a slim folder across the counter.

"We're too small to have our own HR team here," Norris explained, "but you'll find all the information you need is in the folder. Health plans, 401(k), payroll contacts and so on."

He led her along the plush carpeted hallway, past several closed doors. "Meeting rooms," he explained, before opening a door to reveal a comfortable room with tables and chairs, magazines, a pool table, and a kitchenette with tea- and coffee-making facilities. "Lunchroom," he said, then closed the door again.

They continued down to the end of the hall. "I'll give you the basic tour," he said, opening the last door.

He took her on a quick loop through the large research lab inside, stopping to introduce her to several key people as he did so. There were probably a dozen researchers in lab coats scattered throughout the room, working on a variety of tasks. The main thing Kat noticed, though, was the lab equipment. Everything – the microscopes, the computers, the analyzers and storage and refrigeration units – was all state-of-the-art. No expense had been spared in outfitting this place.

Norris ushered her back out into the corridor. "I'm very glad you decided to join our little project," he said. "Chairman Ionescu has asked me to oversee your orientation in person, and I want you to feel welcome here. So anything you need, anything at all, don't hesitate to ask. My office is right down the other end of this corridor."

He started to backtrack toward reception. "The Chairman will be back in the office next week, and I know he's keen to meet with you. See how you're settling in." He stopped at a door halfway along the corridor. "Now I'll introduce you to your team."

The lab inside was smaller, with a single door set into a solid wall on the far side. "That's the darkroom through there," Norris said. "The others will explain."

The two other people in the room looked up when Kat and Director Norris entered.

"Here's the new blood," the director announced, smiling at his own witticism as they crossed the room.

Kat looked at her new workmates, who were observing her with curiosity. One was a woman who looked to be in her late twenties with dark hair cropped short, and big, thick-rimmed glasses. The other was a man; wiry, medium height, early thirties maybe, with sandy hair just long enough to touch the collar of his lab coat, and a little overlong in the front too.

"Monica Rosenbaum. Trevor Gillies." Norris pointed to each in turn. "Meet Katerina Chanter."

"Just Kat is fine." She held out her hand and shook with each in turn.

"If you'll excuse me …" Director Norris looked at his wristwatch. "I'm due in a meeting. These two can look after you from here, and explain everything you'll need to know. We're very glad to have you with us, Kat."

He nodded once, then hurried away.

"So." Monica was studying Kat appraisingly. "I guess we should introduce ourselves properly before getting you settled. I'm local. Born and bred in the Big Apple. I was recruited out of a postdoctoral fellowship at Columbia. You don't turn down an offer from Hema Castus, right?"

"And I'm from Boston, originally," Trevor said. "After MIT I did my five years in the trenches before getting the transfer back east." He gave a comical grimace.

"Trenches?" Kat repeated.

"Yeah. At the main institute, outside Pittsburgh. It's more than an hour out of the city. Hicksville. Seriously, you have no idea."

Kat didn't think now was the moment to mention she'd grown up in a lumber town in the middle of the Appalachians.

"Which school did you go to?" Monica asked.

"University of Virginia."

"They have a good medical school." Monica sounded approving. "And you did your undergraduate there too?"

Kat felt a little awkward clarifying Monica's misunderstanding. "Actually I only have an undergraduate degree, though I was considering doing a masters at some stage."

"Oh." Monica gave her a look, as if mentally reassigning her a position several rungs lower on the academic ladder than she had previously. "So … how did you get on this team, then, Kat?"

Kat was kind of wondering that herself. "I, ah, identified a sample with abnormal platelets."

"No. Way." An incredulous Monica turned to share the moment with Trevor.

"Wow." Trevor put his hands together in a mimed prayer motion, and looked up at the ceiling. "Thank you, thank you."

"Director Norris was telling us about this mythical sample C last week, and we could hardly believe it. I guess it's real! It'll probably be months before we get our hands on it though, if they send it to be cleared through the main institute first."

"How much is there?" Trevor was almost jiggling on the spot, he looked so excited. "Please tell me there's at least half a milliliter."

Kat mentally recalled the color of the sample tube's cap, which indicated the tube volume. "It was a four-milliliter tube."

"Yes!" Trevor punched the air with his fist.

"You have just made his day. Seriously." Monica looked amused.

"Why is it called sample C?" Kat asked, feeling a moment's misgiving. Her surname started with the letter C. "And why is Trevor so excited about it?"

"Doesn't mean anything much, it's just our identifier," Monica said. "You know, sample A, B, C …"

" … through to Z," Kat finished.

Monica gave a short laugh. "Yeah. Theoretically – except we only have two samples. A and B. Three, now, if you count this new one."

"You have no idea how little we get of this stuff." Trevor leaned against the edge of a desk, and wriggled himself into a comfortable position in the manner of someone settling in for a good gossip. "They expect us to do this enormous raft of tests, some of which totally destroy the sample material in the process …"

"Yeah, like the UV-tolerance test," Monica chimed in.

"And when I started in this team two years ago, all they gave me of sample B was one slide."

"One slide. You only had the blood on *one little microscope slide* to work with?" Kat said.

Trevor nodded, obviously happy she shared his disbelief. "I know – ridiculous, right? What do they think we can do with that?"

"I started six months after Trev," Monica said, "and half a year on, he was still growing more material from sample B. That was all he'd been doing. Norris just had him growing more blood, using a special technique he developed at the main institute."

"That's still what I spend most of my time doing," Trevor said. "It's why they recruited me."

"He's a grower, not a shower," Monica said with a grin.

Trevor gave her a dirty look. "I grow more so we have enough for all the tests they want us to do. It's pretty impressive, the colonizing properties of this blood. You basically introduce new plasma and red cells in very small doses, and our samples grow to populate and overwhelm the new material. But it's really, really slow. Used to take me about three months to double a given quantity. You can imagine how much fun it was when I only had one slide's worth to work with. It's been a bit faster in the last year, since my big breakthrough. I discovered the replication rate is increased when samples are exposed to moonlight, of all things." Trevor ran a hand through his hair, pushing it away from his face. "But yeah, a new four mill to play around with is pretty damned exciting, let me tell you."

"Enough, already. Let's show the poor girl her desk." Monica ushered Kat toward an empty workstation. A huge flatscreen monitor dominated it, and beneath there were filing drawers with a key dangling from the top one. A neat pile of notebooks in various sizes and brand-new pens, pencils, highlighters and other bits and pieces were lined up on one side of the desk.

"Mon's been raiding the stationery cupboard for you." Trevor grinned.

"Your computer's all set up. Temporary passwords on the post-it note there …" She indicated a sticky note attached to the bottom of the monitor. "But you're supposed to change them when you first log in. There's a tutorial program you can work your way through to introduce you to our systems. I'm pretty sure there are also some notes in the orientation folder."

"Maybe just spend today working your way through the notes, and ask us any questions you have," Trevor suggested. "It should be pretty straightforward. Then tomorrow, you start shadowing me, and I'll teach you the growth and replication basics, in there." He pointed toward the darkroom door. "All our sample material is incredibly light-sensitive. Just one of the little quirks of this blood type."

"Make sure you soak up the sunlight outside at lunchtime." Monica's expression was droll. "You won't get any around here."

"Yeah." Trevor pushed away from the desk he'd been leaning on to stand upright. "Welcome to Vampire Central. The institute's supposed to be worse, though. When I worked there I heard whispers that there was a huge lab underground, away from the sunlight, and everyone there worked nights."

"Don't be a schmuck." Monica rolled her eyes. "That's got to be an urban myth. You're always going on about what a commute that place was from the city. Location like that, where would they get so many skilled technicians and scientists willing to work nights?"

Kat rested the heel of her hand on her newly allocated desk, the corners of her mouth tilting up as she listened to her workmates bantering. Working in a lab without windows had to get to you after a while, and for Trevor and Monica, humor was clearly a way to dissipate the tension. The fact that they could joke about this place eased some of Kat's own uncertainty about taking up a job like this with such an illustrious employer. Then again, it must be easy to feel confident about your work skills when you were backed by a premier Ivy League education like her two workmates.

She pushed the unhelpful thought aside.

Just take each day as it comes, she told herself. *You can do this.*

Chapter 13

Kat rolled over and opened her eyes reluctantly. No sunlight made its way through the shuttered windows, but the bedside alarm clock told her it was time to get up. She felt like she'd barely slept. Last night she'd been woken by another of those vivid, thoroughly unsettling dreams. Interrupted sleep obviously didn't agree with her, because she'd been left with a feeling of faint nausea … and a splitting headache to go along with it.

This time, in her dream, she'd seen the cloud-blanketed world through the eyes of a giant eagle, flying noiselessly through the night sky. She *was* the eagle at that moment, as it dipped below the clouds, soaring over dark mountain ranges and, finally, over a vast city mapped out in lights; as it flew lower and lower, out of the thermal currents now, drifting past towering skyscrapers and the rooftops below, to alight finally on a tree branch next to a building.

The eagle's great weight caused the branch to bow with a rustling of leaves. Its eyes turned toward the nearby building, looking past the iron balcony railing and through the window to see a dark haired young woman in bed, sleeping.

Just before she'd woken, Kat had realized with a jolt *she* was the young woman in the bed. The apartment window was hers.

She had opened her eyes in the darkness of her room, shaken to the core. The dream had felt so real it was impossible to resist the impulse to get out of bed and go to look out the window. There was nothing in the tree outside, of course, and she felt stupid for having imagined she actually would see a giant eagle perched there on the branch. Despite the proof of her eyes, the feeling of unease had persisted, and she'd pulled the shutters firmly closed across all the windows with a shiver.

Now, as she swung her legs out of bed and sat on the edge, she really didn't want to get up and face the day. Shooting darts of pain pierced the wall of her skull as she pushed herself to her feet with a sigh. Damn – this was exactly the way she'd felt on that morning a couple of weeks ago; the day she'd fainted at work, back in Charleston. She'd been fine for the last week and more, so she'd thought that whatever it was had gone away.

She stood, swaying slightly on unsteady feet, as her head finally righted itself. Probably more due to her stubborn determination than anything else, because despite the way she was feeling, there was no way she was going to call in sick. Not in her first week. That really wasn't the sort of impression she wanted to make on her new employer. Besides, today she was supposed to be shadowing Monica, learning about some of the routine tests they did. It'd make a nice change from yesterday, when, as promised, she'd spent all day in the darkroom with Trevor. She had no idea how he'd survived six months straight of those conditions.

By the time Kat reached work the headache had faded. The nausea and fatigue lingered all morning, though, making it hard to concentrate as Monica explained the various types of tests, and took her slowly through the different procedures for each. She took lots of notes, hoping it would all make more sense when she read them back later.

As she went down to the street at lunchtime, her head was swimming. Going home sick was seeming more attractive all the time. If she wasn't feeling better after eating something, that was exactly what she'd do ... though the idea of food wasn't exactly appealing at the moment.

She started walking, hoping fresh air and exercise would help. On and on she went, for blocks – but with the constant stream of traffic going past, fresh air was in short supply. She passed a donut place, and as she smelled the frying oil her stomach heaved. After two more blocks, she stopped on a corner, giving way to her swimming head. She closed her eyes for a moment, and then opened them and looked up. In a small patch of sky between high-rise buildings, the thin, C-shaped sliver of a crescent moon could faintly be seen. Odd to see the moon here, in the city, in the daytime. It seemed out of place – a bit like her. She sighed, pushing away the unhelpful thought. She'd only just arrived, after all.

As she stood there indecisively, a smell hit her that was impossible to resist. She inhaled deeply, closing her eyes to savor it, and her body turned in the direction that faintest of breezes had come from. Her feet began to move, tracing out a path, reacting to olfactory triggers she was barely conscious of. The scent drawing her toward it at that moment seemed to be the most delicious thing she had ever smelled.

As she stood outside the market on East 86th Street minutes later, purchase in hand, she couldn't even explain to herself what had motivated her to buy the fresh raw ground beef, but the impulse had been impossible to deny. For some reason, her body was asking for – no, *demanding* – meat for lunch, and her mind, in response, had formed the muddled intention of making steak tartare.

She made a beeline for the nearest bookshop, intent on finding the recipe she needed. Her next stop was a tiny shop packed to the rafters with the finest local and imported goods, and she emerged with cornichons, capers and other condiments. She was almost salivating at the thought of the feast that awaited her.

It was a long walk back to work, but she covered the ground quickly, barely aware of the distance. Back in the lunchroom, she found a bowl in the back of a cupboard, and set to work mixing, seasoning, and garnishing, somehow drawing on a precise awareness of how the flavors would blend, how each would complement the other, despite having only read the recipe through once.

Several minutes later, she ate the last of the seasoned beef and relaxed into her chair with a satisfied sigh. That was when she stopped to think about what she'd done. It was like she'd been on autopilot, acting on instinct rather than rational reasoning.

What was *wrong* with her? One minute she'd been considering going home sick, the thought of food totally nauseating ... and the next, she'd been whipping up steak tartare in the lunchroom. And this was after she'd searched out and bought a collection of ingredients she'd never even heard of an hour ago, let alone bought or cooked with before – and she'd searched them out by smell alone.

The memory of her trip to her mom's a couple of weeks ago came flooding back, and how she'd absent-mindedly eaten her way through a whole bag of raw venison on the drive home.

Was it possible her body was craving iron, or something as simple as that? Could that have triggered such a strong reaction? She'd been taking her iron tablets every day since getting the weird blood test results back at Charleston, yet still, she'd been like a sniffer dog going after that meat. She'd heard stories about people eating strange things to get minerals their body was deficient in, but this ... it was beyond weird.

She had to admit she felt fantastic now, though. Filled with vitality as a heated tingling raced through her limbs. It was just like that night she'd eaten the raw venison. The feeling was odd; not unpleasant, but not quite normal. Some sort of protein-induced high.

Well, whatever was causing this, her body seemed to have a clear idea of what food it wanted – or needed. Good evidence for the benefits of following your instincts. She'd heard of retail therapy, so what was this? Food therapy?

"Food therapy." She said the phrase out loud to herself, trying it on for size.

A woman she vaguely recognized from the lab down the corridor, who had just taken a seat at the table next to hers, glanced at her with amusement.

"What did you have, then?"

"Beef," Kat said. She was sure her face was flaming, as she realized she'd been caught talking to herself. She told herself not to be stupid. After all, if it'd been chicken soup, she wouldn't have felt weird talking about it.

"Food therapy would have to involve chocolate for me," the woman said with a smile, unwrapping her sandwich. "No matter what the symptoms, it does the trick every time."

Kat returned the smile, but didn't elaborate any further on her own lunch. She wasn't quite comfortable admitting to the other woman she'd cured herself of a headache and an upset stomach by eating over half a pound of seasoned raw beef.

*

On Thursday night, Kat woke from a sound sleep to find herself bathed in sweat. She rolled over to look at the alarm clock's digital display, and the glowing numbers changed from 12:00 to 12:01 as she watched. It was only a bit over an hour since she'd gone to bed. She frowned to herself in the dark. What had woken her? She usually slept all night without waking – except when she had those strange dreams. That was pretty often lately. But she didn't think it was a dream that had woken her this time.

She was thirsty though. She got out of bed and padded silently into the bathroom to get herself a glass of water from the tap. Drinking it didn't really refresh her. Man, it was hot. Her skin was all clammy, her pajama top sticking to her chest. It'd been cool when she'd gone to bed, but now it was like a heatwave had struck.

She sat on the edge of the bed, debating whether to change into fresh pajamas. Suddenly, a tremor ran through her body, starting in her toes, then moving through her feet and up her legs in a wave of sensation, gaining strength as it flowed on up through her chest and through her head. When the tingling dissipated, it left her skin burning hot, invigorated by the flow of energy through her.

This must have been what had woken her. She gave a shiver, though she wasn't cold. Rolling back into bed, she pulled just the sheet over herself, and lay curled on her side, trying to calm the butterflies in her stomach.

This was only the most recent in a growing list of odd things her body had experienced in the last few weeks. Fainting, and unexplained nausea, and strange protein cravings. It was definitely starting to shake her certainty that there was nothing wrong with her. Even her old workmate Stephanie's suggestion of paying a visit to a doctor for a general medical was starting to sound like a pretty good idea … though she had no idea what a doctor would make of her strange list of symptoms. Or what she'd do if they suggested a blood test. Another batch of bewildered pathologists worrying over her strange blood was the last thing she wanted, and she was hoping, with time, to get all the answers she needed herself, at this new job.

She lay still as her body slowly cooled, waiting to see if the strange sensation would return. But it didn't, and she must have fallen straight into a deep, dreamless sleep because the next thing she knew it was morning, and her alarm clock was waking her.

Whatever had caused the feverish heat seemed to have passed, and oddly enough, she felt wonderfully rested. Definitely an improvement on Wednesday morning's headache. She was glad it was Friday. Her first week had been pretty full-on, with so many brand-new skills to learn. She was looking forward to a couple of days of quiet.

*

Kat arrived home that night lugging a heavy bag of groceries, her supplies for the weekend and the following week, and she shouldered the bag as she pushed open the lobby door. Like every door in her building, it wouldn't open without a protesting squeak of rusty hinges. It was as if nobody else ever used them, though of course that was impossible in a building this size. She lowered the bag of groceries to the floor while waiting for the interminably slow elevator, and as she straightened up the lights flickered.

A sudden chill passed through her. Kat looked around nervously, her gaze skittering over the shadows and dark corners. Quickly, she leaned forward to press the elevator button again, to speed her means of escape, aware at the same time she was being a total idiot. The lights had flickered once, and in a split second she'd cast herself in an Alfred Hitchcock movie.

She made herself take another look around the lobby, calmly this time. Even the shadowy corners. And it was completely deserted, of course, apart from her and her groceries.

Kat bent and picked the bag up again. The solid weight of it in her arms was comforting. Tinned tomatoes, garlic, onions, pasta shells ... you couldn't get much more prosaic than that. She knew it was silly to let herself get rattled. She'd been through the lobby every day this week.

Never at night, a voice in her head reminded her.

It was easy to see what had spooked her. The whole place was old, and though it wasn't actually rundown it was clear it hadn't been maintained for quite a while. The lights were all working – just – but they were dim, leaving shadows in the corners they didn't seem to reach. In fact, they didn't give off much more light than the streetlights outside. Every other day she'd been home before dark, so she hadn't noticed.

The elevator finally ground to a halt in front of her, and with a little surge of relief she pulled open the doors and stepped inside and the wire cage began its ponderous ascent.

The elevator stopped at her floor with a jerk and a grinding of gears. Kat pulled open the doors, and blinked in surprise. A girl was standing in front of her. Kat was sure she hadn't seen her through the grille before the doors opened.

"Hi" she ventured, and smiled. This was the first person she'd met in the entire building in six days. It was nice to see a real person.

The girl smiled back, held out a hand. "Hi, I'm Char. Welcome to the building. Been here long?"

"I moved in last Sunday. I'm Kat." She took the offered hand, and shook it briefly. The girl's grip was cool, firm. Kat stood, feeling awkward for a moment. Char was standing right where she needed to walk.

"Come on, I'll walk you to your door. Want me to take that?" The girl gestured to the bag of shopping.

"No, I'm fine, thanks."

The girl matched steps with her along the hallway. Kat broke the silence.

"So, how long have you lived in the building?"

"A while. Feels like decades."

Kat grinned. "Well, I guess if I have any questions about anything I can ask you then."

"Yeah, whatever." Char gave her a sidelong glance, then looked away again. "You new in town?"

"Yeah, just moved here from West Virginia to take up a job."

"What do you do?"

They had arrived at Kat's door, and she balanced the shopping bag against the wall as she fitted the key to the lock.

"I work in pathology research. You know, identifying blood disorders, stuff like that."

"You work with blood?"

"Yeah." She paused as a wave of defensiveness rippled through her. She was used to people's reaction to her choice of career. They thought it was boring, or even kind of disgusting. She looked at Char, prepared for the same response.

Char was staring at her, eyes faintly glowing, nostrils flared.

Then she grinned, her white teeth impossibly shiny in the dim light of the hallway.

"That's cool."

It wasn't the response Kat had been expecting, and she found herself smiling back at the girl. "Hey, do you want to come in for a minute? I mean, if you have time?"

"Sure. I work nights, but I don't have to be anywhere for hours."

She followed Kat through to the kitchen, and leaned against the bench top watching with interest as Kat emptied the bag, putting items away in the almost empty cupboards, stocking the tiny fridge.

"I don't have much stuff," Kat felt a need to explain. "I traveled here by bus."

Char shrugged, watching her without comment.

After a moment, Kat broke the silence again. "Um, Char, is there a super or maintenance guy in the building? I mean, I wanted to ask about some of the doors. They're kind of hard to open."

"You might have to look after that yourself."

"No super?"

"He's hibernating. Haven't seen him for years."

Kat laughed. "You're exaggerating, right?"

Again, the girl shrugged. After a long pause, she said, "So, you having a … what's it called … housewarming?"

"Not much point. I don't know anyone here."

"No family or friends?"

"Nope. They're all back home."

"Oh, that's too bad."

Kat was surprised by the genuine regret in the other girl's voice.

Char continued, "Hey, don't take this the wrong way, but you should be careful around here. You know, if you don't have someone else looking out for you."

"What, is this a dangerous neighbourhood?"

"No, I mean here – this building."

"Well of course I'll be careful," Kat said, "but you're the only person I've seen all week. I was starting to think there wasn't another human being in the place."

Char seemed to find her comment funny. "You might be right about that."

Kat cocked an eyebrow at her. "The talent is that bad, huh?"

As if in answer, Char touched the stone hanging around her neck. It was a beautiful pink stone, carved into the shape of a heart, and the necklace itself was ornate, old-fashioned; a truly spectacular piece of craftsmanship. Kat had never seen anything like it.

"It's beautiful. Rose quartz, isn't it?"

"Yeah."

"Are you into crystals then? Does it mean something to you?"

"Looking for love," Char said drolly, and rolled her eyes.

Kat raised her eyebrows. "Well good luck with that."

"Thanks."

Char beamed at her, eyes shining. She was an incredibly beautiful girl – perfect skin, thick luxuriant dark hair, and those amazing luminous eyes. Kat couldn't really put her finger on what color they were. With skin like that she had to be young … maybe eighteen or nineteen?

"You know, I don't think you'll have any trouble finding someone when the time is right. And hey, if you come across a spare one you don't want, then toss him my way!"

Char wrinkled up her little nose. "So are you fussy? Or will anything with a pulse do?"

Kat laughed. "You're funny."

Char grinned back at her. "So are you." She stood upright, then yawned, stretching her arms above her head. "I guess I'd better get going. You must have stuff to do."

"I'm just about to start dinner." Kat hesitated. "Do you want to stay and have something to eat? I'm having pasta. I can cook extra, no trouble."

"Thanks for the offer, but I've already eaten today."

Kat pulled a knob of garlic out of the cupboard and reached for a chopping board and knife. When she looked up, the other girl had started to move toward the door.

"I'm outta here."

Kat followed her out, and Char paused in the doorway, her hand on the knob. "Remember to keep your shutters closed at night, okay?"

"Char, I'm on the third floor. I may not be a city girl, but I kind of assumed I didn't have to worry about thieves coming in through a window up here!"

"Can't be too safe, though, right?"

"Sure." Kat smiled. This really wasn't the moment to admit she was already taking Char's advice, even if inadvertently. She'd been keeping the shutters firmly closed every night since her dream. It would definitely sound crazy to admit she was a little freaked out because she thought an eagle was watching her.

"Hey, thanks for coming to say hi," she added. "Like I said, I was starting to think there wasn't another living soul in the place!"

Char smiled goodbye as she pulled the door shut behind her.

A split second later, Kat realized she didn't know the girl's apartment number, even whether she lived on this floor. She opened the door again and stuck her head out, ready to call after her. But the hallway was empty; Char had vanished.

Chapter 14

Char stood in front of her mirror, flicked through a few clothing choices, then pulled out a red silk corset and black top.

She was having trouble with what should have been an easy decision. Should she report the girl? Not report the girl? Having a human around the place who smelled so damned enticing was dangerous on both sides of the equation. Especially a long-legged, big-eyed slender young thing like this one. She reminded Char of a gazelle. Walking goddamn prey.

Char stared at her reflection, her mind wandering, then abruptly frowned and bit her lip. Her sharp teeth broke the skin, and she absently licked away a drop of blood.

Why was she even here? That was the real question. No human had set foot in the building for decades. Her presence was definitely weird.

That'll teach me not to automatically approve every application I get, sight unseen. The laissez-faire approach to tenancy approval had been working fine for her for years, but it looked like her luck had just run out.

She had little to do with humans normally, but there was something about this girl. Something different. A unique quality unconnected to her alluring smell.

To her surprise, Char realized she kind of liked her. And despite herself, she was feeling … protective. She shut down the thought almost before it had surfaced.

This is not my problem, she told herself firmly.

In a moment of decision, she crossed to the phone. The rules were pretty black and white on this sort of thing. No room for creative interpretation. Any aberrant occurrence had to be reported. She dialed the number and waited until she was connected, listening to the clicks and pauses as the line was rerouted again and again. The Directorate liked to do things that way. It was impossible to know where their call center was actually located.

"Yes?" The female voice that answered spoke in their language.

"I need to make a report."

"On which species?"

"Human."

Char gave her details, and after a moment the woman spoke again.

"Stay where you are. I'll have the agent assigned to your zone call you."

While she was waiting, Char glided over to the cold storage unit, took out another two hundred milliliters, and slid it into the warmer. She hadn't been lying when she talked to Kat. She had fed already today, but that smell had sent her completely off balance. She hadn't felt this jumpy in ages.

The thought sent her rummaging in a small, carved chest. She retrieved a moonstone and aquamarine bracelet she hadn't needed to wear in quite a while, and changed her clothes again to match, this time putting on a teal-blue fitted silk top. Then she downed the two hundred milliliters in a couple of gulps. By the time the call came through a few minutes later, she was almost calm again.

The guy's voice was brusque, no-nonsense. Like he didn't have any time for messing around, and wanted her to get to the point as quickly as possible.

"You want to make a human report for North America, right?"

"Yes."

"Okay, what state is the human in? They dead, injured, what?"

"Um, no." Already, this call wasn't going at all as she had expected. "The human is fine at the moment."

"So what are you reporting then?" He sounded annoyed, as if he didn't want to be bothered with whatever petty problem she had, and that protective feeling gripped her again. If someone didn't do something soon there *would* be something serious to report. Probably Kat's death. She resolutely pushed the thought out of her mind, and let his annoyance fuel her own. This was *definitely* not her problem. She wanted nothing more than to pass it on to the appropriate people, though that would only happen if they took it seriously.

"Well I'm sorry if you think I'm wasting your valuable time, but I'm just following the code." Her voice was anything but conciliatory. "I'm making a report because this human has atypical abilities in at least two areas, more for all I know. And she smells like a damned smorgasbord. She had me salivating and I have a low blood need."

"Right then." He sounded resigned. "Run me through the two areas she's shown atypical ability in."

"She has true sight."

"Evidence?" His tone was clipped.

"She's come to live in my building." She gave the street address, then added, "We're a completely non-assimilated community." Silence. "That means we're V-rune protected," she added.

"I know what a non-assimilated community is." He sounded annoyed again. "I know your building. Manhattan, right?"

"Yeah."

"And the other point?"

"I can't scan her. And I mean, not at all. She's completely shielded."

"Well that's not unheard of for a human."

His tone was still more dismissive than she cared for. He was being kind of a jerk, making her jump through hoops just to make a damned report.

"It is for me. I have a pretty high psychic rating. Mind scans are kind of my thing."

"Okay then." He sighed. "So that's three areas, not two. I mean, if you think she reads V-runes. They rate that as a separate skill from having true sight." There was a moment of silence from the other end of the phone. "Look, I'm not gonna lie to you – I think she does need to be checked out, but I'm kind of snowed under right now. I can't get to New York before tomorrow night. Can you take care of her until then?"

"You want me to watch out for her?" Char asked incredulously.

"Yeah. I'm near Detroit. Helluva commute for one little girl. It'd take half the night. I have too much on here to leave right now."

"Yeah, well I have stuff of my own to deal with too. I can really do without this."

Char paused, but there was an unhelpful silence from the other end of the phone.

"Are you still there?"

"Yeah."

She wouldn't be surprised if his mind had already moved on to the other jobs he had on. Places to go, people to see. As far as he was concerned, this was her problem, for now at least.

"She could be dead by tomorrow night. *I* don't want to have to watch her. I'm not trained for this kind of thing." She found herself biting her lip again, and moved her hand to clasp her necklace. It seemed she wouldn't be able to avoid this responsibility, however unwelcome it was. A feeling of helpless frustration welled up in her for a moment, and she firmly quashed it.

Despite the phone line between them, the guy seemed to respond to the uncertainty in her tone, the need for reassurance. He was less abrupt when he next spoke. "Understood. Know anyone who can help you, maybe?"

"Yeah. I do know someone." She spoke reluctantly. "They could even maybe hook her up with some crystals."

"Crystals? What, to ward off bad stuff? Yeah, all right – not that

I can see how it would protect her. I mean, I wear them sometimes, but I don't set much store by that, ah … stuff, myself. Guess you females are all mystical in the unassimilated communities, huh?"

"Yeah, whatever." Char rolled her eyes, knowing he couldn't see her. "I'm not completely nuts. I actually meant crystals as in a rune necklace. If they can see she has friends, it might make someone think twice before trying anything."

"Oh." He actually sounded apologetic. "So you know someone who can get her all runed up?"

"Yeah. My maker. She's a master craftsman."

Sounded like the guy muttered a particularly pithy curse word under his breath on the other end of the line. Obviously she'd surprised him.

"You *are* connected. How old are you?"

Char ignored his rudeness, and treated the question as rhetorical.

Even without her answering, the guy's attitude underwent another change. "I'm so sorry, Arella. When you said you were from Manhattan, I just kind of assumed … I mean, most of them are kids, right? I thought, you know, that somewhere like the Towers would be more your scene. I didn't mean to sound like I was fobbing you off earlier. It's just that I'm stretched so thin out here; it's a big zone to cover. I'll be there as early as I can on Saturday night. Call me if you have any problems, okay?"

He terminated the connection, and Char gave a groan. Spending the night on babysitting duty – this was the last thing she needed. But it had definitely been worth putting up with the rudeness at the start to hear him tripping over himself to apologize at the end. The younger ones always reacted like that when they found they were talking to an arella. She usually found it easier when people didn't know, but once in a while a bit of reverence and respect didn't go astray.

This guy had had a nice voice when he wasn't being an asshole. And she didn't even know his name. She found herself wondering what he looked like. Well, she'd find out soon enough. Tomorrow night … and it had better not be any longer than that.

Chapter 15

Kat flopped onto the sofa with a sigh. She was feeling queasy again, with the beginnings of a headache – even though she'd just eaten. Or was it *because* she'd just eaten? Overfull perhaps? Or just tired after a week at work? She contemplated the quiet weekend stretching before her. She didn't know anyone here in Manhattan yet, and didn't have any particular plans, so maybe some sightseeing was in order. Last week she'd been too focused on finding a place to live to do much.

There was a knock at the door.

She opened it to find Char standing there. She'd changed into an incredible blue-green silk top and tailored pants. Her eyes had taken on the color of her top, and almost seemed to glow in the dimly lit hallway. But besides her change of clothes, there was something different about her mood. It seemed she was kind of agitated about something, even nervous. She was wearing a heavy bracelet on one wrist, and she kept fiddling with it.

"Hi again." Kat smiled her welcome. "I thought you had to go to work."

"Yeah, I do … later." She hesitated, and after the silence had dragged on for a moment more than Kat was comfortable with, she smiled again, and held the door open.

"Well, come on in."

Char peered doubtfully through the door, took a sniff, and stepped away. "No, I'll pass. You've been cooking with garlic. I'm kind of allergic – the smell gives me a headache."

"Oh, sorry."

Char gave one of her characteristic shrugs, then paused again, twisting her bracelet.

"I like your bracelet. Moonstones? And what's the blue stone?"

"Aquamarine." She closed her hand over it, as if to press it more firmly against her wrist. "Listen, you wanna come out? I have to stop by the club where I work, but after that I wanna take you to meet someone."

Kat wasn't the party type, and heading off into an unknown city with someone she'd just met wasn't exactly her style. But she didn't have so many friends here that she could afford to be choosy. Heck, she didn't have *any* friends here. And Char seemed nice. A little odd maybe, but nice.

"I guess so. I mean, I'm not doing anything tonight."

"Great. Let's go then."

"Hang on! Won't I need to change? I mean, I'm not dressed up like you are." She gestured to her jeans and beige turtleneck sweater. Comfortable, but not exactly stylish.

"No, you're fine. You look great. Good enough to eat." Char smiled, showing gleaming white teeth.

Kat raised an eyebrow and shook her head. Make that a lot odd. This girl sure said the weirdest things.

"Okay, if you're sure. I'll just grab my keys."

As they stepped out of the building, Char stopped and scanned the street. "I suppose we should take a cab. We're headed downtown."

"It might be hard at this time of night. I've noticed it gets pretty busy."

"There's one!" Char pointed to a cab that had just turned off Park Avenue into the far lane, but the numbers on its roof weren't lit.

"You have good eyes. But I think it's already taken."

As Char stared at the cab, its roof light lit up, and then it slowed. When there was a break in the traffic, it cut across a lane and pulled up right in front of them.

"Wow, some luck!" said Kat, impressed.

Char ushered her in first and then hopped in beside her, and leaned toward the driver. "Alphabet City," she said. "Avenue C. I'll direct you for the last bit."

Kat got a brief view of Central Park by night as they passed it heading south on 5th Avenue, and then the driver turned left onto East 59th, and cut across to 2nd Avenue, which they followed all the way back down to the East Village. They seemed to cover the distance incredibly quickly, and were soon pulling up at a brightly lit club on a quiet street.

"This where you wanted to go?" The driver sounded doubtful. "There's nothing round here."

Kat glanced at the neon lights on the building in front of them, and spoke under her breath to Char. "What does he mean there's nothing here? We're right in front of a club."

"Most people can't see what's right in front of them," Char said. "Which is the way it should be," she added cryptically. She shot a look at Kat, who was staring up at the neon sign mounted on the wall high above the main door. "What do you think of the name?"

"Bar Sanguine? A little unusual I guess. Why?"

"No reason."

"You sure you're okay?" the driver asked. "Not the best area."

Char handed him a hundred-dollar bill. "Wait here. She's staying in the car." She turned to Kat. "Just stay in the cab, okay? Keep the windows up. Don't go anywhere. I'll be right back."

"Wait … Char?" But Char had already got out of the cab and slammed the door firmly behind her, cutting Kat off.

Char must really think she was out of her depth here in the big city. She seemed convinced Kat'd get herself into some kind of trouble if she set foot outside the car. It was just like when Char had warned her to keep her windows closed in the apartment. It would be annoyingly patronising if it wasn't kind of sweet, coming from a girl several years younger than her.

"Seriously, how much trouble does she think I could possibly get into between here and the door?" she muttered to herself. She watched idly through the cab window as three girls appeared under a streetlight on the corner opposite. They were dressed to kill, a high-heeled triumvirate in clothing that left very little to the imagination – and they had the looks and bodies to carry it off to perfection. They crossed the road together, walking with a sinuous grace Kat had to envy. Now if *she'd* been the one who was balanced five inches off the ground in heels that skinny, there was a good chance her knees would be getting intimately acquainted with the pavement sometime soon. Dancers, they had to be dancers. Or models maybe, with plenty of runway experience. The girls disappeared through the club entrance, leaving the street empty again.

Kat sighed, and shifted on the seat. There was something hard underneath her thigh, and she stuck her hand under to pull out a small cell phone. Char must have left it there by accident and was probably wondering where it was. Maybe she should go inside to give it to her. If three girls like the ones she'd just seen could wander around unmolested, then it couldn't be that bad an area, surely? Kat opened the door and started to get out.

The cab driver swiveled around in his seat. "Hey, what are you doing? Don't you have to stay here?"

"I'm a big girl," Kat said with a wry smile. "I'll be fine."

She closed the car door behind her, and walked toward the club entrance. A huge man stood just outside the door, feet splayed, arms crossed over his broad chest. His gaze narrowed as Kat drew closer and he moved to block the entry.

"I'm sorry, private club." His voice was of the deep and reverberating sort. Definitely the voice of someone you didn't mess with.

"Oh." Kat stopped, feeling suddenly awkward. "I was just looking for Char. She forgot her phone." She held it up, but the big man took no notice. His eyes were fixed on Kat's face, his head tilted to the side, assessing her.

"You don't scan," he said, as if to himself. He frowned.

A gust of wind blew along the street and hit Kat in the back. She shivered, and hugged her arms around herself, wishing she had thought to bring a coat.

The man's nostrils flared, and his eyes narrowed as he examined her more closely. "Who did you say you were?"

"I came here with Char. She said she works here?" *And I guess I should have waited in the cab after all*, Kat added to herself. *Not just because I'm freezing to death out here.* If it was a private club and they wouldn't even let her through the door, that explained Char telling her to wait in the car. She was almost ready to tell the guy not to worry about it and turn and go back to the cab when he spoke again.

"I can't let you go in to the main club. Jumpy crowd tonight. But you can wait through here in the VIP lounge." He opened what looked like a service door set into the wall next to the main entrance, and stood aside to let Kat pass through.

She was about to step forward when an odd reluctance stole over her. Maybe she should wait in the cab instead. A gust of wind blew past her, sending leaves and discarded papers scudding against the brick wall. Kat shivered.

"Are you going in?" the guy asked.

She gave herself a mental shake. She was here now. Why *not* go inside to wait? It was freezing outside.

Kat stepped through the doorway to find herself in a very upmarket space. Soft mood lighting revealed a room in shades of gold and beige, filled with luxurious cushioned lounges, and cabriole-legged tables. There was piped music playing softly, though she couldn't see where it was coming from. No windows – but the paneled walls were decorated with gold-framed murals. It was all very tasteful.

"Don't open the other door. I'll tell Char you're here." He shut the door behind him with a well-oiled click, leaving Kat alone.

She moved toward the middle of the room, closer to the door she supposed must lead into the main section of the club. From beyond the door, the thumping beat of a rock song sounded faintly, at odd contrast with the classical music playing here in the VIP lounge.

She sank onto the nearest seat. Luckily this was just a stop-off, and not their ultimate destination, because after seeing how those girls had dressed to come here tonight she could tell her sweater and jeans were far from appropriate.

There was nothing else in the room to provide a distraction while she waited, so she occupied herself with examining the painted panels on the walls. Now she had the chance to give them more than a cursory glance, she saw they were an unusual mixture of styles; some of the reclining figures draped in robes wouldn't have appeared out of place in an Ancient Greek fresco, but there were also darker figures scattered throughout that lent a more gothic feel.

Kat frowned as she scrutinized one of the scenes depicted. There was something about it that didn't seem quite right – something a little bit menacing about one of the darker figures. Though the artist had done nothing overt, the pose of the man bent over the reclining woman seemed ... predatory. Maybe she was reading too much into it. In any case, the detailed scenes provided fascinating viewing, despite being a little bit creepy.

When the door opened, Kat turned toward it with relief, expecting to see Char. Instead, a girl sauntered in, followed by a laughing group of three: a man with a girl on each arm. After a moment, Kat realized why the girls looked familiar; it was the group she'd seen entering the club earlier.

The laughter died away when they saw Kat, and despite the fact that she'd been asked to wait here, and she'd been there before them, she felt like she was the one who was out of place.

Up close, the girls were even more beautiful, almost surreally so, with their flawless skin and luminous eyes.

The man paused just inside the door, head cocked, and breathed in deeply through his nose.

"Interesting," he said. Then he gave Kat a slow, seductive smile as he shrugged off the girls clinging to his arms and moved a few steps toward her.

"Well what do we have here?" His voice and manner were smoother than smooth, but somehow there was something menacing below the surface. Kat's instincts went on to red alert. She jumped to her feet in a hurry, aware of a sudden tension in the room.

"I'm sorry ... I was asked to wait here for someone."

"So will I do?" His voice silky, he continued his path toward her until he was standing right in front of her, and then he reached out to take her chin in his hand, and turned her head slightly to one side.

"I promise I won't keep you waiting." His glance fell to her neck for the briefest moment, and there was dark suggestion in his eyes when they rose to meet hers again.

Kat froze. The situation had gotten out of hand so unbelievably fast she had no idea what to say or do. Who did he think she was? Maybe he'd been expecting to meet someone else in this room. He was treating her like some kind of ... escort or something, but surely there was no way he could possibly mistake her for one, dressed as she was?

The man smiled again, slowly, watching her. He released her chin, running his thumb across the soft fullness of her lower lip as he did so with the most feather-light of touches, then ran his hand down her arm to clasp her wrist.

"Come, sit with me." He gave her wrist a light tug.

"I'd ... rather not," Kat said breathlessly. "I really have to go." She started to move toward the outside door, but the man didn't let go of her wrist and she was forced to stop with a jolt. She was no weakling, and though he seemed to be resting his hand on her wrist with only the lightest of touches, his grip was unbreakably strong. Panic welled up inside her.

Oh God, this couldn't be happening. Desperately she tried to remember something, anything, from the basic self-defense classes all the girls had done at school so many years ago. *Don't show fear.* Her mind desperately thrust the thought at her. Or was that what you did when facing an animal poised for attack?

"I want you to stay for a little while." The man pulled her by her wrist, and she stumbled and fell onto the sofa. He joined her in one smooth movement, keeping his hand on her arm. "Stay here with me and my friends. What can it hurt?"

The three girls had crossed the room, and now entwined themselves elegantly on the sofa opposite, perfectly posed as if for a magazine shot. Kat's mind filled with inconsequential questions. *How can they just sit there? Why aren't they trying to help me? And why on earth does he want to keep me here when he has half a harem already?*

Kat had no illusions about her own appeal; she supposed she was pretty enough when she was all dressed up, with heels and makeup and her hair done nicely. But right now, in casual clothes with her dark hair pulled into a ponytail, she was a moth compared to the brightly colored butterflies on the sofa opposite.

He was probably just trying to scare her, she decided … though she was a little hazy on the question of why he would want to do that. But he couldn't really mean her any harm. After all, it was a public place. Well, sort of.

"You can't keep me here against my will," Kat said. She wanted the words to come out sounding strong and firm. Instead they were little more than a husky whisper.

"But you want to stay, don't you?" His thumb began making slow circles over the veins of her wrist, going round and round with a light, soothing touch as his eyes locked with hers. His gaze was mesmerizing in a way that made Kat imagine that perhaps, if circumstances were different, she might have fallen under his spell. But at the same time there was something repellent about the feral gleam in the depths of his dark eyes.

"No. I want to go." Kat spoke more firmly, and tried to tug her arm away again. God, he was so strong. Immovably strong. The vague fragments she could remember of her self-defense classes had all centered on using an attacker's own strength against him. But she had to guess that was assuming you could move him at all.

"Are you disagreeing with me?" The man gave another smile, displaying gleaming white teeth. "How refreshing. Your kind will usually do whatever we ask … when we ask nicely." He flicked a glance toward the girls, who giggled in assent.

"My friend will be here soon, with the security guy from the door. He's gone to get her." Kat spoke the words with more confidence than she felt, hoping to scare the guy into backing off through sheer bravado. And it was the truth after all – at least she hoped so. What if the security guy had just been planning on waiting till Char came outside and telling her where Kat was then? *Where are you Char?* she wondered desperately. *What the hell have I got myself into?*

The man raised a supercilious brow. "I would hate to be … interrupted while we get to know each other. Perhaps we should move the party somewhere else?"

He rose lithely to his feet, bringing an unwilling Kat up with him effortlessly. "Shall we take our new friend home, girls?"

Terror froze Kat's feet as he started to walk her toward the external door, and when she stumbled, he wound his arm through hers and brought her close to his side, dragging her along with him. She realized again how incredibly strong he was; he was all but carrying her dead weight beside him, and it didn't slow him down at all. *Oh God, this is really happening. He's going to walk me right out of here, and take me who knows where.*

She closed her eyes in panic for the briefest second as they neared the door. *Please let the security guy be there. Please, please, please.*

As they emerged into the dimly lit street and the cool night air hit her face, Kat gave a sigh of relief that ended on a sob. Char was standing just outside the entrance with a slightly built, fair-haired man, talking to the big security guy. Even the cab was still waiting exactly where they'd left it.

Char and the others with her turned at the soft noise of the door opening, but Kat only got a glimpse of their faces before the man holding her thrust her behind him in one smooth move, and she was enfolded in the arms of the three girls, with one of them placing a firm hand over her mouth. Kat immediately began to struggle, but the apparent slenderness and delicacy of the three girls was deceptive. She was held immobile, completely unable to break free of their iron embrace. Bile rose in her throat and her gut clenched.

The man had moved to block her from sight, but Kat was sure Char had seen her in that instant when she'd first emerged. She couldn't believe her rescue depended on a young girl she had only met tonight, and realized suddenly Char didn't even know her last name. If she were to disappear here in a big city where nobody knew her, far away from her family, she wouldn't be missed for days.

Kat shivered at this thought, while she silently prayed Char could do something. The other man with Char didn't look like he'd be much use, seeing as he wasn't much more than a boy himself. The security guy, though – he was reassuringly massive. Char could get him to help. With a job like this he had to be martial arts trained or something, surely?

"Char-arella, what an unexpected pleasure." The man's voice was smooth, perhaps a touch deferential, and he inclined his head slightly.

"Dominic." There was a moment's pause, and when Char spoke next she sounded like she had moved closer, though Kat's view of her was still blocked. "I'm afraid the pleasure is all yours. We'll ignore for the moment the fact that you were using a private room without our invitation. What concerns me is that you may have inadvertently *taken* something from it belonging to me." Char's voice was glacial, and Kat blinked in shock above the hand covering her mouth. Was this really the same girl she'd shared a cab with minutes earlier? Her entire manner was completely changed.

Dominic stood suddenly rigid, the subtle emphasis in Char's words not lost on him.

"Taken something? Have I? I'm sure you must be mistaken, Arella."

"Give it up, Dom." The new voice, a light male tenor from further away, was one Kat didn't recognize, and must have come from the younger man.

"Shall I make him?" The bass tone of the security guy was easily recognizable.

"I'm a good customer for the club, Arella. Surely things don't need to become unpleasant because of one little girl?" Dominic turned slightly, and jerked Kat forward until she was pressed hard against his chest, his forearm across her throat. With his free hand, he ran a finger down her cheek. "Perhaps we could share her?"

Char's eyes narrowed. "Yeah, sure, Dom, you're on fire with that one."

Shooting a glance over his shoulder, she jerked her head imperiously at the three girls. "Get out of here."

They hurried to do her bidding, throwing sidelong glances at Dominic and the group near the door before silently melting away into the darkness.

"That was a big 'no' to the sharing, Dominic," Char said.

Dominic tensed, but didn't move. The fair-haired man casually strolled forward to flank Char.

"She's mine. Give her back." Char hissed rather than spoke the last three words, and Kat flinched at the venom in Char's voice, though it was clearly not directed at her.

"Oh, have her then." Clearly outnumbered, Dominic gave way with a snarl, and he thrust Kat away. Kat's legs almost collapsed under her, and she fell into the arms of the young man beside Char.

With a last, lingering glance at Kat, Dominic turned and slouched off into the shadows, appearing more like an unruly schoolboy who had been reprimanded for mischief-making than the powerful man who had terrified her moments before.

As soon as he was out of sight, Kat took in a breath in a shuddering gasp. She turned to the man who held her, and his eyes were wide, fixed on her face with the oddest expression. She had the sensation she was looking into his soul. There was pain there, and vulnerability, mixed with a desperate yearning. He raised one hand and gently touched his knuckles to the soft skin of her neck where her pulse was still racing. Then he closed his eyes. A shudder went through him.

When he opened his eyes again a shutter had come down, blocking the reflection of the soul within. He scowled and pushed Kat away.

"Is this why you're taking time off? What did you bring *her* here for, Char?"

Kat recoiled, sensitive to his tone. *What's your problem? You don't even know me.*

"Hey, enough with the temper, kiddo. She's my guest." Char's tone was sharp as she moved in front of Kat and leaned forward to murmur something inaudible into the young guy's ear. His eyes flicked in Kat's direction from time to time, frustration warring with fascination in their gray depths. Like he didn't want to look at her, but couldn't help himself.

Uncomfortable with the scrutiny, Kat turned away and stared in the opposite direction. That was just as bad though, because the big security guy was still standing there stoically, arms folded across his massive chest ... and he was staring straight at her too.

When he caught her eyes on him, he spoke, his voice a deep rumble. "Like I said, jumpy crowd."

The words were innocuous enough, but they were the first anyone had directly addressed to Kat since Dominic had let her go –

and despite his size and threatening appearance, the security guy had spoken gently. It was enough to bring the emotion to the surface for Kat. She just nodded in reply, and blinked against the tears that threatened.

The security guy spoke again. "He's Jonathan." He gestured toward the younger man Char was talking to. "I'm Mac."

"I'm Kat," she said, and gave a watery smile.

Char finished her quick conference with Jonathan, and he headed for the club entrance. Halfway there, he twisted to face them again, seeming lost, almost bereft.

"Be careful, okay?" His words were addressed to Char, but his glance flicked across to Kat, as if to include her in the warning too. His eyes didn't quite meet hers though.

"Or should I say *more* careful?" He disappeared through the club entrance.

The security guy cleared his throat. "Ah, Char-arella, I think you should go before anyone else decides to put in a bid for your merchandise."

Kat tensed, sure the "merchandise" he was referring to was her. Char had claimed ownership of her in a similar way when talking to Dominic earlier. Kat wasn't used to having whole conversations go on over her head, with people talking about her rather than to her. And she certainly didn't like being treated as a possession rather than a person.

"Yeah, that's the plan." Char laid her small hand on Mac's big arm. "And thanks for before."

"You know me. Just stand here and look menacing. Young Jon is the brains, and I'm the brawn. That's what you pay me for, right?"

"Hey, you're smarter than you look. Reckon Dominic knew that I was terrified?"

"Nah, you handled him beautifully, like a real pro – and all on your own."

Char gave a shaky laugh. "I don't want to do it again anytime soon, believe me. And it was nice knowing you had my back."

"Anytime, Arella." He paused, and then continued, his face sober. "You know, that's some kind of trouble you've got yourself there."

Char gave a crack of laughter. "You're telling *me*."

He shook his head disbelievingly. "I mean, the smell … You and I both know Dominic likes to bend the rules, but I've never seen him like *that* before."

His eyes moved to Kat for a moment, then away again. He frowned. "I have to say I'd be tempted myself if I didn't know you'd fire my ass. The kid felt it too." He jerked his head in the direction of the door Jonathan had just disappeared through. "So … you sure you know what you're doing Char-arella?"

"Not really, but life likes to throw us curveballs, right?" Char's tone was light, but there was a serious undertone.

"Okay, well you've got my number if you need me … but I'd advise you not to bring her here again. Not unless you want to get me some backup. I have a bad feeling Dom might come back with reinforcements. You don't want to be here when that happens."

Char swore under her breath. "Okay, we're going."

"Sooner this Directorate guy of yours gets here, the better. This is their game."

Char nodded. "Believe me, I'm counting the minutes."

She grabbed Kat's arm, and hustled her toward the cab.

"I thought I told you to stay in the car," she hissed. "What the *hell* were you thinking?"

Char thrust Kat through the cab door, and followed her in. Kat wordlessly held the phone toward her, and Char took it without saying anything. Char leaned forward to speak to the cab driver, and he nodded and accelerated away from the curb.

Kat began to shake all over, finally reacting to the shock she'd experienced. She pulled her knees onto the seat, and buried her face in them. The beginnings of tears pricked behind her eyelids.

Don't cry, she warned herself. *Don't you dare cry.* But her breaths kept coming in heaving gasps, and right now she couldn't trust herself to answer Char's question. It had sounded rhetorical anyway. After a moment, Char's hand touched her knee, and Kat heard the girl let out a shuddering sigh of her own.

Char's voice was gentler when she spoke again. "I'm sorry. It was my mistake bringing you here in the first place. I'm obviously not cut out for this protection stuff. I have no idea what I'm doing."

It was as if the flippant teenager Kat had first thought her to be was just a persona, a skin she had now shed. And the tough act she had used to face down Dominic had apparently been put on too – which was a pity in a way. Because now she sounded as shaken as Kat felt, and that wasn't exactly comforting.

A few moments passed in silence, and as they moved away from the scene of her recent ordeal, Kat's tension began to slowly melt away, and her breathing returned to normal.

When she was calm again, she lifted her head and turned to face Char. "Who *were* those people?" she asked.

Char didn't answer her immediately. She turned and stared back toward the club rapidly receding behind them. "Kat, I'll explain soon, but first we need to get you out of here. I'd like to take you to see a ... a friend of mine."

"I think I'd rather just go home," Kat said. "I don't feel up to going out anymore."

Char's face filled with dismay. "Kat, you can't go home."

"Look, Char, I'm grateful to you for getting me away from that guy, and I don't want to spoil whatever you had planned for the evening, but I just want to go home. I guess I'm not cut out for big-city nightlife. You don't need to worry about protecting me from anything. I'll be perfectly safe at home."

"No. You won't." Char's denial was firm and unequivocal.

Kat's eyes flew to hers, startled.

"What do you mean? There's no way he has my address or anything. Why would I be in danger at home in my apartment?"

"That's what I'm trying to tell you, Kat. I'm not talking about protecting you from Dominic. I mean, not only Dominic. You need protection from ..." She broke off and bit her lip. "Well, from all of us."

Kat blinked. What did Char mean, all of *us*?

The oddness of some of the comments Char had made at their apartment building earlier that night pricked at Kat's awareness. Then the "private" club, Dominic's inhuman strength, the way he had bargained for her with Char like she was a piece of meat ... it all raced through her mind.

A crawling unease stirred deep within her. She shifted a little further away from Char. Finally she spoke, her voice fracturing the tense silence.

"Who *are* you, Char?"

Char fidgeted with the cell phone in her lap, and didn't answer, so Kat repeated the question in a different way.

"Do you all belong to some sort of strange club? Where you get together and randomly terrorize people?"

Char shook her head slowly.

"Are you ... part of a cult? Satanists?" Kat knew there was a sharp edge to her voice. Accusation. Panic. Both were close to the surface, though it was still hard to see this tiny, adolescent-looking girl next to her as someone to be feared.

"No. Nothing like that." Char's voice was low. "But ... we're not like you."

No kidding, Sherlock. The memory of Dominic's hand gripping her wrist flashed into Kat's mind. Strength like that just wasn't normal. She shivered. What the hell had she got herself into?

Char cleared her throat. "We don't usually talk about this stuff. This is kind of hard for me." She turned to look out the window, as if seeking inspiration. At last she spoke, her voice low and reluctant. "We're not ... human."

Chapter 16

Kat froze, Char's words resonating in her mind. Not human. *Not human.*

"What?" she said faintly.

"Humans have had many names for us over the years." Char's voice was husky. "Dark ones – because we can't tolerate sunlight. And there have been other less flattering designations." Her face twisted into a grimace. "But in the old tongue, our kind called themselves *Tabérin*. It's hard to translate. Kind of just means 'our people'. We live much longer than humans. We're fast, agile, and very strong."

"But how can you not be *human*?" Kat couldn't get past this basic fact. "It's impossible. You *look* human."

"So do you," Char retorted, twisting around to face Kat, "yet you came to live in a building warded with any number of protective runes." She snapped her fingers. "You walked right in the front door, like they were no barrier at all. And your mind is a complete blank to me. That doesn't happen with normal humans. Ever."

Kat blinked, barely taking any of this in. She caught sight of her own face, reflected in the cab's rear-view mirror. Wide-eyed and ghostly pale, like someone who'd had a really big shock.

The air was thick with uncertainty and misgiving as she and Char sat, each frozen into position, at opposite ends of the back seat. They were as far apart as humanly possible. Or should that be inhumanly possible?

"Arella," Kat said suddenly. "Back at the club, that security guy called you Arella. And Char-arella. What does that mean?"

"It's an honorific. A way of showing respect to someone older than you. For a male, they'd use the masculine form, arelli."

"You said … you said your kind lives longer than humans. How old *are* you?"

Char gave a low laugh. "Let's just say that when I was born, this nation wasn't much more than a twinkle in Mother England's eye."

Kat could feel Char's eyes on her, gauging her reaction, but she wasn't ready to return the look. What Char was telling her was fantastic. Incomprehensible. While she'd been talking, Kat had searched for the telltale signs of a person spinning a tall story; the hidden smirk, the dancing smile in the eyes. After growing up with two younger brothers she knew what to look for. But none of those signs was there. Char was deadly serious.

And why on earth would Char – and the rest of the people at her club – have wanted to perpetrate such an elaborate hoax anyway … especially on her? Terrorizing her the way Dominic had earlier – for a joke – wouldn't just have been cruel, it would have been completely pointless.

But the alternative was even harder to swallow. Was it really possible that everything Char had said was true?

Moments later, Char's muffled curse broke the silence in the back of the cab, bringing Kat back to the present with an unpleasant jolt. Char craned her head to peer upward out the back window, as they continued along the city street.

"We have company."

Kat twisted around in her seat. "Where?" She couldn't keep the fear from her voice.

"Coming over the rooftops. I think it's Dominic, and two others. They just waited till we were away from the club." She swore again, then leaned forward and spoke to the driver. He made a sharp left turn at the next corner and was soon speeding past a large suburban park, with trees and basketball courts and play equipment.

"I've asked the driver to go around the park. I'm hoping the trees and open ground will slow them a bit."

Kat turned to look out the rear window, and saw a figure, high above the traffic, leap from the top of a five-story building across two lanes of traffic into the canopy of a large tree below.

She turned back around in a hurry, concentrating on the view of the street ahead. Brake lights, pedestrians on the footpath. Safe. Normal. That leap she'd seen, it wasn't real. It couldn't be real. No normal human could survive a stunt like that.

But they're not normal humans, are they? The whisper of thought couldn't be denied.

A shudder passed through her body, her arms, an involuntary reaction to unspent adrenalin. She pressed her hands together between her knees to stop them shaking.

Char twisted around again to keep watch out the back window, but Kat kept her eyes resolutely forward, her hands clasped together so tightly her knuckles hurt. She didn't want to see anything else.

"What do they want?"

"They're hunting you." Char sounded worried. Very worried. And that couldn't be good.

"*Why* are they hunting me?" Panic splintered her voice.

"Maybe I should have mentioned," Char said, "that our kind feeds on blood."

Kat's pulse was a racing beat inside her head, above the vibration of the car's engine. She shuddered and closed her eyes. New York cabs might be the scene of many unusual disclosures, but nothing could top this. The desire to curl into a ball and hide was almost overwhelming.

Let me wake up. Let this all be a dream.

She opened her eyes, but nothing had changed. She was still in a speeding cab, being hunted as if she had a price on her head. Everything was still hopelessly, awfully wrong.

"Yes," she said shakily. "Maybe you should have mentioned the blood."

"Most of us don't hunt," Char added, as if that made things so much better. "Harming a human is prohibited. We have strict rules against that sort of thing."

Not really comforting, Kat thought. Because clearly the guys chasing them right now weren't playing by the rules.

"There's something different about you, Kat." Char's words came in a rush. "Besides being true sighted and all that. Normal humans – sure, they smell pretty edible, and it's nothing we can't handle. But the way you smell ..." She stopped to let out a long, deep sigh. "I've never experienced anything like it. You bring out the hunger in a big way, and for some of us – the younger ones especially – an urge like that is almost impossible to resist."

Kat's eyes were drawn to the other girl then. Char was just sitting there watching her. Hunched into her corner of the seat, her eyes huge and luminous in the dim interior, she seemed to be waiting for Kat to say something.

Kat tried speaking, actually surprised for a moment when her voice worked properly. "So I'm supposed to believe a bunch of your ..." she couldn't quite bring herself to actually give them a name, "your ... kind, want to drink my blood, and you want to protect me from them."

Char tensed. "I've told you the truth, but you can believe what you damn well like – and if you think I wanted this protection gig, you're mistaken." Her tone was decidedly hostile, tension in every line of her body.

"Well, let's both hope you won't have to bother then," Kat muttered under her breath.

Char's exhalation showed she'd heard the softly uttered words.

Kat sat stiffly back in the seat and faced straight ahead. Char had given her some pretty big things to think about. Not big. Mind-numbingly huge. And she hated being so helpless, dependent on somebody who obviously wished they hadn't been saddled with her.

Kat looked down at her hands, knotted together in her lap. She consciously relaxed them, and opened both hands until they were lying palm up in her lap. Her eyes traced the lines there, and she shuddered as the memory of her trip to the psychic drifted to the front of her mind. Right now, she wasn't feeling strong enough to push it away.

She studied her hands, identifying the gaps the psychic had pointed out. Gaps in her life line, which signaled the coming of a radical change. *Not* that she was going to die. Apparently. Though the psychic hadn't exactly predicted this cab ride from hell, so her reliability was looking a little questionable.

What did "radical change" mean anyway? Moving to New York had been a pretty big change, but nothing compared to sitting in a cab with a … well, a non-human, after being informed there were creatures out there in the night desperate to suck her blood because she smelled especially delicious. Was there still worse to come? More radical change? Or was this it? One future, delivered as prophesied.

She grimaced, and turned her hands palm down. A big part of her found the whole psychic prediction thing easy to dismiss. Yeah, seeing Candice Brown had made her a bit nervous. No one wanted to hear bad things, even if they were ridiculous and untrue. What *were* these predictions, these readings, after all, other than educated guesswork or the product of an overactive imagination?

But a dispassionate, impassive part of her had noted with proper clinical detachment the way the psychic's hand had been shaking ever so slightly as it held hers.

"I need to tell the driver where to take us." Char broke the silence. "We can't just keep driving around the park. And I, uh, I don't think I can protect you by myself." Kat heard the undercurrent of frustration in Char's voice, saw her shifting nervously on the seat.

"I know you probably want out of this situation by now," Char said, "but this … friend I want you to meet – she's powerful. She can help us. Keep you safe."

You're right. I do want out. Kat sighed, thinking better of saying what she was really feeling.

You wanted change, Kat, her inner voice reminded her. *This is it. Embrace it.*

And what other choice did she have? Going home and hiding under the covers in bed apparently wasn't an option if you were more than ten years old, or if you happened to live in a building full of …

She shut the thought off and took a deep breath. *Please let this be the right decision.* "Okay," she said. "Take me to this friend of yours."

Char muttered something to herself. "Thank the Mahra for *that*," it sounded like. Then she leaned forward and murmured new directions to the driver. "Take the FDR …" was the only bit Kat heard.

Char shifted, and leaned back against the seat. "We'll be okay when we get to the Towers," she said to Kat. She didn't sound too sure though.

Kat looked across at her nervously. The trees as they sped past cast flickering shadows on them both. Char's face was creased in a frown.

"Damn," Char added after a pause. "I didn't think they'd actually follow us. I've asked the driver to shut off the air con as well, to make it harder for them to follow your scent."

She twisted around again to check the road behind them, and swore quietly. Her eyes met Kat's, and her lips twisted into a wry smile. "Sorry, I don't mean to scare you. I said I wasn't any good at this protection stuff."

Kat pushed her fear down to the pit of her stomach and tried to think calmly, though that was next to impossible. However unnerving the

He eyed Kat again with a troubled expression, then stood aside to let her exit the cab. Once he had escorted them inside they were stopped again, and waited in a plush lobby while a uniformed concierge put the call through.

"Char," Kat whispered, "why did he suddenly agree to let me come inside? What I said wasn't that spectacular." She wasn't sure why she was whispering, but it was that kind of place, the kind you didn't want to disturb with loud conversation.

Char turned to her and shook her head. "We were speaking our language, Kat. You shouldn't have been able to understand a word we said, and yet you spoke to him in Vardic. And then he switched to Karpat, and you switched again, like it was your native tongue."

"What are you talking about? It was English. We were all speaking English. Weren't we?"

Char just looked at her with bright eyes, and shook her head.

*

The concierge escorted them right to the door of the apartment, and then inclined his head toward Char and silently left them.

Char knocked, and after a moment the door opened. The apartment within was more dimly lit than where they were standing, and as Kat was slightly to the side of Char, at first she couldn't see who had opened the door.

"Charice. I wondered how long it would be before you came to see me." The voice was musical and compelling. Powerful. Old. Both beautiful and dangerous at the same time.

Char inclined her head in formal greeting. "Arella-dara. I'm sorry to disturb you with so little warning. I ..." She looked across at Kat, and reached out to pull her closer, then corrected herself. "*We* need your help."

The woman facing them was tall, with her hair piled high and intricately braided. The total effect was somehow ... regal. She surveyed them both calmly for one, maybe two seconds, her tawny eyes mesmerizing, hard to turn away from.

"And who is this you have brought with you?"

"This is Kat. She's in danger, and I wondered if she could stay here with you tonight … and also perhaps … if you could craft a rune necklace for her. I'm hoping it will provide some protection."

"Why do you believe her to be in danger?"

"Have you smelled her?"

The woman leaned forward, nostrils flaring slightly. "I have a low blood need so I did not notice at first – but yes, now that you mention it. Quite the enticement. She does smell … exotic."

She turned, and gestured to them to pass through. "Very well. Come."

She led the way into a large room lit by a few flickering candles in wall sconces, and filled with ottomans and cushions, and sank gracefully into a pile. "Sit."

Kat sat on the very edge of a cushion with her feet on the floor, knees bent, and Char flopped into another nearby.

"Is that the only reason?" the woman asked.

"No," Char replied. "Well, that's why she needs protection immediately. We were followed as far as the Towers gate by three guys from the club. But she also has … special abilities. I've reported it already, but the Directorate's guy can't get here until tomorrow night, so I've got the job of keeping her safe until then."

"That is very responsible of you, Charice," the woman said, a faint lilt of surprise in her tone.

Char's small face twisted into a perfect replica of an adolescent scowl. "Yeah, well it's not like I was given much of a choice."

She shot a glance at Kat. "Nothing personal, I'm just not keen on being the only thing standing between you and trouble." Her face darkened, as if she was reliving an unpleasant memory.

"So tell me, what are her abilities?" The woman didn't even acknowledge Kat's presence as she asked the question. It was as if

Kat didn't rate. She was someone to be talked *about*, not talked *to*.

"She has true sight, and she's completely shielded from scanning in some way I've never come across before." Char gave a wry grin. "Oh, and she speaks our languages fluently."

"Impressive. Have you considered she might be a danger to us?" Again, the question was directed only at Char.

Char shook her head. "She's not. I can feel it. You know my intuition warns me when anything dangerous is coming my way."

The woman's eyes finally turned toward Kat again, scrutinizing her. It was not the look you gave a person, Kat decided. More the assessing way you'd look at a piece of furniture you were vaguely considering buying. "Perhaps advising the Directorate was not the wisest course of action. There is a certain opportunism to the way they function, and I have often wondered ..."

Char shifted uncomfortably. "I've heard stories too, but I thought that's all they were. And I thought ... with her being human ... I mean, avoiding problems with humans is their primary aim, right? I'm sure they can do a better job of protecting her than I can."

The woman shook her head gently, musingly, eyes still fixed on Kat. Then she tilted her head to the side.

"So, child, you sit there so silently. This evening must have been most distressing for you."

Kat smiled tremulously, and nodded.

"And do you have a longer name, or is it just ... Kat?"

"Katerina, Katerina Chanter."

"Katerina," the woman repeated. "A good, old name." The name sounded richer, nobler when spoken in her musical voice. "Katerina, I am Akilina. You are among friends now, and need not be afraid. Tell me, do you know why you might have the special abilities Charice speaks of?"

Kat shook her head, and Akilina smiled gently.

"Well, child, I will craft a necklace for you. My reading will help us decide how to proceed." With that she rose gracefully to her feet.

"Thank you, Arella-dara." Char also stood. "Will it be a problem for you, that she can't be scanned?"

"You are forgetting, my gift is in the domain of the flesh. I work with material things, not the mind, so I do not scan as you do. Come into my studio, child."

Kat followed Akilina into the next room, feeling a little awkward as she lowered herself onto a cushion next to a low table. The woman's hands were cool as they took hers, positioning her so she was kneeling with her hands palm up, and then clasping her around each wrist, thumbs moving until they had found the pulse points.

Akilina directed a cool glance at Char, who had followed them into the studio. "Leave us now."

Then the elder closed her eyes, and began to hum, a sound of such haunting sweetness Kat couldn't help but let it wash her away. She closed her eyes and surrendered.

*

When Kat opened her eyes she was back in the room they had first entered, nestled into a soft pile of cushions, and Char was sitting in front of her, watching her anxiously.

"Are you okay? Having a reading can be pretty draining. And yours took quite a while."

"I'm fine, I think." She stretched. "Actually, I feel great. Relaxed. A little tired maybe." Again she heard humming from the next room. The sound was coming from Akilina, who kneeled in front of a large bowl, with her hands and forearms immersed, her neck an elegant curve. "What's she doing?"

"She's crafting your rune necklace." Char's voice was hushed, reverential. "She's still in a trance."

"How long will it take?"

Char shrugged. "It varies, depending on the reading, depending on the complexity. That's her gift. She can read a person's past, present and future, their heritage and their destiny, and translate it into runes, and into metal. It's … magical. Mystical. And it's never wrong."

"So what's my destiny?" Kat almost spoke in a whisper. It was as if the talk of magic had cast a spell of its own.

Char shook her head. "We won't know until she's finished."

"Um, Char?" she mumbled.

"Yes?"

"Is she, I mean, is Akilina really okay with me staying here?"

Char nodded.

"It must be late, and I think I really need to sleep now. I'm surprised I'm even considering it given what's happened tonight, because I'm sure I'll have horrible nightmares …" Here she broke off, because even as she said the words, she realized they weren't true. She was tired, and still confused and a little overwhelmed … but she wasn't afraid anymore. Here in Akilina's apartment with Char, she felt safe.

"Anyway," she continued, "is there somewhere I can go to sleep?"

"Sorry, I didn't think." Char instantly looked contrite. "It's after four in the morning. Of course you must be exhausted. But I'm afraid there is no bedroom in the way you would be used to. Elders like Akilina need little sleep."

"No sleeping like the dead?" Kat quipped sleepily.

Char laughed. "No, that's something we leave for your kind. When we sleep, it's more like what you would call catnapping."

"Well, I think I need more than a catnap right now." Kat didn't quite manage to suppress a yawn.

"It's probably easiest if you sleep right where you are." Char gestured at the many cushions.

"That sounds great, if it's no inconvenience." She smiled wearily, finding it more and more difficult to stay awake as the melodious humming continued.

"Will you be staying here too?" she asked drowsily.

Char rose, and went to get something from a chest near the door. She returned to tuck a woven silk throw rug around Kat, who rolled over and curled up on her side. Char moved silently around the room, dousing all but two of the candles. As Kat settled herself and prepared for sleep, Char's soft reply came to her from across the room.

"Sleep well. I'm not going anywhere."

It was good Char was staying too, Kat thought. She was much nicer when she wasn't being so prickly. Kat snuggled into the cushions. She still had so many unanswered questions. Maybe they could talk about things some more, and she would ask her questions … tomorrow.

Within seconds, she was asleep.

Chapter 17

It wasn't a normal dream. When Kat started to share the consciousness of the giant eagle this time, it was annoyed. Even her sleeping
brain knew that wasn't right for a dream. An eagle, even a giant one
– yeah, maybe. But an irritated one? A bit too strange.

It was an odd feeling: knowing she was dreaming, and at the
same time knowing what she was seeing was real. It was just happening to someone else. She shared their thoughts; saw what they
saw, felt what they felt. So, though she was definitely asleep, she –
or rather, the eagle – was also circling around high above the city,
soaring on the thermal currents.

The night-lit city spread out below her like a glittering blanket.
She could focus in on any area at will. A cab driver stopping for
a hotdog after dropping a fare at Gramercy Park, and paying for it
with a crisp hundred-dollar bill he couldn't even remember earning;
the last few patrons leaving a club in an otherwise empty street; and
then she was circling higher again, following something intangible.
A scent carried on the wind? Or perhaps it was just instinct that
later led her to float lower over a wooded hill, with a road leading
through the trees to a large, multi-towered building at its summit.

There – hiding in the thick trees beside the gate. There were the
ones she sought, perched amid the cover of branches, arguing among

themselves. She could sense their anxiety, torn as they were between wanting to wait just a little longer in the hope of their prey emerging, and fear of being caught outdoors as the sunrise approached. But as she plummeted noiselessly toward them through the night sky, some long-buried instinct must have flared to life, because one of them stared fearfully into the darkness and saw her, talons outstretched.

They scattered, fleeing through the trees, heading for their homes somewhere back in the vast city, their desire for their prey overridden by their fear of this new threat.

She floated silently over the gate and alighted on the branch of a large tree within, sure now her target was inside the building. From here, she had a clear view of the building entry, and could keep watch on comings and goings throughout the day.

The sky was beginning to lighten in the east. Daylight was approaching. Kat felt her consciousness separate from the eagle's and drift up and away as the eagle settled itself, hidden within the thick cover of leaves, to wait for nightfall.

*

Kat stirred, and opened her eyes drowsily. Her head was aching, and she had no idea what time it was or how long she'd slept. Her surroundings provided no clue, as shutters covered every window, and the room was lit by candles.

Char and Akilina were talking softly nearby, but she wasn't particularly motivated to move from her cosy nest in the cushions just yet. Her eyelids drifted closed again. She didn't go back to sleep immediately though, and their conversation flowed over her while she lay there half awake.

"Clearly you resent this task, Charice, but perhaps looking after this girl is a good thing. After all, it has finally brought you home."

Char was silent for a while, and her voice was guarded when she replied. "I'm sorry. I know it's been a long time."

"What is a dozen or so years among family?" Akilina's voice was dry, and there was a hint of rueful humor in her words.

"I got the invitations you sent me for Nochistide every year. I wish I could've come. It's just that sometimes, being surrounded by family is too claustrophobic." There was another pause. "I didn't mean that the way it sounded. You know I hate talking about this stuff."

"You feel smothered when surrounded by those who love you. This is part of what I am trying to tell you, Charice. You are letting this pattern repeat again and again. It will destroy you if you let it. For some reason, even after all this time, you do not feel you deserve love, happiness ... or even an end to the pain."

"It's not like that." Char sounded uncomfortable.

"Then explain it to me," Akilina pressed.

"I think ..." Char's voice was low. "Well, part of me doesn't believe in second chances."

"So you do not feel you deserve a family who loves you? You are wrong." There was sorrow in Akilina's voice. "I wish you saw yourself as I do. If you would only ..."

"You can spare me the lecture about how I'm wasting my life," Char cut in rather sharply. "We did that last time, remember?"

"That was not what I was going to say," Akilina replied, a defensive edge to her voice. "But as you have raised the subject ..."

"I really don't want to talk about the club, or Jon, or any of that stuff." Char sounded more tired than angry. "I know you don't approve of the life I lead. For whatever reason, I'm most comfortable surrounded by those who're more dysfunctional than I am."

Akilina was silent for quite some time. "It seems you have made yourself a family after all. One of your own choosing." While she kept her voice light, there was resignation there, and an undercurrent of pain. The sort of pain a parent might feel at losing a child.

There was a fraught silence for a few moments, then Char broke it with an abrupt change of subject. "Anyway, as you said, I'm here now, courtesy of Sleeping Beauty."

"Yes."

The silence went on for so long Kat began to drift off to sleep, and just as she did so, she thought she heard Akilina say softly, "That one is special."

*

Kat blinked herself awake much later, and sat up and stretched. Waking in a dark room was disorienting, and she started to raise her wrist to eye level, then remembered she'd taken off her watch before washing the dishes last night. She had her handbag, but that was about it. Going out with Char had been such a last-minute thing, she hadn't even thought to bring her cell phone. It was still plugged into the charger on her kitchen counter.

Just thinking about her ordinary little apartment made her head spin. Her toothbrush and toiletries were no doubt still sitting there in the bathroom, her leftover pasta in a bowl in the fridge. But Char said her life would be in danger if she went back there ... ever.

"You're awake."

Char moved into her line of sight and extended a hand, effortlessly pulling Kat to her feet. Just as well, because she wouldn't have had the energy to get up by herself. Her head was still spinning, and she was feeling nauseous and light-headed. Again.

"Yeah." She looked toward the shuttered windows. "I'm still getting used to not having natural light in here. I really love these candles of Akilina's, though. They have the most beautiful beeswax smell."

She looked around, stretched. "What time is it anyway?"

"It's about eleven in the morning. I've been waiting hours for you to wake up." Char had a small smile on her face, and there was suppressed excitement in her voice. "Come on."

Char led her into the next room, Akilina's studio, which was ablaze with dozens of candles. The large bowl Akilina had used while in her trance, and the cushion she had kneeled on, had both been tidied away somewhere. There was a cylinder of heavy velvet on the low table.

"Akilina will be back soon, but she's left this for you. It's finished."

Kat looked across at Char. "Have you seen it yet?"

Char shook her head, and Kat dropped to her knees next to the table. She hesitated before reaching out to touch the heavy roll of fabric, reluctant to give concrete form to something they had so far only spoken of. When she finally did touch the velvet, a tingle passed through her fingers. A nervous knot twisted in the pit of her stomach. She almost wanted to laugh at herself for being as credulous as her brothers. *They* probably would have argued, like a pair of good fishermen, that the tingling in her fingers meant something momentous was about to happen. But somehow, she couldn't make light of the sensation. The moment felt weighty. Significant.

Char's earlier words came back to her. *Heritage. Destiny.* The psychic had used the same words in her reading, she remembered. The psychic she had been so quick to write off as being crazy. Somehow *this* seemed quite different. Whatever Akilina had seen, Kat was inclined to trust – because there was nothing at all crazy about Akilina ... and there was something quite special about someone who could form metal with her bare hands.

Kat slowly pushed aside the fabric and lifted the heavy necklace with a soft exhalation of breath. Eyes wide, she examined it closely, awed by its magnificence, while Char peered over her shoulder. Kat had never seen anything like it, never even dreamed such fine work was possible.

The necklace was like the one Char wore, only larger, more detailed, encrusted with smoothly polished stones of every hue. Every inch of gleaming metal was deeply embossed with tiny curling runes. But it was the reverse side that caught her breath, for the metal was formed into a forest, an orchard, a cornucopia. Tiny, perfect flowers were intertwined with leaves and animals, trees and birds, fruit and vines. Akilina's fingers had breathed life into the metal, had recorded the endlessly swirling pattern of creation in its intricate detail.

Char let out her breath in a long, shuddering sigh. "The runes mark you. You are born of the line of the Mahra." Her tone was faintly accusing.

Kat raised her eyes, startled. Char's eyes were glowing, and she frowned as she met Kat's confused glance, then she abruptly stood and stalked around to the other side of the table. She leaned there, on the heels of her hands, scowling at Kat.

"Don't look at me like that. I don't even know what that means!" Kat burst out, defensive for no good reason at all.

Char eyed her moodily, but didn't say anything.

"Who is this Mahra, Char?"

"Who *was* she," Char corrected irritably. "Oh, nobody important. Only a quasi-deity who was apparently your ancestor. Ring any bells?"

"I'm just an ordinary girl," Kat said helplessly.

Char gave a low, humorless laugh. "Well we already know that's not true."

Kat remembered the list of things Char had mentioned when talking about her to Akilina last night. "Special abilities", like being true sighted – whatever that meant. In fact, her so-called special abilities were on the list of things she'd meant to ask Char about today.

"But I don't understand any of it, or know *why* I can do the things you say I can. I'm only human, remember?"

Char gave an exasperated sigh. "Kat, how can you expect me to believe you don't know *anything* about this? I'm guessing you're the result of a pairing between a male of our kind and a human woman. Surely your father taught you something about your heritage? About what to expect if and when you change? You're only really half human, and your latent bloodlines could bring about your transition at any time. Then you won't *be* human anymore, you'll be one of us." Char stopped speaking as the rune necklace slipped from Kat's fingers and fell to the velvet beneath with a soft thud.

Kat was still staring right at Char, but she was seeing something else entirely. The expression on her mom's face whenever she talked about her father flashed before her eyes. If he wasn't human it would explain a lot. Why he'd left, maybe. And why she'd always been different from other kids.

Oddly, it didn't come as a complete shock. Whether or not Kat believed in the psychic stuff, the memory of the fortune teller's words had stayed with her – and most of the woman's predictions seemed to have been eerily accurate. Both her reading of Kat's palms, and the cards Kat had drawn, apparently meant her life was about to change forever. She told Kat she should expect a radical change. A transformation. That she was marked by destiny.

Clearly Candice Brown had been at least a little bit crazy though, especially with the way she'd acted right at the end of the consultation; the whole production about stripping all the rings from her fingers and taking off her gloves to touch Kat's hands with her bare skin. The big theatrical shudder, then all that confusing muttering. And the woman hadn't exactly been forthcoming with explanations of what the heck she'd been talking about. In fact, she'd looked kind of freaked out, and right after that, she'd put her gloves back on and hustled Kat out the door.

Kat would have liked to dismiss the whole thing as a performance – but if so, it had been a pretty damned convincing one. And coming all the way to Kat's home at night to bring her the Arcana – well, it certainly made it credible that Candice actually believed the stuff she'd told Kat, and the universe was punishing Kat in some karmic way for being such a dyed-in-the-wool skeptic. At the time, the psychic's crazy certainty had made Kat nervous, and a little annoyed, but nothing more. Now? Well, she didn't know quite what to believe anymore. Even without any psychic predictions it seemed pretty clear her life was undergoing some radical changes. And there had been the dreams too. Finding out she might not even be fully human made a weird kind of sense.

You won't be *human anymore. You'll be one of us.* Char's words lingered uncomfortably in her head.

Kat shivered, and brought her attention back to Char, who was watching her suspiciously, absorbing her wide eyes and expression of confusion.

Char's gaze narrowed.

"Kat, with these bloodlines, your father has to be a member of our highest aristocracy. The fact you're half human doesn't really matter. You're still *egir'rin* – a true-born princess of the blood. Didn't he tell you *any* of this?"

Kat shook her head slowly from side to side. "How could he have?" she asked softly. "I've never even met him."

Char shook her head in disbelief, and threw her hands into the air with a muttered curse. "Great!" she said. "Just great!"

Chapter 18

Kat was sitting on one of the ottomans when Akilina returned, running her fingers over the rune necklace in her lap again and again. Char was leaning against the far wall in Akilina's studio, glowering at the world in general.

Akilina observed them both dispassionately, and then gestured for the person following her to come through. It was the doorman who had challenged Kat's entry the night before. He entered a little reluctantly, and silently carried the large hampers he was holding through to where Akilina indicated.

As he passed Kat, she smelled the most enticing aromas wafting from the baskets in his hands, and her stomach clenched in response. She still wasn't used to these strange reactions she was having, these cravings. And such an intense awareness of smell. Right at this moment, she felt quite ill, but she knew if it was like the other times, she probably just needed something to eat.

The doorman had gone out of sight to deposit the hampers, but he came past her to leave again. He skirted uneasily around the edge of the room, keeping as far from Kat as possible.

He glanced at her once before leaving the apartment, eyes alight with fascination and disapproval in equal measures. He didn't seem happy about her presence there. He left without saying a word, bowing slightly in Akilina's direction when she thanked him for his help.

"So," Akilina began pleasantly, as the door clicked shut behind him, "who would like to go first?"

Char pushed away from the wall and stalked across to where she stood.

"Kat is *egir'rin*, Arella-dara. A princess of the blood."

"Yes." Akilina's voice was calm and unruffled.

"She knows nothing about her father. In fact, it's quite possible he doesn't even know she exists."

Akilina's eyes flicked across to Kat for a moment, thoughtful and reflective, and then she began to move around the room, lighting more candles.

"Still, Char, I fail to see why you view this situation as a personal affront." Akilina paused in front of Kat. "Well, child, do you like the necklace?"

Kat nodded, and rose to her feet. "It's the most beautiful thing I've ever seen."

"Good." Akilina smiled graciously. "I apologize for Charice. She is not angry with *you*, despite the impression she gives. Are you, Charice?"

Char made a face and flounced into the next room.

Akilina sighed. "It is certainly ... unfortunate for you that your father has never been a presence in your life. Being forced to face such an uncertain future without familial support is less than ideal."

Kat frowned. "I have a family."

"Yeah, *humans*. What use will they be?" Char's disgusted voice floated through from the next room.

Akilina frowned. "Charice, you are not helping." Her tone was gently admonishing. She tilted her head to one side, and beckoned for Kat to follow her. "Come, you must be hungry. I have brought food."

She ushered Kat through her studio and out through another archway. Kat walked into the eat-in kitchen, and hit a solid wall of scent.

Until recently she'd never reacted to food smells so strongly. It was kind of unnerving. It didn't seem to happen all the time – in fact, now she came to think of it, it was whenever she was feeling nauseous. Usually after a night filled with dreams ... or nightmares.

Char had already unpacked most of the contents of the large lidded baskets, and arranged everything on the table. It all bore the appearance of having been delivered directly from the catalogue of some high-end department store in the city.

"I think you might have gone a little overboard," Char observed as they entered, but without rancour.

Kat was faced with a spread of food that easily could have satisfied ten people; fresh fruit, cold meats, smoked fish and cheeses, brioche, muffins and bagels. There was coffee and fresh juice too. It all looked a little odd by candlelight, especially the basket piled with fruit, casting misshapen dancing shadows onto the wall behind it.

"I was not sure what you would want to eat," Akilina said. There was a trace of uncertainty in her voice that ran completely counter to the calm confidence Kat had experienced in all her interactions with her so far.

"You're the first human she's ever entertained," Char said dryly, setting two places at the table.

Her irritation seemed to have evaporated for the moment, replaced by irreverent amusement at Akilina's expense. Akilina ignored her completely, and ushered Kat to one of the places set.

"It's absolutely unbelievable," Kat said, directing a grateful smile at Akilina as she took her seat. "I can promise you I don't eat this well normally. Akilina, thank you for letting me stay, and for everything else you've done for me."

"It is my pleasure, Katerina. It is nice to have an *appreciative* visitor every few decades. In fact, it is a great pleasure having visitors at all." She gave Char a significant look, and took the seat opposite Kat.

"Char, are you eating?" Kat asked, noting that Char hadn't set herself a place.

Char shook her head, and went to lounge against the kitchen counter. "I usually don't."

"Our kind eat little normal food," Akilina explained, "but I thought it would be nice to join you. I like to vary my tastes every once in a while."

"But you do need to ingest something to survive, right?" Kat looked to Char for confirmation.

Char nodded, and gave a wicked grin. "Of course, just not solid food."

Kat decided to stop the questions at that point. She didn't want a more detailed answer just before eating. Especially as her stomach still wasn't feeling the best.

And then she stopped thinking about much at all, because her entire attention was drawn by the food in front of her, to the exclusion of all else. She sat back with a sigh of replete satisfaction several minutes later, and realized she'd just eaten her way through a fairly large portion of cold rare roast beef and several slices of prosciutto without pausing for breath. It was unlike her to eat so much meat first thing after waking. She was more of a granola or oatmeal kind of girl. Well, she used to be.

"You eat with singular focus," Akilina commented, and Kat realized both the older woman and Char had been watching her wolf down food with polite interest. Akilina had cut herself a couple of small slivers of fruit, and a morsel of brioche, but she had barely touched either in the time it had taken Kat to eat a good proportion of the meat on the table.

Kat blushed, and pushed her plate away. "I'm sorry, that's not like me. I don't know why I'm having such strong cravings for certain types of food lately."

"Please, eat whatever you wish, it is all for you." Akilina's smile was kind, and genuinely non-judgmental, as if she had no expectations at all about what a human guest would prefer to eat.

Kat forced herself to eat a muffin and a piece of fruit. The muffin hit her stomach lining like a lump of sodden cardboard. There was plenty of meat left, but despite Akilina's assurances, she didn't want to draw attention to herself by eating any more of it. Her stomach would have liked nothing better though, and the familiar warmth and energy was spreading through her in reaction to what she'd already eaten.

Again, her eyes strayed longingly toward the remaining rare roast beef. Moist and juicy, red-pink and just barely cooked. Her mouth watered at the thought of sinking her teeth into it. She tore her gaze away, annoyed at her lack of control. What *was* it about her and meat lately?

*

"You can't be serious!" Kat knew her voice betrayed her dismay, and she didn't care. The more Char insisted, the more hysterical she felt. "I can't just move out. I can't give up the apartment."

Char faced Kat, her chin jutted out at an angle that advertised to the world the futility of opposition. "Can't, can't, can't." Char shook her head. "Be reasonable, Kat. And don't make it sound so impossible. You can and you will move out. Well, actually, I'll do it for you. There are no windows in the hallway, so it's not safe for you to go back there even during the day tomorrow."

"I've signed a lease, Char, I can't just break it!" Kat locked eyes with Char, who seemed utterly unmoved by anything she said.

"Oh is *that* what's worrying you?" Char airily waved a hand. "Consider it sorted."

Kat eyed her suspiciously, distracted from her protests by this new assertion. "Why do you sound so confident?"

"I know the owner," Char said smugly.

"You *are* the owner, aren't you?" Kat said accusingly in a sudden moment of insight. "I'll bet you own the whole damned building!" When Char shrugged in response, she sighed in defeat, and lapsed into resigned silence.

The lease wasn't what was actually worrying her, and she was frustrated she couldn't express the real reasons for her hesitation to Char. She wasn't even sure of them herself, her thoughts a tangled mess when she even approached the subject. It was difficult to get her head around the repercussions of everything that had swept tsunami-like through her life in such a short time.

She did know that it felt all wrong having someone else go to her place and pack up her things; her hairbrush and toothpaste, books and shoes, even clearing out her fridge … and the fact that she'd only been living there a week made it worse. It was especially hard imagining her life there cleared away without a trace before she'd had the chance to really establish herself. And it highlighted the seriousness of her situation. Her apartment wasn't the only no-go zone; her old life was basically over.

Char must have sensed some of these thoughts, or seen a hint in Kat's face or in her sudden silence. Her expression turned serious, even sympathetic.

"I've gotta go now. Sorry you can't come, but I'll be back soon."

As the door closed behind her, Kat was instantly aware of the change in atmosphere. The apartment seemed more tranquil after she left – but also more empty without her energy to fill the space.

Akilina was kneeling in front of the low table in her studio, studying some illuminated manuscripts. When resting she was so still Kat couldn't be sure whether she was awake. Char had explained how the elders of their kind would sometimes slip in and out of a trance-like state to conserve energy, particularly during the daylight hours when they were most lethargic.

Restless, Kat wandered to the far side of the other room and eyed the door Char had gone through. She didn't want to go back to the books Akilina had been showing her that afternoon. The elder had been curious to test the extent of Kat's knowledge of their languages, and they'd quickly found that while she could speak and understand their dialects, understanding formal written language was a different story.

"I can read it," Kat had said. "It doesn't mean anything though. It's like some kind of strange free verse." Ancient runes like the ones on her necklace were similarly perplexing.

"Language is more than words alone," Akilina had said. "Interpretation of the words you read eludes you because you are unfamiliar with our figurative usages, our syntax."

It seemed the modern, simplified V-runes were the only thing she *could* make real sense of. "Probably because they're so simple," Char had suggested helpfully. "They're designed to be understood even by those without much education. Of course they also contain a concealment charm designed specifically to work on humans, but you're not human."

Kat hadn't said anything at the time, but Char's comment had rankled. In fact, she was still seething about it. She realized she was deeply resentful of any suggestion that she wasn't human. She didn't know how to be anything else. She *felt* human. Her mental image of herself was resolutely, completely, human.

Despite this, well … There was no denying that the talk of special powers, and her father, and an unexpected aristocratic heritage had captured her imagination. Right up until she'd looked at the beautifully illuminated pages of book after book as Akilina had shown them to her, and drawn a big blank. She couldn't fathom the meaning of a single sentence. The words "poetic" and "obscure" came to mind.

She'd excelled at her studies when she was at high school, and been one of the few who left to go on to college in the city. For several years now she'd been a competent, skilled adult. Getting headhunted for this job in New York had been a boost to her confidence too.

But as Akilina returned the beautiful and indecipherable books and scrolls to their shelves, Kat had been frustrated to realize that among her father's people she wasn't much more than a backward child. It was infuriating. Like starting her life all over again from the beginning without getting any advanced credit for the years of schooling she'd already completed.

"Katerina, you are pacing. I may not be able to hear your thoughts but you are giving off a great deal of restless energy." Akilina spoke without turning around, and Kat stopped dead in her tracks.

"I'm sorry," she said guiltily. The last thing she wanted to do was disturb the enviable calm of her hostess.

"There is no need to apologize. It is to be expected." Akilina rose to her feet, and turned to face Kat. "Charice has always been similarly … burdened by her emotions."

"I suppose I'm having trouble processing all this," Kat said.

Akilina tilted her head to the side for a moment, the way she did whenever she didn't understand something Kat said.

"Processing. Ah." She smiled in enlightenment. "An industrial metaphor I think. Charice has always learned the modern turn of phrase more quickly than I." She patted the cushions beside her. "Come, sit with me."

Kat did so, wishing her legs would fold under her as effortlessly and gracefully as Akilina's did.

"Where is your necklace?" Akilina asked suddenly, and Kat blinked in surprise, then pointed toward her handbag in the other room. Akilina moved so fast Kat couldn't even trace the movement, and was seated beside her in exactly the same position an instant later, with the rune necklace held in both hands. Kat felt a jolt of surprise. She supposed she would have to get used to this sort of thing, but right now it was still a bit unnerving.

"Why do you not wear it?" Akilina questioned.

"I've never owned anything so valuable," Kat said, startled into

164

honesty. "I thought it would be best kept for special occasions."

Akilina shook her head gently. "Its value exists only in the wear-ing," she said. "It is *because* it is so special that it should be worn as much as possible." She leaned forward, and Kat bent her head to allow Akilina to fix the clasp behind her neck.

"It's warm!" Kat exclaimed, touching it.

Akilina nodded. "I should have explained the significance of the necklace to you. Our kind does not wear jewelry in the way that a human might. We do not choose to wear a particular piece for its appearance, but rather for its function."

Kat frowned. "But it's so beautiful!"

"There is no reason why beauty and function cannot coexist in an object." Akilina smiled gently, then surveyed her thoughtfully. "It should be worn against the skin, but your clothing covers your neck."

Kat lifted the heavy necklace and, pulling at the neck of her turtleneck sweater, she slipped it underneath, as Akilina nodded ap-provingly. Kat stiffened in surprise, then relaxed as the warm metal settled against her skin and a subtle energy flowed through her. It was the strangest sensation; she was suddenly light, weightless, and her recent frustrations and worries weren't so significant anymore.

"We are a race of strong emotion," Akilina said softly. "Some of us more than others. Passion, hunger, love, rage – all are felt by us with extreme acuteness. If unchecked, our emotions can dominate us entirely. Fortunately, in ancient times it was discovered we also have a unique affinity with the natural world. The Earth's minerals can be extremely beneficial in calming the extremities of our emo-tions. Bringing us into balance, if you will."

"I can feel it!" Kat's eyes were wide with wonder. "I feel light," she added, a little self-consciously. It seemed an odd thing to admit to.

"Good," said Akilina. "Try to center on that feeling whenever you are overwhelmed by things." A shadow passed across her face for a fraction of an instant, and then she smiled. "Are you hungry? I am unfamiliar with how often you need to eat."

"Not yet," Kat reassured her. "I ate so well earlier. Could we open some of the shutters though?" She blushed, hoping Akilina wouldn't read any criticism into what she said. "I'm not used to spending so much time indoors, and you know Char won't let me go anywhere."

"Of course! It is full night. There is no danger to me, and I think we will be safe from any unwanted intrusion here at the Towers."

Akilina's studio didn't have external windows, but there was a large door flanked by windows just through the archway next to the dining table, and Akilina went to it and flung open both shutters and door.

"Thank you," Kat said gratefully, and moved past her onto a sizeable balcony. She took a deep breath of the cool night air. At this height, a strong breeze whipped her hair around her face, and she put up one hand to contain it as she stared out into the night. The glow of city lights lit the sky in the distance, though closer to the Towers darkness marked out the areas dominated by forest and parkland.

Kat had expected this move to New York to bring big change to her life. But she certainly hadn't anticipated everything that had happened since last night. It seemed like a lifetime ago, instead of only a day ago.

An odd sensation assailed her, a shiver running up her spine as she was struck by a rare moment of mental clarity. *Everything I ever knew has changed*, she thought. *I'm not ever going home.* Her conviction about this should have made her sad, but it didn't. In this moment of insight, it all seemed like part of an inevitable cycle. So while this was an end, it was only the end of the beginning. That also made it the beginning of the next stage, if you wanted to look at it that way. Whatever that would bring.

She leaned against the balcony railing, enjoying the cool air, and frowned down at the driveway which led up to the Towers and curved around in front of the building. The shape it made as it arched in on itself ... some recollection tickled at the corner of her mind, a memory struggling to the surface – but she knew she'd never been on the balcony before. She and Char had come by cab, so she certainly hadn't seen things from this height. Still, the driveway from this height and angle did seem oddly familiar.

She remembered the giant eagle of her dream a bare instant before the real thing swooped from the sky and landed next to her with a noisy clatter of claws.

Afterward, she wasn't sure whether to attribute her calmness in the face of this new arrival to the effects of the rune necklace she now wore, or to the knowledge and intelligence in the great bird's glittering eyes. In any case, all she did as she faced its sharp beak and man-sized chest was blink and say, "Hello."

The bird's eyes remained fixed on her unwaveringly for several moments, and then turned slowly to where Akilina stood at the door, silhouetted in the candlelight.

"How unexpected," Akilina said with mild surprise. She was gone in a flash, and then reappeared with a large navy blue silk robe in her hands.

The eagle inclined its great head, and its cream and brown feathers stirred in the wind before its entire shape shimmered and resolved itself into the form of a man, who smoothly donned the offered robe to cover his nakedness, before bowing low over Akilina's hand in the grand manner.

"Most unexpected, Princess." He turned laughing hazel eyes up toward Akilina. "But a great pleasure."

"Indeed." Akilina's tone was noncommittal, but Kat noticed she was smiling ... a little. "Won't you come in?"

Akilina sounded exactly like she was greeting a guest who had come to the front door, rather than an eagle who had flown onto her balcony and changed into a man; a man who even now was wearing nothing but a thin silk robe to cover his nakedness, and seemed completely comfortable with the fact. Was it only Kat who could see the oddness in the situation?

The man preceded them, and Akilina took Kat's forearm in a firm grip and led her inside, closing the shutters and door securely behind them.

"This is a little far afield for you, surely?" Akilina asked as she led the way into the sitting room, and gestured him to a seat. She kept hold of Kat's arm, and Kat, reading between the lines, could tell Akilina wasn't certain enough of the visitor's intentions to take any risks with her safety. So she didn't object when Akilina signaled that Kat should sit close beside her, and kept a protective hand on her arm.

The man hadn't responded to Akilina's last comment, and she went on smoothly, in the same manner one might use when asking about the weather, "So, are you hunting?"

"I was, yes," the man replied calmly.

His eyes darted to Kat and returned to Akilina so quickly it was almost possible to overlook the glance entirely – except Kat had the distinct impression that every part of her had been analyzed, dissected, and catalogued in that brief instant.

"You appear to have caught my rabbit," he said.

"How unfortunate for you." Akilina's tone was chilly.

Her hand slid down Kat's arm to her wrist, where her fingers settled over the pulse points, and Kat felt a dreamy lethargy flow through her.

"Come, there is no need for us to wrangle." The man leaned forward slightly, his expression watchful. "I merely meant to apprize you of the fact that this girl has been marked by my family for many years. No one could reasonably dispute the fact that she belongs to us."

"And yet despite your supposed claim, I appear to be in possession of the prize. Surely there is no disputing that either?" Akilina's fingers tightened possessively on Kat's wrist.

Kat desperately wanted to speak, to protest at the way she was being discussed, objectified. It was like Dominic and Char at the club all over again. But every time she thought about saying something, her mind slowed, and her thoughts floated away in a new direction. All she could do was watch in bemused silence, and listen.

Tension entered the man's face. "We would be willing to … compensate you for her loss."

"That will not be necessary. I have no intention of losing her." Akilina's voice was frosty in the extreme.

The man observed Akilina for a long moment. "What does a princess of the blood want with a human girl? Something beyond the obvious, I presume?"

Akilina's eyes narrowed. "Regardless of what you wild animals may consider normal, *I* am not in the habit of playing with my food before I eat it."

The man sighed, shook his head ruefully. "I meant no offense. Look, whatever your reasons, I cannot let you keep her. I am sorry."

Akilina took in a sharp breath. "You would *fight* me for her?"

"If you insist." The man's voice was clipped.

"I did not take you for a fool, Anton. We are well protected here at the Towers. If you so much as touch me your life will be forfeit."

"And still I would fight for her, Princess. Persisting against insurmountable odds has always been my way." There was an edge to his words, a history left unspoken.

Akilina's hand tightened on Kat's wrist once more. There was a tense silence. "Even when it can only lead to failure … or heartbreak?" Akilina said softly at last. Kat had the definite impression that they weren't discussing her anymore.

"Even then." Surprisingly, Anton's face crinkled into a smile of genuine amusement. "It seems, as always, that we have reached an impasse."

"Should I be concerned if you choose to throw your life away? You assume too much, Anton."

"Perhaps." His smile did not abate, in fact it increased, as if he was enjoying a private joke. "That was always my problem, as I recall."

Both sat silently regarding each other, unblinking, for a long moment, and then Akilina tilted her head to the side thoughtfully. She looked at Kat, then back at Anton. "Perhaps rather than pursuing a path which would almost certainly lead to your death, you could simply tell me why one of the *unalil* is interested in this girl, and I will consider fairly whether your claim outweighs my own."

"A generous offer, but I must refuse. I cannot disclose the nature of my interest." He sounded genuinely regretful.

"Oh, for love of the Mahra, Anton, must you always be so difficult?" Akilina snapped, eyes flashing. She closed her eyes and took a deep breath, as if drawing on an inner core of strength. When she opened her eyes a moment later, she was composed again. "As you do not want to trust me with your reasons, I will trust you first with mine."

Anton leaned forward slightly, watchful and alert.

Akilina met his gaze squarely. "Last night I did a reading on this girl, and fabricated a rune necklace for her."

"Ah yes, your little hobby. I had forgotten." His tone was amused but dismissive, and betrayed more than a touch of condescension.

Akilina regarded him coolly. "It is more than a hobby, Anton. I attained the status of master craftsman more than two hundred years ago."

Anton's eyes widened slightly, and he inclined his head with newfound respect. "Go on."

"What I discovered was surprising. This girl has been raised as a human, but my reading showed she is *egir'rin*."

Anton gave a low whistle. "A blood royal trapped in the body of a human hybrid?"

Akilina nodded once in confirmation. "You know of course how rare new births are, rarer still with so pure a bloodline. We true-born have been dwindling in number for centuries. Hybrid though she may be, I think you will agree this makes her very much *mine* to care for."

"Blood cleaves to blood," Anton quoted softly.

"As it must," Akilina said. "Now perhaps you will tell me *your* reasons for wanting her."

Anton leaned back at his ease and crossed his legs at the ankles. He smiled again, which crinkled the corners of his eyes and made them appear to dance. But he didn't answer immediately.

"Well it sounds like your plan was well thought out," Akilina snapped. "Fly in, fight to the death, and you cannot give me a single reason *why* you are here?"

"I know exactly why I am here," Anton corrected calmly, his smile fading. "My blood-brother has spent more than ten years watching over this girl. He has sacrificed a great deal to protect her. Now, we believe her to be facing a new danger. He has asked for my aid in ensuring her safety. And time is of the essence."

His eyes did that thing again, perusing Kat thoughtfully for the briefest fraction of an instant before returning to Akilina.

"Unsatisfying though it may seem," he continued dryly, "that is all I can tell you at present."

Akilina surveyed him for several long moments, then she gave a decisive nod. "I believe you truly do mean to protect her. Thankfully, falsity was never one of your vices."

Akilina released her hold on Kat's wrist, and clarity blew through her mind like a fresh breeze. Kat was instantly aware that with the removal of the elder's touch on her, whatever had been dulling her impulse to speak had now disappeared.

"I apologize, child," Akilina said. "It was necessary, until I could gauge his intentions." She turned toward Anton. "We have known each other for many years, and as you have seen, Anton is … a little unusual. But you can trust him."

Chapter 19

"They've just rung from the lobby, Mr. Raddberg. The Directorate envoy is here." Portia's voice came through the intercom, brisk and efficient as always.

Raddberg instantly put aside his work and rose from behind the desk. He hadn't actually asked to be advised as soon as the visitor entered the building, but Portia was an admirable assistant. She knew without being told when something was important.

He wanted to be at the elevator to greet the visitor in person. Some might consider this below the dignity of the director of the Hema Castus Institute, but a visit from such a high-level Directorate liaison was rare. If, in fact, this visitor was as well connected as he was rumored to be. Raddberg intended to use the walk from the elevator to his office suite for relaxed conversation if the opportunity arose; to take the chance to assess the situation before the formal reason for the visit was broached.

He took in his visitor's appearance in a quick, sweeping glance as the elevator doors opened, and then returned to the face. The man's mode of dress was old school; dark suit, hand-tailored, and everything from his cufflinks to his shoes was expensive in the most understated of ways. He was a handsome man, and supremely confident of the fact. Wavy dark hair, classical features. There was something familiar about the face, but Raddberg couldn't place it. He found that frustrating. He didn't like to be at a disadvantage

After the greetings were over, he asked whether they had met before, and received a reply in the negative. Still, the face, and the visitor's name – Victor Fortes – definitely teased at his memory. He wished he could place the recollection.

He closed the office door behind them, and ushered his guest to a comfortable wing chair before taking one opposite.

"I'm not sure if we were advised – I believe you report directly to a member of the Mandate Council ... but for which department?"

"Information Acquisition." The man's tone was as bland as the words he spoke, but Raddberg knew department names changed with extreme regularity in the Directorate. Almost as often as the councillors who led them. Information Acquisition was almost certainly a euphemistic way of referring to Intelligence. In his view, that changed things.

Raddberg's eyes tightened a fraction at this thought. The tiny movement would usually have passed unnoticed, but this man noticed. His eyes were alive to the slightest thing body language might betray. Raddberg allowed his face to smooth into an impassive mask. He hadn't reached his current position by being a fool, or by underestimating an opponent. And in his book, *everyone* was a potential opponent – until proven otherwise. Especially so when they came from Directorate Intelligence.

He let Fortes introduce the reason he was here in his own time, and was relieved to be asked a question he could easily answer, though he was careful not to betray that fact by even the twitch of a muscle.

"Yes," he confirmed calmly, "your information is correct. Our number of Level One subjects has increased in the last few years; mainly as a result of bringing several poorly administered external projects back in-house, in line with Directorate guidelines. This suits my own inclinations too. I prefer to keep things more tightly controlled, and on the whole we've found centralizing these projects has served us very well."

Fortes regarded him, unblinking, for a long moment. "Perhaps you were not aware that the subjects for many of those private research projects were acquired using information provided by my department?"

Raddberg knew better than to show any surprise at this. "No, I was not made aware of that fact. Should I assume the Directorate's contribution to these projects was ... unofficial?"

Fortes confirmed this with a quick nod of the head. This indicated to Raddberg that someone in the Directorate had an interest in these investigations, but – until recently – had wanted to keep things at arm's length. Many were still unaware of the complex web that was Directorate politics, but Raddberg was not one of the uninformed. He had never been surprised by the internecine conflict and assassinations, not to mention nepotism and venality at every level. To him, it only seemed natural in an organization where one could not rely on natural attrition for career advancement.

Sometimes it appeared that the only thing everyone in the Directorate agreed on was that the general population should be kept blissfully ignorant of their activities. So when they were involved in murkier matters, they preferred their role to be an indirect one. This wasn't the first time he'd received unofficial advice through official channels – or the reverse, for that matter. It was all about plausible deniability.

Fortes leaned forward. "I'm sure you have dozens of research subjects at present. But there are three in particular we are interested in, one of whom, perhaps, was among those recently acquired. In Predictive Science?"

Raddberg felt a thrill of satisfaction. It was fortunate he had trusted in the instinct that had prompted him to take a closer interest in that division recently, despite his own skepticism about the area.

"The oracles? Yes. We have been working on a Directorate research order in that area. We've been sending through complete weekly transcripts as requested. Was there something in particular …?" He trailed off, uncomfortably aware that his head of Predictive Science was convinced that most of what was in the transcripts was close to useless.

"I know we have received regular transcripts from two of your subjects," Fortes said. "May I ask why there have been no transcripts from the third?"

"We believe the third is not … sane," Raddberg said, choosing his words carefully. "Mostly unintelligible noises rather than actual words. We've even tried UV-exposure treatment, but with little effect. What we have been getting so far doesn't seem useful, and understandably, it's challenging to transcribe accurately."

Fortes eyed him coolly. "Surely you don't think that all useful material comes neatly packaged in rhyming couplets or iambic pentameter?"

Raddberg was annoyed by the put-down, but he didn't show it. "Of course not, but …"

"Perhaps," Fortes continued smoothly, "you should show us everything, and let us be the judge of what is or isn't useful. If you are having trouble transcribing, simply send us full audio files."

"Of course." Raddberg couldn't see any point in refusing the request. Whether or not they agreed with his judgment in withholding the material, the weeks of audio would certainly prove he had told the truth. The woman had proved a frustrating subject.

"Can you perhaps confirm for me – is this third subject a *bestimut* female?" Fortes' tone was offhand, as if the answer didn't matter much one way or the other, but Raddberg noticed that when he nodded in response a satisfied expression passed across the other man's face. Again, he was struck by a distant memory, but he couldn't remember the context.

"Is the gender significant?" he asked.

Fortes shrugged. "We are searching for a particular female, based on information from Ombra Scura."

Raddberg frowned at this mention of their much older sister institute in the Swiss-Italian Alps; the very first scientific facility the Directorate had founded. "We've collaborated on dozens of projects with Ombra Scura. Why didn't they approach us directly? We would have been more than happy to assist them with whatever ..."

"The Vodas has taken a personal interest in this," Fortes interrupted. "All information passes first through him ... via my department."

"The Vodas!" Raddberg couldn't keep the surprise from his face or his voice. How often did one hear of the Vodas, head of the Mandate Council, taking a *personal* interest in something so far removed from council matters?

"The Vodas is interested in many things. We do not question his reasons."

Fortes' tone held a subtle warning, one Raddberg was quick to note. He was already annoyed at himself for his lapse; he had allowed Fortes to see his surprise.

"Of course," he said, his face once more an impassive mask. "Hema Castus is more than happy to assist with whatever you may require."

Fortes gave a curt nod.

"Forgive me." Raddberg paused, and his eyes narrowed slightly. He never forgot a face, and he was sure he had seen this face before.

"You said we haven't met before, and yet I'm quite sure there's something familiar about you."

Fortes returned his gaze with a calculating gleam in his eye, then appeared to reach a decision. Perhaps he had realized belatedly that his rather heavy-handed approach just now had ruffled some feathers, and he wanted to smooth things before his departure. Raddberg was more than willing to let him try.

"Yes, you're correct, we have met once – briefly. I didn't want to confuse today's issue by introducing irrelevancies."

Then he smiled, the move warming the room, lighting every plane of his handsome face. It was a smile that seduced male and female indiscriminately. A smile with the power to creep through the strongest of defenses, inviting the watcher to share the secret, take his side, forgive transgressions, bend the rules ... just this once. How useful such power to manipulate the emotions of others must be, Raddberg thought.

Fortes continued, his tone casual, "Actually, I believe we did meet thirty-two years ago. You were head of Genetics here in those days. You interviewed me for a position."

"Really?" Raddberg's face was alight with speculation, and satisfaction at having his hunch proven right.

"Yes. Of course, life has led me to serve the Directorate in ways other than scientific inquiry, but genetics remains a ... hobby of mine."

Raddberg looked at him thoughtfully. It couldn't hurt to have a well-placed friend in Directorate Intelligence. Even better if that friend really *did* have the ear of the councillor who controlled the flow of information to the Vodas himself. Attracting positive notice from the Vodas was always a wise career move, but difficult for Raddberg, buried away here in one of their far-flung satellite companies. If he allowed Fortes to be the bearer of good news, they would both benefit. And perhaps, if the Vodas was impressed with the progress his Genetics division had been making here at Hema Castus, his researchers might be given permission to undertake field tests, which would be of incalculable value to the project at this late stage.

It wouldn't do to appear too eager though.

"I wonder ..." He leaned back in his chair, giving the impression of being a man at ease, master of his domain. "As a fellow student of genetics, Fortes, perhaps you might be interested in reviewing another of our projects while you are here. I understand how busy you are, but I would be most grateful if the Vodas could be apprized of the progress we have made."

*

The Hema Castus Institute covered three floors, one at ground level and two below. Raddberg had an office on the ground floor, in the center of the building where sunlight never reached. It was for show, mostly. He used it whenever he needed to meet with his human researchers working above ground on the low-security projects – and to meet with human visitors to the institute. It was necessary for the institute to maintain a public profile, a respected position in the human world. One that would never provoke questions.

As the Directorate operated completely in the shadows, hidden from the human sphere, organizations like his were necessary as conduits; channels for information gathering, resource acquisition, and to provide corporate "cover" for the myriad tiny collection agencies the Directorate used to source blood – blood they then refined, denatured, packaged, and distributed among their people.

But the real business of the institute was carried out on the two levels below ground, and it was on the upper of these that his main office was located.

He kept up a flow of light conversation as he led Fortes out of his office suite and back to the elevator, where he raised his hand to the security panel, and spoke the voice command which would take them to a floor not marked on the elevator control panel: the high-security level two floors below ground.

They exited the elevator into a dimly lit concrete corridor, and the guard stationed there bobbed his head respectfully and stood aside to let them pass.

"Here we are." Raddberg stopped at a numbered door, and raised his hand to the security panel next to it. The door slid silently open, and they passed through.

Two researchers in white lab coats turned toward the door as they entered.

"Director." The shorter of the two hurried forward to meet them. "How can I help you?"

"Marcus Clay, meet Victor Fortes. Marcus leads our Genetics division here at the institute." Raddberg turned to Clay. "Marcus, Mr. Fortes may be in a position to ensure news of our progress reaches the Vodas himself." He felt a moment's satisfaction when he saw the way his subordinate's face lit up. They had all worked hard for this. "Will you show him our little project?"

"Of course! Please come through." Clay ushered them over to the inner door, and through into a large chamber, divided down the center by metal bars running floor to ceiling. The light was even dimmer here, spaced to illuminate only the half of the room they were in, and not the cage's interior.

"We keep light levels low. They can't tolerate much." Clay moved toward the bars. He pulled a whistle from the front pocket of his lab coat, and gave one short blast.

A few moments passed, then red eyes began to appear out of the darkness in the far corners of the room as creatures slunk into view, and lined up facing the bars.

"We've had a fairly high attrition rate, due to the complexity of the genetic manipulation we're undertaking, but those you see here have all been merged successfully. They behave as a pack, and are fully programmable, completely obedient." He gestured to them to move back from the bars. "And deadly." He blew the whistle twice.

At once, the creatures became wild, snarling ferociously and attacking each other and the bars that held them with teeth and claws and heavily muscled bodies. The bars reverberated as they were hit again and again. The creatures seemed insensible to pain, continuing unabated even when their coats were wet with sweat and blood, and saliva foamed around their mouths.

Two short blasts of the whistle, and the attack ended. It was like a light had been switched off. The beasts formed a line at the bars again, now blood-streaked and with heaving flanks as they struggled to catch breath.

"They don't stop unless we tell them to. They would fight to the death if we wished it," Clay said. "And they can track anything."

Fortes' lips slowly curled into a smile. A gleam lit his eyes. "The Vodas would certainly be interested in what you have achieved here," he said. "Impressive. Very impressive."

Chapter 20

"Please take as long as you need." Akilina ushered Kat toward the bathroom. "I will have supper waiting when you are finished."

"Thank you." The idea of food was tempting, but the lure of a hot shower was even stronger. Especially now that Char had brought back all her things. Fresh clothes, shampoo ... sometimes simple things were the most important.

Akilina handed her a large folded piece of linen, soft and well-worn with age, and Kat realized she was supposed to use it as a towel. It was edged with a border of the finest, most intricate handmade lace. Kat had no idea how old it must be, but she was sure nothing like that had been made for well over a hundred years, probably longer.

She stepped into the bathroom. It was more modern, though not like anything she'd seen before. There were shelves placed at irregular intervals from floor to ceiling on one wall. Burning candles filled these, and were reflected in mirrors on the other three walls. There was a deep bathtub set into the floor in one corner, and a shower, partially enclosed by clear glass, in another.

When Kat turned on the shower tap it was like being under a waterfall, with a long sheet of water coming out of an opening in the wall, rather than the conventional shower rose. Within the glass enclosure, part of the wall, as well as the floor underfoot, was inlaid with polished river pebbles.

Kat kept her shower fairly short, but even so, by the time she emerged into the kitchen, clean and freshly dressed, she was feeling light-headed. It was well past her normal dinnertime, and she hadn't eaten since that morning. Anton's arrival seemed to have distracted Akilina; she hadn't mentioned food earlier, and Kat hadn't felt comfortable raising it herself.

The smell of meat hit Kat even before she entered the kitchen, and when she saw the cold spread waiting for her she sat down in the seat Akilina indicated with a sigh of satisfaction.

She'd soon demolished several hundred grams of bresaola, barely pausing to wonder how on earth Akilina had managed to get more food delivered at such short notice on the weekend, let alone at what cost. In fact, nothing much crossed her mind except the food in front of her until the first pangs of her hunger had been assuaged.

She sat back with a replete sigh as Char wandered into the kitchen, followed by Anton, who, seeing Kat's plate filled with nothing but cured meat, directed an inquiring glance at Akilina.

"What did Katerina eat earlier? More meat?"

Akilina nodded, and Kat looked up at Anton, her attention caught by his question.

"Has she eaten anything else?"

Akilina looked troubled. "Not much else. I bought more for her because she seemed to like it. Is there a problem?"

Kat pushed her plate away. She ignored the fact that they were discussing her as if she was a child they were responsible for. She was getting used to that. But what Anton had asked made her stop and actually think for the first time about what she'd eaten today. It had basically been unadulterated meat. No, wait, she'd also eaten a muffin and a piece of fruit this morning. The muffin had tasted terrible, if she recalled correctly. And she'd only eaten it out of embarrassment at having devoured an entire meal of meat … as she'd done just now.

Anton was looking at her thoughtfully. "Is this your normal diet, Katerina?"

She shook her head, again embarrassed.

"She made herself a pasta dish last night," Char chimed in helpfully. "With garlic too."

"Really?" Anton's eyes were alight with interest.

"Definitely half human," Akilina said with a delicate shudder. "It makes most of our kind terribly ill," she explained.

Anton took a seat next to Kat. "Katerina, what would you want to eat right at this minute, if you could choose anything in the world?"

Kat blinked as she gazed into his warm hazel eyes, and her embarrassment faded away. It was hard not to relax into the topic of her own strange eating habits when someone so incredibly attractive seemed so *interested* in what she had to say.

"Ummm …" For a moment her mind was completely blank, and then an image came to her from the depths of her memory, an image of incredible clarity. She could remember the exact smells, tastes and textures of the moment, even the direction the wind had been blowing, and how the scudding raindrops had felt as they hit her neck.

"There was one time," she began hesitantly, and Anton nodded encouragingly. "There was one time I went on a hunting trip with my brothers. I had won an archery competition at school, and they bet me that I couldn't bring down a real animal with an arrow." She gave a self-deprecating grimace. "They were right, but not because my aim was off. I saw a deer, only a young one, and I just froze. She was so beautiful, and I realized I didn't want to kill her for a stupid bet. Jez, my brother, was just across from me with his rifle, and when he saw I wasn't going to take the shot, he took it. Anyway, we camped out that night. We'd been walking all day, so we were starving. And we'd barely started to cook the bits of venison when it started raining, so we grabbed everything and took it inside the tent. We were so hungry we ate the meat anyway, and it had the most wonderful flavor from the redbud twigs Ryan had put on the fire."

Anton was still watching her with interest as she finished, but it was Char who broke in with a comment.

"So, basically, you're saying the thing you would most like to eat right now is smoky raw deer meat."

"Ummm, I guess so." Put so bluntly, it sounded pretty unappetising, didn't it? She'd turned to face Char, and away from the soothing influence of Anton's eyes, her embarrassment returned.

"Or maybe steak tartare?" Kat was horrified by the words coming out of her mouth. She'd wanted a second suggestion that sounded *less* aggressively carnivorous than her first answer. "Oh gosh, I can't believe I just said that," she mumbled, thoroughly mortified.

"Katerina, look at me." Anton took her hand, and his warmth flowed into her, calming her. "Given what we are, do you really think you need to be embarrassed about something like that?"

"I suppose not," she murmured.

"Good. All I wanted to suggest was that perhaps as you *are* half human, a more balanced diet might be in order."

"I wonder," Akilina mused. "It seems that her body is choosing exactly the sort of food it wants or needs, and it occurs to me that a dietary change of this sort could be an early indicator of transition. For the blood-made, it is such a rapid, violent transformation."

"And painful," Char added. "Like having your limbs sawed off with a rusty butter knife."

Akilina ignored her interjection, and continued her train of thought. "But perhaps for a hybrid the process is more protracted? I shall have to do some reading to see what I can discover."

She cocked her head then, birdlike, listening to a sound Kat couldn't hear.

"Excuse me," Akilina said, before disappearing in the direction of the entry door. Moments later, she was back. Her expression was serious, a little worried.

"Our doorman informs me we have a visitor. It is your man from the Directorate, Charice. Very resourceful. He seems to have followed you here."

Char frowned. "How?"

"It seems he sought information on your whereabouts at your club."

Anton stiffened, his hand tightening around Kat's.

"Not from any of *my* staff," Char snapped. "They know better."

Akilina turned to Anton apologetically. "We shall have to make the best of it. I, too, would prefer that the Directorate had not been involved. But as they have been it was inevitable they would eventually find us here, and if we had tried to move her, it would ultimately have drawn more attention to both her and us. Perhaps their interest will be innocent enough."

"I do not trust anything about them," Anton said flatly.

"I understand that," Akilina said, "but you don't have any specific reason for thinking they are linked to this ... danger you mentioned?"

"No ... but all that oily politeness hides something unsavory. You know my family lives outside their sphere of influence, and I fail to see how Directorate rule has been so beneficial to the rest of you in the cities."

"The Directorate protect us," Char said. "And they keep us fed. Surely that's worth something?"

"You are young," Anton said. "Still, you must remember what life was like before the Directorate supplied you with measured doses of that denatured rubbish you call food?"

"The Directorate?" Kat asked. "Who are they? And what do they want with me?"

"They are our ruling body," Akilina said. "And as to their interest in you – well, we shall shortly discover that. But you need not be concerned. I am protecting you, and I am not without influence."

Akilina laid her hand gently on Anton's shoulder.

"Perhaps you should simply wait outside on the balcony and listen to what happens. There is no reason for you to draw his attention unnecessarily, as technically you are trespassing within Directorate territories by being here."

Anton let go of Kat's hand, and gave her a last long look before going outside. "You have no need to be afraid," he said. "I will be just outside."

To Akilina, he said, "Be careful."

The tall, broad-shouldered man who followed Akilina into the living room soon after was a little larger than Anton. He was dressed in shades of charcoal and black, in the sort of deliberately unobtrusive style that screamed security. He seemed ill at ease. Kat had seen the respect Dominic and the others accorded Char, and in her own rather unique way Char treated Akilina and Anton with the same respect. This man was behaving like someone who'd just been ushered into the best parlor of his grandmother's rich, elderly friend.

The Directorate man sat gingerly on the edge of the ottoman Akilina ushered him to, but only after all the women had taken seats. Then he was profuse in his apologies; for keeping Char waiting this long, for disturbing Akilina in her home. He used the honorific "arella" to refer to them both, but seemed awkward with it, as if he kept a different sort of company in his usual line of work.

Despite all this, Kat sensed he knew exactly what was going on. More than he initially made explicit, anyway. His eyes kept straying toward the archway leading into the studio, as if he was expecting someone to come through it at any moment.

"Perhaps your friend would like to join us before we discuss the real reason I'm here," he suggested bluntly after a while.

Akilina returned his gaze steadily. "*If* I have another friend here, I really think whether or not they choose to join us would be their decision."

"Of course. My apologies, Arella. Well, let's begin then." He paused as Anton's shadow fell across the floor between them, and glanced up at the elder for the barest instant. Anton stopped in the archway and stayed there, leaning against one wall, as the Directorate man went on in an unhurried way.

"I didn't pay a whole lot of attention to this job when you first rang me." This he directed at Char. "I just logged it like normal, and that was when all hell broke loose. It seems the description you gave me of this girl's abilities has tripped off something in the system, and there's a whole lot of heat coming your way."

He gave a humorless smile, a bare curl of the lips. It didn't reach his serious gray eyes. "Luckily for you, like any big organization, they don't move all that fast. The Directorate's usual response to something like this starts with me. I'm the fastest and the best. I've been asked to take her to the Hema Castus Institute. It's one of the Directorate research facilities – which operates to all intents and purposes as a specialized prison."

Kat drew breath in a gasp. In the blink of an eye Anton and Char had moved as one to block the man's path to Kat with their own bodies.

Apart from being her *employer*, Hema Castus was one of the most ... no, probably *the* most highly respected medical research institute in the country. Was she really supposed to believe that they were some sort of shadow organisation run by supernatural over-lords ...? Her workmate Trevor had been employed at the main institute outside Pittsburgh, and now his words came to mind with a dull thud. *I heard whispers that there was a huge lab underground, away from the sunlight* ... Kat shivered.

Maybe what she'd learned in the last day or so meant she couldn't take *anything* about her normal, safe world at face value anymore. The thought terrified her.

"Out of the question," Anton said coldly.

The Directorate man took in the way Anton and Char shielded Kat with a flicker of amusement, and raised his hand. "You're right to be unimpressed. It's not a nice place." He looked at them soberly. "They weren't specific about the condition she should be in when delivered there, either. That's bad. Not as bad as a kill order, but still bad. It means they don't mind if she happens to end up dead."

Dead? Kat clenched her fists, her stomach a writhing tangle of knots. Her pulse thundered in her ears.

Had this all been an elaborate ruse to trap her? The platelet study; the offer to come and work at the Hema Castus Research Institute; the special attention from Director Norris and the other man who'd recruited her – Ionescu? Surely they'd have had no way of knowing who she was? Still, if the Directorate controlled Hema Castus, and the Directorate wanted her imprisoned, even dead, *everything* took on a much more sinister light. And anyway, why *did* the Directorate want her dead?

The Directorate man didn't seem worried by the three pairs of glowing eyes fixed on him, but looked at her instead. "Sorry," he said, with a trace of rough sympathy. It was the first time he had directly acknowledged her presence since entering the room.

"You can relax. I'm not going to do it," he said.

Gee, thanks. Kat breathed out slowly, watching the man carefully through the gap between Char and Anton. Having them there in front of her was definitely comforting.

The man paused, eyeing the two of them in their protective stances. "You need to make this girl disappear though." He focused on Char. "Two days ago you were less than keen about taking on her protection. Seems that's changed. So, any suggestions?"

"Why are you doing this?" Anton's voice was unfriendly, suspicious.

"I said suggestions, not questions," the man commented dryly, turning to face Anton. "I'm doing this because I may not have a choice about who I work for, but I do have a choice about how I do my job. Okay?" He scanned the faces watching him.

"How do we know we can trust you?" Char said.

The man sighed, obviously realizing he wasn't going to be able to escape without answering a few questions. "Look, I'm no Directorate true believer. You can trust me because I gain nothing by lying and have plenty to lose."

He flipped back the cuffs of his shirtsleeves to reveal matching metal bands secured tightly around each wrist, heavily embossed with symbols.

Char let out a gasp of surprise. "Rune-locked bands. I've never met a bonded convict before."

"Well now you have." The guy looked around at the faces ringing him again, and this time there was less hostility there.

Anton half turned toward Kat. "For the term of their bondage, a bonded convict is the property of the Directorate, with no individual rights. Like a vassal, or a serf, in years gone by. It's a position worse than servitude, worse than mere imprisonment."

"Is it true that your arm bands can ..." Char's voice was hushed, and she broke off and bit her lip.

"Can kill me, at the whim of the Vodas?" the man finished with a bitter smile. "So I hear. I've never wanted to test that fact."

Akilina moved closer. "I understood that the convict system had long ago been discontinued, and there were no more bonded convicts."

"What the Directorate tells the *Tabérin* public and what they do behind closed doors are two very different things," the man said tightly. "All I know is that I've been wearing these bands for nearly a hundred years."

"A hundred years of bonded service!" Akilina was aghast. "Was your crime so severe?"

For a moment, it seemed the man wouldn't answer. When he did speak, anger was mingled with frustration and pain. "My only crime was being made – without Directorate sanction. My maker was sentenced to death, and I got to wear these." He held up his wrists. "But I've served my original term many times over. It was decades before I realized that they never had any intention of letting me go while I'm still useful."

Bitter resignation twisted his face. "Seems to me I'm only going to be freed when there's no more Directorate. And no Vodas. Working toward that day would give me a whole lot of job satisfaction." He looked around at the faces ringing him. "So, we okay?"

"You are suggesting we hide her?" Anton's deep voice cut through the moment of tension, and set the seal on the new collaboration.

"Yes, somewhere outside their influence. Away from the city, if at all possible."

Char and Anton sank to the floor on either side of Kat, so close they were touching her.

Kat knew they were there, but she couldn't feel them. She couldn't feel anything. She was in a hidden, tiny space; a room within a room, boxed in by one-way glass. She could see everything, hear everything, but she herself was separate, unseen and unheard. She cleared her throat, shattering the illusion.

"Why do the Directorate want me dead?"

"They must see you as a threat," Char said. She closed her hand around Kat's arm with a gentle, comforting pressure.

"I'm sorry. When I contacted them it seemed the right thing to do, because of the danger to *you* from *us*. I didn't really consider it the other way around until I got here to the Towers. But basically, you shouldn't be able to read V-runes. You shouldn't be able to see any of our buildings, let alone walk right through the door of them. But you can – and that makes you dangerous."

"Dangerous?" Kat felt like an idiot, echoing what Char said back at her, but it was all her numb brain could do. How could anyone believe she was such a big threat they wanted to *kill* her?

"We are vulnerable during the daylight hours," Akilina said. "Details of where we reside, where we rest through the daylight hours are a secret kept closely guarded from the human community. It is necessary, for our survival."

"There's more to it than that," said the Directorate man. "I don't always get told the full story, but I hear things. I see things. Sometimes I'm even asked to do things. And I have a pretty fair idea that someone within the Mandate Council is acting out a vendetta. In the last ten, twenty years I've seen others like Kat targeted just because they're of mixed parentage. Seems like there's a lot more going on than the Directorate trying to protect our kind from exposure."

"There are others like me?" Kat wasn't sure why she seized on that fact rather than the slightly more important issue of her survival. It rose up like a rock in the rapids that churned around her, and she clung to it. Maybe it was *because* her life was in danger that she desperately wanted to believe she wasn't alone in this.

Belatedly, she noticed Akilina frowning at her admonishingly, and realized it wasn't too wise to confirm anything this guy didn't already know for sure – like her parentage. As far as he knew she could just be a human with special abilities.

The guy shrugged. "It's illegal – not to mention rare – for a male of our kind to father a child with a human woman. But yeah, it still happens."

Kat tensed. Illegal? Did that mean if she suddenly appeared in his life, her father would be branded a criminal by his own people? And if he was some kind of aristocrat like Akilina thought, would he want to know about some half-human kid he'd accidentally fathered? Would he even care?

Suddenly the idea of trying to find him wasn't so appealing – especially given the danger following her around. He wouldn't exactly be happy if she led this Directorate mob right to his door. Unless … for all she knew, he might be *in* the Directorate. She gave a little shiver.

"When she said 'others like her' I believe Katerina meant others … with special abilities like her," Akilina corrected smoothly.

The guy flicked a glance at her. "Sure, yeah. Lots of variations. I've seen 'em all."

Much more than he'd ever wanted to see, by the sound of it.

"So. Whoever she is, whatever she is, she still needs to leave town." The guy's eyes went to Char, then Anton.

"I could go home," Kat suggested softly.

He gave an unequivocal shake of his head. "Out of the question. That's exactly where they'll search for you first. It has to be somewhere not linked to your past. Somewhere untraceable, off the grid."

"I think I can arrange that," Anton said.

The man turned to consider him, as if deciding whether he could be relied upon. Evidently, he liked what he saw. "Good," he said. "I don't want to know the details. It's safer if I don't. But move her as soon as possible. Like tonight. I'll report her missing tomorrow night. That's the longest I can safely delay."

"Will it cause trouble for you? When you tell them you can't find her?" Kat was surprised by the concern in Char's voice as she asked this.

For the first time, as his eyes came to rest on Char, the man smiled, his hard gray eyes softening. "I'll be okay. I have a few tricks up my sleeve."

I bet you do, Kat thought. She frowned, unsure where the thought had come from. Perhaps it was just that he gave every impression of being a man of hidden resources.

Anton cleared his throat. "In the interest of openness and cooperation, do you mind sharing what it is that makes you so useful the Directorate are determined not to let you go?"

"And another question," Akilina said calmly. "As you know, we are very security conscious here at the Towers. My doorman tells me you did not arrive by car. How *did* you get here?"

"Well I didn't fly over the gate." The man smiled blandly in Anton's direction. "So I suppose I must have just appeared at your front door."

Anton stiffened, betraying his surprise. "Something tells me you don't mean that as a figure of speech."

The man disappeared from where he was standing, and in the flicker of an instant reappeared across the room, then returned the same way.

Kat gasped, and there was a stunned silence from the others. One second he'd been there and the next he hadn't. Surely that wasn't *possible*.

The man shrugged, as if to say, 'Now you know what all the fuss is about.'

"Ah," Akilina breathed. "You are of the *zaherin*. I can see why that would make you useful to the Directorate. And dangerous to them once out of their clutches."

"He can disappear from one place and reappear elsewhere," Char whispered to Kat. "It's a rare talent among our kind. I've never seen anyone do that before." Char looked back up at the guy and blushed when she saw him watching her with the hint of a smile in his gray eyes.

"Glad to broaden your horizons," he said.

Anton was clearly less than impressed at the veiled comment about flying that had been directed at him. "About the flying – care to elaborate on what you may have heard? And where?"

"A couple of guys who were hanging around your club – " he nodded in Char's direction, "had a run-in with a giant eagle at the gates just outside here. Of course, you'd know nothing about that."

"Dominic and the others who followed us," Kat said. She looked at Anton with a new awareness. It seemed what she'd seen through the giant eagle's eyes two nights ago hadn't been a dream after all.

"Oh. One more thing I heard while keeping my ears open." The man again directed his comment to Anton, and his expression was serious. "There've been a whole lot of *bestimut* going missing. I mean, that's been happening for decades; it's no secret to anyone that they and the Directorate don't see eye to eye. But the disappearances have been increasing lately."

Anton rose to his full height, eyes glittering. "I believe our shape-shifting brethren prefer the term *unalil.*"

The man shrugged. "Whatever." His mouth twisted in a wry grin. "A dead spade's still dead, right?" He frowned. "Not that anybody knows for sure if all these missing shifters are dead. The important thing is what the Directorate's doing about it."

Anton looked at him questioningly.

"Nothing."

Anton's brow contracted. "So the Directorate could be implicated?"

The man shrugged again. "Not too many pies they *don't* have their fingers in. Just saying, if there's anyone you want to warn, go ahead and warn 'em."

He turned to face the others. "Anyway, that was all I came to say. Wherever you decide to go, do it soon, okay?" He rose to his feet in one lithe movement. "I'll see myself out."

"Wait, how can we reach you … if we need to?" Char asked. There was a hesitancy in her tone that Kat hadn't heard before.

"You shouldn't need to." His voice was hard, the voice of a seasoned professional who didn't believe in taking risks. He must have seen something in Char's face, though, because his expression softened again for an instant. "I mean, it's safer if you don't. You shouldn't call me directly. But if you do need to reach me, you can call this number." He took a card and pen from his pocket and scrawled the digits on the back of the card, which he then handed to Char. "Ask if you can leave a message for Falcon. John Falcon."

And then he was gone.

Chapter 21

Kat sat with her arms clasped around her bent legs and her chin resting on her knees, at that moment very much the child they often seemed to treat her as. Char had already packed all her things for her again, in about two minutes flat, before heading off to tackle Kat's boss.

That was completely Kat's idea. Char had rolled her eyes when she'd expressed concern about disappearing from her job without an explanation. Char did that a lot actually. Once she'd accepted that Kat wasn't going to drop the subject without a fight, she'd come up with a solution that appealed to her sense of irony, and was even now undoubtedly filling Director Norris's head with the impression he'd sent his new recruit on an extended secondment to the main Hema Castus Institute near Pittsburgh, at the request of Chairman Ionescu.

"I don't know why you want to bother though, Kat," Char had said before she'd left. "After what John Falcon told us about Hema Castus and the Directorate, how long do you think you'd have lasted at that place as a researcher before you became the research subject, or worse?" Maybe going to such an effort *was* pointless and unnecessary, as Char claimed, but Director Norris and the others had been nice to her, and tying up the loose ends still made Kat feel more comfortable about the whole thing. Plus, her work colleagues were human, and everything Monica and Trevor had said in the week she'd been working there had left her pretty certain they, at least, had no idea about the unwholesome truth their place of employment was hiding beneath its thick veneer of respectability.

When Kat had offered to help Akilina pack, the elder had smiled at her gently. "No, child, it is a kind offer, but you will only hinder me."

So instead she sat and watched as Akilina darted around the room, packing things into a small trunk. Anton leaned against the far wall, watching Akilina with a brooding expression.

She stopped what she was doing, and turned to face him. "Anton, cease your worrying – this is the best path, the only path to take."

"Are you certain this is what you want to do?" His voice was abrupt. "There may be no going back from this."

"Absolutely certain," Akilina said indignantly. "You should know how grateful I am you are willing to help us, given the danger, and given the … differences between our people. A new *egir'rin*, after so long – this is important to me. And *of course* I must go where she goes. She may need specific tuition, guidance. Only I can provide that. Besides, I have led a quiet life for far too long. It is time for a little adventure, I think."

"Very well then. I certainly do not like the idea of you facing the Directorate and their questions alone." Anton sighed. "If we have been informed correctly it is likely the Directorate will look for her here. I am concerned it will appear rather odd if you are missing when that happens."

Akilina paused to look at him squarely. "If they do come here asking questions, I suggest we have my doorman tell them I have gone on an extended holiday to the Far East. If they suspect I have taken Katerina there, and try to follow us, or send others to apprehend us there, then so much the better."

Anton smiled. "That could work." His expression grew serious. "About these employees of Charice's – she has explained why she needed to take them into her confidence initially. Do you think they can be trusted?"

Akilina tilted her head, considering. "Truthfully, I know little about that part of her life. That has always been the way she preferred it. But I do know they are like family to her, and Charice's gift means her instincts about whom to trust are usually accurate."

Anton seemed satisfied with that. He gave a decisive nod. "Now, for the rest. We need a safe mode of transport, preferably something not linked to any of us. If I was alone, I would fly ..."

"I don't keep a car," Akilina said, "but I have an old friend who bought a Cadillac after the war. He encourages me to use it. He keeps an apartment and car here at the Towers, but lives most of the time in Europe. No one would be able to trace the vehicle to us, or think it odd for it to be missing."

"I know little about cars." Anton frowned, walking across the room to join them. "They need some form of ongoing maintenance to remain operational, do they not?"

Akilina smiled. "Our staff here at the Towers look after that."

"I am happy with that solution then." He gave Kat a thoughtful look. "I am afraid you will need to remain inside the car with the windows closed for the duration of the trip, Katerina, as your scent is so attractive to our kind. Best we make it as hard for them to track you as possible."

*

Akilina's doorman clearly knew his way around the huge garage beneath the Towers. In complete darkness, he stowed their belongings, then somehow disengaged the brake and pulled the car out of its parking bay with a casual hand beneath the fender as if the huge thing was no heavier than a toy. He rolled it over to where they waited in the glow of emergency exit lights at the foot of the ramp, then he bowed low to Akilina and disappeared into the darkness.

"When you said your friend bought this car after the war, I guess you meant the Second World War?" Kat asked.

Akilina nodded and, misinterpreting the reason for Kat's question, hastened to reassure her. "Do not worry, it has been well looked after."

Kat wasn't a particularly car-crazy person, but the rounded lines of this car, and the way the light caught the gleaming paintwork on its immaculate body and the shining metal of the front grille, had her impressed. This Cadillac was beautiful in a way modern cars would never be.

Anton and Char had a brief conference out of Kat's earshot, before Char came over to Kat.

"Well, goodbye. Good luck with it all." Char seemed uncomfortable, and it was clear she wanted to get out of there as soon as possible.

"You're not coming with us then?" Kat kept her tone noncommittal.

"Nah. Not my scene. I belong in the city. Arella-dara will protect you better than I ever could. Take care, huh?"

"Sure. And thanks … for everything you've done." Kat hesitated. She wanted to say something else, to acknowledge the subtext she was sure she could sense. It seemed like there was another whole conversation going on beneath the surface of Char's words that she couldn't quite catch.

Char's white teeth flashed in the near darkness. "Well, I guess I did okay with the protection thing after all. You're not dead." And then she headed for the exit ramp, silently melting away into the moonless night.

Anton stood facing Akilina just off to the side. "Are you sure you can drive this thing?" He sounded worried.

"I'll be fine. It's not something one forgets." Akilina's tone was firm, and didn't invite further comment.

Anton watched wordlessly as she stalked around to the driver's side, before turning to Kat with a sigh and a rueful smile. He opened the rear door and ushered her in, before getting into the front beside Akilina.

It only took a moment for Kat to notice that there were no seatbelts fitted. And a moment after that, as they mounted the exit ramp and sped along the tree-lined driveway away from the Towers buildings and toward the entry gate, Kat realized with a jolt that Akilina was driving without headlights. She wasn't sure if it was to make them less easy to pursue, or because Akilina had simply forgotten, but it was unnerving, being surrounded by the dark night and forced to completely entrust her safety to someone else.

Akilina was driving fast. Very fast. Almost as if the Directorate was on their tail right this minute, rather than a full day behind according to what Falcon had promised them. Each time the car changed direction, or they rounded a corner and the side of the road came frighteningly close to her window, she couldn't help but jump nervously. She'd been presented with several possible options for her own demise in the last two days. Even *one* would have given a reasonable person plenty to worry about. Right now, she didn't know whether dying in a car crash would be better or worse than being taken to a Directorate prison and experimented on, or attacked by a blood-crazed being driven wild by her scent. Hitting a tree at their current speed would probably be the fastest and neatest of the three.

She gave a shudder, and pressed her rune necklace to her chest. She wasn't usually so morbid. The warmth of the metal against her skin soothed her, and she kept her hand to her heart as Akilina reached the main road, turned, and accelerated onto the highway. Things did settle down then, without the constant twists and bends that had been throwing her around.

Slowly, Kat began to relax, lulled by the vibration and rumble of the powerful vintage engine and, over it, the occasional indistinct murmur of conversation from the front of the car. She must have dozed, off and on, as they drove through the night, though she sensed after a while that they were gaining altitude, the car engine laboring as it drove them higher.

Finally, they came to a stop, and moments later the cold air came flooding in as her door was opened to the night. She took a deep, grateful breath, and looked up at Anton, who was standing with his hand outstretched, his expression both relaxed and alert. His brown hair was ruffled artistically by a light breeze, and his eyes shone as they met hers. The fact that he was a creature of the night could be felt rather than seen; he was at ease in the dark that surrounded them. At that moment he had never appeared less human.

"We survived Akilina's driving," he commented as he helped her from the car.

"It was okay as long as we weren't going around corners," she said. "But I'm glad to have my feet back on the ground."

Hazel eyes crinkled into the warm smile she was getting used to. "I won't tell her you said that. Akilina is very proud of her driving prowess."

"Where is she?" Kat asked.

"She has gone ahead," Anton said. "This final part must be covered on foot, but I will carry you. The night is too advanced for us to linger."

Kat nodded, and he scooped her up like she weighed nothing at all, and held her securely against his chest. Then he began to move downhill, traveling through tracts of forest, and past rocks and shrubs, at great speed. The obstacles didn't seem to concern Anton as he effortlessly navigated through the night until they were deep in the wilderness, far from any road or settlement. Though Kat couldn't see clearly, for quite a while it seemed they followed a valley, and then Anton began to climb higher, through the forest, until they were up above the treeline. They traversed a rocky ridge, and then at long last the dark outline of a huge stone and timber building rose up before them. Light spilled from mullioned windows, and Anton set her gently on her feet in front of a large closed door.

"Welcome to our home, Katerina." Anton's teeth flashed into a smile just visible in the darkness, and then he took her hand, and moved to open the door. "Come inside. Everyone is waiting to meet you."

Kat's stomach lurched. She didn't want a big welcome. She was tired; it had been a very long night, and she had a vague memory of having applied a touch of eye makeup hours and hours ago, after her shower. It was probably smudged all the way to her chin by now. Maybe it was stupid for her mind to get stuck on something so ridiculously minor when she was fleeing for her life, but these people were taking a risk by offering her somewhere to stay. It was all kind of a big deal, and under the circumstances … well, okay, so she was no Venezuelan beauty contestant at the best of times – but it *did* seem unfair that their first impression of her would be so far from sensational.

Kat stepped inside, blinking, dazzled by the bright light after the darkness outside. As she faced the semicircle of strangers, it was impossible not to obey her first instinct to take a couple of steps backward.

An instant later, of course, she wished she could have reversed the telling reaction. As expected, she wasn't doing so well with that first impression thing. Just making it crystal clear she didn't want to be here by walking *backward* out the door. Yep, way to go. But looking around the foyer, it wasn't hard to see why she had reacted so instinctively. Everyone was so damned *big* – well, the males were, anyway. She could almost feel the energy coming off them. It was like there was something caged in those bodies; something wild that was only ever a moment from escaping.

This must be what animals felt like when they were caught in the car headlights – right before you hit them. Anton could change from a bird of prey into a man. Did the others have the same ability? And *if* they had a wild side, how well was it controlled? A quiver ran through her. It had been a long night, and she was feeling a bit more vulnerable than usual, and very ... human. Fine. It would still be nice if she could maybe move *forward* this time.

And yet, she hesitated.

Anton's hand touched her shoulder with a gentle warm pressure. "You're safe now, Katerina," he said softly. "You're among friends."

Kat took a small step forward, aware of Anton's solid presence behind her and his hand on her shoulder. Rather perversely, she was annoyed at how reassuring she found it. She forced herself to look at individual faces, and smile like a normal person who wasn't completely out of her depth.

The hooded golden eyes of a gaunt, black-haired man standing slightly off to the side instantly drew her. Was she imagining it, or did he flinch when her eyes met his? There was something ... beseeching in their depths. An apology, a deep misery. And he seemed so familiar – yet she was sure she hadn't ever seen his face before. Odd.

Then, without warning, one of the men was right up in her face, blocking her view of everyone and everything else. She gasped and took a step back again, colliding with Anton, who brought both hands up to her shoulders to steady her from behind.

She had to tilt her head up to see the face of the man towering over her. He must have been several inches over six feet, and every one of those inches was solid, sleek muscle. His eyes were the most frightening thing about him though. They were alight with the same curiosity and hunger she had seen in Dominic's eyes at Char's club. His was the calculating gaze of a predator.

Then he smiled, and that playful curve of the lips transformed him into a tawny-haired god. She realized at that moment how dangerous he was. Though he was very possibly the most beautiful man she had ever seen, there was hardness at his core. She had no doubt that he would kill without a moment's hesitation.

Kat froze as he lifted a loose strand of her hair to his nose, and inhaled deeply.

"Back off, Alek. You're scaring her." Anton's voice came from so close behind her that she could feel the vibration of his chest when he spoke.

The mesmerizing dark blue eyes left hers, and lifted to look over her shoulder. Alek hadn't released her hair yet, and Anton's hands still gripped her shoulders, so she was trapped between them like a petrified rabbit.

"I wondered if she really smelled as good as I'd heard she did." He was still smiling, playing with the hair he held between his fingers. His eyes as they returned to hers were possessive, caressing.

There was a movement in the periphery of her vision, and she realized the dark-haired man had moved forward into her line of sight again. His golden eyes were fixed fiercely on Alek.

Then, moving so fast it was if she appeared out of nowhere, Akilina moved smoothly into place beside Anton.

"And I trust you have satisfied your curiosity now." She reached forward and flicked Kat's hair out of Alek's grasp.

"Certainly, Princess." Withdrawing his empty hand ever so slowly from where it lingered in mid-air beside Kat's face, Alek inclined his head slightly, and an instant later he had moved to the far side of the room.

After one last lingering glance at Kat, he announced to no one in particular, "I'm going hunting." And then he was gone.

A slender woman hurried forward to fill the gap he had left, reaching out to take Kat's hand in a cool clasp. "Welcome." Her voice was soft music after what had come before. "I am Della. Please accept our apologies for Alek's behavior. You are young and lovely, and he is … impulsive."

Della glanced at the assembled group. "Perhaps we can suspend the formal introductions for the moment? You must be tired from your travels, Katerina. Would you like something to drink?"

Della's gentle smile was impossible to resist, and Kat began to relax again, even as her eyes strayed to where the dark-haired man had stood a moment earlier, his strange familiarity a magnetic pull on her attention. He'd seemed like he was ready to spring at Alek; like he wanted to murder him. But the place where he'd stood was now empty. He'd left the room without a word.

Chapter 22

Councillor Leander Ionescu strode into his office and shut the door behind him. His dark eyes took in the younger man seated by the fire. His great-nephew gave a guilty start and rose hesitantly to his feet.

"On your knees," Ionescu hissed. He did not trouble to hide his irritation.

The man sank immediately into the subservient position, knees sinking into the thick rug, head lowered.

Ionescu crossed the room and stopped in front of him.

"You may look at me, Dominic. I'd like to know whether there's even a glimmer of intelligence in your eyes when I talk to you."

Dominic raised his eyes slowly. The councillor could see the reluctance in them. The boy did not want to be here. And he was afraid. As he should be.

The councillor's hand darted out, a lightning-quick movement capturing Dominic's chin in a bruising hold. "I should perhaps be grateful that you have obeyed my order to come here. It seems to be the only thing so far you have been capable of successfully achieving."

Dominic's gaze fell. "Uncle Leo, I—"

"Silence." Ionescu quelled him with a glance. He tightened his grip on Dominic's jaw, forcing him to strain upward. "When you are in this building, you will address me as Councillor, or as Arelli-dar. We may be distantly related but I am also your maker, and I will be respected as such. Do not forget that."

It appeared Dominic had dressed with care for this meeting. Ionescu's sharp eyes took in the fashionable clothes, the expensive watch. "Tell me, Dominic, who pays for your playboy lifestyle?"

Dominic's voice was little more than a whisper. "You do, Unc—, ah, Councillor."

"And ... my memory escapes me. *Where* would you be if I hadn't taken you in and found a use for you?"

Dominic's face twisted in pain. "Dead in a gutter, Councillor."

"Quite." He held Dominic for a moment or two longer, then let him slump back to the floor.

Ionescu crossed to the sideboard, and filled a glass from the decanter there. He returned to the fireside and sank into an armchair.

"So," he said after a moment. He held the glass of ruby liquid up to the firelight, then swirled it and took a sip. From the corner of his eye, he saw the hungry expression in Dominic's eyes as he watched; how his nostrils flared as they caught the rich scent of old blood. So little self-control. The boy was still young.

Ionescu turned to face Dominic at last, his dark eyes unreadable, his face expressionless. "Perhaps you can explain, Dominic, how it is that Katerina Chanter has made several powerful friends among our kind, and has now fled New York, when I gave *you* explicit instructions to befriend her and bring her to me."

Red stained Dominic's cheeks. "I tried, Councillor. I met the night flight at La Guardia as you requested, but she never arrived. I went to the hotel too, that night and again a couple of nights later. She never checked in to the suite you booked."

A twinge of irritation passed through Ionescu. The damned *bestimut* wolf must have interfered somehow. He'd smelled the creature all around her house in Charleston and in the woods near her parents' home at Richwood too. It had been enough to prompt him to engineer her removal from West Virginia, but he still hadn't been sure …

His eyes narrowed as they met Dominic's. "And you didn't think to inform me of this?" His voice was deadly calm.

Dominic swallowed with an effort. His eyes dropped to the rug.

"Clearly, you were engaged in important matters elsewhere, and simply didn't … think at all." The seconds ticked past as Ionescu stared pensively at the fire. He took another sip from his glass. His eyes flicked across to rest on Dominic's bent head.

"And Fate gave you another chance – or sheer dumb luck, many would say – when Katerina appeared at a nightclub you frequent. Yet you failed to seize this chance."

"I had no idea who she was," Dominic burst out. "By the time I'd worked it out, Char-arella was there, and she made it impossible for me to—"

"Instead of charming her," Ionescu continued, as if Dominic had not spoken, "you somehow managed to terrify the girl, and she fled to the Towers, the one place we cannot risk an embarrassing disturbance."

"I tried to stop them reaching the Towers." A sulky note had crept back into Dominic's voice. "I had help. We tracked them as far as the gate, and we were thinking about going inside, but an enormous *bestimut* eagle came out of nowhere and nearly killed us. I didn't even know those things were real."

"I would have been most interested to hear of such a creature being seen so far from its home – but again, you did not think to inform me." Ionescu's voice was silky smooth. "It was not until I heard the Vodas crowing about how he had sent his little minion John Falcon to apprehend a hybrid female in Manhattan that I realized how completely you had failed me." He flicked his fingers against the side of Dominic's head.

Dominic flinched, and looked miserable.

"You have met her, Dominic. So perhaps you can stretch your limited mind to imagining how it made me feel, knowing I had arranged for this luminously lovely creature to come to New York, into *my* care – but through your incompetence she almost fell into the Vodas's hands."

He rose abruptly from his chair, and moved to stand in front of the fire. He placed his glass on the mantelpiece with a soft clink.

"She did get away, though." Dominic's voice behind him sounded faintly plaintive. "The Vodas doesn't know where she is."

"No. But neither do we. The *bestimut* must have hidden her somewhere. For a time the Vodas may believe this –" he waved an elegant hand, "fabrication about them having gone to the Far East, but he is no fool. He has this Char and her nightclub under surveillance. He will use whatever means he has available to track the girl down."

Ionescu frowned as he stared into the flames. *And naturally, he will be expecting my cooperation.* He knew how dangerously fine a line he walked.

He reached for his glass again, and quickly drained it, letting the contents warm the sudden chill he felt; a chill the fire in front of him could not ease.

As head of Information Acquisition, he controlled the flow of information to the Vodas, but each time he failed to pass on something of note he increased his chance of exposure. If any information he had withheld was to reach the Vodas by other means … well, it would not be the first time a councillor had met a sudden and painful death. With ambitious underlings like Victor Fortes snapping at his heels he could not afford to take unnecessary risks.

He turned and saw Dominic was looking up at him, fear replaced by curiosity.

"Why does the Vodas want this hybrid female so badly, Councillor? Why do you want her? Who *is* she?"

"It is not who she is, but who she may become. The stuff of legends. Our most holy trinity. Goddess, Empress, Mother to our race – reborn. With power over the very blood in our veins, if the fools in Predictive Science can be trusted."

Dominic couldn't quite hide his incredulity. "Are you talking about the second coming of the Mahra? Like in that poem?"

"Not poem. Prophecy. It might seem fantastic, but the Vodas believes it absolutely, and sees her as the ultimate threat."

"I think I remember the part you mean," Dominic said. He quoted softly.

"Twixt two worlds she feeds in light,
And seeks her bed by dark of night.
For those who fear and thus oppress,
Great change portend,
All things must end;
For those once wronged who seek redress,
A lasting peace,
And blest release."

Ionescu gave a short nod. "The Mahra Prophecy is gospel to the Vodas, and in his interpretation the first lines tell us that the Mahra will be reborn in one who is hybrid, 'twixt two worlds'. Convention holds, of course, that the reborn Mahra will also be *egir'rin* – a female descendant of the first Mahra."

He turned, leaned a hand against the mantel and stared moodily into the fire. "The remaining lines you quoted, so the Vodas believes, foretell the end of the Directorate at her hands. Which is why he wants her dead." His mouth twisted in derision. "At least I assume that is his motivation. The man is about as trusting as a cobra. He doesn't share such thoughts with me.

"The irony I find in this is that his vendetta, his undiscriminating and overzealous eradication of all hybrids, both male and female, in recent decades is what will bring about his downfall. He has made too many enemies."

Dominic didn't ask the next question, but Ionescu knew what it would have been and answered anyway. The old blood he had drunk had mellowed his mood.

"That is where the Vodas and I part ways, because I do not want to see this girl dead."

He looked down at the heavy gold insignia ring on his right index finger, twisting it absently from side to side. "No. Assuming I can keep her from the Vodas, I have very different plans for Katerina Chanter."

Chapter 23

Kat woke with nervous tension in the pit of her stomach, and the disorienting feeling that there was something she'd forgotten to do. Something …

She rolled over, sat up bleary-eyed among her blankets, and blinked into wakened awareness. Her phone. She'd turned it off before they'd left Akilina's, not knowing if or when she'd be able to charge it again. She groaned as she remembered that last weekend she'd promised to call her mother at nine am the following Sunday. That was today, wasn't it? She should have been looking forward to a relaxing day of sightseeing from her apartment in New York, and instead here she was, in the middle of the mountains.

She fumbled in the near darkness, trying to locate her phone. Her questing fingers found her handbag on the chair beside her bed, and next to it, the phone.

She pressed the power button, and waited for it to start up. Seconds later, a beep signalled incoming data, and the backlit display showed a call had gone to message bank. It was a miracle the damn thing even had reception out here.

Her mom would be waiting for the promised update on her first week in the new job. What time was it now, anyway? It was hard to be sure with the thick curtains drawn across the windows. Kat checked the time display on her phone; it read 10:07.

Damn. Her mother knew she wasn't one for sleeping in late. She must be wondering why Kat wasn't answering. Of course, her mom didn't know she'd been traveling half the night and had only gone to sleep five hours ago. Her head felt like it was full of cotton wool.

Kat blinked again. Her eyelids were like sandpaper. Yeah, she was surrounded by nocturnal creatures, but *she* wasn't nocturnal, and staying up till dawn not once, but twice in a row was completely out of character.

She dialed her mother's number, and listened as the call connected and began to ring. She closed her eyes and flopped back on the bed as her mother answered.

Tessa immediately started with the questions. Was Kat feeling okay? Definitely okay? Because she'd been thinking about Kat's strange blood results, and now she sounded husky ...

No, she didn't have a cold, she assured her mother. Her voice was husky because she'd been out with new friends. And everything else was fine. Totally fine.

That was sort of true. Partly true anyway, and her mom was glad to hear she'd made friends already. That spared her the question of why she hadn't called at nine as promised – her mom assumed she'd had a late night out. *That* bit was certainly true enough.

Work was good, she said. Some new stuff, nothing she couldn't handle.

When the call ended soon after, she turned the phone off again, and stared sightlessly up at the dark ceiling above. This was one of the only times she could remember deliberately lying to her mother. Lying by omission, even if not actually in the things she'd said. Either way, it felt wrong, really wrong.

But what was she supposed to say? What *could* she say? She'd already considered whether her mother could've known her father wasn't human, and dismissed the possibility. Her mother had described him as special … but in her mom's vocabulary that definitely wasn't code for anything supernatural or sinister.

Anyway, she still wasn't sure how she felt about all this herself. Until she worked things out in her own mind, it seemed easier not to tell her mom anything.

Kat briefly considered getting up and going to see whether anyone else was awake. Akilina maybe, as she didn't seem to sleep much even during the day. But after the phone call Kat felt far away from everyone all of a sudden. Removed by a lifetime of different experiences – a very *long* lifetime in the case of the others.

And she was in her pajamas, damn it. Stupid girly ones all covered in flowers. At the time it'd made sense to get changed for bed. Brushing her teeth and putting on her pajamas was something she'd done for herself every night since she was about four years old. Even though she hadn't gone to bed before five am for the last two nights, following her normal bedtime routine was a last vain attempt to cling to some small fragments of her old life. It would be laughable if it wasn't so tragic.

Kat realized she was still holding her cell phone tightly clenched in one hand. In fact, every muscle in her entire body was tense. Obviously, thinking about this stuff wasn't very relaxing. She felt around for her bag, then slipped the phone into the pocket inside. As she withdrew her hand it brushed against something warm, and she pulled out the rune necklace. She'd taken it off and put it away there before going to sleep.

Some instinct made her reach up to clasp it around her neck, and when she released it the warm weight settled against her chest as if it'd been made for no other place. As its energy spread through her body it left complete relaxation in its wake.

The bed was comfortable, she mused. She didn't know why she'd been feeling so negative. Maybe she hadn't slept for quite long enough yet, but she hadn't slept so *well* in ages. And she was wearing her favourite pajamas, the ones with little flowers scattered across them. She loved these pajamas. They reminded her of spring in the Appalachians.

She yawned, and snuggled drowsily back into her blankets. A bit more rest would be good.

She closed her eyes, and fell into a relaxed sleep almost immediately.

Her slumber was not free of dreams though. In the moments between sleep and waking, Kat dreamed she faced the back of an ornate chair of carved wood, inlaid with moonstone and amethyst, lapis and opal. Stretching beyond it was a huge wooden table, also fantastically carved.

The room seemed empty, but then in her dreaming vision Kat's perspective swung around and she saw the figure sitting in the high-backed chair. A woman, with silver links around her arms and legs to chain her in place. Her dark hair curled wildly around her shoulders. Her eyes were closed, face serene.

And then the woman's eyes opened. Even in her dream state, Kat felt the shock of recognition, evoking images of an earlier dream, a dream of a woman imprisoned, caged. The images twisted and wove themselves together, until it was clear they were one and the same.

One woman chained, and imprisoned. One woman with striking, unforgettable eyes. Eyes of glowing gold.

Chapter 24

Victor Fortes had a spring in his step as he approached the door to the Vodas's office suite. He nodded to the guard on duty at the door, and the door was opened to allow him access. He was expected.

Once in the presence of the Vodas, he sank to his knees and lowered his head to the floor.

"You may rise," the Vodas said.

"I have good news, Vodas," Fortes informed him. "The cellular telephone you asked me to monitor just came back online. The girl called her mother. Only for a minute or so, but it gave us enough for a rough triangulation. We know that she is somewhere in the White Mountains region of northern New Hampshire."

"In the mountains?" the Vodas said sharply.

Fortes nodded.

A gleam had entered the Vodas's eye. "These creatures you mentioned, the ones Hema Castus have developed, they can track, yes?"

Fortes smiled. "I anticipated your request, Vodas, and I'm happy to tell you that the Hema Castus Genetics team is on standby. All their resources are at your disposal."

"Good." The Vodas rubbed his hands together, as gleeful as a little boy with a new and destructive toy.

Fortes allowed himself a moment's satisfaction. The Vodas's response was everything he had hoped for. He bowed low. "Unfortunately, Vodas, it will take a little time to transport the beasts to New Hampshire, as they can only travel by night. And we will need special vehicles. But I can give orders for arrangements to begin immediately."

"Do so." The Vodas's voice was impatient. "I want to be there when they're released, Fortes. When our creatures find her and the traitors who protect her, I want to put this matter to rest. Permanently."

Chapter 25

It was only her second night in the mansion, but already Kat felt comfortable in the big, warm kitchen. She sat on her stool next to the bench and watched, fascinated, as Della sprinkled flour onto the counter and distributed it with deft fingers. Kat had never seen anyone make pasta from scratch before. Della had even ground the flour, from spelt grain Akilina had brought them as a gift. Kat settled into her stool and took in her surroundings while Della worked.

The kitchen, with its flagstone floor, and a separate larder off to one side, was like a traditional, pre-electric display room from out of some historic house brought to life. There was a huge wood stove that always had a pot or two simmering away and a large pine table in the center of the room. The wooden benches that lined two walls were scattered with ceramic bowls, stoneware storage canisters, and glass jars. There was a mortar and pestle on the bench, too, and hanging from the beamed ceiling and from hooks on whitewashed walls were bunches of herbs, and an assortment of copper and cast-iron pots, knives, and skillets.

A wooden staircase leading to the main entrance hall was in one corner, and in another, a winding stone staircase leading up to the floors above, where the bedrooms were.

"See how easy it is?" Della glanced up with a smile. "If it wasn't, I wouldn't have remembered how to do it, because it has been an awfully long time." She rolled and cut with quick, precise movements. "There. All done."

She laid the long ribbons of freshly cut pasta to one side of the work surface, gently separating the strands, then moved over to the sink to wash her hands.

"Come, I need basil now. I will show you the garden."

She scooped up a handful of seeds and nuts from a shallow dish on the bench near the kitchen door, and led the way outside. Light spilled through the open doorway into the night, illuminating a semicircle of the garden nearest the house.

"Here we are," Della said, breaking off several branches of fragrant basil leaves. Then she darted off into the darkness, to where Kat could see the outline of a bird feeder, low to the ground. Della scattered the nuts and seeds she had brought from the kitchen, and returned to Kat's side.

"A little treat for a friend of mine." She gave a secret smile. "I harvest the seeds and nuts in the fall."

"I love all this," Kat said seriously. "How you make everything yourself. Not many people do anymore. But where do you find the time?"

Della smiled. "We have lots of it," she said simply. "Too much, if anything. Empty weeks, years, decades … What better way to fill them than by tilling the soil, watching our plants grow, flourish and fruit, and cooking for those we love?" She bent to gather a handful of fine, black soil, and let it trickle through her fingers, an expression of reverence on her face. "It is the only thing with true meaning for me now."

"Oh," Kat said, humbled for a moment by Della's generosity and her honesty. "Well you've created a beautiful garden," she said after a pause. She took a deep breath of the night air, redolent of scented herbs and other growing things. "It even smells good."

"I know," Della said. "Catnip, rose geranium, rue." She let her hand trail past each plant, naming them for Kat as they slowly returned to the kitchen. "Though the scent of rue is not to everyone's taste, it is an effective remedy against fleas. Most of the vegetables are old varieties. I brought seeds with me when we first came from Europe."

Della disappeared through the doorway into the kitchen, but Kat lingered a moment longer in this place where the moisture of growing, verdant things permeated the night air, and the scents of the plants she and Della had brushed against still lingered. She could just make out rectangular beds filled with vegetables and herbs, all immaculately kept and neatly edged. *I have to come here in the daytime*, she thought. It seemed sad that Della, who obviously lavished care on this space, could never enjoy it when the sun was shining.

She turned toward the kitchen door. The warmth and welcome of the enormous, old-fashioned room was almost palpable. Of all the rooms in the house the kitchen was the most alive; the heart of everything. In the evening it was meeting place, workplace, and main thoroughfare in one.

And it was nearly always busy. Busy enough to provide a distraction. While she was there she could bury her apprehensions about what the future held ... for a while at least. Watching Della and Corrin at work, and with the constant comings and goings of the others as they passed through, she didn't have time to dwell on the things worrying her. Like how she was going to deal with the fact that her new job, her safe, normal life, had just been ripped out from under her feet. And of course there was the as-yet-unanswered question of why this organization, the Directorate, wanted to lock her away and maybe kill her – not to mention why they were targeting people like her in the first place. Suddenly, the night air was like a million clutching fingers, cold against her skin, and she shivered.

Kat hurried over to the lit doorway and stepped inside. Into the warmth … away from dark thoughts. She found a bowl of pasta ready and waiting, tossed with fresh basil pesto.

She was getting used to being the only one eating. Well, eating at normal mealtimes anyway – though "normal" in this case was a relative term dependent on whether you kept nocturnal hours. Della and Corrin were constantly preparing food, so she assumed the others must eat. It didn't seem polite to ask what, though.

No, scratch that. It wasn't an issue of politeness. The truth was, she really didn't want to think about what they lived on. What they ate … or drank. Especially as she might have to share their diet one day if Char was right about her going through some sort of "transition." Kat gave a shiver, and concentrated on the food in front of her.

Corrin entered with a basket of pinecones, and Della sat next to Kat with a bowl of them. She began to remove the nuts, shelling them into a second small bowl as she went. Her fingers moved so fast they seemed like a blur to Kat, and she never dropped anything, not a single nut or morsel of shell.

Kat shook her head in awe. "I can't believe you do *everything* from scratch. I guess there are pine nuts like those in the pesto I'm eating?" The fresh nuts and basil made a mouth-watering combination.

Della nodded. "And in my bird mix." She picked up a tiny nut and delicately nibbled on it, looking for all the world like a little squirrel.

Kat stopped eating. "Della, I … well I know I've said this before, but thank you. I don't mean just for the pasta, but for everything. I know I've made extra work for you by being here."

Della gave a tinkle of laughter. "You are thanking me for what comes naturally, Katerina. With our speed and strength, tasks you might see as onerous are no more than the work of a moment. I find it relaxing. Besides, I enjoy having you here."

"We both do," Corrin said from behind Della's shoulder. He reached around her for a couple of the golden pine nuts, and popped them into his mouth.

"It is a novelty for us all, having guests," Della continued. "And especially one who is ..." She broke off.

"Human?" Kat supplied wryly.

Della laughed. "Things are certainly different with you here. But believe me when I say we like taking care of people, and whatever little we have done to make you feel welcome has been a great pleasure."

Kat didn't doubt her sincerity. She'd felt instinctively at ease with Della since the first night, when she'd been led straight to the kitchen, and given a mug of hot, milky chai to drink. Della had glowed with quiet happiness when Kat had commented on how delicious it was. Corrin, too, was completely unthreatening despite his massive size. Pity she couldn't say the same for the other men of the house. Wild, brooding, unpredictable ... None of the words she'd use to describe them was particularly reassuring.

Kat shifted on her stool, and pushed away her empty bowl. "Della, can I ask you a question?"

Della nodded.

Kat flicked a glance at Corrin, who stood with his hands resting on Della's shoulders. She began hesitantly, unsure how to articulate what was in her mind. "When Anton first came to find me at the Towers, he was in the form of an eagle. How does he change shape like that? And ... from some of the things I overheard, I gather Akilina and the others can't take on an animal form. They aren't *unalil*." She said the unfamiliar word the way she'd heard Anton say it during the discussion with Falcon, the man from the Directorate. "But you all are, right? So are Akilina and the others back in the city a different species or something? And the thing I was really wondering, was ..." here she paused for a deep breath, " ... which one am I?"

Corrin gave a slow smile. "That's more than one question."

Della met Kat's gaze with her own, and her expression was serious. "I will answer in the best way I am able, Katerina, but you must first understand that the questions you ask go to the very root of some of the most fundamental problems dividing our people."

She cleared her throat, and reached up to place her hand over Corrin's, where it rested on her shoulder. "We are all one people, all of the *Tabérin,* or so we of the *unalil* believe. And in answer to one of your questions, yes, those of us who live within an *unalil* family and identify ourselves as such all have the ability to take on animal form. That shared experience is what binds any *unalil* family together."

Kat remembered that Char had mentioned the *Tabérin* in that first discussion, in the back of a New York cab. It all felt so far away now.

Della continued, "For some among the *Tabérin,* this ability to embrace and become one with the animal part of our nature is a curse, an aberration. We are seen as a lesser form. As backward, uncivilized, even primitive."

Kat could see the sorrow in her face, and the regret.

"And it is true that we live apart from others, and we choose, in general, a simpler, more traditional lifestyle. What we eat of solid food is by preference seasonal, freshly hunted or homegrown, and prepared by hand. We avoid modern ways, as we feel they disrupt our connection to the Earth's energies. These choices go to the core of who we are."

Well, that answered the food question anyway. They'd pretty much qualify as macrobiotic, if it wasn't for the emphasis on hunting for fresh meat. But Kat could be pretty sure she wasn't going to be offered Pop-Tarts for breakfast.

"As to how our ability works ..." Della paused, seeming to consider how best to express herself. "Perhaps you can imagine the Earth as a huge sphere made up not just of water and minerals and life forms, but also of energy and spirit. That is how we see this world. The rocks beneath our feet, the oceans, the very aether ..." and here her hands lifted to gesture in the empty air above her head, "all are resonant with energy, with life's vibration. Our gift is no more complicated than learning to attune ourselves, keeping our minds and bodies pure so that they are open to these energies of the earth and skies, and can borrow from them and shape them as we wish. Those of us who were not born into this life are assisted in this because the distillation of our maker's abilities is passed on to us when we are made." She frowned. "Does that answer your question at all?"

Kat wrinkled her nose. "Sort of. I mean, in theory."

Della gave a sober smile. "Theory is all the *unalil* talent is for any of the *Tabérin*, until the day a change of form first happens. But once it has – and such channeling of energies can be spontaneous and effortless for a rare few – once that ability has manifested itself, an individual's choices become polarized. Either they hide their talent, and never use it, never even speak of it – or join with a family like ours and leave everything they know behind. Because to be an *unalil* of the *Tabérin* is to be reviled by others of our kind."

"She speaks truth," Corrin said. His jaw clenched. "We also hear from Anton that the Directorate has been specifically targeting the *unalil* in recent years – to what end we do not know. Perhaps, as we live in small groups, isolated from a larger community, they see us as easy prey."

"That is, if they can find us," Della said defiantly. "And if they can catch us."

Corrin's green eyes met Kat's. "As for your last question: what you are, and whether *unalil* or not, this is not something any of us can answer yet with any degree of certainty. But like any of the *Tabérin*, the possibility is there, if you are open to it."

"Perhaps this is something you could also discuss with Akilina," Della suggested. "She could provide a different perspective, as I understand you share an *egir'rin* bloodline."

What Della was suggesting made perfect sense. Kat had a million questions she needed answered, and the elder was the logical person to ask – except Akilina had barely emerged from her bedchamber since they'd arrived. From what she understood, Akilina was engrossed in a bunch of old scrolls that she was hoping might provide information about the "transition" she believed Kat might be going through.

"Akilina's been kind of ... busy," she mumbled. After a moment, another question came to mind. "There was something else I was wondering. Do you ever use that big wooden dining table in the room across from the stairs up in the main hall? I've noticed everyone seems to meet here in the kitchen."

Della smiled, clearly a little puzzled by the sudden change of topic. "Only on formal occasions. Why do you ask?"

Kat struggled to put her memories into words. "I had a strange dream the first night I was here, and that table was in it. But I dreamed of it before I'd ever seen it. The room was ... different somehow. And there was a woman. A woman sitting in a carved wooden chair."

Della came to sit beside her. "What did this woman look like? Do you remember?"

Kat nodded. "She had dark, wavy hair. And golden eyes – like the dark-haired man I met the night I arrived here."

Della exhaled, a sudden sound of surprise. "Amarok. He has ... or rather *had*, a twin sister. Amber." She sighed. "Amber disappeared thirteen years ago, and ... well, we believe her to be dead, though Amarok perhaps has not accepted it even now."

"Oh."

"Her energy must still be strong here," Corrin added. "Perhaps you are susceptible to it?"

"You see?" Della leaned over and let her finger hover over Kat's rune necklace, but without touching it. "You have stones here which enhance psychic vision, and clairvoyance. Amethyst. Also moonstone."

Kat looked down at her necklace herself. Those Della had named were only two among the rainbow cacophony Akilina had woven into the figured metal.

An image flashed into her mind. Amber, in her chair, arms and head in contact with those richly colored stones.

"Was Amber psychic?" she asked suddenly, looking up at Della and Corrin.

Della smiled gently, her eyes shadowed by memories of the past. "Perhaps you could use that word. Our term is seer, or oracle. We've always thought that perhaps that's why she was taken."

Kat felt an involuntary shiver run through her, a sudden chill as the words the psychic had uttered back in Charleston replayed in her mind: *Find her. Find the one who is lost.* The woman couldn't have meant Amber, could she?

Chapter 26

Kat walked out of the stone bathhouse, and shivered as a breeze hit the back of her neck. She was fully dressed, but her hair was still wet, wrapped turban-like in a towel. Della had seemed a bit worried that with her merely-human sense of vision, she might wander off the stone path at night and fall off a cliff or something, so she'd suggested Kat use the bathhouse during the day.

That suited her just fine. Communal bathing might have been common in centuries gone by – it might even be an everyday thing in other parts of the world – but Kat preferred her privacy.

The wind stilled, and she paused halfway along the promontory, enjoying the warmth of the sun against her skin. The view of the valley was spectacular; awe-inspiring when seen from so high.

She turned to look back at the house, though that was hardly an adequate word to describe the enormous stone and wood edifice, complete with towers that blended elements of a fourteenth-century European castle with the architecture of the Arts and Crafts movement. The house was built into the mountainside, and from where she now stood on the promontory she could see its long, wide balcony, above a sheer drop to the trees in the valley far below.

Apart from the house – and the bathhouse she'd just left – there wasn't a single sign of civilization in any direction. She was surrounded by rocks, and forested valleys, and mountain peaks to the horizon. No clouds to break the vastness of the blue sky today; just the faint sickle-shaped curve of a crescent moon. There was no shortage of wild natural beauty, but the isolation took some getting used to. She suspected she'd feel the same whether she stayed for a week or a couple of centuries. This wilderness could never be truly owned.

As she followed the rough stepping-stone path back toward the house, she remembered the garden Della had shown her the night before. It was on the other side of the house, tucked between the kitchen wall and the ridge behind; a sheltered, cultivated space away from the wind, where plants grew even in this rocky and barren area. In small ways, at least, the wilderness could be tamed.

Kat hung her wet towel in her room, then went downstairs with a book in hand and sat on the bench seat in the kitchen garden. She shook out her damp hair, and finger-combed it, hoping the fresh air would dry it before the chill of evening set in.

Around her, all was tranquility and abundance; sun-baked paths and leafy beds. But she couldn't relax. Despite the peaceful warmth, she felt ... uneasy.

Something, or someone, was watching her.

She scanned the garden, but nothing obvious jumped out at her, metaphorically or otherwise, and as an enterprising bee went droning past on its way to the next flower, she shook her head and dismissed the odd feeling. Crazy how an overactive imagination could invent things to worry about even when there was no actual threat – though with everything going on that should hardly come as a surprise.

She was engrossed in her book when something wound itself around her legs.

"Hey, aren't you beautiful?" she said softly, reaching down to smooth her hand over the cat's fur. It stared up at her with almond-shaped green eyes. Then she noticed several low-growing tufts of catnip right below where she was sitting.

"Ah, I know what you're after. You didn't come to visit me at all, did you?"

The cat stalked off regally with the black tip of its tail held high, going to nuzzle the serrated green leaves of another catnip plant before curling up in the sun next to it and licking its paws with complete concentration. It brought its head down to rest on its paws, and Kat was about to return to her book when a little towhee swooped down to land next to the bird feeder, only feet from the recumbent cat.

The bird pecked at the seeds there, and then raised its black head to swallow while looking around, fluffing its chest feathers as it displayed its white belly and russet flanks. The black feathered head dipped again as the bird continued to eat, unworried by the presence of a cat so close by. Kat watched, fascinated, as the little bird flew to the ground, while the cat swished its tail but otherwise paid no attention.

The towhee hopped closer with a flutter of wings, and Kat held her breath, sure the cat would pounce, but it continued to lie there unmoving as the game little bird began to rake its feet backward through the dirt right in front of it, scratching for morsels to eat. The cat rolled over and yawned, and the bird cocked its head, then flew over to perch on a shrub at the edge of the garden where it began a delightful whistling and trilling.

Kat returned to her reading, and after a little while she glanced up to see the cat disappearing through a gap between two shrubs. She leaned back and stretched, noticing the little bird, too, had stopped its singing and flown away, leaving the garden silent and still. Then the odd feeling stole over her again. A prickling at the back of the neck that told her she was being watched.

She turned quickly to check behind her and saw nothing – yet the feeling wouldn't go away. She closed her book, and laid it in her lap. No use trying to read anymore.

It was hard to believe this was only her fourth day here. It felt like longer. Only a week ago she'd been learning the ropes at her new job at the nationally renowned Hema Castus Research Institute, without a single suspicion that it was some elaborate cover organization. And now she was in hiding here in the middle of the mountains, from a danger she didn't fully understand, with her entire future up in the air.

And she was surrounded by deadly predators. She couldn't forget that part. She shivered, feeling a moment's chill despite the sun on her cheek. Remembering the night of her arrival, and two pairs of eyes, one golden and one blue, burning with intensity. Wild ... like the mountain country they lived in.

Maybe they'd be a little more civilized the next time she saw them. Or was that too much to hope for? She hated feeling so apprehensive around them, but unless they toned the whole wild-man routine down a little ...

Della and Corrin she genuinely liked. Several of the others had been kind too – but there was no escaping the fact that the ones who stood between her and danger were anything but safe and normal themselves. Some of them were pretty damned terrifying. Quite beside the fact that they weren't human.

If Akilina was right, *she* wasn't fully human either ... but that thought wasn't particularly comforting. Ever since Akilina had made that idle comment back at the Towers, speculating about whether Kat's cravings for meat were an early sign of transition, she hadn't been able to get the thought out of her mind. For all she knew, she was already changing. Like Char had said, one day she might change completely, so she wasn't human at all anymore. So she was one of them. From some of the things Akilina had mentioned, she was pretty sure the change would come with an unwanted extras package too, like more acute versions of what she was already experiencing. Heightened emotions. And probably – she swallowed – cravings for actual blood. Right now, the thought of *that* almost turned her stomach. All this ... and there wasn't a damned thing she could do about it.

Kat sighed. It was frustrating, this feeling of powerlessness. So much had changed, so fast. She wished she could just accept that her "ordinary" life was a thing of the past. But the truth was, she didn't *want* everything to change. As the spooky psychic had predicted, the Wheel of Fortune wasn't giving her much choice in the matter.

Until this transition actually happened, she was trapped in a scary limbo, completely out of her depth – or at least that was what it felt like most of the time. The human among the predators. The lone pigeon among the cats.

Kat frowned down at the ground, and her attention was caught once again by the catnip plant. Her mouth curled into an unwilling half-smile. A cat and bird playing together. Who would have thought?

Maybe it meant there was hope for her too.

Maybe coexistence with deadly predators really *was* possible.

Chapter 27

Alek's expression was grim as the Ducati purred beneath him, rounding the mountain corners and eating the miles with effortless ease. He scowled, angry at himself as much as anything else. He'd been gone four days. Four days of wine, women and song. Or, rather, nightclubs, women, and something much better than wine, warm and fresh from the source.

He should be feeling replete. Sated. There was nothing quite like a blood-induced high; usually the euphoria would last several days, and he'd get respite from the cravings for a while. But this time, the Bacchanalian pleasures had left him with nothing but a gnawing ache in the gut and a dull sense of unease.

The women weren't the problem. They'd been beautiful. Spectacular even, he acknowledged grudgingly. And so willing to please. He knew how to pick them; every last one toned, and stylish, and pouty as hell. *If* he was being objective.

But however warm and pliable they'd been, they'd left him cold. The whole episode had left him feeling soiled.

The sensation was unfamiliar. And unwelcome. Very unwelcome. He was glad none of the women would retain any memory of their encounter with him. He only wished he could be so lucky.

He leaned into the wind as he raised the speed another notch, and the bike roared in response. Alek was in no real hurry to go home and face the new and unsettling visitor Anton had brought with him, but the demons chasing him were as well worth running from.

After a time, he left the mountain road and turned onto the rutted track that led to his cabin, deep in the hills. He nosed the bike into the garage, and brought it to rest in the space waiting, between his black ZX-14, all muscle and sleek lines, and the K1300R, a pared-back brute beauty glinting silver and orange in the darkness. He'd bought them a few years ago, in a fit of extravagance, but tonight he barely gave them a glance, disillusioned with everything they represented. They were pretty toys, but whatever the bike between his legs, the road always led him to the same place, and it wasn't anywhere he got satisfaction from anymore. No matter how fast or how far he traveled, he couldn't leave this frustration behind. The last few days had proved that.

He moved into the cabin, sparsely furnished and utilitarian. He kept his bikes here, his computer equipment and high-tech toys, a few changes of clothes for his regular trips to the city – not much else. He scanned his surroundings with a scowl, wondering why he even bothered with all this.

Perhaps it was time he actually listened to the others in his family, who told him to give up the modern world of humans and their polluted blood. They chose instead to hunt and feed in animal form, taking strength from the natural world, and peace and balance from being at one with the wilderness surrounding them.

For him ... well, gadgets and satellite internet still held their lure, as did the cities from which they came. Perhaps learning to excel in this new arena was his way of staying connected to an ever-changing world. That, and the fact that he liked the anonymity the internet provided. It was an escape, a release, to set himself free in the currents of a huge system that knew no night or day, that didn't distinguish between human and *Tabérin*.

To test his wits against hackers who didn't care if he was *unalil* or what he was wearing or who he'd just slept with as long as his code was good.

He sat on a stool in front of his computer array, and logged into the system. He scanned emails, and assimilated the latest news stories in mere moments. Then he logged off from the server, and powered down the monitor. He sat, staring at its black blankness for several long seconds.

Usually a visit to the city was a blast. He enjoyed the adrenalin rush he got from speeding along the mountain roads in the pitch dark. He certainly enjoyed the women waiting for him at the other end. But not this time. Every moment of intimacy with the women he'd selected to share his bed had been overshadowed by thoughts of Amarok's damned protégée, and now he was left with a lingering distaste for what he'd done – and clothes smelling of fancy booze, cigarette smoke, and stale perfume.

Even now, his subconscious wouldn't be silent. He closed his eyes and clenched his fists, but still the images came to him un-bidden. Vivid mental conjurings, of slender curves and long, bare athletic limbs tangled in satin sheets. Tangled with his legs as he splayed her body beneath him. And of rose petals, thousands of soft, fragrant rose petals crushed beneath their bodies as they rolled together, entwined. He imagined silk scarves whispering across del-icately flushed female flesh, leaving a wash of sensation in their wake. What he could do to her with a silk scarf …

That image sparked an instant primal response from his body, and he groaned, and with an effort, thrust the seductive thoughts away.

Mouth set in a line of frustration, he stood and stripped off his clothes, wanting to be free of their taint. He left them a jumbled mess on the floor and stepped out into the cool night air, locking the cabin door behind him. Even naked he felt unclean, and as he melted into the darkness he hoped the long, steep run home would take the edge off this confused welter of feelings he couldn't shake.

It irritated him; this frustration, this wanting, this fascination with a slender scrap of a human female who could only bring them all trouble. He'd known that from the instant Anton had led her through their front door. And Amarok, damn him, had done his utmost to ensure the whole family was entangled in this obligation to protect her.

Her face flashed into his mind, clear and perfectly remembered despite the brevity of their only meeting. Big dark eyes raised to his, filled with shock and apprehension. This human girl, this Katerina, had seen right to the hidden depths of him. She hadn't liked what she'd seen.

He would have preferred her adulation, would rather have had her besotted and compliant, watching him with doe-eyed infatuation. Then she would have been easy to dismiss, like all the others. As it was, he couldn't damn well get her out of his mind.

Chapter 28

Ionescu's assistant came running in response to his call, and fell to his knees on the thick rug just inside the door.

"Yes, Arelli?"

"When did this arrive?"

His assistant raised cautious eyes to the scroll Ionescu was holding, with its black and red seal, and the Vodas's unique emblem emblazoned in gold leaf.

"This morning, Arelli. Just before you arrived. It was brought by special messenger."

Ionescu gave a terse nod. "You may go."

He didn't watch as his assistant bowed himself backward out of the room, but instead stood frowning down at the document he held. Official notification that Victor Fortes, one of *his* staff, had been re-tasked. The fact itself was not of great concern perhaps, but that he, a member of the Mandate Council and head of Information Acquisition did not know *why* Fortes would be reporting directly to the Vodas himself was distinctly worrying. And there was something about the way Fortes had been acting lately that made him wonder if in fact this official notification was coming some time after the fact. He had a hunch Fortes had been preparing for this move, doing favors for the Vodas without Ionescu's knowledge, for quite a while.

He exited his office suite moments later, and was fortunate in finding Fortes in the staff library.

Fortes greeted him respectfully, and waited for him to speak first, with an air of complete innocence, as if he had no idea why he might have been sought out.

"I have received notification of your reassignment, Victor."

Fortes inclined his head. "Working with the Vodas will be a great honor, Councillor. Though in truth, I'm just an envoy."

"May I inquire as to the nature of your project?"

Fortes cleared his throat, and gave a good impression of discomfort, but Ionescu recognized it for the act it was. Saw the smugness beneath. "I'm afraid … that's not possible, Councillor. For now, I report only to the Vodas. I'm not at liberty to disclose anything to anyone else. And there is one other thing, Councillor. The Vodas has asked that I be given unfettered access to all records, including your private archive in Information Acquisition, to enable me to conduct research on his behalf."

"Of course. Whatever the Vodas desires." The words were poison to utter, but Ionescu was no fool. Clearly, Fortes had the Vodas's ear, and Ionescu knew if there was the faintest whisper of dissent from him, Fortes would make sure the Vodas heard about it.

"The Vodas thanks you for your cooperation."

The gall of the man, speaking on behalf of the Vodas as if they were an indivisible whole. Ionescu's lips tightened fractionally as he looked down at the man who had just become his biggest threat. In the Directorate, ambition among one's underlings was dangerous. Very dangerous.

"You would be wise to exercise caution in your dealings with the Vodas, Victor. He is a dangerous enemy to any who fail him."

"Thank you for your concern, Councillor, but I'll be fine." Fortes's smile spoke of an unshakable complacency. The confidence of a man who was used to charming all those around him. Who was used to getting his own way … Always.

Chapter 29

Kat tiptoed down the staircase to the kitchen, not wanting to wake anyone.

Being surrounded by people who gave a lesson in fluid dynamics every time they walked downstairs might also have had something to do with it. She felt like a blundering elephant in comparison to the others. Okay, so there probably wasn't much point tiptoeing in a household where everyone else apparently had hearing so acute they could distinguish a rabbit from a hare at five hundred feet – but at least it made her *feel* better.

She had to laugh at herself though. From what she'd seen so far, dawn was the closest thing they had to rush hour around here, with everyone making their way through the dark internal corridors and up the winding staircases to the bedrooms. She was the only one who slept at night, so no matter how loudly she walked, right now she wouldn't be disturbing anyone's rest.

Kat reached the landing, and met Della and Corrin going the other way.

Della smiled at her sleepily. "We're off to bed," she said. "I've left food for you."

Kat smiled in reply, and continued down the stairs. That was definitely one of the main differences between here and Akilina's residence at the Towers; here, everyone did seem to sleep – only, unlike Kat, they did it during the day. According to Della the *unalil* slept more than others of the *Tabérin* because of their closer alignment with the Earth's natural rhythms and energies. And also because using their ability to change form was tiring.

Since she'd arrived, Kat had spent her days rattling around in the huge house with nothing to do other than take long baths and read. Neither provided the distraction she needed. Supposedly she was safe here, but when she was alone her imagination would run wild and she'd jump at the slightest noise.

Unlike Akilina's apartment, huge windows left all the downstairs living spaces and the long hallway flooded with sunlight during the day, and it was in these areas that she spent her time, as well as the kitchen garden. They were beautiful, airy, sunlit spaces, but she couldn't enjoy them. She'd lost count of the number of times in the last few days that she'd wandered from room to room, too edgy to sit down.

She waited for sunset every day with an impatience verging on desperation, because the lengthening shadows, and that moment when the sun finally dipped behind the mountains, meant she could hurry to the big kitchen to meet the others when they rose for the night. Funny, as she'd never really thought of herself as a social animal. At the moment, though, she hated spending so much time with only her own thoughts for company. The more time she spent alone the more time she spent worrying.

When she reached the empty kitchen, Kat took a deep breath. The lingering aromas told her what had just been cooked there. Mushrooms … and toast.

Moving closer she saw a cloth-draped loaf of bread on a board at the end of the bench. She'd seen Della make the bread the night before; scattering flour onto the bench, kneading the dough with quick, sure movements before forming it into a braid and leaving it to rise.

She lifted the silver cover from the plate Della had left to reveal a perfect omelette, filled with wild mushrooms. There were a couple of slices of toast from the morning's loaf in a rack to the side, still warm when she touched them. She had no idea how Della did it. She always seemed to time things exactly so that Kat's food was waiting for her, fresh and piping hot, when she came downstairs.

Kat pulled a stool up to the bench and began to eat appreciatively. After a few mouthfuls she paused, fork halfway to her mouth, and slowly put it down again. She had the strangest sensation, almost a prickling at the back of her neck. A niggling certainty that she was being watched.

She turned slowly, unsure what she was expecting to see. Her eyes widened, and her lips parted in a gasp of surprise. Behind her, a cougar stood on its hind legs, its front paws on the bench so that it was as tall as a man. Its head was turned toward her, unblinking amber eyes level with her own.

Kat leaped to her feet.

What the hell is a huge cougar doing in the kitchen?

Her fingers involuntarily tightened on the handle of the knife she held, and the creature's eyes were drawn to the movement. It bared its teeth in a snarl – or was it a smile? In either case, she couldn't help but notice how long and sharp its incisors and canines were, how lethal the curved claws gripping the bench.

Kat took a step backward, and the cougar dropped to the floor and padded toward her, stalking her as she continued to move away. Kat stopped moving. There was no point in running when it could so easily outpace her.

There was something in its eyes; a consciousness and intelligence which made her sure this was no wild animal.

If it were hostile, wouldn't it have pounced by now?

Then she cursed herself for that thought, because the memories she'd repressed from her last night in Richwood came flooding back … and with them, thoughts of the great wolf she'd known for so many years. Her experiences of the last few days made her question whether it had even been an ordinary wolf.

She'd always imagined it was well ... for want of a better word, tame. Someone's pet – in a very independent, non-collar-wearing sort of way. But it had jumped on her. Despite her having known the wolf for so long, having trusted it ... it had bitten her and made her bleed.

Sometimes she questioned her sanity when remembering that night, because when she'd finally looked in the mirror after stumbling home, the skin where she was sure she'd been bitten was smooth and unbroken.

She focused on the cougar in front of her. She had no idea whether, like Anton, it was more than it seemed to be. She couldn't tell whether it was friend or enemy. But if she had a choice, she wanted to meet it face on. So she forced herself to stand absolutely still, silent and wary as the huge cat approached her. Her thighs and calves were stiff with the tension of holding herself upright as it reared on its hind legs again, mouth opening in a snarling yawn. It brought its huge paws to rest on the bench beside her, and regarded her silently for several long moments. Its eyes held both a challenge and a promise.

Kat realized she had been holding her breath, and she let it out very slowly and softly, as the great cat lowered its head to sniff at her hair, where it was tucked behind her ear. The creature nuzzled her shoulder, then a warm wet tongue licked her neck, her cheek. She shivered and pulled back, angling her head away.

She could feel those eyes fixed on her again, and turned reluctantly to meet them. The cougar was appraising her in a way that was warm, fascinated – not at all animal. And those eyes so close to hers; glowing amber, with a spark of blue near the very center.

It looks like it wants to devour me.

Quite suddenly she was struck with the impression that this was the creature's way of staking a claim over her. That it was possessive, and most definitely *male*. The thought was disconcerting, and Kat flushed and let her gaze drop, breaking the connection.

The cat made a sound between a purr and a growl, then dropped onto all fours again, and its body and long tail slowly brushed past the back of her legs as it moved in the direction of the stairs. The action seemed deliberate, and its tawny fur against her skin was unexpectedly luxurious; thick and soft.

She couldn't help watching as it stalked toward the doorway. A shaft of early-morning light came through the kitchen window and illuminated the creature so that its coat glowed golden, and a second later it was gone, disappearing into the shadows on the stairs with a last flick of its tail.

Kat breathed out shakily, and stared down at her hand, slowly uncurling her fingers from the knife she still held. Her fist had been clenched so hard around the bone handle that her nails had left a row of crescent-shaped impressions on her palm.

She sighed, and eyed her abandoned plate of breakfast – now quite cold. Della might be a culinary magician, but even she obviously wasn't taking visits from wild animals into account when timing her breakfasts.

*

Kat was curled into a chair near a large window in the sitting room, with Della's copy of *A Tale of Two Cities* lying forgotten in her lap when Akilina came into the room just after sunset.

"Katerina?"

Kat looked up inquiringly, realizing she was sitting in the dark. She'd stopped reading when the light became too dim even for her, and had been meaning to go down to the kitchen to ask Della about the cougar she'd encountered that morning, but her mind had gone wandering instead of her feet.

"There is no need for you to sit here in darkness, child." Akilina waved a hand in the direction of a nearby candelabrum, and the wax tapers flared into life.

Kat blinked. "Thanks."

She looked at Akilina with a new interest. She'd seen so little of the elder since they'd arrived, and right now, it was pretty obvious she hadn't come in here just to light candles for Kat. Akilina was hovering, there was no doubt about it. And she seemed … uncomfortable. Did she have news?

Just as Kat was about to ask, Akilina spoke.

"Tonight the family is meeting in full council, and it is my hope that at the meeting's conclusion, you will be formally welcomed."

Her *hope*? Kat tried to digest what that word meant in this context as she put her book on the low table next to her chair and began to stand.

"Okay, I'm ready."

Akilina put out a hand to stop her from rising. "Just the family … and myself."

"Oh." Kat frowned as she sank back to the seat. Nope. It wasn't her imagination. Akilina was *definitely* looking awkward.

"Perhaps …" Akilina added more softly, "you could wait here until you are summoned?" Her eyes were shadowed, but Kat thought she saw sympathy at their depths.

Kat felt stung when she finally made sense of what Akilina was saying. Evidently the family were meeting – without her – to vote on whether or not she could stay. After almost five days here she hadn't even considered the issue to be in question. But it seemed her confidence had been premature. Staying here was by no means a definite thing.

It made her view all of them in a new light, remembering their behavior toward her over the last few days and trying to analyze it. Who would be likely to vote against her? Surely not Della or her gentle giant of a husband, Corrin? She'd spent so much time with them in the kitchen. She'd liked them from the moment they'd met, and she hoped they felt the same way about her. Anton? He'd always been warm and welcoming, and he'd brought her here, after all, so it wasn't likely he'd change his mind and kick her out now.

She'd met another man in the kitchen: Miklós. Tall, slender and melancholy. Every time he saw her he made himself scarce, and she sensed frustration and reproach in his soft eyes when they rested on her. Whatever his problem was, she wouldn't be too surprised if he voted against her staying.

Akilina spoke again. "I am sorry, Katerina. This is customary in a traditional household. But I am sure ... at least I hope ... that you will be welcomed, and that we can stay here, in safety, until your transition."

Kat nodded, and gave a rueful half-smile. "It's okay. I don't exactly have many options. I'll be here ... waiting for the verdict."

Akilina nodded briefly, then said, "Regarding your transition ... I have been researching our ancient records, searching the scrolls for a reference that might tell us what we can expect in the case of one such as yourself. I have found little mention of any human hybrid, much less one with your strong, pure bloodlines."

"Have you seen a reference in the scrolls to something called a Dark Child?" Kat wasn't sure if this was a stupid question, but if anyone could shed light on it surely Akilina could.

"Dark Child?" Akilina looked intrigued. Obviously it wasn't such a stupid question then. "Where did you hear this term?"

"I saw a psychic before I moved to New York. She said that's what *I* am."

"The term is known to me," Akilina said, "though it is rarely used anymore. It is one humans once used to describe certain children; those who were the offspring of a human and one of our kind. Once, humans knew of our existence. Centuries ago, before we hid behind our runes and faded from sight. So yes, you could be referred to as such, though this psychic must be privy to knowledge few humans now possess if she used the term. And if she recognized you for what you are."

"It was mentioned in a book she gave me," Kat explained. "In her family's Arcana." It occurred to her that the Arcana was probably something else Akilina would be able to make a whole lot more sense of than she could. If things hadn't been so crazy since they'd met she'd probably have brought it up sooner.

"Really? I would like to see this Arcana." The gleam of the inquisitive scholar was in Akilina's eyes. "This term is also one I am familiar with. An Arcana is a book filled with secret history, anecdotes, spellcraft – and passed down through the generations in families of power."

Akilina spoke those last few words as if they were everyday, not worthy of special note, but for Kat, it was like another layer had just been peeled away from the reality that she knew, and she wasn't quite ready for the world she saw beneath. "What do you mean, spellcraft? And ... and families of power?"

"Magic, child. As practiced by families of witches." A delicate frown marred the smoothness of Akilina's forehead as she took in Kat's expression. "I apologize. I am forgetting how much of our history and culture you still do not know. The witch families, like those of our kind, have also been forced to hide their true nature from the world."

"I ... but magic isn't real." The minute the words left her mouth, Kat knew that this time she really had said something stupid, because in the last few days she'd accepted the concept of magical runes and beings with superhuman strength who could change shape and light candles with a wave of the hand. Was the idea that there were secret families of witches passing their lore down through the ages really such a leap? When it came right down to it, she'd seen the evidence that magic *was* real with her own eyes – but her rational mind hadn't quite caught up yet.

"There is much I still must teach you," Akilina said. "I should share at least the basics of our modern history, and how we and others were imperilled by the burning times. Perhaps we can also look over this Arcana later, when the council meeting is concluded. For now, though ..." She paused, looking troubled. "There is something else I must speak to you about. You are aware, of course, of your status as *egir'rin*. You are of our royal bloodline, a rare and special distinction. But there has never been ..." She hesitated. "You are the first who was born human. The first who was not raised as one of us, nor given our knowledge."

Kat nodded silently. She knew Akilina didn't *mean* to make her feel inadequate.

The elder appeared to choose her next words carefully. "I have been reluctant to speak of this to you as you have not yet made your transition. But under the circumstances I think I would be remiss in not uttering at least a word of warning ..."

Kat frowned. "About what?"

"You must be careful, in this house. The *unalil* live apart from others of our kind for a reason."

"I asked Della about the *unalil*," Kat said. "She told me that they're looked down on by the rest of you."

"And feared," Akilina added quietly. "Did she also tell you that?"

Kat shook her head. The impression Della had left her with was that the *unalil* were shunned by the rest of the *Tabérin*, without good cause. Clearly there were two sides to every story.

"Their affinity for the wild, even perhaps the savage side of our natures has seen them excel always in any physical sphere." Akilina was very still as she spoke into the hushed room, and her gravity made Kat uneasy. "In the past, some of them were more than willing to exploit that. As fighters, as soldiers of fortune ... and as assassins."

"Oh," Kat said, assimilating this new information. She found it all too easy to mentally cast some of the inhabitants of this house in those roles. Though it wasn't directed at her, she'd felt the controlled menace in them, so it was easy to believe that for other

Tabérin, an *unalil* male was really not the sort you'd like to run into in a dark alley.

"But there is another side to any animal, and the *unalil* are also endowed with charm, with magnetism." Akilina shrugged. "*Unalil* males can be very ... persuasive. Though they have done us a great honor in taking us into their home, an *unalil* male, and one moreover who is blood-made, not true-born of our race, would not make an appropriate consort for a girl of your lineage."

"Consort?" Kat echoed, wrinkling her brow. Where on earth had Akilina pulled *that* one from?

"Yes. Your consort, your life partner. We have a saying for this: blood cleaves to blood. As *egir'rin*, a princess directly descended from the Mahra, your blood will call to one who is your social equal. *Ekal mandu'rin*, that is, a true-born male of our race directly descended from the Mahra's own bodyguard."

"Oh. Right," Kat said faintly. "Well, thanks for clearing that up."

Akilina inclined her head gracefully. "We will speak more about these other matters soon," she said, and left the room.

Kat watched the empty doorway for some time after Akilina had gone. What Akilina had just said made her realize the elder really *was* from a different world. Or a whole different universe.

The consort thing would *definitely* not be a problem. Even the thought that Akilina felt she needed to be warned was a bit embarrassing. After all, it wasn't like she was here on a speed-dating holiday. She was only here because her life was in danger. It wasn't exactly the environment she would choose when looking for a boyfriend. Or consort. Or whatever.

She dismissed the subject with a shake of the head, and turned her mind to the council meeting happening only a few rooms away. It felt a bit too much like the other times when she'd been talked *about* rather than talked *to*, like a child. It hardly seemed fair that her future was being decided in there, yet she wasn't invited. Surely she had a right to know what was being discussed?

She rose from her seat and headed toward what she'd assumed was the formal dining room. The doors to the huge room were usually open, but when she reached them this time, they were firmly shut.

She tiptoed closer, catching a murmur here and there. But the thickness of the solid timber frustrated her efforts to overhear, so she pressed her ear against the door.

Chapter 30

Alek sat at ease at the great table, surrounded by his *unalil* family, legs stretched out in front of him and crossed at the ankle. Across from him, the princess sat beside Anton in a chair brought in for the occasion, leaving Amber and Aron's accustomed chairs vacant as always.

Alek didn't waste a thought on the fact that it was his absence that had broken quorum and made the meeting impossible for the past four nights. Instead, he eyed Amarok moodily, face set in a slight frown.

The man was a damned fool for doing this for so long, for risking himself to play protector. But that was Amarok all over. He'd got the do-gooder gene Alek had missed out on.

Amarok sat slightly hunched in his chair, eyes downcast. It looked like he still wasn't comfortable with so many people and so much noise and was trying to block them out, so Alek may have inadvertently done his brother a favor by delaying the meeting. Given him time to readjust to civilization. Apparently this was the first time Amarok had left his tower room in days.

The big vote on whether to offer the girl sanctuary was already over with. He'd voted against, and Miklós had abstained, but they'd been overruled by the majority, as the rest of the family had been more than willing to pledge their support.

Maybe he was the only one who could see what a bad idea this was. A human female, smelling like *that*, in a house like this. She was temptation personified, but when he'd said as much to Della earlier, she'd looked at him reproachfully. "We're not savages, Alek."

Yeah, maybe he was the only savage here, but seeing her again this morning hadn't taken any of the edge off his reaction to her. She was a living goddamn enticement to sin, every beguiling inch of her. And sin was something he did particularly well.

He glanced at Amarok again, eyes narrowed, and at that moment, Amarok looked up at him, coolly returning his gaze, before returning to his contemplation of the floor. Alek scowled. The returned Prodigal seemed irritatingly calm for someone who'd just foisted a girl with a Directorate target on her back onto his family. Katerina was trouble, plain and simple. A doe-eyed, alluring bundle of the kind of trouble he could sure as hell do without.

With a twist of his lips, Alek turned his attention back to Anton, who was leading the meeting, as he always had since the disappearance of Aron.

" ... brings unique challenges," Anton was saying. "And the most important one is how to ease her transition. As a human hybrid, we can assume hers will be quite different from the change we all went through. Does anyone have any knowledge or experience to offer?"

There was silence around the table. Anton looked from face to face. "Has nobody ever come across a human hybrid?"

"My brother." Akilina's answer was soft, but all eyes turned toward her. "My brother was hybrid-born. Well, perhaps I should say my half-brother. We shared a father, but his mother was human."

"Can you give us any insight then? What do you know about his transition?"

Akilina shook her head slowly, regretfully. "Unfortunately I know nothing of use. He was born well over a century before me, and we never spoke of such things. We have never been ... close."

"Why exactly *are* we getting involved though?" Alek demanded, sitting forward with a frown. "Look, I don't have anything against this girl …"

"Yet you voted against offering her sanctuary," Corrin interjected smoothly, his face expressionless, and Alek turned to glare at him.

"Yeah, and Miklós abstained. What's your point?"

Miklós broke in here. "Offering her sanctuary could bring us a great deal of attention we would prefer to be without – that is, if the Directorate really does want her. We have found an equilibrium through not interfering in their affairs with the assumption that they will not interfere in ours. We cannot even be sure this girl is the one Amber spoke of, or what exactly is so special about her … I think we must consider carefully what we are risking by involving ourselves in this."

Alek eyed him. "What are you, a man or a mouse?"

Miklós looked annoyed. "Neither, last time I checked."

Alek shrugged. "Well that wasn't *my* reason for voting no. Miklós is wondering whether we want to pick a fight with the Directorate. I say hell yeah."

Across the table, Amarok's eyes flew to his. Alek settled back in his chair again, the focus of everyone's attention.

"Come on," he said. "The Directorate have never made any secret of their distaste for the *unalil*. They think we're lesser incarnations because we can take on animal form. And they've used our preference for living in small family groups against us; the fact that we're so scattered has allowed them to pick us off for centuries.

"Now, from what this Falcon guy told you, they seem to be showing their cards pretty clearly – going after human hybrids too. Forget diplomacy, forget equilibrium. We need to band together and use whatever advantage we have against the Directorate before it's too late. We can't wait for them to pick us off family by family. It's time to fight back."

There was a murmur of agreement from around the table, though Akilina stayed silent.

"As I was saying," Alek continued, "I have nothing against this girl, but isn't her transition an area where we should stand aside and let nature run its course? There must be cases where hybrids have been born and not survived transition – or not changed at all, and gone on to lead lives as humans. Shouldn't we just wait to see what happens? If she dies, she dies. If she doesn't ... Well, we can deal with that eventuality if it occurs."

He stopped speaking, and regarded the appalled faces of the others.

"Cold, Alek, even for you," Corrin said.

Alek shrugged. "What? I guess that isn't what everyone wanted to hear, but let's be realistic. If the princess will excuse me saying so, besides being of the *unalil*, the rest of us here are blood-made, not true-born. We made it through the change, but over countless centuries many more haven't. Those who are strong, and ingest strong blood, survive. The weak fail. It's nature at her finest."

Akilina had stiffened at this, her back ramrod straight, but she kept her voice even as she countered Alek's argument. "Nature at her *finest*, and in her infinite wisdom, decreed long ago that the true-born would diminish in number as the millennia passed. Now, the only new births – and even they are tragically few in number – are infants born to human women. Hybrid or not, I feel we must do everything in our power to safeguard the last true-born who remain. In this case especially so; Katerina is a princess of the Mahra's bloodline, *egir'rin*, rarest of the rare – and I mean no disrespect to this house and its inhabitants by the distinction."

She paused, and frowned slightly, eyes downcast. "I think you all know I am not as disinterested as I could be in calling for Katerina's protection. I, too, am of the Mahra's bloodline, and as her direct living descendants, we of the blood alone bear the privilege and burden of our people's salvation.

"I know to some of you the idea of the Mahra being reborn among us must seem a fantasy, a delusional hope." Akilina raised her eyes to scan the faces of the *unalil* surrounding her, and Alek could see several others who, like him, were frankly skeptical.

Akilina's brow creased. "All I can say," she continued, in a voice that was both quiet and forceful, "is that to me, to all who are true-born, it is a very real belief. Our only way of ensuring that it will one day come to pass is to protect our bloodlines. As a new *egir'rin*, Katerina's future is too important to take chances with, and I believe we *must* facilitate her transition by whatever means necessary."

Alek cocked an eyebrow, and sat back again with a lazy grin. "Well, you bluebloods are certainly an endangered species, I'll grant you that. I wouldn't expect you to do anything other than protect your own."

"As you desire to protect your own." Akilina hesitated. "But I would like to make it known how grateful I am that, despite our differences, your family has chosen to join with me in protecting this girl. This matter is … very important to me. And I would also like to stress that I have no love for the Directorate either. Particularly after this targeting of human hybrids has been made so clear. Their fight against the *unalil* has never been my fight. I have no problem with your kind."

"Yeah, you even have *unalil* friends, right?" Alek said, a sardonic tilt to his lips. How the princess must be hating this, having to bury her pride and come here to beg for their help.

Akilina shifted uncomfortably. "Well yes, I do."

Anton broke in smoothly here, giving Alek an admonishing frown. "Alek, I think Akilina has shown herself our friend by the very act of coming here, and trusting her own safety and Katerina's to our household. We have already voted to join her in protecting this girl, despite the possible danger, so let us move on."

He turned to Akilina. "If you have any way of contacting your brother that would be helpful. For those of you who have been absent, Akilina has been reading the scrolls, seeing what she can glean from our writings. Other than that, we should all seek any information that might help us to know what to expect, and keep a close watch on Katerina to monitor changes. We will continue to patrol day and night, though I still think it best to keep this from Katerina until there is a confirmed threat."

"Will we talk to her about the other player?" Della broke in. Her eyes flew across to Amarok. "Whoever was behind the airplane tickets, and her New York job?"

Anton shook his head. "I am not certain it would be to our advantage to draw more attention to the odd sequence of events leading to her departure from Charleston."

Alek snorted. "What, you're worried she might start asking exactly how it was that *we* became involved, and why Anton's arrival in New York was so perfectly timed?"

Anton and Akilina exchanged a glance. It was obvious they'd discussed this issue already.

"Her transition is all she should be focusing on for the moment," Akilina said. "Such a life-changing event ... That is quite enough for her to deal with."

Anton nodded. "We can't be sure exactly how much of this she has pieced together on her own. At the moment, she likely thinks this whole thing started with Char reporting her to the Directorate. And she trusts us," he added.

"But she might not if she learns Rok here is the big bad wolf who's been spying on her for the last decade or more?" Alek knew his tone was sarcastic, and deliberately inflammatory, but he was enjoying this too much to care.

Anton frowned, and shot a look across at Amarok, but the man-wolf just flinched, and hunched even further into his chair.

Alek rolled his eyes. "Whatever. We keep the little lady in the dark wherever possible. Nothing to tell. Got it."

Chapter 31

Kat stared out the living room window into the velvet blackness of the night. She had given up trying to overhear the meeting, and was too distracted to continue reading, so now listened with half an ear for the approaching footsteps of someone coming to get her.

Akilina had said it would be a full family council meeting. Everyone would be there – even the two she hadn't seen since that first night. Alek, the beautiful and compelling one with a fetish for her hair. The one who'd looked like he wanted to have her for dessert. Who knew which way he'd vote? And the other, dark-haired man. Amarok, Della had called him. He was the one who tantalized her memory – all brooding caveman angst. She still couldn't remember who or what he reminded her of, but he'd stood ready to protect her the night she'd arrived. He was the biggest mystery of all.

The first and only time she'd met those two it'd made a lasting impression. Being honest with herself, she had to admit that either one of them, and especially both of them together, were pretty darned intimidating – and it was likely they'd *both* be at this meeting.

She sighed, and turned away from the window. One of the candles Akilina had lit was guttering, its wick too long for a clean flame. She blew it out, and when it continued to glow and smoke, she tried to pinch it out with her fingers and burned them. Not badly, but enough to sting. She pressed her fingertips against the cold window. Stupid thing to do anyway, but she was sure she'd read somewhere about snuffing a flame out like that.

Her mind returned to worrying about the meeting – and why she found these males so unsettling. It wasn't that she was unused to being around men. She came from a family of big men who were into all the stereotypical male stuff; hunting, fishing, sport. Her brothers and Walt were unabashedly masculine. But not like this. Not even in the same ballpark.

These other males didn't walk, they *prowled*. There was no social veneer, no polite distance, no harmless verbal play – let alone any polite conversation.

Even the ones she was most comfortable with, like Anton and Corrin, hid their wildness just beneath the surface, assessing everything that happened around them with a few extra senses besides the five she knew about. It often seemed like they were ready to run, or fly, or pounce at a moment's notice.

It still gave her a jolt every time she saw how *fast* they moved, too, seemingly appearing and disappearing in the blink of an eye. Crossing rooms in an instant. Even when they did slow down, each movement was a study in controlled elegance – like a dancer going through their paces.

There was no fooling herself that they were even remotely human.

She chewed on her bottom lip, frowning thoughtfully. She had no illusions about the role *she* played; undoubtedly there was something unrelated to her going on between Alek and the other one, Amarok, which made him ready to tear Alek to pieces at a moment's notice. For all she knew they were like that all the time, though for her, the whole testosterone- and pheromone-filled atmosphere took a bit of getting used to.

Lost in thought, she was startled when Della appeared at her side. "Oh, I didn't hear you coming!"

"I didn't mean you to. You looked so peaceful sitting there. I didn't want to disturb you."

"Peaceful?" Kat gave a shaky laugh. "I feel like I'm waiting to face a firing squad." Her hand went to her rune necklace. It was becoming a habit to reach for it every time she was nervous, and it had certainly gotten a workout over the last few days.

"Firing squad?" Della frowned, wrinkling her brow. "Oh, you mean guns. No, no, nothing like that. Don't be nervous."

Easy to say, harder to do, Kat thought to herself as she followed Della along the hallway.

The double doors to the dining room had been flung open now, and sounds of soft conversation spilled into the hall. Kat slowed her steps as she approached the door, and her hands clenched. Had she passed the vote? If she hadn't, Della would have said something, surely? The anticipation was killing her. She drew a deep breath and walked inside, and all conversation stopped dead. That really, really didn't seem like a good sign.

The entire household was in two rows, from doorway to table. Akilina stood to one side, her face composed and expressionless. Della flitted off to join Corrin in line as soon as she was through the door, and Kat stood alone, with all eyes intent on her.

Great. I was hoping for something nice and casual. Guess that's not happening.

She swallowed against the lump in her dry throat, and forced herself to step forward. Whatever was in store for her, best to just get it over with.

Anton met her first, and looked deep into her eyes as he took a wrist in each hand, letting his thumbs rest over the pulse points.

"Katerina, welcome. I am Anton, blood-made son of Aron. My blood for your blood. My eyes to guard your back. My walls to shield you."

Relief jolted through her as Anton's words sank in. She was being welcomed! Anton's gaze was filled with compassion, and as his deep voice reverberated through her, a tingling energy passed from his hands along her arms and right through her body to her toes. Though she could understand the meaning of his words, he wasn't speaking English. She had learned to tell the difference now. This language, inexplicably buried somewhere deep within her psyche, was distinguished by its richness and varied cadences.

She almost swayed toward him as he released her and moved aside to let the next two in line repeat the ritual and the phrases; Della, with her light, cool fingers and musical voice, and then Corrin, the giant with the gentle touch. Miklós moved forward next, and completed the ritual with formal correctness, not betraying any of the reluctance to be around her that she was sure she'd sensed in him at their other brief meetings. He was quick to release her and move away, though, as soon as the words had been spoken.

And then there were just two remaining, Alek and dark-haired Amarok. Each was focused on the other, unaware of the silent scrutiny of six pairs of eyes. Neither of them stepped forward. After a moment Alek gave a low laugh, broke the gaze, and shrugged.

"I'll go first, then," he said in English, and moved across to Kat with languid grace. Despite all the people surrounding them she still couldn't help feeling he was … dangerous. There was so much pent-up savagery in him. She let out a shaky breath as his dark blue eyes caught hers and held.

Then his hands slid around her wrists, alive with energy, and she forgot to be afraid. It wasn't just a touch, but a caress that left melting warmth in its wake.

She'd heard the words before, but not spoken like this. His voice was liquid honey, lingering where others like Miklós had hurried, and imbuing each word with textured layers of additional meaning, as what had been stock phrases took on erotic promise.

"Whatever you desire, you need only ask," he added softly at the end, as he lifted her wrist and brushed it with his lips. When her breath caught, he gave a slow smile, displaying sharp white teeth.

His eyes – what was it about them? That feeling of familiarity was there again; as if something in him was calling for recognition, with memory waiting just out of reach. But he was only showing her what he wanted her to see, and she sensed more.

There was something else behind the primal desire to possess, and beyond the accomplished smoothness of a man supremely experienced in enjoying women and being enjoyed in turn. Beneath all that surface fabrication was something she was quite sure he didn't want her to see. He frowned, and abruptly released her and stepped away.

"Kat."

Her eyes had followed Alek, and now she dragged them back to meet the golden gaze of Amarok, last in line to welcome her. As she met his eyes the sense of familiarity washed over her, more intensely this time. But it wasn't his face. There was nothing about the nose, or the high brow, or the over-long hair that spilled across his forehead to spark recognition. Was it just that she'd dreamed of his sister? From what Della had told her, Amber closely resembled him. She frowned. And Amarok had called her Kat, not Katerina. Everyone else here seemed drawn naturally to the formality of her full name.

She realized his hands were outstretched toward her, palms raised, and lifted her own to place them in his. His hands as they cupped hers were as gentle as the down beneath a robin's egg.

"Welcome." The man's voice was husky, as if he didn't use it very often. "I am Amarok, blood-made son of Aron. Our blood for your blood. Our eyes to guard your back. Our walls to shield you."

He spoke the words softly, reverentially. The timbre of his voice told her he wasn't just repeating phrases by rote, he really *meant* them, with a depth of sincerity that was humbling.

He lifted her hand to his lips, as if he planned to place a kiss on her wrist, like Alek had. But instead, he uncurled her fingers, and kissed the tips of her thumb and index finger where she had burned them.

"All gone," he said softly, and she realized there was no discomfort there anymore.

In a strange, unfathomable way, she knew she'd be willing to trust this man she'd never met, even with her life. And that he'd be willing to sacrifice everything to fulfill that trust. She didn't know how she could be so sure of that, but she was.

There was a reticence in him though, a sense of hesitation, and buried deeply in those golden eyes ... was it shame? Kat blinked, and the moment was lost.

It was only as Amarok released her wrists and moved away that she realized the words he'd spoken had been subtly different from the others. His welcome had been spoken in the plural. Had it just been a trick of speech, or was he making those promises on behalf of someone else too?

And then the others all surrounded her, with touches on the shoulder, and less formal conversation. Miklós left first, with a quick nod in her direction. Alek stood to the side, making no attempt to join the group around her. He leaned against the wall with casual nonchalance, amusement in his blue eyes whenever they caught hers. She glanced around quickly, but there was no sign of Amarok – perhaps, like Miklós, he had slipped away as soon as he could.

Della and Corrin were the next to leave. Della gave her a big hug and a sparkling smile.

"Come and join us in the kitchen soon. I'll have your meal waiting."

As the two of them reached the door, Kat turned to find Akilina at her elbow.

"I am glad to see this outcome, child. That you have been welcomed and your protection guaranteed. Come and see me after you have eaten, as we have much to discuss."

Kat nodded, and Akilina left the room with Anton beside her, the two of them engaged in a low-voiced conversation. Kat looked around to see that the room was empty, so she followed in Anton and Akilina's wake.

When she walked into the darkened hallway, she saw Alek leaning against the wall, much like he had been inside.

"So, still here?" His voice was soft.

"Yes." Kat immediately regretted answering. Hadn't his question been rhetorical? Obviously she was still here.

"I thought you might have decided it was best to move on. Once they warned you about me."

"They didn't," Kat said with a frown. "I mean, no one has said anything about you."

"Really? Interesting. They seem to have more faith in me than I do in myself." His eyes were brilliant. "Or perhaps it is you they have faith in …" He took her hand, and brought it to his lips, kissing the back softly this time, his glowing eyes all the while locked on hers. "Princess of the blood."

"I'm not … don't call me that." Kat jerked her hand away, sure he was mocking her.

"Of course. I'm sorry. You haven't been through transition yet. You are still … human." Now he was *definitely* laughing at her.

"Is there something wrong with that?" she snapped.

"Not at all. I like humans very much."

She got the impression there was more than one layer of meaning to his words, and judged silence to be the safest response.

Alek's smile grew. "You know, you might be better off staying human. The *egir'rin* lead such a … curtailed existence. As a princess of the blood, you'd need to limit your contact with the lowly blood-made like us. And another *human* would certainly be out of the question."

Kat glared at him, annoyed Akilina's words had come back to taunt her so soon. "I may not know much about any of this, but I can tell you I'll be making those choices for myself."

Alek looked at her quizzically. "Life is full of things we don't get to choose, little Kat." His voice was almost tender, and Kat noticed he had chosen to use the shortened form of her name after hearing Amarok say it. On his lips it was like an endearment.

"Well, I suppose I'll find out whether that's true soon enough." It wasn't much of a rejoinder, but she really wasn't in the mood for any more witty repartee, especially when all the wit seemed to be coming from one side – not hers. And when all the humor was at her expense. Why had she ever thought Alek a Neanderthal incapable of polite conversation? Everything he said seemed to have ten possible meanings. Talking to him was a minefield.

Alek laughed softly. "Time for breakfast, I think, although for you I suppose it would be dinner. Della and Corrin seem to have adopted you." He turned to move away, and then stopped suddenly, and spoke without facing her, the laughter gone from his voice.

"You know, Kat, I never got the chance to tell you. You do smell … delectable."

"So I've heard," Kat muttered.

He began to walk toward the window at the end of the hallway, and the words were out of her mouth before she could wish them unsaid.

"Where are you going?"

He half turned to face her. "I'm on watch tonight – unless you want company later?" He gave a wicked grin, suggestion darkening his eyes, and she shook her head and abruptly turned to walk away.

Seriously, you've got to get it together, girl, she admonished herself. She was an adult woman, for Pete's sake! It wasn't like she'd never dealt with predatory types before. At that moment, a flash of movement caught her eye as a dark-haired man – Amarok, perhaps – disappeared quickly from view at the other end of the corridor.

"Oh, and Kat?"

Alek's voice behind her drew her attention back to him. She stopped walking, but didn't turn around. She wondered if the other man had heard much of their conversation. She was sure her face must still be flaming red.

"You taste as good as you smell."

She swung around, and caught the barest flash of naked male skin before tawny golden fur shimmered into place, and a cougar leaped through the open window into the darkness beyond.

Chapter 32

Amarok sat, silent and contemplative, on the bench in the kitchen garden. He listened to the noise within, the ebb and flow of life and warmth; Kat coming in through the door from the main hallway and being welcomed by Della with a warm supper; Miklós passing through to grab a bite to eat before heading out to hunt for something more substantial in the peregrine form he favored. He listened, but he did not join them.

The outcome of the family council tonight had been everything he'd hoped for. Kat's protection by his whole family should have lifted the burden he'd been carrying alone for so long. But still, he felt it. A load, weighing him down. A connection that couldn't be sundered.

He listened as she ate, and talked to Della, and laughed. Glad that she could do so. And knowing that he'd do anything, everything in his power, to protect that lightness within her.

A little later, he heard the rhythmic rasp as Della, now alone in the kitchen, began grinding corn. There was the faint sound of footsteps on the stairs, and then Della's welcome for Anton as he entered the room.

"Katerina?"

"She just went upstairs."

"Corrin's not here?"

"Outside somewhere. Not too far. Should I call him?"

"No. Actually, it was you I wanted to speak to."

"Oh?"

Anton fell silent. Amarok could imagine the look on his face, the mute male entreaty.

Then Della, the hint of a smile in her voice, took pity on him. "Can I assume you have no idea what to make of all this?"

Silence from Anton. Perhaps he nodded?

Then Della again, amusement clear now in her tone. "And you believe I might know."

Silence for a moment, and then a rustle as Della searched for a lump of rock salt in the earthenware jar she kept beneath hanging bunches of dried herbs against the window. A small clink as she tossed the salt to Anton, together with a small bowl.

"Here, crush this for me."

Amarok knew he should leave, or enter the kitchen and show his presence, but after so many years on the edge of things, listening but not participating, it was hard to break the habit. And even now, surely, he was listening to what passed between his family members with Kat's interests in mind. Still, as always, the silent protector.

He imagined Anton frowning over the bowl, heard the faint sound of him crushing salt for a few moments, then clearing his throat. "Akilina believes I should ... " Anton hesitated, "forbid the two of them from ... "

"Then Akilina is a fool." Della at her best. Amarok smiled into the darkness. Only a woman could muster quite that tone.

"So *you* do not think ... " Anton sounded relieved.

"No." Della was emphatic.

Anton hesitated again, and Amarok heard the faint brush of fingers as he passed the bowl back to Della. "I worry that Alek might ... disgrace himself," Anton said.

"No." Such certainty from Della. He wished he shared it.

"No?"

Amarok imagined her shaking her head in that very definite way she had. "I think he might find himself instead."

"Oh. So ... "

" ... you should do absolutely nothing." A whisper of sound as she added salt to the cornmeal, and stirred. Amarok had seen her make cornbread so many times, in years gone by, that he knew the process by heart.

"Let things take their natural course," she added.

"It is sometimes difficult. Doing nothing." He could hear the frustration in Anton's voice.

"Doing what is difficult is the mark of greatness." There was humor in Della's tone, but sincerity too.

A huge silent shadow moved toward Amarok out of the darkness, and features became clear as Corrin silently entered the faint light spilling out of the kitchen window, cleaver in hand, with a dead rabbit slung over his shoulder. Astute green eyes traveled to the window, then back to Amarok, sitting alone in the darkness.

Both listened as Anton, inside, cleared his throat again. "I think you flatter me, Della."

A pause, in which Amarok pictured Della shaking her head. "You are a gifted leader, Anton. And you have filled the void admirably." Sadness then tinged her words. "Aron would be proud of how you have kept this family of his together."

"I hope you are right. And thank you." The soft brush of hands against temples, then the unmistakable sound of Anton kissing Della on the forehead. "My best advice comes from the kitchen."

Anton moved away, lingering near the stairs. "No need to tell Corrin I was here."

Amarok saw the corners of Corrin's eyes wrinkle as he smiled into the darkness, then the big man leaned down to press a hand to Amarok's shoulder. "Glad to have you back, brother," he whispered.

When the sound of Anton going upstairs had faded, Corrin

ambled into the kitchen. Amarok followed as far as the doorway, and stopped just outside. Della was still standing where Anton had left her, a soft smile curving her lips.

"Anyone would think I was a fearsome brute," Corrin said mildly, "the way they all act sometimes." He took the rabbit and cleaver through into the larder, and returned to give her a kiss of his own.

Della's eyes met Amarok's for a brief moment before she turned her face up to Corrin's with a loving smile. "Perception is everything."

Amarok turned then, and walked off into the darkness, shrugging away clothes that still chafed unaccustomed skin, and taking on the wolf's form.

When he found Alek a few hundred yards away, the cougar stood on a rocky outcrop staring into the distant night, ears pricked. He didn't move a muscle at the faint sounds of another large animal approaching, or turn to face Amarok as he emerged from a low thicket of shrubs, and loped across to stand on the adjacent rock.

For a while, the two stood side by side, facing the vastness of the dark valley that sloped away from the sheer drop below them. Then the cougar turned and stalked over to a nearby rock, where he changed form.

The wolf followed more slowly, wandering to where Alek sat, long legs sprawled in front of him.

"What do you want?" Alek growled.

The wolf raised his head and howled at the rising moon, the sound reverberating off the rocky surfaces and echoing across the valley.

"Quit playing wolf," Alek said irritably. "Or if you must, then do it somewhere else. I'm supposed to be on watch."

The wolf turned and sat next to Alek as a bank of clouds obscured the moon and plunged the night into blackness. When its light returned, Amarok was sitting beside Alek, his knees to his chin, arms loosely clasped around his legs. He turned to face Alek, who was staring out into the night, a frown marring his handsome face.

"You're in a bad mood," Amarok observed, his voice husky. "So is it me, or is it her?"

"Where does one finish and the other begin?" Alek muttered cryptically, without turning to meet his gaze.

Both were silent for a while.

"Are you here to warn me off?" Alek said at last.

"Would you listen if I were?"

"No." Alek stared out into the night. His eyes narrowed. "You wanted her brought here, Rok. This wasn't my idea." He shrugged. "But since she *is* here ..."

"This isn't a game, Alek," Amarok said tersely. "She's not one of your playthings to be used and then discarded once you've finished with her."

Alek's lips curled into a slow smile. "What's wrong with games? I find they add a little spice to a dull life. Maybe you just have trouble accepting that every game has a winner ... and a loser."

Amarok stiffened, then made a conscious effort to relax again. "It isn't a competition, Alek – and it's hardly the right time for this, with the Directorate after her."

Alek shrugged. "I saw the way you looked at her, Rok. The way you touched her in the council meeting. Like she was porcelain. If you want to provide me with some real competition, you might want to modernize your approach a little. Let her know you're a man."

"Don't make the mistake of judging me by your own standards, Alek." He didn't trouble to hide the dangerous glint in his eye.

Alek finally turned to face him. "You're telling me in well over ten years of playing guardian you've never touched her? That you've kept to a diet of deer, and ... fish, or whatever it is you exist on, and never tasted a single drop of that sweet blood? Never even been *tempted*?"

Amarok sat rigid, unmoving, watching the valley below.

Damn Alek. Damn him for pulling everything down to his own sordid level, and damn him doubly for being right.

Aloud, though, he made no comment, gave no answer.

Alek's eyes roamed over his face. "Do I detect discomfort?" He leaned back, bracing his hands against the rock, enjoying the moment. "An innocent man would have answered. So ... I think you *have* been close enough to feel the beat of that delectable human pulse – or you've wanted to. Either way, the guilt is killing you. You should lighten up."

"Kat and I – we've never been ... like that," Amarok said, the words torn from him unwillingly. "But I've spent too many years watching over her to stand by while you ..."

"While I what?" Alek jumped to his feet and began to prowl around. "Talk to her? Get to know her? Hardly a major drama."

"You normally don't stop there, though, do you?" He felt the beat of his pulse quicken as he fought a rising tide of anger.

Alek shrugged. "Denial isn't good for the soul." He wandered toward the cliff edge. "By the way," he flung over his shoulder, "kissing the fingers ... derivative, but a nice touch."

"She'd burned herself," Amarok said quietly. He met Alek's eyes. "I felt her pain."

Alek was silent for a moment. "Now *that's* a disability I could do without."

Amarok's mouth set in a firm line. "I'll be watching you, Alek. If you do *anything* to hurt her, I'll rip your throat out." Though he spoke softly, his words cut through the darkness like unsheathed claws.

Alek turned sharply. "Over a girl?"

"Over *this* girl? Without hesitation."

"So. Our three hundred years don't count for much."

"Our long history as brothers is why I haven't already sharpened my claws on your hide." Amarok stood and stretched with lithe grace, a dark silhouette in the moonlight. "Luckily for you, I know you're not quite as rotten as you sometimes appear to be." He began to walk away, changing from man to wolf mid-stride in a silver blur. As he padded four-footed into the cover of the low-lying shrubs, Alek's voice came out of the darkness.

"Rok?"

The wolf paused.

"Believe it or not, I don't want to hurt her." Alek moved toward him, and the moon lit the planes of his face. "She frustrates me though." His expression turned savage. "I kind of hope the Directorate does cause trouble for us over this. I could do with a good fight." His fists clenched and he bared his teeth, staring into the distance.

The wolf stood silently as the fierce light faded from Alek's eyes.

"And I'm sorry for what I said when you first came back. About Amber. I know how much you loved her." Alek's voice was gruff, but sincere.

The wolf paused for a moment, head lowered, then slipped away into the bushes.

As soon as he was out of Alek's sight, he began to run, desperate to bury himself within the animal consciousness. This time, though, he could not escape.

He stopped at last, far from home. Far from where Alek stood alone, guarding against the threat of unseen dangers. The Directorate was a fearsome enemy to face, and Amarok already had reason to hate them, if they were the ones who had taken his sister.

He lifted his head, and howled once more to the empty sky. The eerie, echoing cry of animal pain tore through the still night, releasing his frustration, his fear, and regret. For once, he, Amarok the man, was more than a deeply buried fragment within the wolf. More than a paper-thin cutout of a man. He was whole, and he *felt* with every painful fiber of his being.

"I know how much you loved her." Alek's words. In the past tense. As if his twin were really dead. Alek had given him a bad reception when he'd returned, but it wasn't because he thought Amber was still alive. It was because he'd thought Amarok didn't even care enough to search for her.

For years he had been sure – so sure — that she was alive, somewhere. But in truth, his certainty was fed by nothing but hope. Hope – a flimsy scaffolding just barely supporting an emotional ruin. He shut the thought off before it fully formed. After all, hope was what kept him going.

Hope was all he had.

Chapter 33

Kat returned to her room after dinner pleasantly full of venison stew. She dug out the wrapped parcel containing the Arcana from the suitcase Char had packed and went to find Akilina's room, up a flight of stairs and along a corridor.

"Akilina?" Kat knocked gently and poked her head around the edge of the open door. "I've brought the Arcana."

This room seemed larger than hers, perhaps because it was ablaze with candles arranged on every surface. A desk and chair were set against the window, both covered with open scrolls. The curtains were drawn back, the windows open to let in the night air.

Kat stepped inside and looked around, but the room was empty.

"I'm here, child." Akilina spoke from behind her in the doorway.

Kat turned to face her. "Is now still a good time?"

Akilina smiled, and gestured to the edge of the bed. "Of course. Please, be seated."

Akilina herself walked to the window and looked out into the night. "I should like to tell you about how our present society came to be," she said, turning. "Perhaps after that you can ask any questions you may have?" Her eyes met Kat's with a questioning look, and Kat nodded, settling herself onto the bed with the Arcana beside her.

"There have been three races in our world since antiquity: humans; those of power – what you would call witches; and our people, the *Tabérin*." Her voice had taken on the rich timbre of the storyteller. "I will not say we lived always in harmony, but we grew used to one another. That was enough … for a time."

She paused, and turned again toward the window, as if the answers to the problems of her people might be borne in on the cool night air of the mountain. "But our people have not always done the right thing by humans. Far from it, in some cases. Perhaps it should not have surprised us that they would strike back."

"What happened?" Kat wasn't sure whose side she was on in this story, situated as she was between the two parties, but she nonetheless wanted to hear how events had unfolded, even if they'd taken place long ago.

"You have heard, no doubt, of the burning times. More than four centuries have passed since that time when superstition grew throughout Europe, fueled by religious fervor and fear of difference, and witches were hunted down, tried by their village peers and imprisoned or burned. It was irrational mob behavior, as unfounded as it was destructive, for most of the true witches fled and hid, while opportunistic crofters pursued grudges against innocent neighbors. Elderly women. Widows." She spoke calmly as she took a few paces away from the window, but Kat could hear the buried pain of one who had lived through and seen more than she wished.

"And then their attention turned toward our kind, the *Tabérin*, who for centuries had figured in cautionary tales to make their children shiver at night. They had always feared the *Tabérin*, but I can only suppose they were emboldened beyond all precedent, and their witch hunt had become a raging inferno, hungry for new fodder. Perhaps they took advantage of the daylight hours, and made their attack then. At the time I was away with friends, Mahra be praised; deep in the mountains and far from any human settlement."

Akilina's face was sober in the candlelight. "When I returned, it was already over. Our great houses and castles lay empty, abandoned. So many scions of so many of our great families, gone." She let out a shuddering breath. "All across Europe, entire families of our kind disappeared, leaving a changed world for the few of us that remained. You can perhaps imagine the fear, the horror ..." She broke off, and was silent for a time, her hands gripping the back of the chair at her desk.

"And then, in the vacuum caused by the devastation of our aristocratic class, a new group came to dominate. Advisors, liegemen, servants and underlings with the will to survive – they came to those of us who remained, armed with a simple plan: that we hide ourselves from humankind, mark our buildings with magical runes that confound the human eye, and let ourselves fade from their memories. That we hold ourselves apart, and never prey on them or subjugate them as we had in the past, so that we need never again be a cause of their fears or target for their fury. This faction brought in new rules to govern our behaviour, our interactions with humans, professing to represent our interests."

Her eyes sought out Kat, brilliant in the candlelight. "They called themselves the Directorate."

"They've ruled your people ever since?"

Akilina gave a sharp nod. "There were none left to oppose them."

"And their leader is called the ..." Kat paused and frowned, trying to remember the word.

"The Vodas," Akilina said. "It is the title for a role several have filled through the centuries. The title takes the place of any other name, for his identity is always closely guarded to protect him from the ever-present threat of assassination."

"And this Vodas, he wants to kill me because I'm a hybrid?"

"Yes."

Kat shivered. She wanted to understand how everything fit

together, but the realization that there were people out there who wanted to kill her gave her a cold, sick feeling deep in the pit of her stomach.

"We will not let that happen, Katerina." Akilina's voice was gentle. "I hope, especially after tonight, you can take comfort in the fact that there are many who will fight to protect you."

"I know." Kat dismissed her worries about the Directorate through sheer force of will. She reached for the Arcana beside her. "Anyway, I brought the book."

"Ah," Akilina said, taking it in her hands and rifling through the pages. "There is a simple charm at work here, to prevent this information from falling into the wrong hands."

She opened to a particular page and then turned the book so it faced Kat. "Do you see this?"

Kat wrinkled her brow. "It's something complex; I can't really make much sense of it."

"It is giving you that impression," Akilina said, "because it doesn't want to be read. Read again, word by word."

Kat studied the page for a while. "It's a spell!" she said at last. "I think ... a fertility spell."

Akilina nodded approvingly. "It is a simple matter of ignoring the suggestions of the protective charm. It tells you that what is written on the page is uninteresting, or difficult, or obscure. Learn to look beyond that initial impression and the charm will have no effect on you."

"That's how the V-runes work too, isn't it? On the suggestion that something isn't there, like a building, or that something written is incomprehensible?"

Akilina inclined her head in acknowledgement. "We draw our energy from minerals, from the elements; from water, earth, and stone. Witches draw power from the living world. Plants. Animals. Their lore is more formalized, too, in its spellcraft and so on. But apart from that, there are significant similarities in the ways we can draw on and use power."

She turned back to the book. "I would be interested to see if there is any record of hybrids here besides the references to Dark Children you have already mentioned." Starting at the beginning, she flicked through the pages one by one. She raised her brows at the end, and placed the book back on the bed. "I suppose a neat analysis of hybrid transition would have been too much to hope for, though my reading has taught me that the witches are far better informed on our kind than we realize." She gestured to the book on the bed. "This Arcana dwells much more on the fate of those hybrids who never do make transition. Who live their lives as humans, and go on to raise families of their own. But it travels down the bloodline, some of our *Tabérin* power, and the children are perhaps faintly aware of a world beyond the ordinary. So what do they do?" Her wry smile reflected her awareness of the irony. "They're quite likely to marry into witch families."

"It sounds ... complicated," Kat said.

Akilina nodded. "Very," she said.

"So it's possible, isn't it, that I could be like the people they mention in this Arcana, and never make transition? Just stay human?" Even as the words came out of her mouth, Kat wasn't sure what answer she was hoping for. Since this recent upheaval to her life, a big part of her had been wishing it would all just go away. But she'd always known there was something different about her. Always sensed that "world beyond the ordinary" Akilina had referred to, though she hadn't been able to make sense of that awareness until very recently. So could she ever really go back to being merely human?

"Do you wish for that? To stay human?" Kat heard the regret in Akilina's voice.

"I ... I don't know. Maybe sometimes."

"I can only imagine how hard it must be to contemplate this life for one who was not born into it." Akilina's smile was gentle. "But to answer your question, I think you know that your transition has already begun. I wish I could tell you more about how quickly it will happen. About what you will experience. What I have gleaned is that your transition may be influenced by the moon, with symptoms of change becoming stronger with each lunar cycle. And of course your increased appetite for meat is a clear indication of your body's changing needs."

"Oh." Hearing it put so baldly ... well, she couldn't really argue with anything Akilina had said.

Akilina's eyes searched hers. She must have looked pretty glum, because the elder placed a hand on her shoulder, sympathy softening her mouth.

"I'm sorry if that is not what you wanted to hear, child. But your transition ... in my opinion, it is not a matter of if, but when."

Chapter 34

Councillor Ionescu's eyes narrowed as he identified the immaculately groomed man seated in the most exclusive area of the Mandate Council building. It was an area usually only frequented by councillors – outside the Vodas's reception chamber, no less.

"Victor."

Fortes turned at the sound of his name, and his lips curved into a confident smile. "Councillor." He inclined his head slightly as a mark of respect, but did not rise from his chair. Once, he would have been on his knees at Ionescu's feet.

"Does your special project … progress well?"

"Yes. Very well." Again Fortes smiled, the easy, complacent smile of one for whom difficult things are effortless.

Ionescu took the seat beside Fortes. "I know the Vodas has tasked you with locating the hybrid female, Katerina Chanter."

"Oh, is that her name?" Fortes said, his smile just a little too disingenuous for Ionescu's liking.

Ionescu kept his temper with an effort. "Perhaps," he said silkily, "she will not be so easy to find."

Fortes met his eyes, and this time, the younger man did not trouble to cloak his arrogance, his ambition, his casual insolence behind a smile. "Your concern is appreciated, Councillor, but we have resources you could not possibly be aware of. Our plan is already in play. Locating our target …" He paused to look down and delicately flick an invisible speck from one trousered thigh. When he raised his eyes to Ionescu again, they were hard and cold.

"Locating our target and eradicating this threat to the Vodas is only a matter of time."

Chapter 35

A prickling at the back of Kat's neck told her that she was no longer alone in the bathhouse. She slid upright against the stone bath edge.

She *should* be alone, seeing as she'd timed her bath during the daylight hours to guarantee she'd have the place to herself.

There was a quiet hum as gears spun into action, and Kat watched anxiously as covers smoothly slid over the domed skylight. As the shadows increased and the room became dim, candles flared into life in sconces on every wall.

Kat's panic grew. She couldn't keep the dryness from her throat, or stop her heart from pounding extra fast. "Who's there?" she called out.

Her mind, eternally helpful, provided her with headlines for her demise: "Girl found murdered in bath in remote mountain region. No witnesses, no suspects." Or maybe, if they got creative: "Girl's bloodless corpse found in dense forest. No sign of foul play, other than two puncture wounds to the neck." Though of course the whole idea of headlines was ridiculous. She wouldn't even make the news. Her name would probably languish on a missing person's list somewhere, because out here they'd never even find her body.

Kat shivered, and then turned quickly to see Alek on the other side of the room, leaning against the wall. He seemed completely relaxed, as if he'd been leaning in that exact position for some time. Of course, he hadn't.

"You scared me!" she said, fear making her voice sharp.

Then it occurred to her that maybe that'd been his intention. He *had* made that comment after all, last time she'd seen him; something about the others warning her about him. He seemed to enjoy making her uncomfortable. Probably, the best way to handle him was to show as little reaction as possible. If she could manage that.

Alek straightened and sauntered toward her as if he had all the time in the world. His chest was bare, a towel draped around his waist.

Good to know he isn't carrying any weapons, Kat thought irrelevantly. Then she gave herself a mental slap in the face, and pulled her focus back to eye level, hoping the heat in her cheeks wasn't visible in this light.

She didn't move, but watched him warily as he came to a stop a few feet away, towering over her. God, he was huge. Broad shoulders tapering to a narrow waist, every inch of him lithe muscle. Viewed completely objectively, Alek was pretty damned gorgeous. But she didn't trust him as far as she could throw him … assuming, of course, she could lift well over two hundred pounds.

"Don't look so suspicious," he said lazily. "I'm just here to take a bath."

Yeah, sure you are.

"And you typically do that in the middle of the day?" Kat didn't bother to hide the sarcasm.

He glanced in the direction of the darkened skylight, which minutes before had allowed sunshine to spill through into the room. His lips twisted in a mocking smile. "Evidently."

Kat's eyes narrowed. "Well, I'll let you have the place to yourself."

He shrugged, as if it didn't much matter one way or the other. "I don't mind sharing, so don't rush on my account."

Yeah, like hell I'm sharing a bath with you.

He was about as subtle as a brick to the head. Okay, so he was better than the average guy running with the "How about it, Sweet Pea, you and me?" line. Just barely.

"It's no trouble, I was pretty much finished anyway." Her voice was deliberately calm. *We're just discussing the weather here, buddy. You're not gonna get another rise out of me.*

But then he stood there. And didn't move. She stayed motionless in the concealing water as several long, awkward moments ticked by. Maybe he didn't realize this whole communal bathing thing was completely new for her. On the other hand, maybe he did. If it had been Della, or Akilina, she might have felt differently. Maybe. But with someone of the opposite sex …

"Would you mind turning away for a moment?" she asked finally, sure her face was blazing.

He raised perfect eyebrows in an artistic show of surprise. "Of course."

He turned to face the far wall, and Kat could have sworn that the gleam in his eyes was not at all innocent. She slipped her robe over her shoulders and belted it securely in front of her. Whatever game he was playing, she didn't know the rules and didn't want to learn them.

"Well, enjoy your bath." She bolted for the door without looking back.

As soon as she was through into the antechamber, she was furious, both at herself for letting him unnerve her, and at him. She couldn't be completely sure whether he *had* been trying to frighten her when he'd come in like that, so unexpectedly. Maybe he didn't realize how intimidating he was. But he could have used some basic logic and worked out that being under constant threat might make her a little on edge, couldn't he? Sneaking up on people was …

well, unfriendly, to say the least. And the rest of his behavior had to have been calculated to make her squirm. He'd succeeded, damn him.

Kat grabbed her clothes from the antechamber, but didn't waste time putting them on. That could wait until she was safely in her own room with the door bolted.

She stepped outside in her robe, and blinked in the bright sunlight. *Definitely* daytime. Alek should have been asleep or resting, like the others. And they couldn't go out in the sunlight, as far as she knew. So how had he made it to the bathhouse in broad daylight?

And *why* had he come? It had to be deliberate. A predatory male thing. He must have known she'd be there, and hadn't been able to resist ...

Kat wrinkled her brow, knowing it was the most logical conclusion, but unable to accept it. He was *obscenely* good-looking, and it wasn't like he'd have any trouble finding willing women.

Had she somehow given the impression last time they met that she was ... interested? The way she remembered it, she'd made her annoyance pretty obvious, and when he made a sort-of pass, she'd turned it down. So ... either he was desperate to prove his powers of seduction worked on her, or teasing and innuendo were the only way he could relate to the opposite sex. Maybe – just maybe – this whole performance he put on every time he saw her was a wild, territorial, testosterone-driven male way of being friendly. Or something.

Kat sighed. To say she didn't know Alek all that well was an understatement. With no point of reference, no idea how he normally behaved, she might never work out what motivated him.

A breeze touched the dampness on the back of her legs, and she realized she'd been in such a hurry she hadn't stopped to dry herself. Or put shoes on. The stone walkway was rough beneath her bare feet, and she stopped to untangle her shoes from the pile of clothes she held, and slip them on.

Her brief pause gave the cougar following behind time to draw level. The giant cat passed so close by her on the narrow path that its fur brushed against her bare skin, sending a shiver of sensation up her damp legs. It continued past, and disappeared behind some rocks near the house.

Well, that answered one question anyway. Kat didn't need to re-trace her steps to know that the bathhouse would now be empty. And it confirmed what Akilina had told her, about the *unalil* working as the *Tabérin's* assassins. Being able to move during daylight hours would give them a big advantage over their targets.

She knew there was nothing behind her, but instinct made her take a quick glance anyway – and she saw the panties she'd dropped on a rock beside the path when she'd pulled her shoes out from among her clothing. Great. Just great.

She hurried to snatch them up, though the damage had already been done. The horse had already bolted … or in this case, the marauding Alek-as-cougar had already seen her red and white polka dot panties.

Could it get any worse than that?

Chapter 36

Kancamagus Highway cut deep into New Hampshire's White Mountain National Forest, and it was there, in the dead of night, on an unsealed forest track leading to Big Rock campground, that Victor Fortes awaited the Vodas's arrival.

The three huge trucks lined up at the forest edge gleamed black and silver in the moonlight, every inch of them reinforced and customized to allow the transportation of a deadly live cargo.

A distant sound, the whine of an expensive engine as it rounded a corner, heralded the approach of a vehicle, and soon its headlights were visible, approaching slowly along the tree-lined track. The car pulled up behind the nearest truck, and Fortes hurried over, making sure he was the one to open the door for the man who was the supreme leader of the Directorate. The Vodas stepped down onto the leaf litter and gravel in his ceremonial hooded cloak.

"How many are there?" The Vodas's cloak brushed the ground as he strode over to the nearest truck. Fortes had rarely seen him so energized.

Fortes motioned to Marcus Clay, the genetic engineer who had accompanied the truck convoy from the Hema Castus Institute to oversee the deployment of his "creations."

Clay hurried over, and bowed low before the Vodas. "Almost a hundred, Vodas. We lost a few on the way. They are sensitive to certain sounds. To light."

The Vodas barely nodded before turning back to Fortes. "And the car, Victor?"

"New York plates, and rune-marked to avoid detection by any human passersby." Fortes led the Vodas to where the vehicle was parked close to the trees. "If you could take care, Vodas, not to enter the back seat of the vehicle. Clay has yet to give the creatures the scent of our target."

He should have known, though, that the Vodas – who had already shown a marked preoccupation for the details of this case – wouldn't be satisfied without getting a little closer to the primary scene than the outside of the vehicle. He watched impassively as the Vodas opened the back door, took a deep, lingering breath, and then straightened up and stepped back from the car.

"Yes. I smell her."

The Vodas seemed exhilarated by this proof that they were close, and swung around to survey the rest of the scene. "Well, what are you waiting for? Begin!"

Clay hurried to obey, a couple of assistants hurrying to join him as the truck ramps were lowered, and heavy cages rolled down and placed in long rows on the forest road. The Vodas paced back and forth along the rows, delighting in the growls of the creatures and their futile attempts to escape the enclosing bars.

Fortes moved to the Vodas's side, bowing before trying to wrest his attention from a snarling creature with its slavering muzzle straining against the bars of the cage, its eyes fixed on the Vodas.

"Vodas, if perhaps we could wait over here ..." He gestured to where a rudimentary dais had been erected, topped with what he hoped was a suitably grand chair. Fortunately the Vodas appeared satisfied, and allowed himself to be shepherded away.

They watched together as Clay and his team went from cage to cage, checking each animal's GPS chip was active and transmitting, and brought the rabid beasts to attention with the blast of a whistle. Then, one by one, the cages were unlocked, and each animal was exposed to the scent in the Cadillac's rear seat. Finally, the process was complete. Row after row of brutish muscled forms crouched silent and still in front of their cages, each with the same strangely attentive glow in their eyes.

Clay turned toward the dais and bowed low. "At your command, Vodas."

The Vodas gave a crow of laughter, and stood up. "Very good!" He walked over and paraded in front of the creatures, strutting back and forth like a general assessing his troops. "Very good," he said again.

He snapped his fingers at Clay. "How will they hunt her?"

"Upon hearing two blasts of the whistle, they will split into three packs," Clay explained, "each traveling in a different direction. Then they will proceed, valley by valley, until they pick up her scent."

"And when they find their prey?"

"They will destroy her."

There was a momentary hush, as the beasts stood still as carved stone, waiting, and the Vodas wheeled around, one arm raised above his head.

Clay raised his whistle to his mouth.

As always, the deep hood on the Vodas's robe left his face mostly hidden, but Fortes caught a glimpse of his mouth, the lips curved into a cruel smile.

"Release them."

Chapter 37

Char looked up, and pushed her chair back from her desk when Jonathan entered the room. "There you are." She rubbed her eyes, and gave a catlike yawn. "So was Mac right?"

Jonathan nodded. "Definitely gone."

Char grimaced. "So what are we supposed to make of the abrupt departure of the Directorate team after several days of around-the-clock surveillance?"

"They've decided to leave us alone?"

"Huh. Wishful thinking. No." Char narrowed her eyes. "Something must have changed. I think they've found another play. Another way in."

Jonathan nodded. "Makes sense. But do you think they really know how to find Kat?"

Char suddenly doubled over, pressing her hands to her temples.

"Char? What is it?" Jonathan's concerned voice cut through the din of club noise, before the sound was muted. She realized he had shut the door to her office.

"Char?" His voice sounded loud in the relative quiet, as he came to take a seat beside her. "Are you okay?"

Char didn't answer at first, concentrating on taking long, deep breaths to calm the familiar churning in her stomach. Finally, she

opened her eyes. "I think so." She blinked uncertainly. "Maybe."
She shuddered. "That was horrible."

Jonathan frowned. "A vision?"

"Yeah, but not …" Char broke off and bit her lip, staring sight-lessly at the wall opposite. "It was about the others. Normally it's about me. But this time … Akilina and Kat are in danger."

"What danger?"

Char didn't answer, still in the grip of the after-chill.

"What danger, Char?"

She was dimly aware that his voice was more insistent than it perhaps should have been. He was probably just worried.

"I don't know!" She stood, and swayed a little before Jonathan shot an arm out to steady her. She blinked again, a little confused to find herself in her familiar office, in her club, with the night's festivities in full swing right outside the office door.

Jonathan scrutinized her face, then raised his hand to her fore-head for a moment. "You're pale, Char, and you feel all cold and clammy. Sit down again, and don't go anywhere."

Char sat, but only because his hand on her shoulder was pressing her gently down. When he had left the room, she found herself reaching for her phone, and dialing a number.

A woman answered after only a couple of rings, and Char's confidence plunged for a moment. She hadn't considered the possibility that a woman might answer, that he might already have a woman in his life.

"Hello?" she said hesitantly. "My name is Char. I wanted to get a message to John Falcon."

Char was sitting in exactly the same place when Jonathan opened the door and hurried back into her office a little later. She was staring at the wall, her brow wrinkled in thought.

"Here," he said, pressing the warm, dark liquid into her hand. "Drink up. A couple of hundred should make you feel better."

Char tilted the glass and drank. Warmth flowed through her,

replacing the awful bone-deep chill. When the glass was empty she placed it on the table and rose to her feet in one swift movement.

"I have to go," she said abruptly, sudden decision firming her voice. "With the surveillance team leaving so suddenly, and now this vision. The signs aren't good, are they? Akilina's my maker. I have to find her."

"Go *now*?" Jonathan's expression was an odd mixture of desperation and burning focus. "Char, it's only two hours till sunrise. You can't just take off without a plan or any place to wait out the daylight hours!"

"I have to try," she said. "I have to warn them."

Chapter 38

Kat hurried down the stairs to the kitchen, glad the sun had set, and eager to have someone to talk to. She'd been on edge all day, worrying, thinking. She still wasn't any closer to a decision on exactly what she should tell her mom about all of this. Technically, she had a story prepared; the one Char had invented, about her being seconded to another lab outside the city. But when she imagined actually lying to her mom … it just didn't feel right.

Then again, last time they'd talked she'd made an art form out of having a conversation without saying much at all, even while half asleep. *I could give lessons,* she thought glumly. *Evasiveness 101.*

Her mouth twisted in a wry grimace as she rounded the corner and went down the last few steps two at a time. She ran into a solid wall of stationary male just as she reached the bottom.

"Oh!"

She took a step backward, and when she realized it was Alek she'd run into, she kept right on going until she hit the edge of the stair tread with her heel. Why did it have to be him, of all people?

He took a step or two toward her, and her breath caught as adrenalin rushed through her. *There's no need to be ridiculous,* she admonished herself. *Della is probably right around the corner. Or Corrin.* Though right at this second, there was no sign of either of them.

For a long moment, they just stared at each other.

"Don't look at me like that," he said softly. He lifted his hand, and caressed the line of her jaw with the backs of his fingers. Her skin tingled where he touched it, and an unfamiliar hunger flamed into life and began to smoulder deep inside her.

Kat swallowed, her throat suddenly uncomfortably dry. "I don't know how I'm looking at you." *You are such a liar. You see him and you want to run the other way. It's got to stop.*

He smiled, but there was a hint of sadness in it. "As if I'm about to spring at you. As if you're afraid of me." He paused. "I don't want you to be."

She could tell his words were sincere, which was a nice change. No innuendo.

Alek went on talking. "Ironically, your fear brings out the worst in me, and I become something even *I* don't recognize."

Kat didn't say anything. What could she say to that? She didn't know him well enough to even be sure what that meant. She may only have seen his worst side, but she didn't *know* what his best side was. So far she hadn't been keen to stick around long enough to find out.

He tilted his head, blue eyes suddenly shining with a slumberous, sensual light. She'd seen that expression before. It sent her imagination tumbling into dark and unfamiliar territory, making her face heat. One minute he had her wanting to flee to safety, and the next … She swallowed again, struggling to marshal her wayward thoughts. She didn't want to be feeling this right now.

"Would it help if you knew I've never done anything to a woman that she didn't want me to do?" Alek asked.

God, that she could certainly believe. A melting heat pooled in her belly, liquid and deep, and she tensed, fighting the unwelcome response. Damn him for the pictures he was putting in her head. He may have been gorgeous, but his behavior around her was so completely over the top. He really did take sexual aggressiveness to a new level.

"Alek, you don't need to tell me about your ..."

He laughed. "I meant what I said about fulfilling your desires Kat. If you'll let me. So if you want a back rub one night ..."

And here we go with the seduction routine, Kat thought. *Maybe I am getting to know him after all.*

"Umm ... yeah, well if I don't get murdered or kidnapped by the Directorate in the next little while I may keep that in mind." She might have sounded a little sharp, but he was too intense for comfort, and she *did* find him unnerving, whether he was trying to intimidate her or turning on the charm. But if she was being honest with herself, what unnerved her most was her own reaction to him. Not to the Alek who was trying his damnedest to seduce her with his words; to the man she sensed hiding beneath the smart comments and overconfidence.

"You're privileged, Kat. Usually I don't offer. Usually they beg me. And then later, they beg for more." He gave a wicked grin.

Kat didn't smile. She eyed him thoughtfully. "I think you like trying to shock me."

He shrugged in response. "I think you don't want to believe the offer's genuine." There was an edge to his voice, as if she wasn't responding the way he'd hoped she would.

Kat blinked. What offer? What in heck had they been talking about, before ... Oh, that's right, the back rub. If that was really what he had been offering, which she doubted.

"Okay. Whatever." She took refuge in silence, and then realized he was holding his hand out in her direction – like he wanted to shake hands.

"Friends?" he asked, with a spine-melting smile, and at that moment Kat thought she could forgive him anything. A split second later, she realized that the fact he could get that sort of response with one smile was exactly *why* he was trouble with a capital T. She could really do without his lightning-quick changes of mood. They made him very disconcerting to be around. He was a heck of a lot easier to keep at a safe distance – emotionally speaking – when he was being obnoxious. When he was being *nice* he was pretty much irresistible.

She squared her shoulders, and quoted his own words back at him, a challenging glint in her eyes. "*If* the offer's genuine."

He continued to hold his hand out, his eyes warm, and after a moment's hesitation, she reached out to clasp it with her own. It was an attempt at trust, and it felt like the beginning of a new chapter. As strong fingers tightened around hers, a thrill raced through every vein and rendered her arm boneless. She almost swayed where she stood.

This, she thought, *could definitely get complicated.*

*

"Katerina? Katerina? Wake up." The voice was soft, but insistent. A gentle hand shook her shoulder.

Kat blinked, disoriented at having been woken from a sound sleep.

"What …?" she mumbled. Then she sat bolt upright, a testament to her heightened state of nerves.

Akilina was obviously the one who'd shaken her awake. The elder stepped back now to stand next to Della, who held a single candle. In its flickering light, the others were assembled, forming a ring around the bed. Her sleepy mind wondered what they were all doing in her bedroom.

Her eyes traveled to Alek, uncharacteristically grim tonight. Then Amarok, golden eyes glowing with concern, and Corrin, who seemed more tense and alert than he ever was in the kitchen. Finally her eyes came to rest on Anton, who stepped forward, bringing someone with him.

"We have a visitor," he said, his deep voice resonant in the silent room.

Char stepped forward into the candlelight, and Kat's eyes widened in surprise. A moment later this turned into a frown. Char was pale and she looked exhausted.

"Hey." Char's mouth twisted into a half-grimace, half-grin.

"Tell her what you told me," Anton prompted.

Char looked to Akilina for confirmation, and Kat saw Akilina give the smallest of nods. Char turned back to Kat.

"Kat, I have visions sometimes, normally warning me of some sort of threat I'm going to be facing. But just recently I had one … about you and Akilina. Nothing specific, but I believe you're both in danger."

There was silence. Everyone seemed to be waiting for Kat's response – though she didn't really know what to say.

"Um, didn't we know that already?" Kat asked, bewildered that this news – which was hardly news – had warranted a family meeting in the middle of the night.

One of the men gave a crack of laughter, quickly stifled. It sounded suspiciously like Alek.

"I think the Directorate have found some way to follow you here," Char said.

A shiver ran down Kat's spine, and it had nothing to do with the chill of the night air. But, perversely, she found a morsel of comfort in the news. Char had said she was in danger, and danger didn't mean *dead* – otherwise Char would have said "mortal peril" or something. So obviously Char didn't think she was going to die. That was good news, right? She'd come a long way in the last week if she was able to put a positive spin on something like this.

"It doesn't look good." Char shifted uncomfortably. "The Directorate had my club under surveillance after you all left. But they cleared out suddenly about a day ago. I called the guy from the Directorate, Falcon. He said they've got something big going on at the Hema Castus Institute. Some project headed by a guy called Victor Fortes. They're all excited about it ... but unfortunately he doesn't know any details." She looked frustrated. "Still, it's something to go on."

Anton spoke next. "Unfortunately, that is not all, Katerina. I found Charice while I was patroling tonight, and brought her here. But before I saw her I came across something else worrying." He frowned. "A pack of animals. They disappeared into the bushes when I flew overhead, but on my return I asked Miklós to fly out and investigate further."

"Where?" Amarok spoke in a low growl, and Kat realized it must be the first time the rest of the family was hearing this.

"Not close, thankfully," Anton said. "I was doing a sweep of the outlying valleys. Judging by their location, they were working their way in from the nearest road."

"Plenty of rock and mountain between them and us, then," Amarok said. "Good. That will help."

Anton nodded. "Difficult terrain – even for the gifted."

"Tell me about it," Char muttered under her breath.

"What were these animals you saw?" Corrin asked. "Why do you even think they are a threat?"

Anton was silent for a moment. "Instinct, mostly." Frustration marked his face. "I did not see them for long," he said. "They were gone so fast. But I think there was a bobcat ... and a couple of coyotes."

"Together?" Corrin asked disbelievingly.

Anton gave a wry smile. "I found it strange too, to say the least, which is why I asked Miklós to investigate. And we are a little outside the preferred range for either species, so high in the mountains. I know it sounds odd, but I got the distinct impression they were a scouting party."

"And they are not ... like us?"

Anton shook his head emphatically. "They are not of the *unalil*. I am sure of that. Something seemed ... wrong about them."

"It's got to be related in some way to what Falcon mentioned, presumably?" Amarok asked, his voice low and serious. "Some twisted hybrid the Hema Castus Institute have developed?"

Anton sighed. "I had considered that. Again, we have no way of being sure, but it is probably safest to assume the worst. We may know more when Miklós returns."

"So I suppose," Alek broke in, his tone dry, "we can be confident that it wasn't our big-city visitor here who kindly led the pack of wild animals to us. Seeing as, so she tells us, the surveillance at her club was ostentatiously withdrawn right before she headed in our direction."

There was silence. Char's eyes were downcast. Obviously the possibility she might have been followed had occurred to her too.

Alek's blue eyes were icicles as he looked at Char's bent head. "I've no doubt we should be considering it a major achievement that you made it here without getting fried in the noonday sun," he said scornfully. "Lily-white and intact."

"Nice welcome, Alek," Corrin said after an uncomfortable pause.

Alek shrugged. "You were all thinking it."

Char shot a glance at him, her face stricken. "I was careful. I … I'm pretty sure I wasn't followed."

"Guess we'll find out soon enough," Alek said, leading to another awkward pause.

At least I'm not the only fish out of water anymore, Kat thought, listening to this interchange and reading between the lines. Char had been ill at ease from the first moment she'd seen her tonight. Clearly out of her element; a city dweller, without the well-honed instincts all the others relied on to survive out here.

As the other odd one out, Kat had a pretty fair idea how Char was feeling. In an act of solidarity, she broke the uncomfortable silence with a question. "Char, how did *you* know where to find us? Did Anton tell you where we were going before we left?"

"Certainly not." There was a note of gentle reproof in Anton's voice. "That would have placed you at great risk if Charice had been forced to betray the information."

"Charice is linked to me, child," Akilina answered softly. "I am her maker. We can always find each other when we need to." Something in her tone gave Kat to understand that this was something the tiniest child in their culture would have known.

"Oh," Kat said. Some sort of mysterious blood link. Well that wouldn't have occurred to her, now, would it? At moments like this she was keenly aware of what she'd missed out on by not knowing her father – the one who, according to what Char had told her, was supposed to teach her all this stuff.

Amarok cleared his throat, and stepped a little closer to the bed. "Well ... perhaps the threat is not too immediate. Anton only saw a few of them, and they are still a long way off."

"It is worse than that." Miklós's voice came from the doorway, and all eyes turned toward him as he strode into the room. "I did as Anton asked, and there are many more of these creatures than he imagined. I found two packs, each more than twenty strong, at my rough count. While they are still not close, both are headed in this direction."

Miklós came to stand beside Anton, and his eyes were troubled as he glanced down at Kat, still sitting in bed. "I flew back as far as the car you brought Kat in, Anton. It was surrounded by fresh tyre tracks from several large vehicles. That is almost definitely where the incursion of these creatures began. The stench of them was all around the car, particularly strong in the back seat."

Kat's stomach clenched. So these twisted hybrids, these beasts that Anton instinctively felt were in some way *wrong*, had been sniffing around the seat where she'd sat only days ago. The thought made her skin crawl.

"Judging by the smell, several *dimamar* males had also been there," Miklós added.

"The *dimamar* are those who are blood-made of our kind, not true-born," Della explained to Kat quietly.

"It is clear then. They are hunting her." Alek's comment was greeted by a tense silence, as everyone came to terms with this new certainty.

Kat swallowed nervously, and looked up at Anton, hoping to see something in his face that would give her comfort. But he'd turned to Corrin.

"I think it is time for more support out there. A few extra pairs of eyes and ears. Could you go to Saskia and Andreas, explain the situation, and ask for their help?" Anton's voice was grave.

Corrin inclined his head. "Of course." He moved across to Della, and embraced her quickly with a few whispered words before slipping from the room.

Kat shifted, turning toward Della. "Who are Saskia and Andreas?"

"Friends," Della said. "Old friends. Saskia and Andreas and their family are *unalil*, like us. They live some hours away, but they are the closest neighbors of our kind."

Kat wrinkled her brow. "But ... they don't even know me."

Alek gave a savage laugh. "This isn't just about you anymore, Kat. This is an attack on all of us. We *unalil* have little love for the Directorate."

There were murmurs of assent, fearful and angry mutterings.

Anton raised a hand to hush them. "You all understand the need for increased vigilance in light of this confirmed threat. Now, at least, we have a clear idea of what to watch for during our patrols, and which direction they will come from." He reached out to clasp Kat's shoulder, and as always, his touch was warm and comforting.

"Perhaps it would also be helpful ..." Anton broke off, and looked across at Alek with a frown. "Katerina, purely as a precaution, it would be beneficial for you to do some combat training. Some self-defense – and perhaps we could begin to teach you how to channel ambient energy in the *unalil* way, if you show an aptitude."

"Okay," Kat said.

"Anton, is that really necess—" Akilina began.

"Yes," Anton said shortly, cutting her off. "It is."

He turned back to Kat. "Of us all, Alek is most seasoned at combat in a man's form." Anton hesitated. "So if you are willing …"

"Sure," Kat said. She couldn't suppress a fresh quiver of nerves though. Because Anton suggesting combat training could only mean one thing. And that Alek had been chosen to teach her; well, that was just her luck. Particularly since she was pretty sure she was going to make a complete fool of herself.

Anton's eyes traveled across her face, reading her uncertainty, her fear.

"You need not be concerned, Katerina – we will all protect you."

But despite the poor light cast by the flickering candle, Anton was close enough for her to see him clearly. He looked very worried.

Chapter 39

Alek chose a flat area behind the house for their evening lesson, sparsely covered with coarse grass, and surrounded by rocks. Somewhere out in the darkness, several of the others were out on patrol. Anton wasn't taking any chances, given the immediacy of the danger.

Alek stood opposite her, a step away in the moonlight. "We could start with theory, or ..." he spread his hands, "you could show me what you've got."

The look on his face as he said it, his calm arrogance and clear assumption of superiority ... well, it got in her throat. It really did. She wanted him to take her seriously. She wanted to wipe that look off his face.

Kat tilted her chin at him combatively. "I have two brothers," she said. "I'm not totally useless. I can fight."

Alek grinned, and crooked his finger at her. "Come."

So Kat gave him everything she had, letting the blows rain down on his chest, his upper arms. She even aimed one at his chin, but he easily turned his head away at the last instant, and she swung into empty air.

A moment later, though, when she realized he wasn't blocking, wasn't defending himself at all, she stopped and stepped back, rubbing her sore fists.

Alek just stood there smiling at her.

"You didn't feel that at all?"

"It was like a gentle massage," Alek said. "Kind of tickled."

"Great. So I have a future career as a masseuse."

Alek raised a brow, and gave a small shrug. "It's a starting point."

Kat shook her head, annoyed at her own ineffectiveness. Frustrated by Alek's amusement. She could see it all over his face.

"I'm not laughing at you," he said. "You did pretty well, but you're fighting like a human."

"How else should I be fighting?" Kat demanded.

"You have great strength in you," Alek said quietly. "Hidden in your core. Any physical exercise is based more on mental discipline, the discipline to tap into the strength within and draw from the energy around you, than on raw physical prowess."

"So I'm mentally undisciplined." There was a sarcastic edge to her reversal of his words.

Alek ignored it. "Yes," he said, "but only because you have no training. We're about to change that."

He turned to face out into the night, and then swung back to face her, arms straight by his sides, fists clenched. "Imagine energy is flowing through our bodies all the time. From the air around us, from the earth beneath our feet. But in your case, it's flowing straight through you, unchanneled ..." he opened his hands, let his fingers spread wide, "and dissipating."

"All right." She was willing to play "let's suppose" for a minute. What Alek was saying sounded pretty strange. Kind of a repeat of Della's explanation of how the *unalil*'s shape-changing ability worked. But strange or not, she couldn't discount all the incredible stuff she'd seen with her own eyes. If figuring out how this channeling stuff worked meant she could set candles blazing from across the room like the others could, she was willing to put in the effort, because that was a pretty cool trick.

"Your aim is to identify the flow of energy through you. Call on your inner strength to harness it. Hold it, and let it build within you, then when you are ready, channel it outward. Think you can do that?"

Kat shook her head mutely.

Alek sighed. "This is a crucial skill. Essential for anything requiring physical strength, but also for defending, for shielding yourself."

"So it's not about being strong, but about being a good conduit?"

"Exactly," Alek said.

Great. So at least she'd earned her gold star for logical extrapolation. "But it's just words." Kat knew she sounded defeated. "I don't have the first idea how to start doing what you just described."

Alek gave her a sharp look. "This is no time for self-pity, Kat. Trouble is coming, and you have to be ready."

Was that his idea of a pep talk? She wasn't feeling sorry for herself, she was just feeling a little … overwhelmed. Which was completely different and, as far as she was concerned, totally justifiable.

"Just give it a try." Alek took a step back, and beckoned impatiently. "Again."

Kat rushed at him, but if anything her flailing fists were even less effective this time, as her heart really wasn't in the attack. Knowing that the best punches you could muster barely tickled your opponent wasn't exactly confidence-inspiring.

Alek waved her away after a moment, and grinned. "Oh boy. This is why I didn't want to start with the theory. Once you've actually felt it, you won't ever forget."

He gestured to a rock a few yards away, one that formed a natural seat. "Okay, let's take a different approach."

Kat walked over and sat down. Alek didn't sit, though, but went around behind her and she craned her neck to see what he was doing.

"Relax." His breath tickled her ear, and his hands were a warm weight on her shoulders. "Your tension is blocking you, making it hard for you to look within yourself with the awareness we need for this exercise."

She was tense. How surprising. And it was *completely* unrelated to the fact that this "friends" thing they were supposed to be trying was not working. Not for her. The slightest touch from Alek had her reacting in a way that was more than just friendly, and she was positive he knew it.

She shifted beneath his hands. "You touching me isn't really helping me relax."

Alek gave a warm chuckle.

Yeah, clearly he knew *exactly* what he was doing. And he was enjoying this far too much.

"Close your eyes," he said. "Concentrate on my hands."

That wouldn't be hard. She couldn't think about anything else anyway. She did close her eyes though, and the night faded away as her focus shifted entirely to the warmth of the hands touching her, their firm weight bearing down on her shoulders.

And then ... it was hard to explain, as it was like nothing Kat had ever felt before. It was as if Alek started drawing energy through her, waves of it, passing from her legs where they touched the stone she sat on, through her torso to her shoulders and head. Waves of tingling warmth, leaving boneless relaxation in their wake.

After a few moments of this, Kat's head lolled sideways to rest against Alek's forearm. "Who needs massage when you can do whatever that is." Her voice came out on the husky side.

"Concentrate," Alek admonished softly. She could feel his breath on her hair, and then he spoke, a warm whisper in her ear, sending shivers through her body. "Akilina would like to wrap you in cotton wool to protect you from the world," he said, "but you're stronger than that."

Slowly, subtly, the sensation changed, as if the wave of energy flowing through her had spent itself, and was ebbing to a finish, and at almost the same moment that the flow finally stopped, it turned and began to run the other way, at first a harmless trickle of energy flowing into her, then a rising tide pressing down on her, and still it built and grew until a tsunami was drowning her, engulfing her.

She lashed out with a cry, thrusting that bruising force away so she could breathe again. And then she opened her eyes.

Alek was picking himself up from the ground ten feet away. His nose was bleeding, but his expression was amused.

He sauntered over to her. "Tell me again that you don't know how to channel your energy outward." His lips curled in a slow smile. "Or maybe you'd prefer to tell me I'm the best teacher you've ever had."

Kat jumped to her feet as he stopped in front of her, her eyes drawn to the trickle of blood running down to his upper lip. "I didn't mean to hurt you."

"Oh, you didn't." A careless grin, as he wiped the blood from his face. "This, from the girl who was pummeling me with her fists a minute or two ago."

He had a point, but seeing him bleed had been enough to kill any desire to prove how tough she was. She looked at him broodingly for a moment, taking in his smug self-satisfaction.

"You wanted that to happen!" She couldn't keep the accusatory note from her voice.

Alek shrugged. "You learned something, didn't you?" His eyes locked on to hers. "The first sensation you felt was the energy you normally have running through you, unnoticed and unchecked. I just amplified it slightly so you could feel it. And the second, that was a little demonstration of what's possible when you actually channel that energy."

"But I don't know what I did." Kat frowned. "I don't think I can do it again."

"When you need it, you'll know." Alek sounded utterly confident that his lesson had had the desired outcome. That she'd assimilated this new skill, even though she didn't understand the first thing about it.

She wished she shared his certainty.

*

Kat rolled over in bed yet again, wriggling her toes, and even rubbing her feet together to try to create some heat. Cold weather often lingered well into May here in the mountains, and today, the temperature had dropped soon after nightfall. Though it'd been warm enough in front of the fire downstairs earlier in the evening, it was freezing in her bedroom. This wasn't the sort of place where the beds were equipped with electric blankets, unfortunately, so she'd been lying awake for quite a while, mentally cursing the cold.

Her mind replayed the impromptu conference that had happened right here in her room the night before. What Anton had reported seeing was unsettling. Knowing there was a group of creatures out there after her blood had her wound very tight, a cold ball of fear coiled deep in her gut.

And then there was the news Corrin had brought when he arrived home earlier this evening. He'd smiled when he saw her in the kitchen, but he and Anton had gone into a huddle soon afterward, talking in subdued voices. They'd both looked grim.

After the men had left the room, Kat asked Della what was going on, and watched how Della's eyes flew to the door the others had just left through with a guilty expression.

"Did Corrin manage to get in touch with your *unalil* friends?" Kat asked. She didn't like making Della uncomfortable, but she felt within her rights to press for an answer since they'd all been placed on high alert last night in her presence.

"No." Della picked at some invisible spot on the edge of the kitchen bench for a long moment, and then looked up at Kat with a sigh. "That's what he was telling Anton." She looked toward the door again, and when nobody came through it, she spoke hurriedly. "It looks like nobody has been living in their house for months – but all their belongings are still there. Corrin believes they may have met with foul play, and Anton agrees."

Kat pushed away the memory of Della's concerned face with an effort, and rolled onto her back. She gave a frustrated sigh. Too many thoughts running through her head. It was no wonder she couldn't sleep. She'd probably be lying awake all night. She could almost see the hours spreading out endlessly in front of her. Thinking about not sleeping was always worse than not sleeping.

A noise from the window caught her attention, and she tensed. Was it just the whistling of the wind? Even the slightest of sounds was amplified by the silence of the room and her overactive imagination. But it was stupid to worry with two of the best protectors a girl could hope for nearby in the dark somewhere, with animal-honed senses to watch and listen for even the slightest sign of trouble.

Then it came again. A faint squeak. Metal hinges. Definitely the window, being slid open inch by inch behind the thick curtains. She gulped in a breath and held it, lying silent and tense in the big bed. The curtain was pushed aside, and for an instant the dark shape of a giant cat was silhouetted against the window. There was a soft thud as cushioned paws hit the floor of her room.

"Who's there?" Despite the sudden lurch in her stomach, she was perversely happy to note that her voice didn't shake at all. She didn't *sound* afraid, whatever that counted for.

She couldn't see a thing as she lay there, poised to jump out of the bed, but after a moment, the reply came from out of the darkness.

"It's me – Alek."

Soft footsteps padded across the room as he came toward her. "I could hear you tossing and turning from outside."

"So you thought it'd make me feel *more* comfortable if you came through my window uninvited?" Kat said, more than usually disgruntled because of the scare he'd given her. "I thought you had to ask my permission to enter or something."

He paused, and gave a low ripple of laughter. "Sounds like you've been watching too many movies. And how would that work here? You're in *our* house, after all. You walked into the lion's den with your eyes wide open."

"Well it would still be polite to ask," she said, annoyed. "It's called good manners – not something you seem to have heard of."

He chuckled, not at all put off by her grumpiness, and continued toward her, sounding perfectly sure-footed in the darkness.

Something suddenly occurred to her. If he'd just changed form, then that meant ... "And I think you should go and put some clothes on."

"Don't worry, I'm not cold."

Obviously, as far as *he* was concerned, nudity was the most natural and normal thing in the world, and maybe she would have thought so too under specific circumstances ... Say, if you were getting a full-body spray-tan, or a remedial massage. But not when the weather was arctic, or when the person in question was an uninvited adult male in your room at night.

"So why can't you sleep, Kat? Are you finally becoming nocturnal?"

"No!" Kat said crossly. She didn't want to mention her fears to Alek, as if giving voice to them would make them more real. "I guess I'm used to central heating. Actually, I'm a bit cold." By rights, he should be too, prancing around naked in an unheated room with a bare wooden floor.

She couldn't see his grin in the darkness but she could sense it was there.

"You won't have any trouble with the cold after you change," he observed.

"*If* I change."

He laughed, and the sound filled the dark room. "Wait here, little icicle. I'll get something to warm you."

He disappeared into the darkness, moving so silently that she couldn't tell whether he'd gone back out through the window or left through the bedroom door. Moments later he was back, and something heavy and incredibly soft was being spread over her.

"What *is* this?" she wondered out loud. "I've never felt anything like it."

"Sable," Alek replied.

"Real fur?" Kat was horrified for a moment.

Alek chuckled. "Yes, real fur – but don't worry, it was made using furs from animals that didn't need them anymore."

"Oh." Kat was silent for a moment, digesting this. "Where did you just go to get it?"

"My room – it's from my bed."

She really didn't want to engage with the idea of Alek's bed right now. "Well, thank you," she said a bit abruptly. "I hope you got dressed while you were there too."

"Yup. Covered from neck to ankle. Just to satisfy your prudish sensibilities."

Kat didn't dignify that with a response. In the darkness she had no idea whether he was telling the truth anyway.

"This rug is wonderful," she ventured after a pause, "though my feet are still cold."

"I can fix that."

The covers lifted, and a warm male body slipped in behind her.

"What are you doing?" Kat jerked away from him until she was on the other side of the bed.

He followed her. "You mean that wasn't an invitation?" His voice was a low purr, and she could feel the heat of his breath against the side of her face.

"Alek, I don't want you in my bed – fully dressed or ... or any other way." She was sure she sounded strangled, and a little breathless. The way she felt. He was warm, he was sexy … he was too damned close.

"Where *do* you want me then? Fully dressed or any other way?"

How he managed to sound suggestive and mocking at the same time she didn't know. Images flooded unbidden into her mind, and she firmly quashed them. Messy, messy, messy. She didn't *do* casual flings.

"Don't be ridiculous. I don't *want* you anywhere at all. And you know this whole seduction thing you've got going doesn't do anything for me," she added.

Liar, liar.

"What does then?" The words could have been suggestive, but his interest seemed genuine.

Kat sighed. She knew she'd probably be calling herself ten kinds of idiot tomorrow, but she was sure that letting things go in the direction Alek wanted to take them was a really bad idea. He was too intense, just … too much for her to handle right now.

Pity the irrational part of her didn't quite agree. The part that was like a foolish moth drawn to a very dangerous flame. If *that* half won, she'd probably be finding something creative to do with all that body heat of his.

Not worrying about what's out there searching for me in the darkness.

Kat shivered.

"You did say 'friends,' remember? How about we try that? Now get out. Please."

In a quick move, his arms came around her and pulled her toward him, and away from the edge of the bed.

"Hey!" she squealed.

"Calm down. You were about to fall out of the damned bed." For a brief moment he held her securely against him, the length of his body touching hers, searing her with his heat. Then he was gone from the bed, and the blankets settled back around her, sealing her in a warm cocoon.

Kat gave the tiniest of sighs, not much more than a gentle exhalation. This was for the best. It really was. But the bed felt very empty all of a sudden.

"Are you still there?" she asked after a long pause.

"Mmm," came Alek's reply out of the darkness near the window.

Another long moment passed. "Aren't you supposed to be keeping watch, anyway?" she said drowsily.

"Miklós and Anton are patrolling. You're quite safe."

"So you didn't see anything out there tonight?" She found herself needing the extra reassurance, and couldn't quite keep the apprehension from her voice.

"Nothing. Try and get some sleep."

She felt safer having him close by. A personal guard to ward off unseen dangers out there in the dark night. Close, but not too close, because when he was invading her space his presence was anything but calming.

"I'm *not* a prude," she mumbled sleepily after a while, her response still faintly indignant despite the delay in her making it.

A low chuckle was the only reply.

That was the last sound she remembered before sleep overtook her, and her dreams were turbulent. She was running, running along never-ending corridors, and in and out of windowless rooms, in a subterranean network without end. And all the while, she heard a woman sobbing, pleading, calling to her. The woman's voice echoed through the corridors, but no matter which way Kat turned, no matter how fast she ran, she could never find her.

When she woke, early morning sunlight was streaming in through the window where the curtains had been hooked back on both sides. The air of the room was still cold against her face, but she was snug beneath the covers, with Alek's huge sable rug tucked in around her. But her night-time visitor was long gone.

Chapter 40

"Are you ready?" Miklós's voice was courteous as he held Kat's door open for her.

Kat nodded, blew the two candles out, and walked out of the dark room. She had someone guarding her day and night right now, and she wasn't sure she liked it. Anton had also asked her to stay inside whenever possible, and as if that wasn't bad enough, she had to do without sunlight in her own room too, to make sure whoever was guarding her wouldn't be inadvertently put at risk.

Right now it was time for the one exception she'd begged Anton to allow – her visit to the bathhouse. This one trip she was allowed to make outside the house was a bit like being on day leave from prison … except in this case her "jailers" were trying to keep her alive.

Ever since this latest threat, they'd been so careful and gentle around her. If she were being absolutely honest, she'd say they were solicitous to the point of annoyingly overprotective. It was driving her a little crazy. But though she might not have wanted someone watching her or outside her door every minute of the day and night, she was certainly grateful they were all putting their own safety on the line to protect hers.

Amarok was out there somewhere right now, patrolling, and Miklós had also been out already and scouted around to make sure the coast was clear. Now he was waiting patiently to escort her to the bathhouse.

She was guiltily aware of what she'd thought about him at the beginning. Miklós was one of the *unalil* she'd found most unwelcoming, but she seemed to have broken through whatever barrier had been between them. Now, she would actually say that she liked him. She liked all of them.

Amarok, though, gave reserve a whole new meaning. Since the council meeting he'd barely spoken two words to her. If she actually caught his eye he'd smile – but generally, he seemed to make sure that wherever she was, he wasn't. That meant he was the only one she really hadn't gotten to know. But she still had the odd instinct that she already knew him, that she could *trust* him.

"Are you ready?" Miklós asked again, patiently. Kat realized she had stopped in the doorway to her room.

"Sorry, I guess I was daydreaming." She smiled at Miklós as she moved on past him, and watched as he shut the door behind her. Suddenly, a chill of foreboding went through her, and she swayed where she stood.

"Are you all right? You look a little pale." Miklós's concern was obvious.

"It's nothing. I'm fine."

Kat mustered a smile and followed Miklós down the dark internal corridor. She paused at the top of the stairs, overcome by a strange tension. She was suddenly reluctant to go down the stairs. Frowning, she made herself follow Miklós as he led the way. There couldn't possibly be anything to worry about when he'd just preceded her.

She slowed her steps slightly and let him go out of sight around the corner as they neared the bottom. Whether or not *they* cared about privacy, if she knew in advance someone was going to change she was happier giving them some space.

Kat stepped over Miklós's discarded robe at the bottom of the stairs, and emerged into the sunlit hallway just as Miklós swooped out the door, a beautiful peregrine in flight. Besides that, nothing. Absolutely nothing out of place, nothing strange or unexpected. She tried to shake off the odd feeling, but it lingered.

She walked through the door, overcome with apprehension about what she might find waiting for her outside, but again … nothing. Nothing but the dull drone of insects and the whisper of the wind.

Miklós flew overhead as she walked to the bathhouse. She wondered if he realized she was moving slowly because she was scanning every rock along the path, examining every grassy lump she passed by, in case it concealed something it shouldn't have.

As she reached the bathhouse, the wind stopped, and the stillness of the afternoon seemed suddenly oppressive. Kat hurried inside with a sigh of relief. She was completely overreacting to all this. It was ridiculous. With both Amarok and Miklós keeping watch, there was absolutely nothing to worry about.

She turned around in the dimly lit antechamber to find Miklós shrugging into another robe.

"Miklós, ah, would it be okay if you waited out here?"

He raised a brow. "Certainly." He moved to poke his head into the main room and light all the candles for her, taking a moment to cast a glance around the large room. The skylight dome had been covered since this new permanent-guard regime of Anton's had come into effect, and Kat sighed, resigning herself to a bath by candlelight even while the afternoon sun was shining brightly outside. If Miklós noticed her sigh, he didn't say anything.

"Thanks," she said.

He smiled, and took a seat on a bench against the wall. "Take your time." He closed his eyes.

Kat moved inside, and though Miklós had just checked it, her niggling sense of unease made her glance around again, just to be doubly sure the room was empty. Of course, it was. Nothing but four walls, and the warm, welcoming bath set into the middle of the floor.

She took her clothes off, folding them and leaving them in a neat pile on the floor, preferring that to undressing in the ante-chamber where Miklós was. She looked around the candlelit room. It could be considered romantic, she supposed, but given what she was imagining in every shadow right now, she found it a bit creepy.

She gave a shiver, and hurried to immerse herself in the steaming water, as if, like a protective blanket, it would shield her from harm. Washing quickly, she sank deeper until the water covered her breasts and lapped against her collarbones, and rested her head against the edge of the bath with a sigh.

All this nervous energy was getting to her. Like today, seeing shadows in every corner and danger around every turn. Imagining being attacked every five seconds just wasn't healthy.

Finally, immersed in the warm water, she began to relax and think more calmly.

The threat to her could have been exaggerated, right? For all she knew, Char's non-specific "vision" had been brought on by stress. As for Anton ... well, maybe his instinct about the creatures he'd seen was as unreliable as hers was. She'd had a completely weird feeling about coming downstairs today, and there had been abso-lutely nothing there.

The hard edge of the bath was digging into her head a little, and she moved to compensate.

I need a bath cushion. The mundane thought made her smile, and she closed her eyes. Her sleep had been fragmented the past few nights, and she was starting to feel the effects.

Despite the hardness of the stone edge against the back of her head she must have drifted off to sleep for a brief moment, because she woke with a start to what sounded like a cascade of droplets pouring into the bath. Except Kat hadn't moved a muscle.

Not two steps in front of her a man stood in the middle of the bath, his clothes in tatters. Tangled fair hair clung wetly to his cheeks and neck as water streamed off him.

Kat drew in her breath in a gasp.

Every inch of his skin was horribly marked, disfigured by welts and swollen, blistering flesh.

He stepped toward her, red-lidded eyes focused with ravenous intensity on her bare neck and chest. His mouth opened in a snarl of savage pleasure, and pointed teeth lengthened as they were bared for attack.

She scrambled backward, away from him, onto the cold stone. She tried to cry out, tried to scream for help, but her traitorous throat clenched shut, and her scream came out as a strangled dry rasp.

With a guttural growl he was on her, his fingertips sinking deep into the flesh of her upper arms in a bruising grip. Too fast for escape, and though she struggled to tear herself away, struggled to remember anything, even a fraction of what Alek had taught her, the knowledge eluded her. He was much too strong to break away from, but she kept straining against him with all her might, her breath catching as a sob finally escaped her lips and tears of helpless frustration welled up in her eyes.

In that moment the stakes became crystal clear to her, and she knew that despite all her thoughts about the threat facing her, she wasn't prepared for this moment. She didn't want to die. Not yet, not here, not like this.

I'm going to be murdered in the bath after all, she thought dully. *No headlines*. Inexplicably, that made her sad. It was her last conscious thought before he struck.

Chapter 41

Kat's mind flickered slowly back to consciousness. She was in the antechamber of the bathhouse, wrapped in a robe, and being cradled gently in Amarok's arms. Her neck was stinging, and she felt completely drained, too groggy and light-headed to comprehend that she had indeed been drained, quite literally.

Amarok was crying, his tears warm and wet on her face. She felt bad about that. It didn't seem to her that he knew her well enough to cry for her. She wanted to say something, but neither her mind nor her voice would cooperate in forming words to soothe him. She tried to move but whatever part of her body usually made that happen wasn't working either.

Then others arrived to cluster around them, hands comforting her with gentle touches. Della and Corrin were first. Della was aghast, and buried her face in Corrin's chest, clutching his robe while he stroked her hair.

Miklós arrived next, bringing Alek with him. As Miklós donned a robe Alek stalked over to her and surveyed her with angry, dispassionate eyes. He bared his teeth.

"Where is he?" he snarled.

Miklós jerked his head at the door leading into the main room. "Still in there, cowering in a corner. Seems he has realized he would have to go through sunlight to escape. He does not appear to favor that idea."

"I'm going to kill him," Alek growled as he sprang toward the door.

Miklós was faster, and blocked his way. "No! Wait for Anton. We don't even know who he is. We have to question him."

It seemed, for a moment, that Alek would fight his way past. Then he subsided, and began to pace back and forth, putting on the robe Corrin handed him with an impatient shrug.

Della gave a sob, and spoke in a near-whisper. "This is awful, I can hardly bear to look at her. So pale and still. Is there anything we can do for her?"

Alek stopped pacing suddenly, and spun around. "Couldn't we feed her? Our blood holds our strength and ability to heal, and we know it works the same way on humans too."

Miklós moved over to Kat, face grim. "It can't hurt." He touched a finger to her cold cheek. "It might be the only thing which can save her now … if we are not too late."

Anton strode into the tight circle surrounding Kat, Akilina just behind him. He dropped to his knees beside her and stared into her face intently, one hand on her cheek while the other rested on Amarok's shoulder.

"She is definitely alive in there somewhere," he said, after a long pause. "I am sure of it." He looked to Akilina. "What do you think? Your blood is the purest, the strongest. You would be the best choice."

Akilina studied Kat, her brow creased in worry. She nodded once. "I can certainly try." She began to roll her trailing sleeve, baring her wrist.

"Wait!" Della stepped forward, her face twisted into an odd expression, between hope and worry. "Perhaps we should consider first … I mean, what will this do to her?"

Akilina looked up, her face pale and set. "Truthfully, we cannot be sure. I have read everything I can find and there is almost no information on those like Katerina, who are half human. A human who had lost so much blood would need to ingest a great deal of ours to have a chance of recovery, and it would certainly provoke their change." She sighed toward Kat's lifeless figure. "That is, if they survived."

"We know that," Alek said impatiently. "Most of us made our change under similar conditions."

"But Katerina is halfway to being one of us already," Anton pointed out quietly.

Akilina nodded. "In a way, yes, and we have not ascertained what, exactly, will bring about her full transition. Perhaps my blood will precipitate it, or perhaps it will have no effect other than to heal. I do not believe it will harm her. If we fail to act, though, she will very likely die."

"I think being one of us is a heck of a lot better than being dead," Alek growled. "If the princess is willing to feed her, I say we stop talking about it and let her get on with it."

Della bit her lip, then nodded and stepped back. One by one, the others all nodded too, and Anton moved aside to let Akilina take his place, kneeling next to Kat.

"Turn her head a little this way," she said to Amarok softly. And then she brought her wrist to her lips, and broke the skin.

Kat felt rather than tasted the first flow of warm blood that entered her mouth and trickled down her throat. A sweet lassitude flowed through her, followed by a hot surge of energy. And then she could taste it, taste starry constellations, history and power and flowers in fresh earth. Her hands, which had lain lifeless by her sides a bare moment before, rose suddenly to hold Akilina's wrist in place with an iron grip, acting on deeply buried instinct. Her eyes fluttered closed, and she continued to take swallow after swallow of the life-giving liquid that made every cell hum and every sense sing.

Function returned to her brain slowly, and the words that floated to the surface first were far from lyrical. *Why on earth*, she thought, *did I ever waste my time on steak tartare?* And then she drifted off into a bliss-state where words didn't matter at all.

*

"Sunset," Anton said softly. "Finally. Should we move her to the house now?"

Kat knew she was being lifted in someone's arms, but the sensation was one of utter weightlessness, like she was floating.

"Are you still okay, Rok? Do you want someone else to take her now?"

She opened her eyes in time to see an emphatic shake of Amarok's dark head, and then she was carried swiftly along the promontory path to the house.

Soft voices spoke nearby as she was settled gently into her bed.

"Anton, are you sure you will not reconsider letting Charice see her? She is imagining the worst." The pleading note in Akilina's voice was unfamiliar.

Anton sighed. "I am sorry, but it is out of the question with things so fraught. She will have her chance to explain later, but right now Alek, for one, is dangerously close to the edge of control, and we have him on a short enough leash as it is."

Then the voices faded away, and the door closed with a soft click. Kat turned her head to the side, dreamily aware that the room was ablaze with candlelight, with dozens on every available surface. The sweet scent of beeswax hung in the air.

Her eyes met Della's, and a moment later, Della reached for her hand, stroking it with cool fingers.

"Katerina? Can you hear me now?"

Kat nodded, and smiled. She felt utterly relaxed and at peace.

"Thank goodness. You have been drifting in and out for a couple of hours." Della pressed her hand gently. "Is there something you would like? Something to eat or drink, perhaps, if you feel well enough? Or anything else?"

"No, I ... I'm not hungry." She *was* sleepy, though she was pretty sure she'd done nothing but sleep for the last few hours. What she couldn't really remember was why.

"If you change your mind, just ask." Della smiled tenderly, and then looked over Kat's head to the person sitting beside the bed on the opposite side.

"Rok, are you okay?" she asked, a wealth of meaning in her tone.

Kat turned her head to see Amarok sitting on a chair against the wall. He was in shadows, set back from where she was propped up on dozens of soft pillows. It seemed odd to her that he had been chosen to sit at her bedside when she barely knew him. He nodded silently.

"Well, try and get some rest then, Kat. Rok is right here. Call if you need anything," Della said, addressing the last comment to both of them equally, then she left the room quietly.

Chapter 42

Downstairs, Alek was pacing the length of the hallway, again and again, his cougar ever-present and threatening to break free.

Anton moved over to him, and placed a hand on his arm. "Miklós and Corrin are bringing him now. Do you want to leave?"

Alek shook his head, and turned toward the door with a snarl, watching silently with glowing eyes as a bedraggled fair-haired man was hustled inside and through to the family council room between Corrin and Miklós. That was him. The bastard who'd attacked Kat. Alek clenched his fists, as fury burned white hot within him, hungry for an outlet. He wanted to slash, and tear, and maim.

The man was almost a head shorter than the two who flanked him, and much slimmer. His head was lowered as he walked, and he let them direct his steps, not seeming to care where he was led. He was smaller than Alek had expected. Any one of them could have pulverized him before he'd laid a finger on her, if only they'd been there. The thought of Kat, alone and in need, sent him to a very dark place.

Alek tracked the man with his eyes until he went through the doors and out of sight. Anton kept his hand on Alek's arm the whole time, both a restraint and a calming touch.

"So, are we going to do this?" Alek ground out.

Anton sighed. "Yes, I suppose we must."

"Don't sound so unwilling," Alek growled, as they moved together toward the open double doors. "I, for one, will *enjoy* tearing the little rat apart as soon as you've done your questioning."

Inside, the whole family was assembled with the exception of Amarok. Miklós and Corrin still flanked their prisoner, who slumped miserably, his pale hair sticking out in all directions, gray eyes fixed on the floor. Akilina hovered near the door, until Anton nodded to her. "You can go and get her now."

Akilina soon re-entered with Char, who looked pale and tense. Her eyes flashed around the room as soon as she entered, as if seeking out the source of the current trouble she was embroiled in. When she saw the man seated between Corrin and Miklós, she seemed confused at first.

"What are *you* doing here?" she asked. Then, as she took in the fact that the men flanking him each had a heavy hand resting on his shoulder, her expression became incredulous. "Jon? It was *you*? But why?"

Jonathan shrank into his chair. He looked up at Char, his gray eyes pools of anguish. "I couldn't resist, I swear I couldn't. You know I've always found it hard. I wanted to stop, but ..." He faltered, and dropped his head into his hands.

Alek leaped across the table with a growl, and grabbed Jonathan by the throat, dragging him out of his seat. "You think we don't all feel it? That we don't think about it every minute we're with her? The only difference is, *we* have willpower, you spineless little maggot."

Jonathan began to choke as Alek's hand constricted his windpipe.

"No!" Char cried.

Alek turned to her with a growl, without releasing his grip. He was quite willing to strangle the little bastard, right here and now. "No? Who is he to you?"

"No," Char said again, more softly, an expression of heartbreaking sadness twisting her face. "If you decide he must die, then I must do it."

"Charice?" Akilina turned to face her, comprehension dawning in her eyes. "No, he cannot be ..."

"He's mine," Char said, her voice firming. Her chin went up. "He must have followed me here. I am his maker, so I share the blame for his transgressions. I bear responsibility for his life ... and his death."

Alek dropped Jonathan back into the chair with a thud. He leaped from the table and prowled over to stand in front of Char. So she wanted to share the blame? That was fine with him.

"If he followed you, you have put us all at risk," he snarled.

"Oh, my little one," Akilina said brokenly, searching Char's face for a reason. "Why did you not tell me?"

Alek watched Char scan the faces around the table. Some were judgmental, most serious, and one or two just seemed disappointed.

"Well," she said, "you can all worry about what to do with both of us later. There are more important things to worry about right now, like the fact that Kat is still in danger. I had another vision."

If she hadn't had everyone's full focus before, she had it now.

"You are quite sure?" Anton asked, his eyes intent on her.

Char nodded. "Unfortunately, I've never been more certain of anything," she said grimly. "It wasn't over with Jon."

Alek swore aloud. This just kept getting better. "Ironic that you came here to warn us ... and the only danger is the one you brought with you."

"That's not true, Alek." Anton's voice was quiet. Reasonable. "The Directorate clearly have their own way of tracking us, and they were hunting Kat before Char arrived."

Miklós rose from his seat to stand by Alek's side.

"We know what the threat is," Miklós said. "I say we go hunting for this pack Anton saw."

Alek kept his eyes on Char. "I still think we should decide what to do about this other matter first. There's no point half of us leaving on a hunting mission when there's a known *enemy* at home."

Char met his eyes this time, and shrugged defiantly, as if to say "Do your worst." Oddly, this took the edge off his mood, and though he continued to glower at her broodingly, he didn't say anything else.

"We all want to blame someone," Della broke in, "you most of all, Alek. But I truly do not believe Charice *meant* to bring danger to us, or to Katerina."

"I didn't," Char said clearly. "I admit my fault, but I swear my offense was unintentional."

Murmured discussion broke out around the table, and after a few moments of this, Anton cut in.

"Assuming we accept you were innocent of bad intention, Charice, what do you propose we do with *him*?"

All eyes turned toward Jonathan, who lifted his head at last, eyes glittering with a feverish brightness. "I know I deserve to die for what I have done. But I want to make it right."

"What do you propose?" Anton asked.

"This pack of animals you were talking about – they attacked me." Jonathan shuddered. "They're a hundred times more dangerous than I will ever be. If you want to hunt them, I can help you find them."

Chapter 43

Kat turned her head quickly when Akilina and Anton entered her room. She struggled to sit upright, but her body didn't seem to be cooperating. What was wrong with her?

"How are you feeling?" Akilina asked.

Kat gave a tired smile. "A bit strange." She looked across at Amarok, still keeping his vigil beside her bed.

Akilina moved closer. "You are very pale." She frowned. "Your pulse remains irregular."

"Yes. I think it must be a flu or something." Kat collapsed against the pillows again. The effort of supporting herself was too much. Her eyes fluttered closed.

She heard Akilina ask Amarok a soft question.

"She has been like this the whole time," he said, voice tense. "Drifting in and out. She doesn't seem to have any idea what happened."

Kat felt a hand press lightly against the inside of her forearm, and then heard Anton's voice. "She is barely here. I am surprised she was able to talk to us a moment ago."

I am here, she wanted to say, but her lips wouldn't form the words. Just too ... tired.

Akilina spoke then. "I do not understand it. There is such

strength in her, and she took a great deal of my blood earlier. Yet she is clearly failing." She sounded frustrated. Helpless.

Kat felt like she was floating by them all on a fluffy cloud. No need to worry. No, no need to worry. All good here. She wanted to giggle, but it didn't seem appropriate. There was something dark, though, a shadow in the corner of her mind, but she couldn't quite …

She drifted off into a dream, and she was back in the place with the endless, empty corridors and locked doors, deep beneath the ground. A woman was calling her, and her feet traced out a path, following the beckoning call around corners and through doors, deeper into the maze, until finally she found her.

The woman with the tangled hair and golden eyes was sitting cross-legged on the concrete floor of a bare cell. *Amber*. Her dreaming subconscious supplied the name. *Amber*.

When Amber saw Kat, her pale face creased into a frown.

"Not yet," she said softly, "but soon."

And then Kat dreamed of the bathhouse, and the dark shadow was back, and she felt cold stone at her back, and a gut-clenching fear, and she couldn't escape him. Couldn't get away …

Kat blinked her eyes open to find herself lying in bed, in her room full of candles, with Akilina and Anton bending over her. The two of them exchanged glances. Akilina reached out and took Kat's hand.

"Katerina? You do not have the flu. Do you remember anything about what happened today?"

Kat smiled mistily. "I've been having the strangest dreams. Scary ones. I was having a bath, and …" She hesitated, and a shadow passed across her face.

Frowning, she turned to Amarok. "I remember Amarok carrying me." She paused uncertainly. "But I don't know why." She continued to gaze at him, searching those dark gold eyes. "You were crying!" she said in wonder, and tears filled her own eyes at the memory. After a moment, she blinked, and turned to stare at the far wall, where the many flickering candles made complicated patterns of light and shadow.

She heard Anton speaking softly to Amarok. "Miklós and Alek have already left, and you can join them, if you are willing to leave Katerina in our care now."

She felt Amarok's presence behind her, and a hand on her shoulder, and then he was gone.

Kat rolled back over a little later, and found herself alone with Akilina. The elder was still holding her hand.

"I think I drank your blood," Kat said candidly. "Unless I dreamed that too."

"Katerina, you were attacked," Akilina said gently. "You lost a large amount of blood. We … well, we thought you might not survive. Offering you my blood was our only hope."

"I know." Kat looked up at her trustingly. "I don't mind. But I wonder, will I … will I change now? How does it work?"

"I do not know, child," Akilina said. "For a human, ingesting our blood after they have been drained of their own brings them closer to becoming one of us – that is, if they drink enough and are strong enough to survive the change. But for you … what we are has always been within you. Whatever happens now, we have to believe that things are as they must be."

"Yes, I suppose we do have to," Kat said. Her eyes blinked shut for a long moment, and it was an effort to open them again. She felt exhausted.

Worry creased Akilina's smooth brow. "You are still weak," she said carefully. "I think perhaps you should feed again. Would you like to?"

Was she ready to deal with this? Kat found the question oddly confronting, and she was silent for a long while, intently focused on the candles beside her bed. The flickering flames didn't hold any answers though. Her mind remained a jumbled mess, the path ahead twisted and confusing.

"You know," she said, almost conversationally, "it seems wrong to want to." She looked up at Akilina. "I almost think I should be resisting the impulse, as if it's a naughty indulgence I would be better off without. An unhealthy craving." Her voice faltered. "But I think ... I need it."

After a moment, she let go of Akilina's hand, rolled her whole body to the side, and stared blindly at the wall. *Would you like to?* Too hard to answer that question, make sense of that question.

Her eyes slowly closed, and she heard a faint rustle as Akilina sat in Amarok's chair to keep vigil beside the bed.

And then, it was as if she watched herself from the outside, as her resting form instinctively took on the curved pose of a child in utero. She seemed to have no control over her own responses as her lips parted and a whisper came out on a soft exhalation.

"Yes, please."

*

Kat woke and smiled, stretching luxuriously like a cat. She felt strong, rested, and ready for action. Automatically, her hand went to her neck, fingering the place where she had been bitten.

"It's gone," she murmured to herself thankfully. She turned her head, and saw Della sitting beside her bed.

"Hi," she said. "What time is it?"

"Just before midnight," Della said. "You have been sleeping ever since Akilina fed you again."

Kat frowned. "Does it make her weaker?" she asked.

Della smiled. "You need not worry about her. She is old, power-ful – and will recover her strength after a rest. Charice is with her."

"I haven't seen Char since before everything happened, have I?"

Della shook her head. "No. Tempers were ... a little high among some of us. She would like to see you." She glanced around. "She arranged all these candles in your room before we brought you in.

She seemed sure you would like them. But … it was decided that seeing her might upset you."

"Upset me?" Kat was surprised. "No, I'd like to see her." She paused. "I remember what happened, you know." She did remember, and what was strange was how detached she felt about it. She could run through the whole incident in her mind without fear or emotional trauma. "Where is he? The one who attacked me?"

"He is under guard, downstairs." Della hesitated. "From what Charice has told us, it appears you have met him once before."

"Who is he?" Kat asked, mystified.

"It was Jonathan, from her club."

Kat's mouth formed a round O of surprise.

"Charice is his maker, as it transpires. He followed her here."

"Oh," said Kat. "That weird blood-link thing. Is … is that why they didn't want her to see me?"

Della nodded. "You did not recognize Jonathan, then?" she asked, curious.

"No," Kat admitted. "With all the injuries and burns all over him, he looked terrible. Nothing like when I first met him." She gave a brief shudder at the memory of the disfigured man in the bathhouse.

Della tilted her head and gave Kat a quizzical look. "What injuries?"

Kat grimaced. "Cuts, scratches, animal claw marks maybe." She paused, thinking. "I suppose it must have been those animals Anton saw who attacked him?"

But she was speaking to candles and thin air, because Della had flitted to the door and called for Anton.

He arrived moments later. "What is it?" he asked.

The two of them had a whispered conference in the doorway, and Anton eyed Kat thoughtfully before crossing the room to stand beside her.

"Katerina, are you able to … talk about it yet?" His eyes were watchful, careful.

"The attack, you mean? Yes, I don't mind," Kat said. "I don't actually remember anything after he sprang on me anyway." She shrugged, unable to explain why she was so calm about it.

Anton nodded. "We have questioned the man who attacked you. Jonathan. He told us he climbed the rock face to our east, and hid inside the bathhouse in the time between our night patrol going inside, just before dawn, and our day watch beginning. He hid there through the day, and then submerged himself under the water when he heard Miklós come to the door, and stayed there until you had entered. In hindsight it appears we were not as careful as we could have been. As we *should* have been – and for that I apologize."

"Well," said Kat, reasonably, "you were expecting some strange pack of animals, not one man. That's why he was able to sneak in."

"Perhaps," Anton said, his expression contemplative. "I did have a question about one aspect, though. You told Della that when he attacked you, he was unrecognizable because he was so disfigured by injuries and burns?"

Kat nodded, unsure where Anton was going with this. She looked inquiringly at Della, who stood beside him.

"When Miklós entered the bathing room, Jonathan barely had a mark on him," Della explained softly. "His clothes were a complete mess, but *he* was completely uninjured." She looked troubled.

"But you *all* heal faster than humans, don't you?" Kat said, bewildered.

"Not during the daytime," Anton said grimly. "That is when we are at our weakest, with little regenerative power. And if we have the misfortune to be exposed directly to the sun, even for a couple of seconds, the burns take hours to heal – at a minimum. Usually a whole night."

Kat was silent for a while, and then she raised questioning eyes to his. "Does it make a difference whether you've just fed? I mean, he ... obviously he drank my blood, right?"

Anton and Della exchanged a meaningful glance.

"Exactly," Anton said.

*

Kat sat perched on a kitchen chair, swathed in the sable rug Alek had lent her. Della had insisted on that before letting her come to the kitchen. But she was feeling fine – better than fine – and she wished they would all stop treating her like an invalid.

Her eyes were shining bright, silently following Della's quick movements as she placed several cloths on the bench top, and wrapped and knotted food within them. Kat rubbed her cheek against the softness of one corner of the rug. The sable made her think of Alek, then of Amarok, and Miklós too, out there in the dark somewhere.

"You must truly be of our kind," Della observed. "I have noticed you do not talk much. Or ask questions, although you must have many. After all, you almost died tonight."

"I've always been like that." Kat suddenly felt self-conscious.

Della continued darting around the kitchen, from pot to sink to larder. It was funny how someone so active could be so restful to be around.

"So, why don't your kind talk much? Or ask questions?" Kat asked after a while.

Della glanced across with a quick smile. "It spoils the journey if we find out too much about each other too soon. We may, after all, be in each other's lives for a very long time." She scattered a handful of nuts onto a clean wooden board, and began to chop them, the silver blade a blur.

"The journey?"

"Life. Better it be a journey into the great unknown, full of twists and turns we do not expect." She stopped what she was doing, and looked squarely at Kat. "So keep your secrets, whatever they may be. Unless, of course, you would rather not." She went back to her chopping and mixing.

There was silence between them for several minutes, but it was not an uncomfortable one.

"You can smell him on me, can't you?" Kat said at last with quiet resignation, her fingers tightening on the thick, soft fur wrapped around her.

"Of course," Della replied calmly. "We all can. Beside the fact that he has always been extremely fond of that particular rug."

"Oh." Kat sat silently for a moment. "He's very … intense. Is he like that with everyone?"

Della paused to think for a moment. "Not exactly," she said finally. "Not in quite the way I imagine he is with you."

Kat's eyes fell to the flagstone floor, and she began examining the cracks and ridges and joins. "You know … nothing is happening. With me and him. Honestly."

"I know. But it is *your* journey, Kat. Not anyone else's."

Kat's eyes flew up, surprised at Della's tone. There was no condemnation in it, no judgment. Just understanding, and decade upon decade of wisdom. They exchanged a look, a smile.

"Thanks," Kat said.

Then they both turned toward the door as hurried footsteps descended the stairs. Anton entered the room. "Miklós has returned. They have found the pack. There are at least thirty of them."

"That many?" Della said in dismay.

Anton nodded tersely.

"How far away?" Della asked.

"Not far enough." His expression was grim. "Rok and Alek are keeping watch on them from the top of the escarpment, but they will not approach until Miklós and I return. Even with the four of us, they will have a huge advantage."

"Do you have to fight them?" Della asked softly.

Anton nodded. "We have to head them off before they find the southern pass – otherwise they will have a clear path into our valley."

He flicked a look across at Kat, who was listening intently, eyes wide, and mustered a comforting smile for her. "There is no need for you to worry, Katerina. From what Jonathan has told us, these creatures cannot bear the sunlight, so we need only hold them off until dawn. Anyway, I must go. Miklós is waiting."

"Here." Della handed him the wrapped food parcels. "For you, and the others."

Anton took them, and smiled his thanks.

Kat reached out to detain him as he moved past her. His hazel eyes met hers.

"Thank you," she said.

He gave a quick nod, and a half-smile.

"Be careful!" Della called as he left the room.

She immediately turned to Kat. "You mustn't sit around here worrying about them. As soon as you have eaten your meal I will take you back to bed."

Kat dutifully picked up her fork as Della placed the plate in front of her, hoping if she at least *looked* like she was trying to eat, Della's mother hen impulses would be calmed. She took a small mouthful and chewed slowly, then swallowed, keeping her expression neutral. She didn't want Della to know that the meal she had lovingly prepared was about as appetizing as sawdust, and caught in Kat's dry throat as it went down.

It wasn't that the food was bad, just that it seemed wrong to be sitting here, eating a meal, while the others were out there getting ready to fight. That not worrying thing? So much easier said than done.

Aware Della's eyes were still on her, Kat took another bite. Her eyes were on her plate, but she couldn't see it. Instead, the faces of those out there in the night formed a procession in her head. Anton and Miklós, Amarok and Alek – she felt their absence from the house as a physical ache. The enormity of the knowledge that right now they were preparing to tangle with a pack of aggressive deadly beasts – for *her* – was difficult to assimilate. Nobody had ever, *ever* done anything like this for her before.

"Della?" she asked as a sudden question surfaced in her mind. "Do you and Corrin ever go out on patrol like the others?" She realized she had no idea what animal form Della *or* Corrin took. "I was just wondering since tonight, they're so outnumbered."

The mortification that flooded Della's face made Kat instantly regret opening her mouth without engaging the tact filter.

"We are neither of us fighters," Della said. "Most *unalil* prefer to do combat in animal form. That is where we are fastest, and strongest. And those who take on the form of a flying creature have a huge advantage, of course. Except ..." She broke off, and Kat hurried to fill the awkward pause.

"You don't have to tell me. I'm sorry for asking."

"No, it's just ..." Della's eyes flickered across to the door, as if she was worried Corrin might enter and overhear them. She continued hurriedly. "You have seen me in my animal form, Katerina. That day you were in my garden." She gestured toward the outside door. "I wound myself around your legs."

Kat certainly remembered the elegant cat that had pushed past her to get to the catnip. "But that means Corrin ..." An image popped into her mind of the little bird, smaller than a robin, that she had also seen foraging for food that day. The "friend" Della had referred to as she scattered seeds and nuts on the bird feeder. "Oh!"

"He rarely speaks of it, but I know that in times of trouble, it is a source of great regret to him that he cannot transform into something ... larger. Please do not mention it to him."

Kat nodded. "Of course."

"How is the food?" Della asked, changing the subject, and Kat brought her mind back to the kitchen, and the plate in front of her, with an effort.

"Delicious, thank you."

She was guiltily aware that if someone had asked her what she was eating right now, she wouldn't have had a clue. She kept eating though, until most of the plate was empty. Then she pushed it away, and cleared her throat.

"Della, would you take me to see Jonathan?"

Della looked shocked. "You want to see him? Is that wise?"

Kat shrugged. "I don't know about wise, but …"

"I've heard he's been asking to see you too." Della hesitated. "When Miklós found you, he … Jonathan … he was crouched over your body, weeping."

Kat wrinkled her brow. "It's hard to explain," she said, "but I have to see him. We're … connected now. Please, Della."

Della thought for a long moment, and then nodded reluctantly. She led the way up to the main entrance hall, and then down another narrow flight of stairs to a locked door.

"Corrin's with him," she said. "Wait here."

Kat heard the murmur of voices, and then Della reappeared and ushered her into the windowless room. Corrin and Jonathan stood on the far side of the room, and Corrin gripped Jonathan's wrist with both hands.

As soon as he saw Kat, though, Jonathan jerked toward her with a cry, and flung himself to the floor at her feet. Corrin still had hold of his arm, and quickly moved to pull him away, but Kat stopped him with a firm shake of the head and a raised hand.

She couldn't have pinpointed where it was coming from, but a torrent of compassion and forgiveness flowed from somewhere deep within her. The thought of doing anything but forgive was untenable. She knew Jonathan would never, ever hurt her again. Her certainty on this point was absolute.

She bent, and laid her hand on Jonathan's fair head with all the grace and wisdom of a grandmother comforting a child. As he sobbed, she smoothed his hair gently. He tilted his head up to meet her eyes, and reached up to take her hand in both of his. Kat looked down at him as he gazed at her in adoration, his eyes drenched with tears. There were no words uttered, but after a long moment Kat let out a deep sigh and lifted her other hand to touch his hair again.

"I know," she said softly. "I know."

Chapter 44

The silvery moon was high in the night sky as the huge eagle and smaller peregrine flew down to join the cougar and wolf keeping watch at the cliff's edge. A moment of unspoken communication, and then the wolf and cougar, Amarok and Alek, turned away and disappeared into the darkness.

Alek padded silently into the clearing on the valley floor, the gray wolf by his side. The barest instant passed in which they were unobserved, and then the pack of intruders they had been watching scented them, and wheeled around to attack.

Moonlight glinted on crazed eyes, and slavering muzzles drew closer, and then the pack were on them in a snarling, seething mass.

Even when Miklós swooped into the fray, the attackers didn't break off. Bigger and more aggressive than ordinary bobcats and coyotes, they appeared to think and act as a unified force, turning and snarling as one. Alek twisted and turned as he ran, with Amarok by his side, keeping to the higher ground. Even so, they were hard pressed, and the tearing beak and claws of their winged defender seemed to do little to halt the determined attack of the pack.

Then the giant eagle dived out of the dark sky, creating a division, cutting three of the creatures off from the rest of the group. Alek growled, pacing back and forth until he and Amarok had driven those three back into a space enclosed on several sides by rock. The two coyotes and the bobcat backed up until they were against the rock face, snarling their fury as they realized they were trapped. They showed caution, but no fear. Seeing a sudden gap, they raced past Alek in unison to rejoin their pack, but when he leaped to give chase he saw a streak of silver-gray, as Amarok ran to block them. The creatures backed up again, hackles raised.

Alek leaped, and took down the bobcat in a snarling mess of claws and sharp teeth. Close beside him, he saw Miklós plummeting with claws outstretched to land on the back of one of the coyotes. Clearly the peregrine didn't realize there was another coyote close beside the first, and when the second beast sprang to defend its pack mate, its teeth and claws tore through feather and flesh, into his unprotected breast. Alek was still occupied with the snarling bobcat and couldn't help his brother, but Amarok whirled with a flurry of claws, and sprang at the throat of the nearest coyote, giving Miklós the chance he needed to release his hold on the animal's back. He flapped awkwardly away, streaming blood behind him.

There was a screeching cry overhead, and both Alek and Amarok stared toward the sound. They disappeared in the direction the eagle had indicated, with the rest of the pack joining the injured and chasing in pursuit of them.

They fled, with the pack at their heels, while Anton swooped and wheeled in front of them, close to the steep rock face. Then he fixed his eye on Alek, and gave another screech, and Alek broke away to follow where he led. Just in front of them, on the cliff face – what was it Anton wanted to show him? And then Alek saw it, far above his head. A fault line in the rock. A jagged crack between the giant slabs, faintly visible in the moonlight.

Anton must be desperate to consider such a thing, but clearly he hoped to apply just the right pressure at the fault line to bring the rock face tumbling down and block the pass. And Alek saw that this was indeed what his brother intended when Anton landed on a tiny rocky outcrop high up on the cliff face and changed form.

Whether geotechnical wizardry or brute force or a big dose of luck was the deciding factor Alek could never be sure, but fortune certainly favored Anton's desperate plan that night. An ominous rumble sounded high overhead, rushing ever closer, and Alek leaped clear and began to run as tons of rock began crumbling away from the mountainside and falling to the valley below.

He kept on running as the rock fall continued, and when he was clear, he whirled around and looked back. High above him, Anton had resumed an eagle's form and swooped away from the havoc he had wrought. And far below, Alek saw the swirling gray form of Amarok as he ducked and twisted, dodging boulders big enough to kill. The bobcats and coyotes had broken off their pursuit and were scrambling to find cover away from the pass. Several didn't escape the rockslide, and lay where they fell, limbs sprawled at odd, broken angles as a thick layer of rock and dust covered them. Then, with an almighty crack, a last, huge piece of the mountainside broke away and went bouncing down to the valley floor. High above him, Alek heard the eagle let out a terrible screech as the wolf was buried from view.

*

Alek stood on two feet alone in the shadows, looking down at the scene of devastation. Dust from the rock fall hung in the air below him like a pall of smoke as Anton carried Miklós into the moonlight. Alek grinned, exhilarated by the adrenalin still coursing through him. He felt ready to go another round. "You missed all the best action after that early stunt," he called to Miklós. "One coyote you could perhaps manage alone, but two? A pipsqueak peregrine like you? What were you thinking?"

He moved to Anton's side, and looked down into his injured brother's pale face.

"We will have to carry him home," Anton said. "He is badly hurt."

"I can hear you," Miklós protested weakly, with a trace of annoyance.

"Good. It is the truth," Anton snapped.

"Rok?" Alek questioned, suddenly noting his absence.

Slowly, Anton shook his head, his expression grim. "We should search for him now."

"Let me," Alek offered, taking Miklós in his arms.

They reached the dust-shrouded valley moments later, and Anton stiffened at the sight of a pair of legs and half a torso beneath a jumble of rocks. He gestured to Alek, and they started moving closer.

"Looking for me?" Amarok asked, appearing silently at his side.

Anton spun to face him. Amarok was favouring one foot, but appeared otherwise unhurt. "I can hardly believe it," he said weakly. "You are alive."

Amarok slung his arm across Anton's shoulders. "Yes," he said in a casual tone, "but did you have to drop half the mountain on my foot?"

Anton didn't smile. "Look." He gestured toward the sprawled body visible through the moonlit dust eddies. "For a moment I thought it was you."

Amarok frowned, and they all approached the rock fall. When they had cleared the rocks from the body and revealed the face, Anton squatted back on his haunches. "I ... how could this have happened?"

Amarok shook his head in disbelief. "There's no mistaking him. It's Andreas." He bent down, and did his best to straighten the bent and broken limbs. "Andreas always took the form of an owl. Always. Not a coyote or a damned bobcat."

"Show me," Miklós whispered. Alek kneeled and held him closer, and he looked down at their fallen friend with sick horror, then turned away.

"Will you hold him?" Alek said abruptly to Amarok, and carefully passed Miklós to him.

"Come on," Alek said grimly to Anton, moving further in among the tumbled rocks. On the far side of the rock fall he could hear howls and baying from the survivors, as they regrouped and ran off into the night.

Picking through the rubble in the darkness, with Amarok following close behind, they soon revealed two more crushed and bloodied bodies. One was Saskia, the other they didn't recognize. Both had evidently changed from snarling beasts to their true forms upon death.

"Do you think that all of them are ..." Amarok trailed off, seemingly unable to finish. "Who would do this? Turn friend against friend?"

"The Directorate. And their Hema Castus Institute." Savage rage boiled through Alek. He hurled a lump of rock into the darkness and listened to it shatter. "Damn them to hell."

*

Alek entered the hallway first on their return home, Miklós in his arms. He was alive with suppressed energy in the candlelight, unconcerned about the scratches and claw marks on his arms and cheeks. It was Miklós who had got the worst of it. A deep cut slashed the length of his blood-covered torso, and he held his arm across his chest to protect broken ribs. Alek helped him into a chair in the hallway as soon as they were through the door, and he sat there, trembling with pain and exhaustion. Anton followed with Amarok moments later.

Della hurried down the stairs to greet them. "Thank the Mahra, you have returned safely."

Anton gave her a tired smile.

"Did you stop those creatures?" Della asked.

"Some." Anton fell silent.

Della's eyes narrowed as she looked from face to face. "What aren't you telling me?"

"They were *unalil*," Amarok said softly, coming to stand between them. He lifted a hand to Anton's shoulder. "But … changed somehow. Made crazed and vicious. When they died, they changed form. Saskia and Andreas were among the dead."

"What?" Della's eyes filled with tears. "No!"

Amarok engulfed her in a rough hug.

"We took out perhaps half," Anton said. There was no satisfaction in his words, just bare statement of the facts. None of them could triumph in the death of a friend, however justified.

"We will be revenged for this." Alek's voice cut like shards of ice. His rage had crystalized, become a cold and fearsome thing. "They've picked a fight with the wrong pack."

Della pulled away from Amarok and turned to face Anton, brushing the tears from her eyes. "Tomorrow night is the full moon."

Anton nodded. "We have no idea how that will affect these creatures, but it is certainly possible their aggression will be heightened. We have blocked the southern pass into the valley, but it is only a matter of time until the survivors find their way around. We will leave at dusk – it will take them much longer than that to make it this far."

Della breathed out in a shuddering sigh. "Saskia and Andreas. And perhaps their whole family. It is hard to comprehend … Is there nothing we can do to bring back the ones who are still living? To calm this, this madness in them?"

Anton slowly shook his head, the healer in him regretting his answer.

"How is she?" Alek asked, abruptly changing the subject. They all knew who he was referring to.

"Headstrong and much recovered," Della said. "She insisted on seeing Jonathan."

A bolt of pure fury shot through Alek, and he strode forward to glower at her. "She *what*?" He didn't know, at that moment, if he was more angry at Kat for her rashness or fearful for her safety.

Della winced. "I know, brother, I know. But, surprisingly, she survived the ordeal. She is a remarkable young woman. She is in her room now, and I have convinced her to rest in a chair, though she insists she cannot sleep." She touched Miklós gently on the shoulder. "Be well, brother. Katerina has been worrying. I will go and tell her you have all returned."

"That reminds me." Anton turned to Alek as Della disappeared up the stairs. "There was no time to tell you earlier." He briefed Alek on Jonathan's miraculous healing and Alek gave a low whistle.

"He told us he'd been attacked, but I guess we all assumed he hadn't been badly hurt. He looked completely uninjured. What are you thinking? That Kat's blood healed him? She *is* a princess of the blood, so Akilina says. Or would be, if she changed."

"Yes, but at the moment, she is still human," Anton said. "Such healing power should not be possible."

Alek shrugged, and raised his eyebrows. Where Kat was concerned, it seemed *anything* was possible.

Anton turned his attention to Miklós. After placing a hand on the other man's wounded chest, he grimaced and shook his head. "You have lost a great deal of blood, brother. Take mine to speed your healing."

"Let me." Akilina's clear voice rang through the hallway as she descended the main stairs.

Anton began to protest but she shook her head firmly.

"Let me," she said again, with quiet strength. "I am *egir'rin*. It is both my duty and my privilege."

Anton frowned, then gave a short nod and moved aside to let her tend to their injured brother.

"You heard what I said to Della? The Hema Castus Institute has somehow twisted and changed others of the *unalil*, our friends among them. It is they who attacked us."

Anton fell silent, and Alek saw the tender way the princess looked at him. There was definitely a history between them, one Anton had never spoken of. He wondered what it was.

Anton brushed a hand across his eyes, shook his head. "I have no appetite for more killing. We will have to leave at dusk."

Akilina laid a hand on his arm.

"Go. I will take care of Miklós – you have much to organize."

Chapter 45

"Thank you for helping me pack ... again." Kat smoothed her hand over a folded pile of sweaters and tops and looked up at Akilina with a glimmer of a smile. "I've only just unpacked, and now it's all going back in the suitcase."

"You are still recovering, child. It is my pleasure to help you." Akilina crossed the room, and returned with a stack of Kat's books. As she slid these into a bag, a flat package dropped to the floor. Akilina retrieved it, and held it up.

"Thanks." Kat gave a rueful laugh as she took it. "It's my mother's."

Homesickness suddenly blindsided her, and she sank to the bed, desperate for a glimpse of her mother's young laughing face. Something from home, to distract her from the grim reality of her present situation.

Kat unwrapped the paper carefully, and lifted the drawing free while Akilina kept packing. The room's curtains were drawn tight against the setting sun, and the candlelight didn't provide much illumination, but still Kat's eyes drank in the details only she could see in the picture; the vibrance in her mother's face, her happiness as she basked in the presence of the unseen artist. "Tironek Vasilei," she whispered to herself.

Akilina stopped what she was doing. "What did you say?" she asked sharply.

"Tironek Vasilei," Kat repeated more loudly, suddenly self-conscious. She sometimes still forgot how good Akilina's hearing was. "It's my father's name."

In an instant Akilina was beside her, looking at the picture Kat held, then at Kat in wonder.

"Your father drew this? Are you sure?"

Kat nodded. "It's a drawing of my mother. The only thing she has from him."

Akilina took the picture in her own hands, touched a finger gently to the words at the bottom. "That is not his name. At least, not Tironek. It was a nickname. One he chose himself. Tironek – peasant, and Vasilei – prince. Two halves of a man eternally in conflict."

Kat stared at her. "You know my father?"

"Yes, child, though it is many, many years since I have seen him. Vasilei was never at ease with his rank ... or with the name chosen for him at birth." Akilina stared down at the portrait. "I remember how much he loved to draw."

Kat's lips formed the question soundlessly. "Who?"

Akilina slowly put the picture aside, and reached for one of Kat's hands. Her touch was ... different from the time she'd held Kat's hands to do the reading. This time, she seemed unsure, almost tentative, as if she hadn't reached out to another in quite this way for a very long time.

As if she had been waiting for centuries, and had long ago given up hope that this day would ever come.

"My child, we are family." Akilina's eyes shone with unshed tears. She lifted Kat's hand, and pressed it to her heart with both her own. "Vasilei – the man who drew that picture – he ... he is my elder brother."

Chapter 46

When dusk fell, Kat gave up the pretense of trying to rest. She'd promised Akilina that she'd try, but her whole body was wired and tense, and she was filled with a strange restlessness. It was as if she had an excess of energy and it was searching for an outlet.

She headed out of her room and went downstairs, taking the steps two at a time, stopping when she reached the entrance hallway. The doors at both ends were open to the dusk, and a faint, cool breeze made them swing on their hinges. Bags and corded trunks, her own among them, littered the floor. She could see Akilina's scrolls. A neat satchel with Della's plant seeds and favourite kitchen tools. The others seemed to be taking surprisingly little given they were packing up an entire household.

Mortification washed through her as she realized the obvious. Because of where they lived they *couldn't* take much. Only what they could carry. Shaken by the thought, she walked through into the big meeting room, with its beautiful, ornately carved chairs and table. She looked with fresh eyes at the carved wooden lintels above the doors, the woven rugs on the floor. Every stone in this huge and beautiful house, every stick of wood, every piece of furniture and kitchen bowl, must have been brought in by hand. She'd been here such a short time and already *she* didn't like the thought of leaving it all behind. How must they feel?

The house around her was quiet and still, with no candles lit to dispel the gloom of approaching night. As she approached the doors leading out onto the long stone balcony – the one with the view to the valley – a sudden prickle of unease brought her to a dead stop.

They were supposed to be leaving at dusk. That was right now. So where the hell *was* everyone?

Her eyes were drawn to the window, and the sky outside. Beyond the balcony baluster, silhouetted against the last faint glow of lingering daylight, she saw the swooping form of a giant eagle, with a peregrine close by his side.

Then she heard it; faintly at first, but quickly becoming louder. Her faint prickle of unease became a crawling apprehension that made every hair on her body stand on end. Because there was no mistaking the sound that was drawing ever closer. The excited baying, the mournful howls of wild creatures as they grouped and closed in for the kill.

Cold dread swept through her, chilling her to the bone. The pack was here.

"Katerina?"

Akilina, fearful and urgent, called to her from the hallway. Kat swung around and ran back to the door. Akilina stood at the bottom of the staircase, and her apprehensive face filled with relief when she saw Kat emerge from the meeting room.

"Come back upstairs, child. Run!"

But it was much too late for escape. The hair-raising howls were right outside now, and then bobcats and coyotes, more huge and hideous than anything Kat had ever seen in nature, came tearing through the front door. And they kept coming, an endless snarling swarm, with a cougar and great gray wolf fighting tooth and claw in their midst.

The eagle swooped screeching through the far door, a fearsome, whirling mass of feathers and talons, and clattered onto the flag-stones, but the hallway to the house was already overrun.

All this happened in mere seconds. The tide of creatures sweeping between Kat and Akilina; bags left ready for their departure overturned and scattered. Mere moments, as Kat watched, frozen in the meeting room doorway. It was all unbelievably fast, leaving no time to think or feel or move. No time to escape, or hide.

They were hopelessly outnumbered. Another instant, and the creatures would be at her and Akilina's throats.

All Kat remembered of that moment afterward was her icy detachment. Her utter absence of fear. And the fact that she stopped thinking, trusted in instinct, and began to act.

And time, that fickle creature that so often runs away from us, was her friend that day. It slowed to the barest trickle as she spread her hands wide and drew in power while her mind took stock of the scene. She watched as if in slow motion as two coyotes leaped toward her. Tracked their arcs through the air.

She pulled curling rainbow strands of energy from the air, the stones beneath her feet, the mountain below, until she was brim-full and overflowing. Until she spilled forth incandescence and became a new thing, a glowing creature of power, a mythic thing of flaming wings and claws and beak that burned with fire.

When she moved at last, she was faster than thought. Faster than clemency or forgiveness. A searing and relentless force for justice.

Only afterward, when she'd collapsed naked on the cool stone floor, did she register the acrid odor of burned fur and flesh. Only then could she see and understand the carnage she had wrought, and recall the shocked awe on the faces of Akilina and the *unalil* as she laid waste to their attackers in a moment.

They left with the sound of distant baying in their ears as still more of the beasts gathered in the valley far below, looking for a way to ascend. They fled while they still could. It was all a blur to Kat, utterly spent, exhausted in both body and mind.

She was carried at speed through the night, swathed in Alek's sable rug; held so securely and carried so smoothly through the hilly terrain that more than once her eyes closed and she drifted off to sleep, and when she stirred, she heard just the whistle of the wind speeding past. Sometimes, when she stirred, she heard the others' voices, fragments of conversations.

" … impossible surely. And so incredibly *fast*." That was Anton. And then Della, soft with wonder. "Was she a phoenix?"

Later, she traveled a short distance along mountain roads on the back of a big motorcycle, her arms around Alek's waist. That she was awake for.

Then she was transferred in darkness to the back of a car. Leather seats, her nose told her. Lulled by the twists and turns of the road, she slept again.

She saw the shining golden eyes first, then the pale face and tangle of hair that were so familiar to her now, asleep or awake. The features were softer, and female, but unmistakably like Amarok's.

Amber.

Amber sat cross-legged behind metal bars in the middle of a bare cell, illuminated by harsh electric lights. Kat sensed there were people nearby, outside the bars, but Amber paid them no attention. She seemed to look straight at Kat. To recognize her.

You are coming.

Not question, but statement. The words were not spoken aloud, but were projected straight into Kat's mind.

Amber's face broke into a smile of such sweetness and beauty that Kat felt her heart catch in her chest. Then Amber lifted her hand, and motioned as if to swat her gently away.

Kat felt herself drifting on eddies unseen, out of Amber's cell and along a corridor, then up; one level, then two, through several doorways and along another endless corridor. Finally she floated out through an entrance foyer, and into the moonlit night.

As she rose up, up and away, the three words above the front door, and the inverted ankh symbol were indelibly etched in her sleeping mind.

Kat came back to wakening awareness with snatches of conversation in her ears. She heard a voice she didn't know through a half-open car window, interspersed with murmured questions from Anton.

bien sur … trois heures du matin … pleine lune … lumière …

Kat turned her head, and found Akilina beside her. "Where are we?" she asked drowsily.

"Near Sherbrooke," Akilina said. "Just over the Canadian border."

The answer didn't mean anything to Kat, but she lifted her head a little from her reclining position. She saw a sleek aircraft a short distance away in the middle of an expanse of tarmac, bathed in moonlight, and guessed they were at an airport.

She bolted upright. "I have to talk to Amarok. To Anton. All of them."

"What is it?" Amarok's voice came from the passenger seat in front of her.

Kat blinked, the memory of her recent dream fresh in her mind. "It's Amber," she said. "She's alive. I know where she is."

*

The group gathered in the shadow of the dark aircraft hangar, tense and silent.

"The timing couldn't be better." Amarok's voice was low, and almost vibrated with anticipation. "This opportunity seems heaven-sent."

Miklós nodded. "We know these appalling *unalil* mutations of theirs are otherwise engaged." He slung an arm around Amarok's shoulders in solidarity. "With any luck, the place will barely be defended." He broke into a smile filled with a savagery that shocked Kat.

"I kind of hope they put up a bit of a struggle." Alek grinned, his expression every bit as savage as Miklós's and much more gleeful. "Make this worth our while."

Anton shook his head. "I'll forget you said that. My priority will be retrieving Amber and getting the rest of you back out unharmed."

"No!" Alek made a frustrated movement forward, and Miklós put a restraining hand on his shoulder. "Our friends, our brethren – what of them? Anton, we can't let them continue to create these mutations, these abominations of beasts by modifying *unalil*. I'm sure I can do something; break into their computer system, plant a virus maybe, depending on how good their encryption is. This may be the only chance we get to strike back against years of persecution."

Anton held up a calming hand. "If we see a chance to destroy their genetic research pertaining to the *unalil*, that would be an added bonus. Other than that, the less direct conflict, the better. We don't honor the fallen by getting ourselves killed."

Alek gave a low growl, but with Miklós's hand now clamped to his shoulder he had no choice but to acquiesce.

Char rejoined the group from the direction of the darkened airport building.

"So?" Anton looked at her inquiringly, ignoring the others. "Were you able to contact Falcon?"

"Yes. Thinks we're crazy to even consider a jailbreak at Hema Castus, and he's even crazier if he helps us, but …" Char shrugged, and gave a rather smug smile, "I convinced him to anyway. The good news is, he's been there. To the low-security parts. He confirmed there are definitely a few highly secured levels below ground. Bad news is, he has no idea what's in those sub-ground floors, which is why he thinks this idea is just too risky."

"So basically, we'd be going in blind," Alek said.

There was a moment's fraught silence.

"I've told you already," Kat said quietly. "I've seen Amber, in some sort of cell. Seen all the corridors leading to her. I know I can find her."

Anton gave her a gentle smile, the kind bestowed upon an overambitious child. "I know you think you can."

"And I know you don't mean to be condescending." Kat heard the sharpness in her own voice. Physical exhaustion was having a definite flow-on effect on her ability to be tactful. She hadn't had time to process her feelings about what had happened to her back in the mountains either. What she'd *done*. So far, she'd tried to banish her recollections of the bloody massacre. But her total annihilation of the genetic monstrosities that had attacked them back in the mountains had changed her. Knowing that she had a weapon inside her, the ability to transform into something formidable and fiery and deadly, made things ... *different* now.

"If you believed Kat when she told you where Amber was, why won't you believe she can find her?" Char asked. "Surely she's proven herself?"

Anton cleared his throat. "The risks are so great, if we get this wrong."

Akilina had been listening in silence, but now she broke in. "Consider, too, that it would require Katerina to accompany you inside." Her eyes met Kat's. "The idea of you going into that place, into such danger ..."

"I think Katerina has shown she is more than able to defend herself, and probably the rest of us too if need be," Miklós said, with an expressive glance in her direction. "Personally, I would be honored to have her as our guide."

Alek gave a crack of laughter. "Two days ago I wouldn't have said this, but my money's on Kat in a fight. Those Hema Castus research stooges won't know what hit them."

Anton gave him a reproving look. "She is still so new to her ability. So untried. I do not ..."

"I know you're only trying to protect me, both of you," Kat included Akilina in her comment, "but I'm going with you, Anton." There was a steely glint to her eye that she didn't trouble to hide.

Anton raised his hands in surrender. "Very well then. Let us discuss strategy. As Miklós said earlier, the timing is good. We know they won't be expecting us, and given that Hema Castus has to pass for a normal research facility, they won't be heavily fortified, at least on the ground level. At night, there are unlikely to be any human researchers to worry about, which is another important consideration. So I think we should go in as soon as possible."

"Tonight," Amarok said quietly, emphatically.

Anton frowned. "It will depend on whether there is a suitable airstrip near the institute though."

Akilina looked from one to the other, and finally her eyes came to rest on Kat, and she gave a defeated sigh. "If you are certain this is what you choose to do, I shall talk to the pilot." She pulled an obscenely thick roll of bills out of a concealed pocket somewhere, and then disappeared across the tarmac toward the plane.

Looked like chartering a plane didn't come cheap.

"He's logging the new flight plan," she said when she returned soon after. "Come, let us board now." She motioned for them all to follow her. "Our pilot tells me that he can have us in western Pennsylvania in less than two hours. I gave him a mental nudge to avoid any problems with the TSA about our border crossing. As far as he knows, I have been chartering flights with him for years."

Char was in front of Kat when she mounted the steps to the aircraft door, and she turned back as she reached the top step. "Kat?" Her voice was pitched low.

"Yes?"

"I know I went in to bat for you back there, and I'm the last person who should be doubting anyone's visions, but ..." Char's forehead wrinkled into a frown. "You *are* sure about this, aren't you?"

Kat nodded. "As sure as I can be," she whispered back.

They squeezed along the narrow central aisle, and sat opposite each other. Kat sank into the luxurious high-backed seat with a sigh, and glanced toward the window. It was big and round, like a ship's porthole, but there was nothing to be seen in the dark airport outside, besides the row of lights that would guide their pilot on takeoff.

"I've had so many dreams about this," Kat said softly to Char. "About Amber. I feel like I know that place backward. It *seemed* real."

Char kicked off her shoes and curled her feet up under her on the cream leather, doubtless breaking any number of aviation safety guidelines. She breathed out softly, eyes flickering toward Kat for an instant. She bit her lip. "Let's hope so."

*

The full moon was starting to sink behind the mountains by the time a diminished group gathered on a ridge just above the Hema Castus Institute. They had a clear view of the back of the building, but that didn't mean much; there were few lights on after hours – at least in the visible above-ground sections which, according to what Falcon had told Char, were populated during the daytime largely by human researchers.

Akilina had gone to find a spot higher up the mountain with a view of the front entrance, and Kat turned to see if she could find her. The night sky was beginning to lighten as a first distant reminder that morning approached, and Kat could just make out Akilina, a silent dark sentinel silhouetted against the sky on the ridge overlooking the institute. Before Akilina had left them, Kat had asked her if she wished she were joining them.

"I? No." Akilina had sounded faintly discomfited. "I would only hinder you if I were. I was not raised to a life of physical combat. These men are natural fighters, and it seems that perhaps you have something of that too, while I, truth be told, am happiest with my scrolls."

Char and Jonathan were already in position several miles away, watching the road leading in. Della and Corrin were a little closer to the main entrance, ready to run interference if the need arose.

Anton looked into each tense face. "Amber will not spend another night in that place. Alek is with me. Amarok and Miklós, you are with Katerina. Are we all clear on the plan?" He was met with terse nods. "Any last comments?"

Alek's voice came out of the darkness. "It is a far, far better thing that I do, than I have ever—"

"Thank you, Alek." Anton cut him off. "My request was not for quotations. I think we are all familiar with how that one ends."

He pulled Amarok and Miklós aside for a final quiet word, as Kat stood and racked her brains, trying to think where Alek's quote was from and how it ended.

Then she remembered. The lawyer guy who sacrificed himself at the end of the Dickens novel, *A Tale of Two Cities* … He'd said that line right before he went to the guillotine.

Kat peered into the darkness, her pulse beating a nervous rhythm in her chest. She really couldn't see much by the faint light of the setting moon, but that didn't stop the compulsion to keep watching the building far below.

Yes, she was clear on the plan. Go in, leave the complicated stuff like disabling guards and security systems to the others, and lead Amarok and Miklós to where Amber was being kept. Anton had been quite emphatic about the fact that if she was going in, she wasn't to face any more risk than absolutely necessary, and she was fine with that, because this was all about Amber as far as she was concerned.

She reached for her rune necklace, and pressed its comforting warmth to her chest. She'd felt so sure about this, earlier in the night, with Amber's image so clear in her mind. But that certainty had lessened after they arrived at the institute, and evaporated completely the minute the others started splitting into their smaller groups and melting away into the darkness.

Anxious questions beat against the confines of her mind, demanding to be answered.

What if somebody was caught?

Worse, what if she'd been wrong, and Amber wasn't even here?

Alek had delivered his words in his usual mocking way, so he obviously hadn't been serious about being some kind of sacrifice. And Anton had as good as promised they'd all be coming out of this alive.

Even so, she shivered. She had no intention of backing out, but she didn't like thinking about the danger they were facing. She'd seen the admiring glances the others had been sneaking at her. Most of them had her pegged as some kind of hero, when she had no clue how she'd done her miraculous flying instrument-of-death act, and had a sick suspicion that she'd never be able to do it again. That meant that if she *was* wrong about this, some of them – maybe her, maybe Alek – might not make it out.

Looking around, she realized she was now alone with just her team, Amarok and Miklós, on the silent ridge top. Anton and Alek had already melted away into the night.

It was time.

Chapter 47

Alek lowered himself through the ventilation shaft and dropped nimbly to the concrete floor far below, silent as a cat. A moment later, a soft noise told him Anton had also arrived.

The room around them was dark and still, and Anton made a move as if to go in search of the door, but Alek grabbed his arm.

"Wait!" He wasn't quite sure what had prompted him to hiss the warning to Anton. Some odd instinct, a distant memory triggered by the faint, bitter odor of burnt almond. "No flame," he said softly. "Do you still have that flashlight I gave you?"

Beside him he felt Anton bend to fumble in a pocket in his pants leg.

"Never used," Anton said wryly. "I hope the battery is still functioning."

The narrow beam played over their surroundings, illuminating the large storeroom, one wall of which was lined with row upon row of metal cylinders.

They moved closer, and Anton bent to read the label on the nearest cylinder, but Alek already knew what it would say.

"Hydrogen cyanide." Anton frowned, his face stark in the angled light of the torch. "I hardly like to speculate on what they use this for."

"Or, perhaps, what they're planning to use it for." Alek's voice was very grim. He raised his hand to hover over the release valve. "We can't just leave it here."

"No." Anton's jaw contracted. "Be quick. I will wait by the door."

Alek nodded silently, and sped along the rows, leaving cylinders softly hissing in his wake as they emptied their poison into the silent room.

He joined Anton in the dark corridor outside, pulled the storeroom door closed behind them, and locked it. "Done. Now let's go and find some action."

Alek and Anton met up with Miklós, Amarok and Kat next to the elevator near the main lobby. The area was dimly lit by after-hours security lighting.

"The guard room?" Anton asked tersely.

"Cameras and sensors disabled," Amarok said. "We've left the human guard 'sleeping' peacefully. There are other guards on this floor out on their rounds, but from what I can see they stay in their allocated areas. They shouldn't concern us."

Anton turned to look at the black security panel next to the elevator. His eyes narrowed. "How is this operated?"

Amarok raised his hand in front of the panel, which lit up for a moment and then went dark again. "I'm guessing we're not on their invitation list." He looked at Kat. "Any ideas?"

She shook her head slowly, regretfully. "Sorry."

Alek swore softly.

They all stood silently for a moment.

Alek suddenly cocked his head. "I hear something."

Anton frowned. "You and Miklós go – Amarok and I will wait here with Katerina."

Alek nodded, and he and Miklós headed off down the corridor.

"Here," Alek whispered a moment later, pointing to a closed door.

Miklós took up position on the other side of the door. After a silent count, Alek tried the handle, and the door swung noiselessly open.

The room within was fully lit but unoccupied. On one side it contained a small waiting area furnished with two comfortable chairs and a low table spread with journals. On the other side, facing the door, was a large desk. A small plaque on the front of the desk advertised the name of its usual occupant in a modern font: *Portia Cerquoni.*

There was another door beyond which was slightly ajar, and they both moved toward it. A name plate indicated it was the office of the institute director, Zeth Raddberg. From inside, faint rustling noises could be heard; papers being gathered and sorted. Then brisk footsteps coming back in their direction.

Alek jerked his head at Miklós, who moved noiselessly into position on the other side of the door.

The door was pulled further open, and a woman moved through it, her hair, clothing, and entire bearing proclaiming her to be every inch the corporate secretary.

In a flash, Alek whipped an arm around her upper body, pinning her arms to her torso, and pushed her back against the wall. "Portia?"

Pupils dilated in big, dark eyes. The woman's eyes flashed from Miklós to Alek. "Who are you? We – we're closed to visitors."

Alek almost smiled. He had to give her credit for maintaining her poise under the circumstances.

"Better you ask *what* we are." Miklós moved a step closer. "We are *unalil*. We don't keep business hours." He tilted his head to one side as he considered her. "And I doubt you do either."

Alek felt her flinch. And she had also reacted – just for an instant – to the news that they were *unalil*. She was doing a good job of hiding it, but finding out who – or what – they were had increased her tension.

Portia moistened her lips with her tongue, giving a brief flash of perfect white teeth. "Why are you here? I don't want any trouble."

Alek smiled. "No need for trouble, if you're feeling cooperative. We just need you to give us a hand with a security panel."

"Yes." Miklós echoed the smile, a hard light in his eyes. He walked across and grabbed her arm for emphasis. "It's completely your decision whether it's attached to you at the time or not."

Portia met Miklós's eyes. "Hurting me won't help you get where you want."

Alek raised a quizzical eyebrow. "No?"

"No." She raised her chin. "Access to the lower floors requires both a hand scan and voice command."

Miklós's hand tightened on Portia's arm, and she winced.

"What exactly do you think we're looking for?" Alek asked, jerking his head at Miklós to indicate he should back off.

"You're of the *unalil*. You've come for your people, surely? You've discovered what they're doing to them. Their so-called research subjects. Someone was bound to." Her eyes flashed at Alek, a militant sparkle in their depths.

"And if, perhaps, we were looking for another who has certain special abilities, and may not be grouped with the other *unalil* imprisoned here? A woman?"

Genuine surprise crossed Portia's face. "Not with the others? There's only one other department besides Genetics that keeps that kind of prisoner. I don't know if any of them are *unalil*, but there is a woman. In Predictive Science. Two floors down, east wing."

Alek met Miklós's eyes. What she'd just told them was consistent with the impressions Kat had shared with them all before they'd come in. Portia Cerquoni was telling the truth. No attempt at subterfuge.

Miklós moved back toward her, his expression suspicious. "Why are you telling us all this?" he demanded.

Her mouth tightened, and Alek thought at first that she wouldn't answer. Finally, her lips softened, and she gave a tiny sigh. "I have a family too. One the Directorate doesn't know about. Working here, staying on the inside is my best chance of keeping them alive."

Alek smiled suddenly, and swung her away from the wall. "Well, well," he said, and looped his arm around her. He clasped his hand around her wrist, immoveable as a vice, keeping her firmly beside him as he turned in the direction of the door. "Portia Cerquoni, I have a feeling we're going to get along just fine."

Chapter 48

The elevator door slid open on the institute's second subterranean level, and Alek was through it in a flash, dispatching the guard stationed there before he had time to react.

Portia drew back against the elevator wall, pupils dilated with sudden fear. "This is as far as I can go," she said. "Please. They'll kill me if they find out that I helped you."

Miklós's lips twisted in a humorless smile. "We would have killed you if you had not."

"All clear!" Alek called softly from outside. "He's out for the count."

"You may go," Anton cut in. He gave Portia a brief smile. "Thank you for your assistance."

Portia inclined her head in acknowledgment, and her eyes followed them as they exited into the corridor.

"I hope you find your friend." Her words came to them softly as the elevator door slid shut. The elevator began to move once again with a whir.

"I thought she seemed nice," Kat said.

Alek gave her a look.

"What?" Kat frowned at him.

"This isn't a social call, Kat."

She didn't dignify that with a reply, just gave him a withering stare.

Alek turned back to the fallen guard with a grin. "The Directorate should really look at improving the diet they provide for their people." He nudged the guard's body with one booted foot. "Definitely inferior. He might as well have been human for all the fight he put up. Couldn't knock *me* out that easily."

Miklós tilted his head to look at the closed eyes and unconscious face. "Nor me."

"Just … move him somewhere," Anton said impatiently.

Alek dragged the guard's body around a corner, and then they all gathered around Anton.

"Katerina, do you recognize where we are? And can you lead Miklós and Amarok to Amber?"

Kat glanced around quickly. She'd seen this corridor several times before in her sleeping visions, and the confirmation that what she'd dreamed was real swept away her earlier doubts in a wave of renewed confidence. "Yes." She could do this. She knew she could.

"When you find Amber, get her out of here. Alek and I will do what damage we can to their genetic research section."

Amarok frowned. "Will you need our assistance? Portia said the director is visiting that section, and there will be others with him."

Anton shook his head. "Your priority is you getting Amber – and yourselves – out safely. Alek and I can manage the rest."

Kat didn't need a translator to work out the subtext. As well as getting Amber to safety, Anton wanted *her* out of harm's way as soon as possible, and Amarok and Miklós had probably been tasked with making that happen.

Amarok nodded reluctantly, and the two groups exchanged grim smiles before heading off in different directions.

Chapter 49

Anton hunched his shoulders as they entered the large server room. "I hate it down here. Underground and surrounded by concrete."

Alek shrugged. "If you spent more time in human buildings you'd get used to it."

Anton grunted. "I suppose *you* do not feel like the walls are closing in on you."

Alek made no reply, just gave a low whistle as he surveyed the long, humming racks of storage arrays. So much possibility. He felt the thrill of discovery, the buzz of a new challenge infect him.

"Well, see what you can do," Anton said. "I wish I could be more help."

Alek grinned, crossing to the nearest workstation. "You are helping. You're making me look good."

Anton grunted again. "Nice to see you in your element, brother."

Alek made no reply as he leaned over a keyboard, fingers moving in a blur. "Not encrypted," he said after a moment. "Just a password."

Anton went outside to check the corridor was still empty.

"Aha," Alek said a moment later. Anton returned to lean over his shoulder.

"Evidently they weren't expecting unwanted visitors down this far. Looks like I can get access to everything from right here. See this?" He pointed to the document open on the screen. "They've chipped all the *unalil* hybrids. They control the whole pack via satellite link."

Anton's face darkened. "I know what I said outside, but I am glad we do have the opportunity to strike back against these murderers for what they have done to our friends. If you truly understand how to wield this technology against them, destroy them. Destroy it all."

"With pleasure." Alek's mouth twisted in a crooked grin. "First, I think we need to broadcast a little revision to their project parameters."

Anton nodded, then paced back to stand guard in the doorway. Alek glanced at him as he leaned against the doorframe, tension in his shoulders and neck giving the lie to the casual pose. "To think of our friends, families torn apart, made into automatons to do *their* bidding. Unforgivable." His hands curled into fists.

Alek shook his head, his attention back on the screen as his fingers flew across the keyboard. "Take out your frustration on that collection of RAID units over there." He gestured toward a bank of cabinets across the room, covered with LED lights which flickered in the dim room. "Their data backup system," he added briefly in explanation.

Anton wasted no time in complying; pulling out the hard drives within and methodically crushing them one by one, as if each was no thicker than a sheet of paper.

A short while later, Alek leaned back with a satisfied sigh. Hacking into a system, taking control and making it his own, had never felt so good. Because this time, it was personal.

He glanced across at Anton. "Finished?"

Anton nodded.

Alek made a final keystroke. "And, execute script. Beautiful. That should keep them busy for a while."

"I hope so." There was no sympathy in Anton's voice. "Now let us pay a visit to the Genetics division."

*

Anton stopped dead when they reached the security panel at the numbered door they knew housed the laboratories they wanted access to.

"Damn. Another hand scanner." His face darkened. "Do you think Portia knew?"

"Doesn't matter, 'cos there's been a recent change to the algorithm in their biometric recognition software." Alek winked at Anton, then held his hand up to the panel. God, he loved moments like this. The panel illuminated briefly and then, smoothly and silently, the door slid open.

There were three men within the brightly lit room, and they rose instantly to their feet, startled surprise replaced by shock, then for one of them, anger, smoothly erased. It was this last man who took a step forward and faced them. "If you had requested an invitation during business hours, gentlemen, I would have been happy to oblige."

"You are very kind, Director Raddberg." Anton spoke with a controlled icy politeness Alek had rarely heard. "Of course, we take issue with the fact that for some of our kind, entry to Hema Castus seems to have been made mandatory, even when an invitation has certainly *not* been sought."

Raddberg didn't move, or flinch, or look away. He and Anton eyed each other. "Yes," Raddberg said at last. "A regrettable necessity. So where does that leave us?"

"Unfortunately," Anton said, "we need to destroy your laboratory and all your research. You understand, of course."

The short man behind the director leaned forward and whispered something urgently in his ear. Raddberg nodded once in response, not taking his eyes off Anton.

"And you understand, of course, that I can't permit that."

"I love a good impasse," Alek murmured from behind Anton's shoulder. And then Raddberg bent, and in a lightning-quick move hurled his metal chair straight at Anton's chest. Adrenalin surged as the pair of them dodged and twisted out of the way, and the chair crashed harmlessly into the wall behind them.

The three men had used the moment's distraction to disappear through an inner door.

"Pen-pushers," Alek scoffed. "Is that all they've got?" He wished they'd stayed and fought properly, because he was itching for a physical clash.

They crossed to the door, and opened it to reveal a dimly lit room, bisected by silver bars, floor to ceiling. Raddberg and the others were clustered at the far end of the room, and as Anton and Alek entered, the shorter man pressed a button on the concrete wall, and the bars began to retract into the ceiling.

"There they are," Anton said softly, looking into the dark depths of the cage. "The ones they didn't send out after us. Poor damaged souls."

Glowing red eyes began to appear out of the dark corners of the cage as several beasts slunk closer to the rapidly retreating bars, though they still kept to the shadows.

"Yeah." Alek touched his shoulder briefly. "There's nothing we can do for them, right? Besides making damned sure this doesn't happen again."

Anton shook his head.

The short man raised a whistle to his lips, and Alek felt Anton tense beside him.

"And so the hunter becomes the hunted," Alek said in an undertone. He could feel the inevitability of what was about to happen, and it seemed fitting, even appropriate that the warped and corrupted forms of their brethren, those who had been *unalil*, would be the instruments of death in this endgame.

The whistle sounded once, and the beasts formed a line where the bars had been, glowing eyes intent on the whistle blower.

Raddberg smiled smugly, secure in the knowledge of the deadly weapon they were about to unleash. "Goodbye, gentlemen."

The short man blew the whistle again; two short shrill blasts.

The creatures wheeled as one snarling body, and leaped to obey the command they had been engineered to obey with a ferocity which would only abate on death – their victim's, or their own.

They attacked their enemy.

Exactly as Alek had programmed.

Chapter 50

All was quiet in the corridors of the Predictive Science division. Too quiet. Empty offices were left fully lit, as if the occupants had been there just moments before.

Then, in the distance, they heard a burst of laughter, and the sound of glasses clinking. Amarok motioned to Miklós and Kat to follow, and they rounded a corner and moved a little closer to the noise. Kat concentrated on her feet, on tiptoeing silently behind the others, on controlling her breathing. She allowed herself only short shallow puffs, worried that even the sound of a deep breath might be too loud.

Miklós paused after a few steps and cocked his head, listening. Then he shook his head dismissively. "It's nothing," he whispered. "Toasting someone's promotion."

Amarok raised his nose, sniffed the air. "With old blood." The rich scent of the Directorate's beverage of choice was unmistakable. "They should be there for a while. Suits our purposes."

They moved quickly away from the sounds of revelry and Kat breathed a sigh of relief as they turned into another angled corridor, moving deeper into the underground network.

Finally, she stopped outside a locked metal door. "This is it. I'm sure of it."

Amarok nodded, jaw tense.

No biometric scanners here in Predictive Science. By the look of things, there hadn't been much change since the 1960s.

Kat looked over her shoulder, straining her ears for any footfalls, for the slightest sound announcing someone was coming. She looked back at Miklós and Amarok, who were now flanking the door. What were they going to do? Surely they weren't going to tear it off, because if anybody was close enough to hear …

"Ready?" Miklós asked.

Amarok nodded, and together they pushed, until the metal buckled and door hinges twisted with a protesting groan, and the lock broke free of the concrete wall. Amarok lifted the door to one side, and they passed silently through.

Kat let out the breath she'd been holding, and with a last quick glance back along the corridor, she followed them through. So far so good.

The first room they entered was filled with audio equipment, blinking red lights and a faint hum indicating that something was currently being recorded. Amarok strode over to the main power switch and ripped it from the wall. The lights blinked out and the room went quiet.

Amarok stood, tension radiating from him as he stared blindly at the wall. Kat hung back, feeling suddenly uncomfortable. As if she was witnessing something that was too private for her eyes.

Miklós went to Amarok's side, and placed a hand on his shoulder. "So," he asked again. "*Are* you ready?"

A shudder passed through Amarok, and he raised both hands to his face, then let his fingers rake through his hair. He turned to Miklós at last, face ravaged by uncertainty. "I don't know. All these years she's spent waiting for us, waiting for *me*, and I didn't come for her. I'm afraid of what we'll find."

"Don't think about it," Miklós said gently, and turned Amarok in the direction of the door. "We're here now."

He twisted to look at Kat, and motioned for her to follow.

The first cell contained a ragged, barely clothed male, who crouched near the bars, mumbling to himself. He looked up as they approached, and Kat stifled her instant response, which was to recoil in horror from the emaciated features and the madness in his eyes.

"Oooh," he crooned, "have you got food for me? Have you got food? Have you got food?"

When they didn't answer immediately he went on talking to himself, paying no further attention to them. It was awful, heartbreaking – and Kat felt tears well up in her eyes. Tears of pity and sympathy, yes, but also tears of angry relief. Because they were here now, and they would be able to help these people. They *had* to help these people.

"If he was at full strength, he'd be able to break through these bars in moments," Miklós muttered. "Any of us could. They're not even silver. They must be starving them of blood to keep them weak."

Amarok soberly watched the gibbering mess in front of them who must once have been a man, and at last he shook his head. "We'll get them out," he said. "All of them. As soon as we find Amber."

"She's at the end," Kat said quietly, wishing they didn't have to go past cells housing these other tortured souls to get there.

The inmate of the second cell was waiting at the bars for them, clutching a worn blanket around his throat with one hand, so it fell to his ankles like a shabby cloak. "Who are you?" he asked querulously. "I don't know you. I haven't seen you before."

"We are friends," Amarok said.

The man eyed them suspiciously for a moment or two, and then his eyes fixed on Kat and his face cleared. "You have come for the girl," he said. "I hear her screaming every night, in here." He tapped his head with one bony finger. "Always screaming." He shook his head sadly. "But never a sound."

There was a bundle of rags and curled blanket in the center of the third squalid cell. A bundle topped with tangled dark hair that would otherwise have seemed too small to be the one they were looking for. Kat gasped, shocked at the difference between the woman she'd dreamed of and the one before them now.

Amarok let out a strangled moan and tore out the bars nearest him and then he was beside her, cradling her fragile form in his arms, carrying her out of her broken cell. She was too light, far too light, her arms and legs birdlike where they protruded from the blanket, and marked all over with mottled scars.

Kat had expected something different. Expected to be welcomed maybe, to be spoken to as a friend. Not faced with this cold, thin figure who didn't even open her eyes to acknowledge them. Even when her brother's tears fell to wet her face and closed eyes, and Miklós tucked the blanket more closely around her and enclosed them both in his arms, Amber did not move, or wake, or speak.

But Kat could see her pale face and neck between the strong arms that encircled her slight form, and at Amber's throat, there was the faint flickering beat of a pulse.

*

Della and Corrin were waiting for them at the building entrance, and Della let out a little sound between a gasp and a sob as Amarok – somewhat reluctantly – passed his sister into her arms.

Della looked down at Amber, tears shining in her eyes, and then she looked up at Amarok and Miklós before her eyes came to rest on Kat. "Thank you," she said.

"We have to go back and get the others out," Miklós's said, his voice grim, and then he and Amarok headed back inside.

Della lifted a hand away from her precious burden to give Kat a quick squeeze on the shoulder, and then Corrin slung his arm around Kat's shoulders and drew them all deeper into the shadows.

"I was going to take you back to where Akilina was waiting," Corrin said, "only she headed past us in a tearing hurry a little while ago, saying something about Charice being hurt."

"Come on," Della whispered. "I would still feel more comfortable if we moved back up the ridge. I want Amber as far away from that place as possible. And you, Katerina."

Corrin led the way as they picked their way up over the rubble. They stopped when they reached a good vantage point, and Della sat down on a rock and adjusted Amber so her head was cradled against her shoulder.

"What happened to Char?" Kat asked in a normal voice, glad to be a safe distance from any listening ears.

"Jonathan came back to explain what happened," Della said softly. "The director's assistant came out through the front entrance down there, and she told us she had your permission, which we thought sounded plausible."

In the faint light, Kat saw Corrin's face break into a smile. "It appears," he said, "that Charice is not so trusting. She saw Portia's car approaching on the road out, assumed she had fought her way past the two of us, and threw herself bodily into the task of apprehension. Portia, apparently, has finally been farewelled with minor scratches and bruising, but Charice is nursing two fractures in her leg. From what Jonathan told us, last he'd seen, Akilina was offering her blood to aid the healing, and Charice was ... refusing."

"Have you ..." Kat's throat was dry, and she swallowed before continuing. "Have you seen Anton and Alek yet? Are they out safely?"

Corrin shook his head. "No sign of them," he said. "I think they are still inside."

Chapter 51

In an isolated corner of the Hema Castus Institute, a fire exit door swung open, and a security guard slipped through it and into the night. The cigarette butts littering the ground outside were testament to the fact that he'd done this before.

He was oblivious to the fact that this was where Anton and Alek had entered the building via an air vent such a short time earlier; oblivious to the disturbance that had so recently occurred two floors below. As a habitual smoker, he didn't even notice the odd smell of toasted marzipan lingering near the building wall.

He moved a few steps away from the building, and cupped his hand to light his cigarette. He smoked it quickly, while staring out into the night, and then turned and carelessly tossed the glowing butt back toward the wall.

It arced through the air, a tiny orange glow, and hit the air vent at ground level in a shower of sparks.

*

Della grabbed Kat's arm when the first explosion broke the stillness.

They watched as plumes of orange-tinged smoke and clouds of billowing dust rose into the air, and flame engulfed one wall of the

Hema Castus Institute. Slowly, the wall toppled inward, and several more explosions rumbled through the building. Kat felt the vibrations run through the ground beneath her feet, and she sank to the ground and clung to Della's arm.

Kat heard Della's gasp as she stood suddenly, pulling Kat up with her. "I want to take Amber away from this," she whispered urgently.

Corrin gave a short nod. "Go. We will join you as soon as we can."

They embraced briefly and then Della ran off into the night, cradling Amber to her chest.

Corrin and Kat turned back to the building below, and as the dust settled, the scene became clearer. Kat felt a sick apprehension as she looked at the remaining half of one exterior wall, which listed at a drunken angle above a crater of rubble and flickering flame. The rest of the building had collapsed in on itself.

Again she sank to the ground, and rocked slowly back and forth as her shocked eyes surveyed the devastation. No one, *nothing* could possibly survive such destruction.

She dimly realized Corrin was speaking to her, but her brain wouldn't register the words until he squatted in front of her and held her face in both hands, speaking directly to her.

"Katerina, I have to go down there. I have to. Do you understand?"

She nodded dully.

"Stay here. Do not move. I will be back soon."

She didn't even register that he had gone, her eyes focused only on the flames, and the faint tremors as remaining masonry crumbled and fell.

She couldn't have known. *How* could she have known? But still the guilt clawed through her, needing the barest foothold. Because she was the one who had brought them here, and they were all still inside. Miklós and Amarok and Anton. And Alek. Alek was down there buried in the burning rubble. And it was her fault.

She let out a sob as her eyes moved over the scene of devastation again and again, searching for something, anything that would give her hope, and found nothing at all.

Then something changed.

An indefinable increase in energy, a subtle charge to the night air which caused the hairs on the back of her neck to stand on end.

She swung around.

Alek stood a few paces away, a half-grin curving his lips. She sensed the exhilaration, the raw adrenalin rolling off him in waves. The energy and triumph of a warrior returned.

"Everyone's out safely. Even the other prisoners."

Kat made a low sound, deep in her throat, and then she ran to him and flung her arms around him. Needing the bodily contact to convince herself they were all safe; Alek was here, he was real, and unhurt.

Alek's heat and vitality surrounded her, sang to her senses, and melted away the cold core of worry which she hadn't even realized had been chilling her from deep within as she waited for news on the dark mountaintop.

After a long moment, Alek pulled away a fraction. "Worried about me?" His smile was both teasing and tender. He raised a finger to smooth the side of her face.

Kat let out a little sound, and tilted her chin up to meet his hand. Alek's eyes darkened, deep blue and fathomless, and she was drowning, swimming in a sea of sensation, and he her only connection to land.

Then he bent his head, and their lips met in a kiss.

He wasn't slow, or even very gentle. All the fear, and frustration, and unresolved tension that had been building up within her became liquid fire and molten heat, igniting them both and spilling over into a potent, urgent melding of lips that sparked a trembling, unfurling awareness deep within her body.

His arms slid around her, caressed her, but in this he was too tentative, and her hands tangled in the back of his shirt, pulling him closer, wanting him closer still. He clasped her hips at last and pulled her right into him, moulding her body to his so her breasts were crushed against his chest, her hips pressed against his thighs. One of his hands slid beneath the waistband of her jeans with a gentle inward pressure, and she reached up to cup the back of his head with her free hand, fingers slipping through the soft hair at his nape. He groaned against her lips and, tilting his head, deepened the kiss. Demanding, plundering, giving unreservedly.

How had she ever resisted this? Why had she thought she could? It was as if at the most primitive, physical level, something in her was attuned to him, and his particular energy and inner rhythm fused perfectly with her own so that, together, they formed a soaring song. A harmony of spirits surpassing words, defying practicality and logical thought.

She couldn't have said how long the moment lasted. It seemed at once an eternity and a bare instant; but while it lasted the world fell away and it was only the two of them, two heated bodies, entwined there on the mountaintop.

But slowly, so slowly, lingering lips pulled away. Alek's hold loosened, and he released her. Kat blinked, and came back to the real world with a jolt, aware once more of the hard rocks beneath her feet. The wind whispered across her face, cooling fevered cheeks and kiss-swollen lips.

"Damn." Alek's breathing was unsteady, his hand coming up to tenderly cup the side of her face. "Can't believe I'm the one saying it, but this isn't the right time or place."

And suddenly, she didn't want him looking at her, with her emotion nakedly displayed on her face. And she didn't want to see his face either; didn't want to see or respond to what she might find there.

She turned away, and pretended to look out into the night. She'd practically jumped the guy. It was only natural that he'd responded.

She blinked again, and was almost surprised to find she was blinking away tears.

So, you're emotional, she told herself. *Not really surprising, with Amber's rescue and thinking everyone was dead and all.*

But that reason didn't really ring true.

The tiniest crack of a twig underfoot signaled Corrin's return.

"Katerina?" His voice sounded close by. Only a moment more till he saw them.

"Yeah," Kat agreed, her voice a little husky. "Definitely not the right time."

Alek walked a few steps away after Corrin rejoined them, and frowned down at the ruined institute building. An instant later, he was back at Kat's side, and had taken her hand in his.

Her breath caught. A quiver passed right up her arm as memories of what had happened between them moments earlier flooded through her. But as he held up her wrist between them she realized it was her bracelet that had caught his attention.

"Can you show me this?"

She nodded and pulled her arm away, then fumbled for the clasp by feel.

"Let me." Alek took her hand back in his again, and had the clasp undone almost immediately. "Also, I couldn't help noticing…is that a cell phone in your back pocket?"

Kat wordlessly reached around and pulled it out. She was still feeling too raw about their recent encounter to make a light comment about how he came to be so intimately acquainted with the contents of her jeans pocket.

"Stupid!" Alek said as he took the phone, and then seeing her expression, added, "Not you, me. I should have thought to ask you before now. Nobody else in my family of technophobes would even have thought…" He held up the phone. "This is probably how the Directorate tracked you. We've got to get rid of it."

He pocketed the phone, then held the thin gold bracelet up to get a better look at it. "This is engraved, right?"

"My name and birthday," Kat said. "Why?"

"Are you particularly attached to it? I promise I'll get you something to replace it."

Kat looked at the bracelet dangling between his fingers. Her grandmother had given it to her for her sixteenth birthday. Nine-carat gold; some mass-manufactured thing that wasn't worth much given what her grandmother could afford. She knew even at the time it was because Grandmother was convinced she was some kind of tomboy who would lose anything more valuable.

Kat remembered her rebellious feelings on initially putting it on. At first, she wore it because she knew her grandmother didn't expect she would, but after a while it had become habit.

"Might be useful if the Directorate were to find it with your cell phone in the rubble of that building down there when they get around to cleaning up this mess." Alek shrugged. "Just a thought."

"They'll assume the worst," Corrin added, nodding thoughtfully. "Good thinking."

"Go ahead." Kat felt barely a twinge of guilt as she answered. "I won't really miss it."

She turned away, and stood watching the flames flickering over the ruins down below, their orange radiance brighter than the faint pre-dawn glow of the approaching sun.

She felt, at that moment, like a phoenix reborn.

Chapter 52

Alek turned slightly from his seat on the narrow stone ledge to acknowledge Amarok's silent arrival before returning to his task of watching the people scurrying like insects to and fro across the darkening square so far below.

"So many Parisians intent on going to light their candles and say their prayers," Alek said, after a moment.

Amarok shrugged. "It is one of the world's most famous churches. Most are probably tourists." He paused, leaning against the cool stone behind him. "Notre-Dame Cathedral. Interesting place to choose for reflection. Are you planning a conversion?"

Alek's teeth flashed in a sudden smile. He reached out to pat the winged and horned stone gargoyle which jutted out of the building facade beside him. "I'm just keeping this one company."

He frowned and looked up at Amarok. "Any change?"

Amarok shook his head briefly. "Amber still sleeps."

Alek nodded.

"Now that I have my sister back, though, I find I am free to consider other matters." Amarok's voice was measured. Deceptively calm.

Alek's eyes flashed upward, glinting in the twilight. "Oh?"

"Once you told me in relation to a particular matter that I should, ah, 'modernise my approach.' I believe those were your words. Behave more like a man."

Alek's eyes narrowed. "I remember the conversation."

"Fair warning, brother," Amarok said. And then he was gone.

Alek watched the reflected lights from Petit Pont ripple across the Seine as a breeze disturbed the river's surface.

"Damn." He reached out to the gargoyle beside him and ran a hand over its rough, cold back. "Who would have thought Amarok had it in him?"

Somewhere off among the jumble of city roofs, a dog started barking.

"Claws out," Alek said softly into the night.

Chapter 53

Kat leaned against the cool metal of the narrow black balcony, and watched as the last of the daylight faded from the river. The quai d'Anjou was empty below her; despite being in the heart of Paris it seemed only the more dedicated tourists, like those coming to gawk at Hôtel Lambert, found this quiet corner of the Île Saint-Louis, especially once the sun was gone. It didn't boast any major draw-cards like the nearby musicians on the main banks of the Seine, who attracted groups of evening strollers. Or the Notre-Dame, on the neighboring Île de la Cité.

"Kat?"

The quiet voice behind her startled her. She swung around.

Amarok stood framed in the doorway, dark hair smoothed away from his brow, a charcoal V-necked sweater moulding his chest and upper arms.

"Oh. Hi." She smiled. Apart from the trip here, she'd barely seen Amarok since Amber's rescue. He'd hardly left his sister's room, and Kat hadn't felt right about intruding on the others as they sat vigil by her. After all, she didn't even really know Amber outside those strange dreams, and she wasn't sure that counted.

"Has there been any change?" she asked hesitantly. "Amber, I mean?"

Amarok shook his head. "She will swallow when we feed her, and she is much improved physically, but she hasn't opened her eyes yet. The main part of her trauma was psychological. Recovery will take time."

He moved aside, and gestured to her to precede him through the doorway.

Kat walked back inside, and sank into a carved Rococo armchair. Amarok sat on the edge of a settee just to her left, looking strangely out of place against its graceful curves. Kat found herself taking a closer look at him in the light. Tonight, Amarok seemed different. More muscular, more relaxed than the troubled, gaunt man she'd met that first night.

"I realized I haven't had the chance to thank you for bringing my sister back to me, though words hardly seem adequate to express how I feel."

Kat felt the warmth of embarrassment wash across her cheeks. "I didn't actually *do* anything."

"You believed." Amarok leaned forward and took her hands in his. "As you probably know, Amber has a special gift, and she reached out to you. You heard her. And you answered. For that you will always have my gratitude."

"You're welcome," Kat mumbled. She looked away, suddenly shy. Now would probably be the right time to pull her hands away from his, to break the contact. But the moment passed, and her hands were still resting in his, warmly enclosed.

"Kat, I have a confession to make. Something I should have told you much earlier."

She looked up and her eyes were caught in his golden gaze for a long, charged moment. His thumb gently moved across the soft skin of her inner wrist, and she found herself leaning closer, until all she could see were his shining eyes, so oddly familiar. And then she could smell him, male musk and pine, and his eyes darkened to glowing amber, and suddenly, she knew.

"Oh!" she breathed, a soft exclamation. "It's you."

She didn't need his nod of confirmation. Now, she did pull her hands away with a frown, and pressed them flat against her thighs. "But I ... I'm not used to you like this."

"I could change for you," he offered. "Would fur make you more comfortable?"

She gave a slight smile at this, and shook her head. "I think I can adjust."

Then an inevitable memory intruded. Her whole body stiffened, and her eyes flew to his. "The last time I saw you as a wolf, you *bit* me!" Her hand went to her neck, the memory of that night still so strong that she could almost feel the place where his sharp teeth had grazed her.

He met her accusing gaze squarely. "I did."

It almost seemed as if he wanted to say more, but Kat's memory was already replaying that night; the way her legs had frozen in fear, making her powerless to run, and, later, her burning sense of shock and betrayal. And anger came boiling, churning up from somewhere deep within, and before she could even register the emotion her hand had swept up and connected with his cheek in a resounding slap.

For a moment, they just stared at each other. Neither said a word. And Kat knew full well that for one of his kind, her clumsy slap must have appeared to be in slow motion, so easy to avoid if he'd wanted to.

Amarok looked away first. "I deserved that."

"Why did you do it?" Kat whispered, her throat tight with emotion.

Amarok gave a rueful smile. "I knew you were leaving. I was afraid of losing you. With the emotional bond we already shared, a taste of your blood was my guarantee I'd be able to find you again."

Kat breathed out in a long sigh. "You could've just asked, instead of attacking me." She eyed him distrustfully. "It's not as though I'm squeamish about blood. Pathologist, remember?"

"We … hadn't quite advanced to the point of conversation at the time," Amarok said quietly. "I think you know that nothing like that will ever happen again. And I sincerely regret frightening you."

Kat sat silently for a moment, digesting what he'd said. "I suppose," she said tartly, "you think I have to forgive you if I've already forgiven Jonathan, seeing as what he did was so much worse."

Amarok gave a faint, humorless smile. "I don't think there are rules about this sort of thing. I believe the decision as to whether to grant or withhold forgiveness is entirely your prerogative."

"And if I were to withhold it?"

He bowed his head, shoulders tense. "Then I would respect your decision."

Kat gave a faint smile. "I really think you would." She sat back, eyes clear, decision made. "I'm not sure it would help anyone if I decided to make a big issue of this, though. And I'm pretty sure you've been feeling bad about the whole thing. Besides, I've *missed* you, damn it!"

Unexpectedly, her eyes filled with tears, too many to blink away or hide, and Amarok slid to his knees in front of her, his face reflecting his anguish.

"Oh, Kat." His voice broke on the words as he reached for her hands. "I'm so, so sorry."

And she wanted to laugh, or make some joke to break the tension, but instead the tears kept streaming down her cheeks.

Amarok released her hands and slid his arms behind her to pull her against his shoulder as she sobbed. And when she finally stopped, he smoothed the wetness from her cheeks with gentle fingers, and framed her face, and pressed his lips to her forehead.

She gave a watery smile.

"Better now?" he asked.

She nodded, and gave a little hiccupping sigh. "You know," she said after a moment, "you're the closest thing I have to a best friend, wolf-man." A martial light entered her eyes. "Don't you *ever* shut me out again."

*

Later that night, Char came to visit Kat in her room. She took a chair near the tall window, where moonlight streamed through and silvered the figured satin and ornate gilded timber. She seemed surprisingly at home in the rich surroundings, sitting with one bare foot tucked beneath her and the other leg swinging over the arm of the chair.

"So, still miss that apartment in New York?"

Kat made a face. "Staying in this place is like living in a museum. It's just ... too perfect. I keep thinking I'll break something and then find out it's a priceless antique. I'm expecting a camera crew to come around the corner any minute now and tell me I'm in a costume drama or something." She looked down at herself. "Not that I'm dressed for it."

"Museum?" Char looked affronted. "There's no need to make me feel old."

"Well what *is* the story with this place?" Kat asked.

Char shrugged. "Built in the seventeenth century to the design of Louis Le Vau, the guy who later designed the Château de Versailles ..."

"I get it," Kat interrupted. "It's old, and obviously historically significant and all that, but who was the guy who met us and gave Akilina the key?"

Char grinned. "The secretary to the Ukrainian ambassador. Technically, this house is held in trust by the Ukrainian government. They're trustees for a very old company which bought this place a couple of hundred years ago, a company which just happens to be wholly owned by Arella-dara."

"Akilina owns this house?" Kat was startled. The thought that her aunt had a fully furnished mansion like this sitting empty and at her disposal in the center of Paris kind of brought home exactly how different their lives were.

"Well, yeah. In a roundabout sort of way. Nothing the Directorate could trace back to her though, so don't worry." Char held out her hand, and examined the glossy black-red nails with a critical frown. "Oh, that reminds me." She looked up. "Arella-dara wanted me to ask you to go and see her. She's finally tracked down Sabine."

"Oh." Kat felt a flutter of nerves at this mention of the woman she knew Akilina planned for her to live with here in Paris. Another of her aunt's blood-made daughters. "What's she like?"

Char raised a brow. "Sabine? She's a good choice for you, seriously. Great job, fully assimilated with humans. Stable. Normal." She gave a self-deprecating shrug. "Nothing like me."

Kat was about to say something when a knock on the open door distracted them both.

Char looked across at the door, and sprang to her feet. "Hey, I'm gonna go now."

Alek stood in the doorway, his size and presence at odds with every part of the refined elegance of the room. Next to him, the furniture looked feminine, almost flimsy.

He moved to one side to let Char pass, and then advanced a step into the room and paused, looking at Kat. He seemed tense. On edge. "Can we talk?"

Kat wasn't really surprised he was asking. Because they hadn't yet. Talked, that was. Not since that night at the Hema Castus Institute – and Kat's awkwardness grew every time she saw him. Every time she thought about what had happened. What she'd *invited* to happen.

"I was just on my way to see Akilina." Kat seized gratefully on the excuse Char's visit had provided. "I think it's something important."

"After that, then?" Alek's eyes followed hers. "This is important too." He seemed to want her promise, and stood with feet planted just inside her doorway waiting for her answer.

"I ... yeah. Sure. I'll come and find you later."

He gave a nod of acknowledgment, and then he was gone, and Kat breathed out in a shuddering sigh. Clearly she wasn't going to be able to put this off much longer. *Whatever* it was that had happened between them that night, it had to be put to rest, one way or another.

*

Kat found it a struggle to keep her attention on what Akilina was telling her; where she'd be living, details of her new job, plans to introduce her to Sabine tomorrow night. It was all important stuff, and she nodded and smiled at appropriate intervals, but her mind kept wandering back to the more pressing issue: Alek.

Luckily the discussion with Akilina didn't take long, and as Kat closed Akilina's door behind her and started back along the hallway, she felt her decision crystalize and take shape.

No more avoidance.

She'd find Alek, and she'd get this over with. There was absolutely no reason to be so timid about a discussion any adult should be capable of having. And anyway, now she'd actually *promised*.

She realized she didn't know where Alek's room was, or even if that was where she'd find him, so she headed for the stairs. Della would know. Della always knew.

As she rounded the corner into the main hallway, though, she saw Amarok slumped in a chair, elbows on knees and face buried in his hands. He looked up as she approached.

"Everything okay?" Kat felt a sudden surge of sympathy. She rested a hand on his shoulder and felt the muscles bunch beneath her touch as he moved.

Amarok nodded, gave a tired smile. "It's just Amber. Nothing new, but still ... no change. It's hard. I want to be *doing* something."

Kat took a chair beside him. "You were the one who told *me* – it's going to take time. You can't *make* it happen; you have to *let* it happen."

Amarok gave a half-smile. "When did you get so wise?"

Kat smiled back, and leaned her head against his shoulder. Yeah, so this time they weren't sitting side by side watching the moon rise on a hillside in the Appalachian woods, but being with him still felt pretty much the same. Companionable. Safe. It was good to have her friend back.

"You know, I might be wrong," Kat said suddenly, sitting up straight. She'd had a sudden thought.

Amarok looked at her questioningly.

"About not making it happen. Amber's recovery, I mean."

"What are you thinking?" He was definitely intrigued.

"You told me before that you can feed her, right?"

Amarok nodded. "But she still hasn't opened her eyes, or uttered a word. Anton calls it a protective coma." Pain creased his face.

"Do you think, um …" Suddenly her idea seemed wildly presumptuous, but she had to say it anyway. "Maybe if we give Amber some of my blood, it might help her?"

Amarok looked at her, shocked. "Your blood?"

"Yes." She paused, then added softly, "It healed Jonathan, remember? Anton thought that wasn't usual, so maybe there's something special about …"

"You would do that for my sister?" There was a shining light in Amarok's eyes.

Kat nodded. "Of course. If it would help her." It wasn't really any different to making a blood donation to the Red Cross, was it?

"But healing Jonathan almost killed you." Amarok sounded tortured by the memory.

"I'm not suggesting you drain me, Amarok." She would have smiled, to show him she was joking, only he didn't look like he was in the mood for funny. Not about this subject, anyway. "I meant maybe … give it to her in a cup? Or something?"

The next thing she knew, Amarok had seized her in his arms and was carrying her upstairs and along a corridor at great speed, bannisters and wall panelling passing her in a blur. Then he shouldered his way in through a door that had been left ajar, and placed Kat on her feet at Amber's bedside. Anton was in the room, and he looked up at them inquiringly as if to ask what all the fuss was about.

"Kat wants to give Amber her blood," Amarok announced, and he sounded at once proud, and awed, and hopeful.

"Is this true?" Anton asked.

Kat nodded. "I don't know if it will help," she added, not wanting Amarok to get his hopes up, though it looked like it might already be too late for that.

"We would never have asked," Anton said seriously, "but you have offered."

The arrangements were made very quickly; a glass was procured, and a strong-smelling oil that Anton told her was essence of clove was applied to the inside of her wrist.

"It will help to numb the area," he said.

Kat turned away for the next bit, and despite the scented oil, she did feel a sharp pain in her wrist, and then the cold rim of the glass was pressed against it.

The seconds ticked past, and then, "Done," said Anton. "Do you mind …" He hesitated. "Our saliva accelerates healing, so do you want Amarok or I …"

Kat thought for a moment, wincing at the sting as the night air hit her wrist. She knew she healed fast even without any help, but it might still take minutes. "Amarok," she said.

Amarok moved to her side, and she watched with a strange fascination as he bent his dark head and, almost reverently, lowered his lips to her inner wrist. When he released her, the sting, the pain, was gone, and her skin was unbroken and smooth, but faintly smeared with pink.

She and Amarok watched as Anton raised the cup to Amber's lips and slowly, very slowly, helped her to drink, watching each time she took a small sip to make sure she was swallowing. Careful not to waste a single precious drop.

Amarok turned to Kat when the cup was emptied, and dropped to his knees in front of her, taking her completely by surprise. His head was bowed, but his voice was clear and ringing. "For what you have done for my sister, I thank you. In all domains, though I roam near or far, my loyalty is yours to command." He spoke in the old tongue, lending a weight and formality to his utterance.

Kat looked down at his kneeling form and felt a burgeoning consciousness stirring awake within her, stretching incorporeal limbs as it spread to seamlessly enrobe her like raiment she'd been born to wear.

So it begins. And it is meet. It is fitting. The words sounded within her, in a new voice, one that perhaps had always been there, observing, in some corner of her mind.

When Amarok spoke his final words, Kat realised Anton had come to stand beside them.

"Brother, I witness your oath of fealty," Anton murmured.

"And I accept your pledge in all honor," Kat replied, in a voice that was hers and yet not hers, rich and full and overbrimming with confidence, though she had no idea where she'd plucked the words from.

And then Anton mirrored Amarok's actions. By now she was leagues beyond being shocked at having a man dropping to kneel before her. Anton's words were steeped with respect as he too made his oath with Amarok. "While I have strength to fight and soul to plight, they, and my loyalty, are yours to command."

Kat felt the early prickle of tears in response to the gift of trust he was bestowing on her.

Anton then disappeared from the room, only to return with Miklós, Della and Corrin in his wake, all of whom approached her with something like wonderment. And then each pledged themselves to her in terms that were uniquely their own, with Della avowing her loyalty "in times of famine and times of plenty" and Corrin promising "fidelity uncorruptible", and Miklós swearing himself to her "with soul unfettered and heart unburdened".

And through it all, Kat was divided in two. Half of her, the untried girl, in silent awe at the momentous enormity of the situation, and the other half, an old, old soul, responding to what was her due with unruffled serenity.

Then it was over, and they all slipped away, leaving Amarok and Kat by the bedside. The charged atmosphere slowly returned to normal, as the two of them focused on the frail body lying unmoving in the bed. After more than ten minutes had passed, Kat stirred herself.

"I'd better go now, and leave her to rest." There wasn't really anything else to say or do. She knew, and he knew, that they'd tried something, and it hadn't worked. She stood and looked down at Amber's pale, still face with a twinge of regret. Was she wrong to accept all these promises of loyalty, these pledges, when she couldn't deliver the miracle they were obviously hoping for?

"Where are you off to?" Amarok asked softly, tearing his eyes away from his sister and looking up at her.

"The kitchen. I was on my way to see Della when I ran into you earlier." Now that she was heading back downstairs, the reminder that she was going to go and find Alek and have this talk she'd been putting off was enough to bring back the nervous excitement she'd been feeling earlier. She should have been able to talk to Amarok about this. After all, she'd shared her deepest desires with him over the years. Her intimate worries and fears.

Yeah, but that was when he didn't talk back. And you didn't know he was really a man.

It did make a difference, and Kat realized that Alek was one topic she certainly didn't feel comfortable discussing with Amarok. It felt too ... private.

The expression on Amarok's face now made her frown.

"Come on," she said lightly. "You've got to stop torturing yourself about this. Right now the best thing you can do for Amber – and yourself – is to think positively."

Amarok shook his head. "It's not Amber. I'm worried about you."

Kat blinked. "*Me*?"

Amarok stood in one lithe movement, and took both her hands in his. She could feel the restrained strength in him despite the gentleness of his touch. He looked down at her, his golden eyes serious and thoughtful. "I know it's none of my business, but there are certain things I need to tell you about Alek."

"Oh." Kat's eyes dropped to the floor. So this was what it felt like to suddenly find yourself in the middle of a discussion you'd had no intention of having. Awkward. *Very* awkward.

"Alek ... seems intrigued by you." Amarok's hands tightened fractionally on hers. "I think you probably know that. But you're one in a very, very long line of women who have attracted his attention over the years."

Kat looked up. "I'm not an idiot, Amarok." Her voice was almost fierce. Whether that emotion was directed at him or Alek ... or even herself ... she couldn't be quite sure.

"All right." Amarok released her hands, and held his palms up in the universal sign of acquiescence. "I won't say any more. I just don't want you to get hurt, okay?"

"I'd better go." This time, her voice was carefully neutral. "And please don't worry about me. I'll be fine." She turned and walked away.

What Amarok had said didn't change anything. She'd basically known all that anyway, right? She'd be a fool if she thought there was a chance of anything real with someone like Alek. Clearly he was no saint, but in all fairness, *she* was the one who'd stupidly thrown herself at *him* – not the other way around. She still had to get this discussion – confrontation – whatever, out of the way. For her own peace of mind as much as anything else.

As expected, Della was able to tell her exactly where to find Alek's room. "You may not find him there, though," she added. "I think he has gone out."

"Oh, okay – thanks." Kat hoped it sounded like she didn't care much one way or the other, but as soon as she left the kitchen she headed straight upstairs. He wouldn't have gone out, would he? Not when he'd been so insistent on talking to her? When he'd known she was going to be looking for him later?

The door to his room was ajar, and she knocked softly. There was no answer, and she pushed the door open and walked inside. Clearly, the room was empty. So she should leave.

But her feet seemed more inclined to be governed by curiosity than common sense as she moved over to the dressing table. It was almost empty in true Spartan, masculine style. There was hardly anything in the room to signal there was someone actually living here. The bed was perfectly made, with the familiar sable rug folded and draped neatly over the foot of it.

On a chair beside the bed, though, there was a small book, open face down. Faded black leather cover, well worn through many years of use. *Don't touch it. It doesn't belong to you,* her conscience nagged, but it was no more than a whisper. She was already reaching for the book.

Kat absently marked the open page with the frayed ribbon attached to the spine, and began to flick through. The book was meticulously divided into dozens of sections, each marked with a separate handwritten tab, some in a script she couldn't read, probably Russian. Cities, towns, far-flung localities from around the globe arranged alphabetically – and each section listed names, addresses. Sometimes telephone numbers. Often scrawled notes had been added in pencil.

Every single name was female. Julieta López in Buenos Aires. Niamh Mullins in Dublin. Liisa Nieminen in Helsinki. Miyuki

Inoue in Kyoto. Josette Durand in Montréal. Page upon page upon page.

Kat swallowed against the wave of nausea rising from her stomach. She'd heard of little black books, but this one gave the term a whole new meaning. There must have been *hundreds* of names in here.

She quickly flicked back to the page marked by the ribbon. It was neatly labeled with a tab marked *Paris*.

She sank onto the edge of the bed, suddenly not trusting her legs to hold her anymore. She closed her eyes, and took several deep breaths. In, and out. In, and out.

She opened her eyes, and stared blankly at the far wall. Why was this a shock to her? The only surprise should be that he kept such meticulous records. But she couldn't help feeling betrayed. Misled. All those very normal female emotions.

Damn him, he'd stood in her doorway less than an hour ago and made her think that maybe, just maybe, there *was* something for them to discuss. More fool her, because straight after that he'd gone to meet up with some other woman.

And suddenly, nothing seemed more important than having the discussion with Alek that she'd been so keen to put off earlier. Even if she only ended up confirming what seemed so glaringly obvious now, she had a burning need to know for sure. To know that he wasn't even *worth* caring about.

But where had he gone? She looked back at the open page. The names all looked like they'd been there for years, but against one there was an address written in pencil. And it looked like a fresh entry. She memorized the street name and number, then carefully placed the book face down on the chair as it had been when she'd come in.

Then she smoothed the bed covers where she'd wrinkled them slightly by sitting, and left the room.

Chapter 54

The Vodas rose from the ornate chair in his reception chamber and stalked toward the man bent over in a deep bow just inside the door. "Dead? You are certain?"

Councillor Ionescu raised himself from his low bow, and nodded. "Absolute certainty, of course, is impossible without a body. But the bracelet and cell phone we found indicate that Katerina Chanter died in the fire."

In the dim lighting the Vodas preferred, only his glittering eyes could be seen beneath the deeply cowled ceremonial hood. "But not how or why she came to be there." The Vodas framed it as a statement, but Ionescu felt compelled to answer anyway.

"No, Vodas."

"A question I would have enjoyed putting to the institute director, Raddberg, had he lived." The Vodas turned away from Ionescu and paced toward the far wall, his irritation evident in every line of his well-cloaked body. "He may have provided us with some useful research recently, but he was undoubtedly also playing his own game, damn him. Fortes discovered he had a captive class-one oracle at Hema Castus, and he clearly was hiding her most valuable prophecies from us. Who knows what else he was planning in his petty little struggle for power."

Ionescu judged it best to stay silent. The Vodas was as paranoid as he was vindictive, and his personal penchant for torture and interrogation was well known, and broadly applied. Innocent or not, Raddberg was lucky he'd died.

"And the fire. Accidental?"

"It appears so, Vodas. It was sparked by an explosion of gases the institute had stockpiled."

The Vodas swung suddenly back toward Ionescu and eyed him narrowly. "Bring me the dead child's bracelet. I have a fascination for such trinkets."

Only Ionescu's long training allowed him to respond without a tremor. "I fear that will be impossible, Vodas. Full details of the item were recorded when we found it, but the bracelet itself has subsequently disappeared."

"Disappeared?" the Vodas hissed.

Ionescu bowed low once again. "Rest assured, Vodas, I am investigating the matter. I am certain I will discover which of our people is disloyal to you."

Ionescu began to rise, but a sudden weight prevented him as the Vodas gripped his shoulder and pressed him down with bruising force.

"Remember, Ionescu." The Vodas's voice was a thin, cutting blade. "Disloyalty is the thing I despise above all else. Anyone foolish enough to betray me can so easily be replaced, no matter how elevated their position."

The Vodas kept up a steady pressure on his shoulder, forcing him to stay down, like a dog at its master's feet.

"Of course, Vodas." Ionescu kept his head lowered. His voice he could control, but he did not want to risk the Vodas seeing anger in his eyes.

"You know, Ionescu," the Vodas said softly, musingly, "if Katerina Chanter was ever to reappear, alive and well, your position could become … uncomfortable."

Chapter 55

The queue for the ChaCha Club stretched right back along rue Berger to the next street corner. One glance told Kat that this was a collection of Paris's most fashionable and beautiful, and she, dressed again in her jeans, could never hope to blend in. Three serious-looking bouncers stood guarding the entry. It wasn't the sort of place you could sneak into … but feeling the way she did, Kat had no intention of waiting in line. She folded her map of Paris and shoved it into her back pocket, then squared her shoulders and walked straight past the waiting Parisians to where the bouncers stood behind a red-roped barricade.

One turned toward her and gave her a quick once-over with a distinctly bored expression. He pointed to the end of the queue. *"Faites la queue."*

Very helpful, I can see there's a queue, Kat fumed silently. The guy turned away with a superior sort of smirk which pretty much told her that queue or no queue, people dressed like her weren't admitted to clubs like this anyway. She didn't make the grade.

Kat felt a red wall of anger slam into her. She took a step forward, until the thick red rope of the barricade was touching her thighs.

"Excusez-moi, Monsieur?"

He turned toward her, making no secret of the fact that he considered it a personal affront that she was still there bothering him when he had better things to do.

Kat pressed her rune necklace flat against her chest. *Calm down,* she counseled herself. *You can do this.* A warm wave of confidence flowed through her, easing her tension and washing away some of her anger.

She looked deep into those condescending brown eyes, and spoke with quiet force. "There's someone inside I have to see. I need you to let me in *now*, please."

The guy blinked, and looked confused for a moment. He gave her a foolish grin, then turned and moved the barricade aside and ushered her through with a murmured "Mademoiselle." Kat was inside before she had time to wonder whether "please" was the magic word that'd made him change his mind. Maybe she'd just got lucky with the one guy in Paris who was actually *more* helpful to English-speaking Americans?

Alek wasn't anywhere to be seen near the main bar or dance floor, and Kat began looking through the smaller rooms to the sides. The decor was sophisticated art deco; dark-patterned wallpaper, large gilt mirrors and plush red-upholstered chairs. One room even had a baby grand piano.

At last, in an intimate lamp-lit corner, she saw him. He looked perfectly at home lounging on a striped red satin sofa – and so did the fifties-styled siren curled around him. Another girl, her dark hair cropped into a short, fashionable bob, pouted at something which had just been said, then kneeled on the sofa next to Alek and wound her arms around his neck, leaning in close to whisper in his ear with cherry-red lips.

And Alek – the traitor – looked up at the brunette with a smile turning up the corners of those damnably kissable lips.

Kat felt sick to her stomach. She didn't wait to see any more. Her legs moved automatically, and she didn't even register where she was until she was back on rue de Rivoli heading home. She stopped, halfway. Stopped and looked down at her hands, now shaking with emotion.

Why was she running away, like a fearful child? At the very least, she should have marched up and punched Alek right on his arrogant nose. A *hard* punch, too, with a force that he couldn't simply laugh off, like he had her other pathetic attempts when he'd been training her to fight. Where was this fearsome power she was supposed to have when she needed it? Where was her burning alter-ego, the searing creature of myth? If ever there was a time for some serious risen-from-the-flames smiting-action, this was it. She spread her fingers, impatiently willing something to happen, trying to force a change, and then clenched them in frustration. Nothing. She felt absolutely nothing.

She held her hands up to look at them in the moonlight, and they were undeniably ordinary. Just a pair of hands. Not fiery, flaming wings of justice. It was ridiculous, of course, to think she'd be able to summon such a transformation for such an unworthy purpose, no matter how goddamned angry or upset she might be. And right at this moment, she was plenty doubtful about whether she'd *ever* be able to find her way back to that power again. Not without someone to guide her. Not without Alek. *That* was the hardest part to swallow.

She stumbled home, by the light of the streetlamps and a high, pale moon. Her feet seemed heavy, her vision blurry. It was only then she realized that for the second time that night, her cheeks were wet with tears.

Back in her room, she didn't let herself brood over what she'd just seen. It wouldn't help matters, wouldn't solve anything. Instead, she tried to put Alek out of her mind entirely, but as she stripped off her clothes and put on her pajamas, she was weighed down by a sense of leaden misery. Stupid. So damned *stupid*.

She was sitting on the edge of her bed in the dark when there was a gentle tap on the window.

"Who is it?" Kat called out.

"Amarok."

Guided by the faint glimmer of moonlight, she moved toward his voice and opened one of the doors leading to the narrow balcony. He'd be able to see she'd been crying, but she didn't care. "Now's not really a good time," she said.

He took in her expression in one sweeping glance. "I could feel you were upset." There was an unspoken entreaty in his voice. *Let me comfort you. Share your pain.*

Clearly he wasn't going to say "I told you so" and for that she was grateful. But she couldn't share this. Not now. Not with him.

"I'm going to bed," she said woodenly. "You should go."

She returned to the bed, but as she reached it, a shimmering glow from the balcony caught her eye. Then a muffled patter of wolf paws approached her. With that presence, that achingly familiar smell all around her, recognition swamped her defences in a sudden deluge that completely submerged the rational part of her mind as it made direct communion with her psyche.

She reached for him, desperately clung to him, slid her arms around his neck and buried her face in the fur of his cheek as she sought the comfort only he could offer and took sanctuary in his steadfast strength. This was what she'd missed. *This* was what she needed. He'd known without her asking. Her tears overflowed again, cleansing and restoring her as they were lost in his thick, soft coat. Soon, she crawled into bed and slid beneath the covers, and her wolf lay atop the bed, warm beside her. She curled her arm over his neck, sliding her fingers deep into his fur, tracing them through the softness of his undercoat again and again as she absorbed the solid reassurance of his presence.

At last, she was ready for sleep.

"Goodnight," she whispered drowsily.

And only then did he leave her, treading his way to the moonlit balcony on near-silent paws, and pushing the door shut behind him.

*

Kat woke to a hand on her shoulder, and opened her eyes to see Della's apologetic face, illuminated by the candle she held.

"What time is it?" she mumbled, as that was the only thing her sleepy brain was interested in right at that moment.

"Just after midnight," Della said, then, "Amber has woken. She is asking for you."

Kat sat up in a hurry, the bedclothes dropping to pool around her waist. "Really?" Exultation flooded through her at the knowledge that maybe she'd helped bring this about.

*

It was crowded at Amber's bedside. Not everyone was there, but Corrin was, and Amarok and Miklós, each holding one of her hands. Anton stood at the foot of the bed. Kat had never seen so many shining eyes and beaming smiles.

Each came to thank her on their way out of the room, touching her shoulder, or giving her a huge smile, expressing their gratitude. Clearly they all believed her blood had been instrumental in Amber's return to consciousness, that their faith in her had been justified. She wished she could take more reassurance from that herself.

Before long, the room was empty except for her and Amber, and they stared at each other, wide-eyed. Kat could see that Amber was as struck by this face-to-face meeting as she was. Clearly, whatever she had seen in her dreams of Amber, Amber had experienced in some form too. They had never met – at least not while Amber was awake – but there was an instant connection between them, as if they already knew each other.

Amber raised her head up and spoke at last, in a voice so impossibly soft that Kat had to lean over by the bedside and lower her ear until it was inches from Amber's mouth.

"We are bound together," she said. Each word came slowly, huskily. "I am to guide you through what is to come." She fell back to the pillow, clearly exhausted by the effort of speaking just these few words.

After a pause, her eyes slid sideways and met Kat's. "But you must own your present before you can face your future."

And then her eyes fluttered closed. When she didn't stir for the next few long seconds, Kat called to the door, and Anton and Amarok hurried back in.

Anton went immediately to Amber's bedside and placed a hand against her temple. "I am sorry," he said after a pause, speaking directly to Amarok. "She has slipped out of consciousness again. It may be some time before she wakes fully, but this interlude was a very good sign."

The look on Amarok's face, the tentative hope mixed with fearfulness and apprehension, almost broke Kat's heart. She took three steps toward him and gave him the tightest hug, and after tensing for the most infinitesimal moment, he returned the embrace.

"Well, it's a start," she said at last. Amber certainly wasn't recovered yet, but her recovery was headed in the right direction.

"Yes," Amarok agreed, and his arms momentarily tightened around her.

"Come," he said at last, releasing her, and his eyes were once more dark with torment. "You should rest. Let me walk you back to your room."

Chapter 56

Alek prowled into the kitchen, and gave Corrin a glowering look from beneath his brows.

The big man grinned, and got up from his seat next to Della. He ran a hand over her hair and gave her a lazy kiss. "I believe I was just leaving," he said.

When he was gone, Alek appropriated a vacant stool and sat across the table from Della. "She's asleep," he said.

"Katerina?" Della asked.

Alek nodded moodily.

"Well, it is late, for her. She came looking for you earlier."

"I know. We were supposed to talk."

"You've missed a great deal of excitement, you know. Some of us have sworn ourselves to Katerina. She gave her blood to Amber tonight."

"Did she?" *This* was news. Kat couldn't possibly have known how greatly selfless generosity was revered by their kind. Customarily, an offer of blood was a political act; a judiciously bestowed honor tantamount to an offer of patronage. "And what of Amber now?"

"She woke very briefly. She asked to see Katerina, but after they'd spoken, she slipped back into a coma."

"That's something." He had the grace to feel happy for Amarok. Whatever their differences, he wished him nothing but well when it came to his damaged sister.

Della nodded. She fetched a mug, and filled it with milk from a steaming saucepan. She pushed it across to him.

Alek held up a hand. "No. I've just eaten."

"Well *finally*," Della said. "You've never gone so long before. You were as grumpy as a cat with a sore paw."

Alek massaged his temples with long fingers, and sighed. "Kat ... complicates things for me," he said at last.

"I can imagine." Della wrinkled her nose. "Why not, you know, grab someone in an alley and then afterward wipe their memories and leave them on a park bench somewhere?"

Alek winced. "That seems so ... brutal."

"Well," Della said sensibly, "feeding from humans is hardly compulsory."

Alek shifted restlessly, and frowned. "It's what I've always known."

"But with these girls of yours, you do not actually, you know –"

"No," Alek said tersely. "Not anymore," he amended, after a pause.

Della took a sip from her own mug of milk, and looked at him thoughtfully. "I believe Amarok has finally revealed the truth about himself to Katerina."

"I guessed as much." Alek looked up. "Any idea how she took it?"

"It would not have been polite to listen," Della said delicately, "but Anton happened to be passing by and he swears he heard a slap."

Alek gave a low laugh. "I'm sure the shifty bastard deserved that."

A crease appeared on Della's forehead. "Surely that is a little ... unfair. Amarok has been through a great ordeal."

Alek simply shrugged.

"The two of you are not seriously going to *compete* over this, are you?"

"You know *my* answer." He gave a grim smile. "Serious would be an understatement. As for Amarok ..." Alek tilted his head and regarded her through narrowed eyes, "well, you'd have to ask him that. The man plays his cards very damned close to his chest."

"While you, my Alek, wear your heart on your sleeve – during those periods of time when you let it be seen you actually have a heart." Della spoke lightly, but she reached across and rested her hand on his forearm.

Alek didn't shrug her away. Instead, he reached his free hand into a pocket, and retrieved something that he placed on the table between them. "I'm even considering this," he said.

Della looked at the heavy gold ring, with its elaborately carved carnelian lion's head, and her eyes widened in surprise. "Your father's?"

Alek nodded, face grim.

Della reached out tentatively to touch the carved lion with one finger, her action cautious, almost fearful. She quickly pulled her hand back again. "It is your legacy to choose or deny, Alek, but do you know what this could mean? What you would be risking?"

Alek nodded again, his eyes serious. "But I think," he said softly, "she'd be very much worth it."

Chapter 57

Kat didn't think she'd be able to get back to sleep after Amarok returned her to her room, but she did, and she slept in till eight o'clock. Her sleep was troubled though, filled with unsettling dreams.

She dreamed she was trapped behind a one-way mirror, looking out onto a formal ballroom where Della and Corrin, Anton and Akilina and all the others were dancing and laughing, dressed expensively in clothes out of the pages of a history book. And Alek … Alek was there, looking impossibly debonair. Smiling and graceful and endlessly flirtatious as he danced with a procession of partners. One beautiful woman would curtsy and mince away and another would come immediately to take her place, simpering and fluttering her fan. And Kat, afraid and alone, called and called. But none of them could hear her. Nobody came.

When she woke, the atmosphere of her nightmare lingered. All the exhilaration of Amber's partial recovery was gone, and she was full of dark thoughts.

She swung her legs out of bed with a sigh. After fleeing by night in fear of her life, and crossing an ocean and half a continent, and being cheated on by some stupid guy who she wasn't even really involved with, was a nightmare or two really surprising?

The morning outside was clear and mild, so after eating the breakfast Della had left for her, Kat headed out to do some sightseeing. There was so much still on her list that she hadn't managed yet – easily enough to keep her busy and out of the house all day, which was exactly what she wanted. What she *needed*.

Her first stop was the Jardin des Tuileries behind the Louvre, which was an easy walk. She wasn't able to enjoy the flower borders and immaculate landscaping though. Thoughts of Alek kept intruding.

She wished she could be cooler about this thing with Alek. Less hurt. There certainly hadn't been anything official going on between them. Yes, he'd said he wanted to talk, and given how he'd always been around her, how much attention he'd always paid her, she'd stupidly assumed that meant something it clearly hadn't meant. Her bad. Still, every time she thought about him in the arms of those women last night, smiling down at them, she felt the bitter sting of betrayal.

After wandering aimlessly around the garden for a while, she found a bakery in the streets nearby and bought a baguette with ham and cheese that she took back to the garden to eat. By early afternoon, she'd made her way to the Musée d'Orsay, and she spent a couple of hours among the Impressionist masterpieces there, and then navigated her way to the Luxembourg Gardens.

She picked a quiet spot to sit overlooking one of the spectacular flowerbeds near a large fountain, and ate through the entire box of expensive chocolates she'd bought while walking along the Boulevard Saint-Germain.

Plenty of people around her were visiting the garden by themselves, and quietly reading a book or newspaper on one of the many well-positioned benches. Most looked like locals enjoying the late-afternoon sun.

Kat found it hard to enjoy the moment though. Dark thoughts and worries lurked like shadows in the corners of her mind. The sun glistened on the water splashing out of the fountain nearby, and she wondered how much longer she'd be able to enjoy it for. Heat, light, life – the sun was something she took so much for granted it was difficult to imagine ever being forced to hide from it.

Morose. You're being morose.

Pity telling herself that didn't take the feeling away. She wasn't like all these people, content with their beautiful surroundings. Not anymore. She flattened the chocolate box, and pulled out her map. She was over the whole solitary sightseeing thing. She was even sick of feeling sorry for herself.

She consulted the map with a frown. Akilina's house on Île Saint-Louis really wasn't *that* far. On the other hand, she was sick of walking, and she hadn't used the Metro yet. So, Odéon looked like the closest station to here, and then she could get off at Sully Morland, only a few hundred feet from her front door, and be home and showered and changed by the time Sabine arrived for their big meet-and-greet after sundown.

Of course, it wasn't quite that simple; she'd reckoned without the complication of multiple lines and platforms, so she was feeling flushed with success when she emerged from the Metro station near home, having changed platforms and trains at Châtelet without getting lost. Mastering her little sub-section of the Paris subway was pretty much the most satisfying thing she'd achieved all day.

She'd be home with barely enough time to get ready for Sabine's visit. She could certainly avoid Alek until then.

*

Della's stew smelled wonderful, and Kat's stomach gave a rumble of anticipation as she sat down at the kitchen table. The meeting with Sabine had taken longer than expected, so she was starving.

Amarok seemed to be brooding about something as he leaned against the kitchen wall and watched her eat. "You liked this Sabine?" he asked abruptly.

Kat nodded. "She seemed very nice. Unthreatening." She made a droll face. "Almost like a human."

"Good." Amarok gave her a worried look. "We do need to take Amber somewhere secluded for her continued recovery. The plan is for us to leave tomorrow night. But I wanted to be sure that you were happy with arrangements here first."

Kat wrinkled her nose at him. "I have a princess of the blood – who also happens to be a relative – watching over me now. I think you're off the hook."

Amarok chuckled, and the corners of his eyes crinkled up in the first genuine smile Kat could remember seeing from him. It lit up his face, and made him seem younger.

"You're right," he said. "Old habits die hard." He tilted his head and looked at her consideringly. "You're sure, though, that you're happy with the princess's plans for you?"

Kat looked at him quizzically. "Which of her plans in particular?"

Amarok raised a brow. "All of them."

Kat eyed him thoughtfully. "She has a very old-fashioned approach, but I think she means well, most of the time." She gave a rueful sigh. "Yes, she can be a bit … over the top. But I'd certainly be in trouble without her help. Once I'm settled with Sabine, she plans on going to stay in some château outside Paris for the foreseeable future, just in case I need her."

Amarok took her hand, and held it between both his own. "You have many friends, Kat. Others who are also happy to help you in any way you need."

"I know." She reached up and gave him a spontaneous hug. "And I'm very grateful. Just go and be with your sister. I'll be fine. Promise."

He kept his arms around her for a moment after hers had relaxed, enclosing her in his strength, and warmth, and safety. Finally he nodded, and moved his hands to the sides of her shoulders. He gave her a long look with those tawny golden eyes. "Remember, even when I'm not with you I'm never too far to come if there's trouble. If you need me."

"I'll be counting on it," Kat said softly.

*

Later that evening, Char was lounging on Kat's bed relating her own plans for the future.

"Can't go back to New York. Too many uncomfortable questions from the Directorate waiting for me. But Jonathan and I are gonna try our hand at a new club in York, and Mac'll join us after he winds things up for me Stateside."

"York, as in York, England?"

Char grinned and nodded. "New York, York. Seemed appropriate, and there's a good clientele there from what I hear." She looked up at the door, and rolled her eyes. "Déjà vu. Gotta go."

She was out the door before Kat could say anything, and when Kat's eyes followed her path, she saw Alek waiting just outside in the hallway. Her heart sank. *Showdown*, she thought.

As soon as Char had gone, Alek walked in, walked right up to her with all the feline grace and controlled menace of a lion. "I've been looking for you since last night. We still haven't had that talk." His eyes were impossible to avoid.

"I know," Kat said lightly. "Well, here I am."

Alek frowned, watching her intently. "Your aunt thinks it'd be safer if we all left you alone in Paris with this blood-made progeny of hers, Sabine. Less likely that way for the Directorate to track one of us back to you and realize you're still alive."

He made an impatient gesture. "Her suggestion is that my family all leave together. Amber needs a quiet place to rest and heal, certainly. But we don't all need to stay with her. If some of us – one of us – stayed in Paris, we could keep watch. Protect you. I know you don't always see eye to eye with the princess, so ..."

He reached out to take her hand, and the tide of warmth that washed through her demonstrated yet again the strength of the physical pull Alek exerted without even trying. Luckily her mind was in charge of the big decisions – not her body.

Kat let her forehead crease in a tiny frown, and gently tugged her hand away. "Actually I do agree with her about this. A fresh start is a good idea."

Alek stiffened, a trace of tension in the set of his jaw. "That's what you want? A fresh start?"

Kat shrugged. "Seems best, after everything." She kept her voice even. Unemotional. "You all have lives to lead too. I'm very grateful for all that you and your family have done for me and my aunt, but I really don't need protecting anymore. My problems have already taken up enough of your time."

Alek moved closer, cupped her face in his hands, and her breath caught as he stared down at her with those electric blue eyes. "Kat, little Kat, only a few days ago I really thought we were getting somewhere, and now there's this wall between us again."

Kat forced herself to breathe out. He was close enough that she could almost imagine the warmth of her breath touching his chin, his lips. She took a step backward, back to safety. Away from the heat of his hands, from their mingled breaths and the magnetism of his touch.

"You're always trying something, Alek. Always coming out with a line."

"A shallow pool offering no reflection?" There was bitterness in his voice, but also, unaccountably, a rueful acceptance. "That may have been true once, Kat, but not anymore. I've never hidden the way I feel about you. If you trust in nothing else, trust in that."

He took a step toward her, again closing the distance between them. "And is it so one-sided between us?" His eyes at that moment were such a deep, dark blue that she thought she would drown in them. "When you're not so guarded, you give me reason to hope that the feelings between us are mutual."

Kat stared up at him, trapped. He was referring to the way she'd behaved that night. When they'd kissed. When *she'd* kissed *him*. There had been a connection between them; a spine-tingling, world-altering bond. They both knew it.

Physical chemistry, whatever you wanted to call it. That part, at least, she couldn't deny, damn him. But he was an extremely attract-ive man, and for all she knew, he'd shared that kind of chemistry with any number of other women. She didn't want to be just another one in his list of conquests. Another name against the 'Paris' tab in his little black book.

She let out a shaky breath. "Everything's always one step away from sex with you, Alek. Sometimes it's nice to have someone you can just talk to, without all that pressure."

His eyes darkened. "Someone like Amarok?"

The flippant way he came out with that annoyed her. "Like Della. Like Amarok. Like lots of people, Alek. People who are my *friends*." And she turned on her heel and walked out of the room.

As final lines went it probably wasn't that impressive, but he must have got the message anyway, because he didn't follow her. Alek and she had already tried the friends thing, and it clearly hadn't worked.

For one thing, friends were supposed to be people you could trust.

Chapter 58

The last of the hugs had been exchanged and farewells said in the front entry of the great house. There was a kiss on the brow and assurances of ongoing support from Amarok; a big hug from Corrin; smiles and kisses to the back of her hand from Anton and Miklós, before they left to carry Amber down to the waiting car. From Della, kisses and tears, and from Alek a remote expression and brief handshake which was harder to take than all the rest put together.

Char and Jonathan had already left without much fanfare as soon as the sun dipped below the horizon, on their way to make the Channel crossing.

Akilina looked across at Kat as the last echo of the closing door died away. "I think that you will miss the *unalil*. And perhaps one in particular?" Her eyes held a compassion Kat hadn't really been expecting.

A tide of tears threatened to rise within her, and she turned away from Akilina while the sensation slowly subsided. After a long pause, she shrugged. "The house is certainly quieter." She kept her tone noncommittal.

"Better a safe distance between you, child. You know of course that such a relationship – if one had occurred – would have been ill-fated. You are destined for one of another class entirely."

Kat mumbled something affirmative in reply, and made some excuse to go upstairs. The moment she reached the first landing, though, she wished she'd had the guts to say something to Akilina. It was time she challenged this assumption the elder seemed to have that she was just going to go along with some sort of arranged marriage when the time came. *If* the time ever came, because the whole deal was undoubtedly contingent on her not being human anymore. She stopped walking, almost resolved on going back and discussing it now.

It wasn't the first time Akilina had brought up the idea, which was antiquated, and insulting, and just plain ridiculous. Okay, so she was grateful for the help her aunt was providing in getting her re-established in a new country, but just knowing they were related didn't mean she welcomed Akilina's involvement in planning her entire life, especially seeing as they'd met for the first time a couple of weeks ago.

She sighed, and continued on up the stairs. Yeah, Akilina might have the wrong impression about how cooperative she really was about this matchmaking stuff, but it didn't seem worth challenging her over it right now. Given what they'd just been discussing, and Akilina's annoying perceptiveness, it would look suspiciously like she was fighting for the right to be involved with one of the *unalil*. The whole situation was embarrassing enough without that.

Back in her room, she tried to read, but couldn't concentrate. After a while, she wandered over to the window and stood looking out into the night, but without really seeing anything. The others had probably left Paris behind by now. Like she'd told Akilina earlier, the house did feel empty. Abandoned.

Tomorrow night she'd be leaving too, moving into the spare room in Sabine's little two-bedroom apartment in Montmartre. And the day after that, she'd start her new job in the pathology lab at the American Hospital where Sabine worked.

As she gripped the sill, her hand brushed against something and she looked down. A neat little box was resting there, tied with a ribbon – and her name was on the lid in masculine handwriting. Handwriting which looked kind of familiar.

She fumbled with the knot in the ribbon, trying to pretend to herself that she didn't know who it could have been from, but the truth was she *did* know. The handwriting was the same as in the black-covered journal in Alek's room. But why would he have left her …

She pulled the ribbon free and lifted off the lid, letting out a gasp when she saw the bracelet nestled in the velvet interior. Links of gold, delicately wrought and embellished with tiny flowers of all descriptions. Hanging from the center, an intricately carved rose quartz birdcage captured a tiny heart, carved to look like a baby bird.

I promise I'll get you something to replace it. Alek's words, as they watched flames play over the ruined Hema Castus Institute. As his kiss still burned on her lips.

Kat closed her eyes.

I've never hidden the way I feel about you. If you trust in nothing else, trust in that.

She could still remember the way he'd been looking at her when he'd said that. Even at the time, she'd heard the sincerity in his voice, seen the truth in his eyes, *known* how much more than just physical this was. But she'd fought against believing it. Everything in her had rebelled against believing in him.

True, trusting Alek didn't make any logical sense given what she'd seen at the ChaCha Club that night. *Could* there be another explanation? Her head still said no, but somehow her heart told her he wasn't involved with anyone else.

Complicated, Kat. You always knew anything to do with Alek was going to be complicated.

Her hand closed around the stone-caged heart as she fought the lump in her throat and the tears pricking her eyelids.

Pain, confusion, loss. They all swirled through her, an over-whelming tide. She leaned her forehead against the cool glass of the window, and let out a shuddering breath.

What she'd experienced with Alek was so raw, wild, and won-derful it was pretty damned scary. Distrusting him had been easier. Pushing him away had seemed safer.

And now it was too late to change her mind.

Chapter 59

Kat sat perched on the edge of a cream leather sofa, looking up at Sabine, who was a neatly pressed vision in her white nurse's uniform. The windows and white shutters flung open onto the narrow balcony behind her let in the fresh night air and faint sounds of a Montmartre evening, though at this hour the window boxes of cascading geraniums could barely be seen.

"Tell me again how you will get there." Sabine waited expectantly.

Kat smiled and recited obediently. "I get on the Metro at Abbesses, change at Saint-Lazare, then get off at Anatole France and walk to the hospital from there."

Sabine gave a satisfied nod, her sleekly styled dark hair barely moving. "Good. I would prefer to come with you, but as you are working daytimes of course it is impossible. And you will remember the shutters?"

Kat nodded. "I'll close them before I leave." Living with someone who worked opposite shifts – and was sunlight-intolerant – did present its challenges, though she'd already had a bit of practice with Akilina and the others.

Sabine flashed her a sudden smile with her perfectly glossed lips. "I'm going to enjoy having you here, *chérie*. It's company for me.

Though you would not believe the list of instructions Arella-dara has left me with. You are very precious to her, you know."

Kat shifted in her seat, embarrassed. "It's taking some getting used to."

"Me, I'm happy she has something to take her mind off Charice. The pair of them, their relationship is very … how do you say? Dysfunctional."

Kat wanted to ask more, but Sabine scooped up her handbag and jacket, clearly in a hurry to go to work.

"I must go, *chérie*. Call if you need to, and you have Arelladara's number at the château."

When Sabine had left, Kat wandered through the apartment restlessly. There was nothing to occupy herself with, as all her things had already been unpacked and put away by faster hands than hers. Sabine kept the place immaculate, and Kat felt like she shouldn't touch anything in case she accidentally disturbed some perfectly arranged vignette.

She finally found herself sitting on the bed in her new room, gazing at the hand-drawn picture of her mother. At her father's scrawled name in the corner. And at the delicate gold bracelet circling her wrist.

So much had changed. Recent events had seen the shearing of her connections to her old life, one by one. Her family in Richwood, the place she lived, even her sense of self. And it was still hard getting her head around Akilina being her aunt, which gave her a tangible connection to these people. That discovery was just another one of a million silken threads being woven every day, binding her into a chrysalis not of her own making, and pulling her inexorably toward a new life. A non-human life – which it seemed her father had known, and rejected.

Akilina had shared what she knew about her brother with Kat, but it was frustratingly little. She had told Kat that he'd had a human mother like her. He was a hybrid just like her. And he'd made his transition, and become one of the *Tabérin*. Akilina related her memories of occasional visits from him during her childhood. Arguments between him and their father. "He was deeply uneasy about what we are," Akilina had recalled. "Father was endlessly frustrated by his rejection of his birthright. Position, and power with all its trappings – he wanted none of it, hence the name he chose for himself: Peasant Prince."

But despite the fact he'd been born human, Kat couldn't imagine it had been easy for her father to choose to live among humans, so perhaps it wasn't surprising that he'd left. Knowing what he knew. With memories of the life he'd once led, so different to her mother's. A wave of sadness washed through her for what might have been for her parents. For what might have been for her as a child.

And for her and Alek. Alek, who was probably a thousand miles away by now, and still mad at her.

She sighed, and ran her tongue over her teeth. Still the same, though her gums had been aching off and on for the last couple of days. She ran an experimental finger along the gum line above her incisor. Definitely tender – but no swelling. Yet. They'd all assured her there would be swelling when something was really happening. And until something *did* happen, she remained vulnerable.

Stop it, Kat. She could almost hear Amber's admonishing voice in her head. She was thinking about the future again. Worrying about the future.

Own your present. Amber's words hadn't made sense at the time, but she'd had plenty of time to think them over since then. Owning her present, living in the here and now, not constantly fearful of what tomorrow would bring, or yearning for power she hadn't quite grown into yet. That was all she had to do. It was as simple and as complicated as that. She did, after all, have a full-time worrier about the future in Akilina. And Sabine, with her list of things to watch out for. Her detailed instructions from Akilina on how to take care of Kat. Plus, Kat had a band of loyal *unalil* friends ready to back her if she ever needed it. Plenty of combined firepower there.

She needed to release her worry. Let it go.

Oddly, that thought process did help her, and she felt an instant lightening of her mood. She was starting a new job in one of the most beautiful cities in the world. She had free accommodation in a beautiful apartment in a vibrant part of Paris, and a newly discovered aunt who lived to make her life go smoothly, and had the means to ensure it did. Thinking about it like that, her life was actually pretty fabulous.

Own your present.

Kat's eyes returned to the picture of her mother. There was something she absolutely had to do before she went to bed.

She went and fetched the cell phone Akilina had given her, and brought it back to the bed. There were only three contacts listed. Three numbers she could safely call without compromising her safety. Sabine's cell phone, Akilina at the château, and her mom's new cell number. What must her mother have thought upon receiving an unexpected parcel: a cell phone, together with instructions to keep it charged and keep it near her at all times, waiting for Kat's call? However much she hated it, Kat had to accept that this spy-stuff, this paranoia or whatever you wanted to call it was a necessary part of her life now.

Kat closed her eyes for a moment to collect her thoughts, then pressed the call button, and held the phone to her ear while she waited for it to connect.

Tessa answered almost immediately.

"Sweetie, I've been going out of my mind," she said as soon as Kat had said hello. "Where are you? You didn't call on the weekend. I tried to call your cell phone and the number was disconnected. Then you sent me this phone. Are you in trouble?"

Kat imagined her mother leaning over the breakfast counter, phone in hand, with the mail holder that stored the unpaid bills just behind her shoulder. She'd seen her stand like that to take calls a million times. To Mom, back in Richwood, it was just a normal Thursday evening like any other.

It all seemed so far away now. It *was* far away.

"A lot has changed. A new opportunity came up for me," Kat said. "It was very, ah, sudden." *And when did I start using "sudden" as a euphemism for fleeing for my life?* She sighed, and pressed a hand to the comforting warmth of her rune necklace.

"I'm working at the American Hospital now, Mom. Everything's…fine."

"So where *are* you?" Tessa asked again, her tone insistent, and Kat realized she still hadn't quite replied to that part. Putting it off wouldn't make it any easier. She took a deep breath.

"Well, I'm finally getting to do that travel you wanted me to do," she said. "I'm in Paris."

Acknowledgements

So many people helped bring *Dark Child* into being.

The entire team at Momentum books have been wonderful, but I'd especially like to thank my publisher Joel Naoum, my editor Ali Lavau, and editorial assistant Tara Goedjen who have engaged with the characters and story and polished them till they shone. Thanks also to Jon Macdonald for his fabulous cover designs.

I'm very grateful to my agent, Sophie Hamley of Cameron's, who believed in me and kept me believing in myself through many drafts and revisions.

Heartfelt thanks to my beta-gals and sisters, the two Rebeccas, Esther, Alice, and Kerri-Ann, who read the earliest drafts and provided comments, endless encouragement, and even nanny services at times. Sincere thanks also to Fran, who helped carve order from the chaos at home, and listened to me natter on and de-stress over cake and endless cups of tea as this novel came into being.

I wouldn't have fared nearly so well without you all.

And finally, my family, and wonderful parents; you have always, always been there for me, and have supported *Dark Child* from the very beginning. Thank you all.

www.ingramcontent.com/pod-product-compliance
Lightning Source LLC
Chambersburg PA
CBHW030759260626
47169CB00001B/114